Assassin's Creed®

Black Flag

OLIVER BOWDEN

PENGUIN BOOKS

PENGUIN BOOKS

Published by the Penguin Group
Penguin Books Ltd, 80 Strand, London WC2R ORL, England
Penguin Group (USA) Inc., 375 Hudson Street, New York, New York 10014, USA
Penguin Group (Canada), 90 Eglinton Avenue East, Suite 700, Toronto, Ontario,
Canada M4P 2Y3 (a division of Pearson Penguin Canada Inc.)
Penguin Ireland, 25 St Stephen's Green, Dublin 2, Ireland (a division of Penguin Books Ltd)
Penguin Group (Australia), 707 Collins Street, Melbourne, Victoria 3008, Australia
(a division of Pearson Australia Group Pty Ltd)
Penguin Books India Pvt Ltd, 11 Community Centre, Panchsheel Park,
New Delhi – 110 017, India
Penguin Group (NZ), 67 Apollo Drive, Rosedale, Auckland 0632, New Zealand
(a division of Pearson New Zealand Ltd)
Penguin Books (South Africa) (Pty) Ltd, Block D, Rosebank Office Park,
181 Jan Smuts Avenue, Parktown North, Gauteng 2193, South Africa

Penguin Books Ltd, Registered Offices: 80 Strand, London WC2R ORL, England

www.penguin.com

First published 2013

014

Set in 12.5/14.75pt Garamond MT Std
Typeset by Jouve (UK), Milton Keynes
Printed in Great Britain by Clays Ltd, St Ives plc

PAPERBACK ISBN: 978-0-718-19375-1
OM PAPERBACK ISBN: 978-0-718-17815-4

www.greenpenguin.co.uk

Black Flag

PART ONE

I

I cut off a man's nose once.

I don't recall exactly when it was: 1719 or thereabouts. Nor where. But it happened during a raid on a Spanish brig. We wanted her supplies, of course. I pride myself on keeping the *Jackdaw* well stocked. But there was something else on board, too. Something we didn't have but needed. *Someone*, to be precise. A ship's cook.

Our own ship's cook and his mate were both dead. Cook's mate had been caught pissing in the ballast, which I didn't allow so punished the traditional way, by making him drink a mug of the crew's piss. I must admit, I've never had it happen before where the mug of punishment piss actually killed the man, but that's what happened with the cook's mate. He drank the mug of piss, went to sleep that night and never got up. Cook was all right by himself for a time, but he did like a nip of rum, and after a nip of rum was apt to take the night air on the poop deck. I'd hear him clomping about on the roof of my cabin, dancing a jig. Until one night I heard him clomping about on the roof of my cabin and dancing a jig – followed by a scream and a splash.

5

The bell rang and the crew rushed to the deck where we dropped anchor and lit lanterns and torches, but of cook there was no sign.

They had lads working with them, of course, but they were just boys, none of them knew how do anything more culinary-minded than stir the pot or peel some spuds, and we'd been living on raw grub ever since. Not a man among us knew how to do so much as boil a pot of water.

Now, not long back we'd taken a man-of-war. A tasty little excursion from which we'd bagged ourselves a brand spanking new broadside battery and a hold full of artillery: cutlasses, pikes, muskets, pistols, powder and shot. From one of the captured crew, who then became one of *my* crew, I'd learnt that the Dons had a particular supply ship on which served an especially adept cook. Word was that he'd cooked at court but offended the queen and been banished. I didn't believe a word of that but it didn't stop me repeating it, telling the crew we'd have him preparing our meals before the week was out. Sure enough we made it our business to hunt down this particular brig, and when we found it, lost no time in attacking it.

Our new broadside battery came in handy. We drew up alongside and peppered the brig with shot till she broke, the canvas in tatters and the helm splintered in the water.

She was already listing as my crew lashed and boarded her, scuttling over her sides like rats, the air heavy with the stink of powder, the sound of muskets popping and cutlasses already beginning to rattle. I was in among them as always, cutlass in one hand and my hidden blade engaged, the cutlass for melee work, the blade for close finishing. Two of them came at me and I made short of the first, driving my cutlass into the top of his head and slicing his tricorne in half as the blade cleaved his head almost in two. He went to his knees with the blade of my sword between his eyes but the problem was I'd driven it in too deep, and when I tried to wrench it free his writhing body came with it. Now the second man was upon me, terror in his eyes, not used to fighting, obviously, and with a flick of the blade I sliced off his nose, which had the desired effect of sending him back with blood spraying from the hole where his beak had been, while I used two hands to finally wrench my cutlass out of the skull of the first attacker and continue the good fight. It was soon over, with as few of their crew dead as possible, me having given out special instructions that on no account was the cook to be harmed – *whatever happened, I'd said, we had to take the cook alive.*

And as their brig disappeared beneath the water and we sailed away, leaving a fog of powder smoke and a sea of splintered hull and bobbing bits of broken ship behind us, we gathered their crew on the main deck to flush out the cook, hardly a man among us not salivating, his belly not rumbling, the well-fed look of their crew not lost on us. Not at all.

It was Caroline who taught me how to appreciate good food. Caroline, my one true love. In the all-too brief time we'd spent together she'd refined my palate, and I liked to think that she'd have approved of my policy towards the repast, and how I'd passed on a love of the finer things to the crew, knowing as I did, partly due to what she'd shown me, that a well-fed man is a happy man, and a happy man is a man less prone to questioning the authority of the ship, which is why in all those years at sea I never had one sniff of mutiny. Not one.

'Here I am,' he said, stepping forward. Except it sounded more like, 'Beer I bam,' owing to his bandaged face, where some fool had cut off his nose.

2

1711

But, anyway, where was I? *Caroline*. You wanted to know how I met her.

Well, therein lies a tale, as they say. Therein lies a tale. For that I need to go much further back, to a time when I was just a simple sheep farmer, before I knew anything of Assassins or Templars, of Blackbeard, Benjamin Hornigold, of Nassau or the Observatory, and might never have been any the wiser but for a chance meeting at the Auld Shillelagh one hot summer's day back in 1711.

The thing is, I was one of those young firebrands who liked a drink, even though it got me into a few scrapes. Quite a few . . . *incidents*, shall we say, of which I'm none too proud. But that's the cross you have to bear if you're a little over-fond of the booze; it's rare to find a drinker with a clean conscience. Most of us will have considered knocking it on the head at one time or another, reforming our lives and perhaps turning to God or trying to make something of ourselves. But then noon comes around and you know what's good for that head is another drink, and so you head for the tavern.

The taverns I'm referring to were in Bristol, on the south-west coast of dear old England, where we were accustomed to fierce winters and glorious summers, and that year, that particular year, the year that I first met her, 1711, like I say, I was just seventeen years old.

And, yes – yes I was drunk when it happened. In those days, you'd have to say I was drunk a lot of the time. Perhaps . . . well, let's not exaggerate, I don't want to give a bad account of myself. But perhaps half of the time. Maybe a bit more.

Home was on the outskirts of a village called Hatherton, seven miles outside Bristol, where we ran a smallholding keeping sheep. Father's interests lay with the livestock. They always had, so having me on board had freed him from the aspect of the business he most despised, which was making the trips into town with the merchandise, haggling with merchants and traders, bargaining, cutting deals. As soon as I'd come of age, by which I mean, as soon as I was enough of a man to meet the eye of our business associates and trade as an equal, well, that's what I did. And father was all too glad to let me do it.

My father's name was Bernard. My mother, Linette. They hailed from Swansea but had found their way to the West Country when I was ten years old. We still had the Welsh accent. I don't suppose I minded much that it marked us out as different. I was a sheep farmer, not one of the sheep.

Father and Mother used to say I had the gift of the

gab, and Mother in particular used to tell me I was a good-looking young man, and that I could charm the birds off the trees, and it's true, even though I do say so myself, I did have a certain way with the ladies. Let's put it this way, dealing with the wives of the merchants was a more successful hunting ground than having to barter with their husbands.

How I spent my days would depend on the season. January to May, that was lambing season, our busiest time, when I'd find myself in the barns by sun-up, sore head or not, needing to see whether any ewes had lambed during the night. If they had, then they were taken into one of the smaller barns and put into pens, lambing jugs we called them, where father would take over, while I was cleaning feeders, filling them up again, changing the hay and water, and mother would be assiduously recording details of the new births in a journal. Me, I didn't have my letters then. I do now, of course, Caroline taught me them, along with much else that made me a man, but not back then, so that duty fell to Mother, whose own letters weren't much better, but enough to at least keep a record.

They loved working together, Mother and Father. Even more reason why Father liked me going into town. He and my mother – it was as though they were joined at the hip. I had never seen another two people so much in love and who had so little need to make a display of the fact. It was plain to witness that they kept each other going. It was good for the soul to see.

In the autumn we'd bring the rams through to the pasture to graze with the ewes, so that they could get on with the business of producing more lambs for the following spring. Fields needed tending to, fences and walls building and repairing.

In winter, if the weather was very bad, we brought the sheep into the barns, kept them safe and warm, ready for January when lambing season began.

But it was during summer when I really came into my own. Shearing season. Mother and Father carried out the bulk of it while I made more frequent trips into town, not with carcasses for meat, but with my cart laden with wool. And in the summer, with even more opportunity to do so, I found myself frequenting the local taverns more and more. You could say I became a familiar sight in the taverns, in fact, in my long buttoned-up waistcoat, knee breeches, white stockings and the slightly battered brown tricorne that I liked to think of as my trademark, because my mother said it went well with my hair (which was permanently in need of a cut, but quite a striking sandy colour, if I do say so myself).

It was in the taverns I discovered that my gift of the gab was improved after a few ales at noon. The booze, it has that effect, doesn't it? Loosens tongues, inhibitions, morals . . . Not that I was exactly shy and retiring when I was sober, but the ale, it gave me that extra edge. And after all, the money from extra sales made as a result of my ale-inspired salesmanship more than covered the cost of the ale in the first place. Or at least that's what I told myself at the time.

And there was something else, too, apart from the foolish notion that Edward in his cups was a better salesman than Edward sober, and that was my state of mind.

Because the truth was, I thought I was different. No, I *knew* I was different. There were times I'd sit by myself at night and know I was seeing the world in a way that was all my own. I know what it is now but I couldn't put it into words back then, other than to say I felt different.

And either because of that or despite it I'd decided I didn't want to be a sheep farmer all my life. I knew it the first day, when I set foot on the farm as an employee, and not as a child, and I saw myself, and then looked at my father, and understood that I was no longer here to play and would soon go home to dream about a future setting sail on the high seas. No, this *was* my future, and I would spend the rest of my life as a sheep farmer, working for my father, marrying a local girl, siring boys and teaching them to become sheep farmers, just like their father, just like their grandfather. I saw the rest of my life laid out for me, like neat workclothes on a bed, and rather than feel a warm surge of contentment and happiness about that fact, it terrified me.

So the truth was, and there's no way of putting it more gently, and I'm sorry, Father, God rest your soul, but I hated my job. And after a few ales, well, I hated it less, is all I can say. Was I blotting out my dashed dreams with the booze? Probably. I never really thought about it at the time. All I knew was that sitting on my shoulder, perched there like a mangy cat, was a festering resentment at the way my life was turning out – or, worse, actually had turned out.

Perhaps I was a little indiscreet concerning some of my true feelings. I might on occasion have given my fellow drinkers the impression that I felt life had better things in store for me. What can I say? I was young and arrogant and a pisshead. A lethal combination at the best of times. And these were definitely not the best of times.

'You think you're above the likes of us, do you?'

I heard that a lot. Or variations of it, at least.

And perhaps it would have been more diplomatic of me to answer in the negative, but I didn't, and so I found myself in more than my fair share of fights. Perhaps it was to prove that I was better than them in all things, fighting included. Perhaps because in my own way I was upholding the family name. A drinker I might have been. A philanderer. Arrogant. Unreliable. But not a coward. Oh no. Never one to shrink from a fight.

And it was during the summertime when my recklessness reached its height; when I would be most drunk and most boisterous, and mainly a bit of a pain in the arse. But on the other hand, all the more likely to help a young lady in distress.

3

She was in the Auld Shillelagh, a tavern halfway between Hatherton and Bristol, which was a regular haunt of mine, and sometimes in the summer when Mother and Father toiled over the shearing at home, when I'd make more regular trips into town, regular to the tune of several times a day.

I admit I hadn't taken much notice of her at first, which was unusual for me, because I liked to pride myself on knowing the exact location of any pretty woman nearabouts, and besides, the Shillelagh wasn't the sort of place you expected to find a pretty woman. A *woman*, yes. A certain type of woman. But this girl I could see wasn't like that: she was young, about my age, and she wore a white linen coif and a smock. Looked to me like a domestic.

But it wasn't her clothes that drew my attention. It was the loudness of her voice, which you'd have to say was in complete contrast to the way she looked. She was sitting with three men, all of them older than her, who I recognized at once: Tom Cobleigh, his brother Seth and Julian somebody, whose surname escaped me, but who worked with them – three men with whom I had traded words if not blows before. The kind who looked down their noses at me because they thought I looked down my nose at them, who liked me no more than I liked them, which was not a lot. They were sat forward on their stools and watching this young girl with leering, wolfish eyes that betrayed a darker purpose, even though they were all smiles, thumping on the table, encouraging her as she drank dry a flagon of ale.

No, she did not look like one of the women who usually frequented the tavern, but it seemed she was determined to act like one of them. The flagon was about as big as she was, and as she wiped her hand across her mouth and hammered it to the table, the men responded with cheers, shouting for another one and no doubt pleased to see her wobble slightly on her stool. Probably couldn't believe their luck. Pretty little thing like that.

I watched as they let the girl drink yet more ale with the same tumult accompanying her success, and then as she did the same as before, and wiped her hand across her mouth but with an even more pronounced wobble this time, a look passed between them. A look that seemed to say, *The Job Is Done*.

Tom and Julian stood, and they began, in their words, to 'escort' her to the door, because, 'You've had too much to drink, my lovely, let's get you home, shall we?'

'To bed,' smirked Seth, thinking he was saying it under his breath even though the whole tavern heard him. 'Let's be getting you to bed.'

I passed a look to the barman, who dropped his eyes

and used his apron to blow his nose. A customer sat down the bar from me turned away. Bastards. Might as well have looked to the cat for help, I thought, then with a sigh banged down my tankard, stepped off my stool and followed the Cobleighs into the road outside.

I blinked as I stepped from the darkness of the tavern into bright sunlight. My cart was there, roasting in the sun; beside it another one that I took to belong to the Cobleighs. On the other side of the road was a yard with the house set far back, but no sign of a farmer. We were alone on the highway: just me, the two Cobleigh brothers, Julian and the girl, of course.

'Well, Tom Cobleigh,' I said, 'the things you see on a fine afternoon. Things like you and your cronies getting drunk and getting a poor defenceless young woman even drunker.'

The girl sagged as Tom Cobleigh let go of her arm and turned to address me, his finger already raised.

'Now just you stay out of this, Edward Kenway, you young good-for-nothing. You're as drunk as I am and yer morals just as loose; I don't need to be given a talking-to by the likes of you.'

Seth and Julian had turned as well. The girl was glazed over, like her mind had gone to sleep even if her body was still awake.

'Well,' I smiled, 'loose morals I might have, Tom Cobleigh, but I don't need to pour ale down a girl's throat before taking her to bed, and I certainly don't need two friends to help me at the task.'

Tom Cobleigh reddened. 'Why, you cheeky little bastard, you, I'm going to put her on my cart is what I'm going to do, and take her home.'

'I have no doubt that you intend to put her on your cart and take her home. It's what you plan to do between putting her on the cart and reaching home that concerns me.'

'That *concerns* you, does it? A broken nose and a couple of broken ribs will be concerning you unless you mind your own bloody business.'

Squinting, I glanced at the highway, where the trees bordering the dirt track shone gold and green in the sun, and in the distance was a lone figure on a horse, shimmering and indistinct.

I took a step forward, and if there had been any warmth or humour in my manner, then it disappeared now, almost of its own accord. There was a steeliness in my voice when I next spoke.

'Now you just leave that girl alone, Tom Cobleigh, or I won't be responsible for my actions.'

The three men looked at one another. In a way they'd done as I asked. They'd let go of the girl, and she seemed almost relieved to slide to her haunches, placing one hand on the ground and looking at us all with bleary eyes, evidently oblivious to all this being discussed on her behalf.

Meanwhile I looked at the Cobleighs and weighed up the odds. Had I ever fought three at once? Well, no. Because if you were fighting three at once then you weren't so much fighting as getting beaten up. But come on, Edward Kenway, I told myself. Yes, on the one hand, it was three men, but one of them was Tom Cobleigh, who was no spring chicken, but about my father's age. Another one was Seth Cobleigh, who was Tom Cobleigh's son. And if you can imagine the kind of person who would help his father get a young girl drunk, well, then you can imagine the sort of person Seth Cobleigh was, which was to say a maggoty, underhand type, more likely to run away from a fight with wet breeches than stand his ground. And what's more, they were drunk.

On the other hand, I was drunk, too. Plus they had Julian who, going on looks alone, could handle himself.

But I had another idea. That lone rider I could see in the distance. If I could just hold off the Cobleighs till he arrived, the odds were likely to shift back in my favour. After all, if he was of good character, the lone rider was bound to stop and help me out.

'Well, Tom Cobleigh,' I said, 'you got the advantage over me, that's obvious for anyone to see, but, you know, I just wouldn't be able to look my mother in the eye knowing I'd let you and your cronies abduct this pretty young thing.'

I glanced up the road, to where that lone rider was getting closer. *Come on then*, I thought. *Don't hang about.*

'So,' I continued, 'even if you end up leaving me in a bloody heap by the side of this here road, and carry that young lassie off anyway, I'm going to have to do all that I can to make it as difficult for you as possible. And perhaps see to it that you go on your way with a black eye and maybe a pair of throbbing bollocks for your troubles.'

Tom Cobleigh spat then peered at me through wizened, slitty eyes. 'That's it then, is it? Well, are you just going to stand there talking about it all day, or are you going to attend to your task? Because time waits for no man . . .' He grinned an evil grin. 'I've got things to see, people to do.'

'Aye, that's right, and the longer you leave it the more chance that poor lassie has of sobering up, eh?'

'I don't mind telling you, I'm getting tired of all this talk, Kenway.' He turned to Julian. 'How about we teach this little bastard a lesson? Oh, and one more thing before we start, Master Kenway, you ain't fit to shine your mother's shoes, you understand?'

That hit me hard, I don't mind admitting. Having someone like Tom Cobleigh, who had all the morals of a frothing dog and about half the intelligence, able to reach into my soul as if my guilt was an open wound, then stick his thumb in that open wound and cause me even more pain, well, it certainly firmed up my resolve, if nothing else.

Julian pushed his chest forward and with a snarl advanced. Two steps away from me he raised his fists, dipped his right shoulder and swung, and I don't know who Julian was used to fighting outside taverns, but somebody with less experience than me, that's for sure, because I'd already taken note of the fact that he was right-handed, and he couldn't have made his intentions more obvious if he'd tried.

The dirt rose in clouds around my feet as I dodged easily and brought my own right fist up sharply. He shouted in pain as I caught him under the jaw. And if it had just been him, the battle would have been won. But Tom Cobleigh was already upon me. From the corner of my eye I saw him but was too late to react and, next thing you know, I was dazed by knuckles that slammed into my temple.

I staggered slightly as I swung to meet the attack, and my fists were swinging much more wildly than I'd have liked. I was hoping to land a lucky blow, needing to put at least one of the men down to even up the numbers. But none of my punches made contact as Tom Cobleigh retreated, plus Julian had recovered from my first strike with alarming speed and now came at me again.

His right fist came up and connected with my chin, spinning me about so that I almost lost my balance. My hat flew off, my hair was in my eyes and I was in disarray. And guess who came in with his boots kicking? That worm, Seth Cobleigh, shouting encouragement to his father and Julian at the same time. And the little bastard was lucky. His boot caught me in the midriff and, already off balance, I lost my footing. And fell.

The worst thing you can do in a fight is fall. Once you

fall it's over. Through their legs I saw the lone rider up the highway, who was now my only chance at salvation, possibly my only hope of getting out of this alive. But what I saw made my heart sink. Not a man on a horse, a tradesman, who would dismount and come rushing to my aid. No, the lone rider was a woman. She was riding astride the horse, not side-saddle, but despite that you could see she was a lady. She wore a bonnet and a light-coloured summer dress, and the last thing I thought before the Cobleigh boots obscured my view and the kicks came raining in was that she was beautiful.

So what, though? Good looks weren't going to save me now.

'Hey,' I heard. 'You three men. Stop what you're doing right now.'

They turned to look up at her and removed their hats, shuffling in line to hide the sight of me, who lay coughing on the ground.

'What is going on here?' she demanded to know. From the sound of her voice I could tell she was young and, while not highly born, definitely well-bred – too well-bred surely to be riding unaccompanied?

'We were just teaching this young man here some manners,' rasped Tom Cobleigh, out of breath. Exhausting business it was, kicking me half to death.

'Well, it doesn't take three of you to do that, does it?' she replied. I could see her now, twice as beautiful as I'd first thought, as she glowered at the Cobleighs, who for their part looked thoroughly mortified.

She dismounted. 'More to the point, what are you doing with this young lady here?' She indicated the girl, who still sat dazed and drunk on the ground.

'Oh, ma'am, begging your pardon, ma'am, but this is a young friend of ours who has had too much to drink.'

The lady darkened. 'She is most certainly *not* your young friend, she is a maidservant, and if I don't get her back home before my mother discovers she's absconded then she will be an unemployed maidservant.'

She looked pointedly from one man to the next. 'I know you men, and I think I understand exactly what has been going on here. Now you will leave this young man alone and be on your way before I am of a mind to take this further.'

With much bowing and scraping, the Cobleighs clambered aboard their cart and were soon gone. Meanwhile the woman dismounted and knelt down to speak to me. Her voice had changed. She was softly spoken now. I heard concern. 'My name is Caroline Scott. My family lives on Hawkins Lane in Bristol; let me take you back there and tend to your wounds.'

'I cannot, my lady,' I said, sitting up and trying to manage a grin. 'I have work to do.'

She stood, frowning. 'I see. And did I assess the situation correctly?'

I picked up my hat and began to brush the dirt from it. It was even more battered now. 'You did, my lady.'

'Then I owe you my thanks and so will Rose when she sobers up. She's a wilful girl, not always the easiest of staff, but, nevertheless, I don't want to see her suffer for her impetuousness.'

She was an angel, I decided then, and as I helped them mount the horse, Caroline holding on to Rose, who lolled drunkenly over the neck of the horse, I had a sudden thought.

'Can I see you again, my lady? To thank you properly when I look a little more presentable, perhaps?'

She gave me a regretful look. 'I fear my father would not approve,' she said, and with that shook the reins and left.

That night I sat beneath the thatch of our cottage, gazing out over the pastures that rolled away from the farm as the sun went down. Usually my thoughts would be of escaping my future.

That night I thought of Caroline. Caroline Scott of Hawkins Lane.

4

Two days later I woke up to the sound of screaming. In a rush I dragged my breeches on and hopped out of the room with my shirt unbuttoned, still pulling my boots on over bare feet. I knew that scream. It was my mother. Moments later her screams had died down to a sob, replaced by my father cursing. The soft cursing of a man who had been proved correct.

After my fight at the Auld Shillelagh I had returned to the tavern in order to do something about my cuts and bruises. To numb the pain, so to speak. And what better way of doing that than with a drink or two? Thus, when I'd eventually arrived home I'd been in a bit of a state. And when I say 'state', I mean 'state', as in a man who looked as though he'd been in the wars, which I had: bruises to my face, my neck, my clothes ragged and torn. But also 'state', as in a man who had had far too much to drink.

Either one of these two things were likely to make Father angry, so we'd argued, and I'm ashamed to say I used some choice language in front of my mother. And of course Father was furious about that, and I felt the back of his hand for it. But what had really enraged him was that the brawl, as he called it (because he wouldn't accept that I'd been protecting a lady's honour, and that he would have done the same in my position) had all taken place during the working day. What he saw was them, exhausted from their labours, and me, getting drunk and into fights, sullying the good name of the Kenways, and in this particular case storing up even more trouble for the future.

'The Cobleighs.' He'd thrown up his hands in exasperation. 'That lot of bad bloody eggs,' he'd said. 'It would have to be them, wouldn't it? They won't let it go, you know that, don't you?'

Sure enough, I rushed out to the front yard that morning, and there was Father, in his workclothes, comforting Mother, who stood with her head buried in his chest, sobbing quietly, her back to what was on the ground.

My hand went to my mouth, seeing what had greeted them: two slaughtered sheep, their throats cut, laid side by side in the blood-darkened dust. They'd been placed there so we'd know they weren't the victims of a fox or wild dog. So that we'd know the sheep had been killed for a reason.

A warning. Vengeance.

'The Cobleighs,' I spat, feeling rage bubble like fast-boiling water within me. With it came a sharp, stinging guilt. We all knew it was my actions that had caused this.

Father didn't look at me. On his face was all the sadness and worry you'd expect. Like I say, he was a well-respected man, and he enjoyed the benefits of that respect; his relations even with his competitors were conducted with courtesy and respect. He didn't like the Cobleighs, of course he didn't – who did? – but he'd never had trouble before, either with them or anyone else. This was the first time. This was new to us.

'I know what you're thinking, Edward,' he said. He couldn't bear to look at me, I noticed; he just stood holding Mother with his eyes fixed on some point in the distance. 'But you can think again.'

'What am I thinking, Father?'

'You're thinking it's you who has brought this upon us. You're thinking about having it out with the Cobleighs.'

'Well? What are *you* thinking? Just let them get away with it?' I indicated the two bleeding corpses on the dirt. Livestock destroyed. Livelihood lost. 'They have to pay.'

'It can't be done,' he said simply.

'What do you mean it can't be done?'

'Two days ago, I was approached to join an organization – a trade organization, it was called.'

When I looked at my father I wondered if I was seeing an older version of myself and, may God strike me down for thinking it, but I fervently hoped not. He'd been a handsome man once, but now his face was lined and drawn. The wide brim of his felt hat covered eyes that were always turned down and tired.

'They wanted me to join,' he continued, 'but I said

no. Like most of the tradesmen in the area the Cobleighs have said yes. They enjoy the protection of the trade organization, Edward. Why else do you think they would do something so ruthless? They're protected.'

I closed my eyes. 'Is there anything we can do?'

'We continue as before, Edward, and hope that this is an end to it, that the Cobleighs will feel their honour has been restored.' He turned his tired, old eyes on me for the first time. There was nothing in them, no anger or reproach. Only defeat. 'Now, can I trust you to get this cleared up, while I see to your mother?'

'Yes, Father,' I said.

He and Mother made their way back into the cottage.

'Father,' I called as they reached the door, 'why didn't you join the trade organization?'

'You'll learn one day, if you ever grow up,' he said without turning.

5

In the meantime my thoughts returned to Caroline. The first thing I did was find out who she was, and by asking around Hawkins Lane I learnt that her father, Emmett Scott, was a wealthy merchant dealing in tea, who would no doubt have been seen as *new money* by most of his customers, but nevertheless seemed to have inveigled himself into high society.

Now, a man less headstrong than myself, less cock-sure, might well have chosen a different path to Caroline's heart than the one I opted for. After all, her father was a supplier of fine teas to the well-to-do households in the West Country; he had money, enough to employ servants at a good-sized house on Hawkins Lane – no smallholder he, no getting up at five a.m. to feed the livestock for him. He was a man of means and influence. What I should have done – even knowing it would be futile – was try to make his acquaintance. And much of what subsequently happened – so much – could have been avoided if I had at least tried.

But I didn't.

I was young, you see. And no wonder the likes of Tom Cobleigh hated me, I was so arrogant. Despite my social status I thought currying favour with a tea merchant was below me.

Now, one thing I know is that if you love women, which I do, I'm not ashamed to say, you find something of beauty in every woman, no matter whether or not they're what you might call classically beautiful. But with Caroline it was my misfortune to fall in love with a woman whose outer beauty matched the inner, and of course her charms were likely to catch the attention of others. So the next thing I discovered about her was that she had caught the eye of Matthew Hague, son of Sir Aubrey Hague, Bristol's biggest landowner, and an executive in the East India Company.

From what I gathered, young Matthew was our age, and as self-important and jumped-up as they come, thinking himself much more than he was. He liked to wear the air of a shrewd businessman, like his father, though it was clear he possessed none of his father's aptitude in that area. What's more he liked to think himself something of a philosopher and often dictated his thoughts to a draughtsman who accompanied him wherever he went – pen and ink at the ready to write down, whatever the circumstances, Hague's thoughts, such as, 'A joke is a stone tossed into water, laughter the ripples it makes.'

Perhaps his utterings were deeply profound. All I know is that I wouldn't have paid him much mind – indeed, I would have joined in with the general derision and laughter that seemed to accompany mention of his name – if it hadn't been for the fact that he'd showed an interest in Caroline. Perhaps even that wouldn't have worried me so much, but for two other factors. That Caroline's father, Emmett Scott, had apparently betrothed Caroline to the Hague boy, and also the fact that the Hague boy, possibly on account of his condescending manner, his tendency to make vital mistakes in even the most simple business dealings and his ability to wind people up, had a minder, a man named Wilson, who was an uncultured brute of a man, but very big, with one slightly closed-up eye, who was said to be tough.

'Life is not a battle, for battles are there to be won or lost. Life is to be experienced,' Matthew Hague had been heard to dictate to his skinny draughtsman.

Well, of course, for Matthew Hague there was precious little battling going on. Firstly, because he was the son of Sir Aubrey Hague, and, secondly, he had a dirty great minder following him everywhere.

So, anyway, I made it my business to find out where Caroline would be one sunny afternoon. How? Well, that was a case of calling in a favour, you could say. You remember Rose, the maidservant I'd helped save from a fate worse than death? Well, I reminded her of that fact one day when I followed her from Hawkins Lane to the market, and then as she made her way through the stalls, deftly avoiding the shouts of the stallholders with a basket in the crook of her arm, made my introductions.

She didn't recognize me, of course.

'I'm sure I have no idea who you are, sir,' she said with little startled eyes darting in all directions, as though her employers might come a-leaping from the aisles between the stalls.

'Well, I know exactly who you are, Rose,' I said. 'And it was me who took a beating on your behalf outside the Auld Shillelagh last week. Drunk as you were, you remember the presence of a good Samaritan, I hope?'

She nodded reluctantly. And, yes, perhaps it's not the most gentlemanly thing to do, to use a young lady's unfortunate circumstances in such a mercenary fashion to . . . well, I wouldn't go as far as to say *blackmail*, but as leverage, but there we have it. I was smitten, and given that my penmanship skills were none too clever, had decided that a face-to-face encounter with Caroline was the best way to begin the process of winning her heart.

Charm the birds out the trees, see? Well, it worked on traders, and on the occasional young lady I encountered in the taverns. Why not on someone of high-born stock?

From Rose I learnt that Caroline enjoyed taking the air at the Bristol docks on a Tuesday afternoon. But, she said, with a quick look left to right, I should be wary of Mr Hague. Him and his manservant, Wilson.

Mr Hague was most keen on Caroline, so Rose said, and was very protective of her.

So it was that the following morning I made sure I took a trip into town, moved my goods as quickly as possible, and then made my way down to the harbour. There the air was thick with the scent of sea salt and manure and boiling pitch, and rang to the cries of seagulls, as well as the endless shouts of those who made the docks their place of work: crews calling to one another as they loaded and unloaded ships whose masts rocked slightly in the gentle breeze.

I could see why Caroline might like it here. All life was on the harbour. From the men with baskets of freshly picked apples or pheasants hanging on twine round their necks, to the tradesmen who merely deposited baskets on the quayside and hollered at visiting deckhands, and the women with fabric, persuading jack tars they were getting a bargain. There were children who had flowers or tinder to sell, or who ran through the legs of sailors and dodged the traders, almost as anonymous as the dogs that slunk around the harbour walls and snuffled at the piles of rubbish and rotting food swept there from the day before.

Among them all was Caroline who, with a bow in her bonnet and a parasol over one shoulder, with Rose a respectful few feet behind her, looked every inch the lady. And yet, I noticed – I kept my own distance for the time being, needing to choose my moment – she didn't look down her nose at the activity around her as she so easily could have done. From her demeanour I could tell that she, like me, enjoyed seeing life in all its forms. I wondered did she also, like me, ever look out to a sea that glittered with treasure, masts of ships tilting gently, gulls flying towards where the world began, and wonder what stories the horizons had to tell?

I am a romantic man, it's true, but not a romantic fool, and there had been moments since that day outside the tavern when I'd wondered if my growing affections for Caroline were not partly an invention of my mind. She had been my saviour, after all. But now, as I walked along the harbour, I fell for her anew.

Did I expect to speak to Caroline in my sheep-farmer's clothes? Of course not. So I'd taken the precaution of changing. Trading my dirty boots for a pair of silver-buckled shoes, neat white stockings and dark breeches, a freshly laundered waistcoat over my shirt and a matching three-cornered hat instead of my trusty brown one. I looked quite the gentleman, if I do say so myself: I was young, good-looking and full of confidence, the son of a well-respected tradesman in the area. A Kenway. The name had something at least (despite my attempts otherwise), and I also had with me a young scallywag by the name of Albert, who I had bribed to do a job for me. It doesn't take much grey matter to guess the nature of the job: he was to help me impress the fair Caroline. One transaction with a flower girl later and I had the means to do it, too.

'Right, you remember the plan,' I told Albert, who looked up at me from beneath the brim of his hat with eyes that were so much older than his years and a bored heard-it-all-before look on his face.

'Right, mate, you're to give this spray of flowers to that fine-looking lady over there. She will stop. She will say to you, "Ah, young fellow, for what reason are you presenting me with these flowers?" And you will point over here.' I indicated to where I would be standing, proud as a peacock. Caroline would either recognize me from the other day, or at the very least wish to thank her mysterious admirer, and instruct Albert to invite me over, at which point the charm offensive would begin.

'And what's in it for me?' asked Albert.

'What's in it for you? How about counting yourself lucky I don't give you a thick ear?'

He curled a lip. 'How about you taking a running jump off the side of the harbour?'

'All right,' I said, knowing when I was beaten, 'there's half a penny in it for you.'

'Half a penny? Is that the best you can do?'

'As a matter of fact, Sonny Jim, it is the best I can bloody do, and for walking across the harbour and pre-senting a flower to a beautiful woman it's also the easiest half-penny's work there ever was.'

'Ain't she got a suitor with her?' Albert craned his neck to look.

And, of course, it would soon become apparent

exactly why Albert wanted to know whether Caroline had an escort. But at that particular moment I took his interest for nothing more than curiosity. A bit of chit-chat. Some idle conversation. So I told him that, no, she had no suitor, and I gave him the spray of flowers and his half-penny and sent him on his way.

It was as he sauntered over that something he was holding in his other hand caught my eye, and I realized what a mistake I'd made.

It was a tiny blade. And his eyes were fixed on her arm, where her purse hung on a ribbon.

Oh God. A cutpurse. Young Albert was a cutpurse.

'You little bastard,' I said under my breath, and immediately set off across the harbour after him.

By now he was halfway between us, but being small was able to slip between the seething crowds more quickly. I saw Caroline, oblivious to the approaching danger – danger that I had inadvertently sent into her path.

The next thing I saw were three men, who were also making their way towards Caroline. Three men I recognized: Matthew Hague, his skinny writing companion and his minder, Wilson. Inwardly I cringed. Even more so when I saw Wilson's eyes flick from Caroline to Albert and then back again. He was good, you could tell. In a heartbeat he had seen what was about to happen.

I stopped. For a second I was totally flummoxed. Didn't know what to do next.

'Oi,' shouted Wilson, his gruff tones cutting across the endless squawking, chatting, hawking of the day.

'Oi, you!' and he surged forward. But Albert had reached Caroline and in one almost impossibly fast and fluid gesture his hand snaked out, the ribbon of Caroline's purse was cut and the tiny silk bag dropped neatly into Albert's other hand.

Caroline didn't notice the theft but she couldn't fail to see the huge figure of Wilson bearing down upon her and she cried out in surprise, even as he lunged past her and grabbed Albert by the shoulders.

'This young rapscallion has something that belongs to you, miss,' roared Wilson, shaking Albert so hard that the silk purse dropped to the harbour floor.

Her eyes went to the purse and then to Albert.

'Is this true?' she said, though the evidence was in front of her eyes, and, in fact, currently sat in a small pile of horse manure by their feet.

'Pick it up, pick it up,' Hague was saying to his skinny companion, having just arrived and already beginning to behave as though it was he who had apprehended the knife-wielding youth and not his six-and-a-half-foot minder.

'Teach the young ruffian a lesson, Wilson.' This was Hague waving his hand as though attempting to ward off some especially noxious flatulence.

'With pleasure, sir.'

There were still several feet between me and them. He was held fast but Albert's eyes swivelled from looking terrified at Wilson to where I stood in the crowd and as our eyes met, he stared at me beseechingly.

I clenched my teeth. *That little bastard*, he had been about to ruin all of my plans and now he was looking to me for help. The cheek of him.

But then Wilson, holding him by the scruff of the neck with one hand, drove his fist into Albert's stomach and that was it for me. That same sense of injustice I had felt at the tavern was reignited and in a second I was shoving through the crowd to Albert's aid.

'Hey,' I shouted. Wilson swung to see me, and though he was bigger than me, and far uglier than me, I'd just seen him hit a child and my blood was up. It's not an especially gentlemanly way to conduct a fight, but I knew from experience both as giver and receiver that there was no quicker and cleaner way to put a man down, so I did it. I led with the knee. My knee into his bollocks, to be precise. So quick and so hard that where one second Wilson was a huge snarling bully about to meet my attack, the next he was a snivelling mewling heap of a man, his hands grasping at his groin as he landed on the floor.

Heedless of Matthew Hague's outraged screaming, I grabbed Albert. 'Say sorry to the lady,' I ordered him, with a finger in his face.

'Sorry, miss,' said Albert obediently.

'Now hop it,' I said and pointed him off down the harbour. He needed no second invitation and in a trice was gone, prompting even more protestations from Matthew Hague, and I thanked God that at least Albert was out of the picture and unable to dob me in.

I had saved Albert from getting a worse beating but my victory was short-lived and I certainly didn't get the time to enjoy it. Wilson was already on his feet and though his bollocks must have been throbbing something rotten, he wasn't feeling anything at that moment except rage. He was quick, too, and before I had time to react had grabbed me and was holding me firm. I tried to pull away, dipping one shoulder and driving my fist up towards his solar plexus but I didn't have the momentum and he used his body to block me, grunting as much with satisfaction as with the effort as he dragged me bodily across the harbour, people scattering before him. In a fair fight I would have had a chance, but he used his superior strength and his sudden rage-fuelled spurt of speed to his advantage, and in the next moment my feet were kicking in thin air as he flung me off the side of the harbour.

Well, I had always dreamed of taking to the high seas, and with the sound of laughter ringing in my ears I pulled myself to the nearest rope ladder and began to climb out. Caroline, Rose, Hague and his two men had already gone; I saw a hand reach down to help me up.

'Here, mate, let me help you with that,' said a voice. I looked up gratefully, about to clasp the hand of my Samaritan, only to see the leering face of Tom Cobleigh peering over the harbour's edge at me.

'Well, the things you see when you're out without your musket,' he said and there was nothing I could do to prevent his fist smashing into my face, sending me off the rope ladder and back into the water.

6

Tom Cobleigh had made himself scarce, but Wilson must have doubled back. Chances are, he saw to it that Hague and Caroline were okay then made haste back to the harbour and found me sitting on a set of steps licking my wounds. He passed across my light and I looked up to see him, heart sinking.

'If you've come back to try that again,' I said, 'I won't make it quite so easy for you this time.'

'I have no doubt,' he replied without so much as flinching, 'but I'm not here to pitch you back in the sea, Kenway.'

At that I looked sharply at him.

'That's right, boy, I have my spies, and my spies tell me that a young gentleman by the name of Edward Kenway has been asking questions about Caroline Scott. This same young gentleman by the name of Edward Kenway was involved in a fight outside the Auld Shillelagh on the road to Hatherton last week. That same day Miss Scott was also on the road to Hatherton because her maidservant had absconded and that you and Miss Scott had cause to speak following your altercation.'

He came so close I could smell the stale coffee on his

breath. Proof, if proof were needed, that he wasn't in the slightest bit intimidated – not by me nor by my fearsome reputation.

'Am I on the right lines so far, Master Kenway?'

'You might be.'

He nodded. 'I thought so. How old are you, boy? What? Seventeen? About the same age as Miss Scott. Me thinks you're nurturing a bit of a passion for her, am I right?'

'You might be.'

'I think I am. Now, I'm going to say this once and once only, but Miss Scott is promised to Mr Hague. This union has the blessing of the parents . . .' He hauled me to my feet, pinning my arms to my sides. Too wet, too bedraggled, too exhausted to resist, I knew what was coming anyway.

'Now, if I see you hanging around her again, or trying any more stupid stunts to try to get her attention, then it'll be more than a dip in the sea you get, do I make myself clear?'

I nodded. 'And what about the knee in the goolies you're about to give me?'

He smiled grimly. 'Oh, that? That's personal.'

He came good on his word, and it was some time before I was able to get to my feet and make my way back to my cart. It wasn't just my tackle that was injured – my pride had taken a beating, too.

7

That night I lay in bed, cursing my luck. I had blown my chances with Caroline. She was lost to me. All thanks to that greedy urchin Albert, not to mention Hague and company; I had suffered once more at the hands of Tom Cobleigh, and father had looked at me askance when I'd arrived home, a little later than usual and, even though I had had a change of clothing, a little more bedraggled into the bargain.

'You've not been in those taverns again?' he said darkly. 'So help me God, if I hear you've been dragging our good name –'

'No, Father, nothing like that.'

He was wrong; I'd not been to the tavern on my way home. In fact, I'd not gone within sniffing distance of an ale house since the fight outside the Auld Shillelagh. I'd been telling myself that meeting Caroline had had an effect on me. Quite literally a *sobering* effect.

Now, though, I didn't know. I began to wonder – perhaps my life was there, in the beer suds, around the sloppy grins of easy women with hardly any teeth and even fewer morals, and by the time of my thirtieth summer hauling wool to Bristol market I'd be numbed to it; I'd have forgotten whatever hopes I had of one day seeing the world. Gradually the lure of the taverns asserted itself once more.

And then two things happened that changed everything. The first came in the shape of a gentleman who took his place next to me at the bar of the George and Dragon in Bristol one sunny afternoon. A smartly dressed gentleman with flamboyant cuffs and a colourful necktie, who removed his hat, placed it on the bar and indicated my drink.

'Can I get you another, sir?' he asked me.

It made a change from 'son', 'lad' or 'boy'. All of which I had to endure on a daily, if not hourly, basis.

'And who do I have to thank for my drink? And what might he want in return?' I asked guardedly.

'Perhaps just the chance to talk, friend,' beamed the stranger. He proffered his hand to shake. 'The name is Dylan Wallace, pleased to make your acquaintance, Mr . . . Kenway, isn't it?'

For the second time in a matter of days I was presented with someone who knew my name, though I had no idea why.

'Oh yes,' he said, beaming (he was at least of a more friendly nature than Wilson, I reflected), 'I know your name. Edward Kenway. Quite the reputation you have around these parts. Indeed, I've seen you in action for myself.'

'Have you?' I looked at him eyes narrowed.

'Why, yes indeed,' he said. 'I hear from the people I've spoken to that you're no stranger to a bit of a ruck, but even so you can't have forgotten your fight at the Auld Shillelagh the other day.'

'I don't think I'm going to be allowed to forget it,' I sighed.

'Well, I tell you what, sir, I'm just going to come straight out with it, because you look like a young man who knows his own mind and is unlikely to be persuaded one way or the other by anything I might have to tell you. Have you ever thought of going to sea?'

'Well, now that you come to mention it, Mr Wallace, I had once considered leaving Bristol and heading in that direction, you're right.'

'So what's stopping you?'

I shook my head. 'Now *that* is a very good question.'

'Do you know what a privateer is, Mr Kenway, sir?'

Before I could answer he was telling me. 'They're buccaneers given letters of marque by the Crown. You see, the Dons and the Portuguese are helping themselves to the treasures of the New World; they're filling their coffers, and it's the job of privateers either to stop them or to take what they're taking. Do you understand?'

'I know what a privateer is, thank you very much, Mr Wallace. I know that you can't be put on trial for piracy, so long as you don't attack ships belonging to your own country, that's it, isn't it?'

'Oh, that's it, Mr Kenway, sir,' grinned Dylan Wallace. 'How would it be if I leaned over and was to help myself to a mug of ale? That'd be stealing, wouldn't it? The barman might try to stop me, but what if I was doing it with impunity. What if my theft had the royal seal of approval? This is what we are talking about, Mr Kenway. The opportunity to go out on the high seas and help yourself to as much gold and treasure as your captain's ship will carry. And, by doing so, be not only working with the approval of Her Majesty Queen Anne but *helping* her. You've heard of Captain Christopher Newport, Francis Drake, Admiral Sir Henry Morgan – privateers all. How about adding the name Edward Kenway to that illustrious list?'

'What are you saying?'

'I'm saying how about becoming a privateer, sir?'

I gave him a studying look. 'And if I promise to think about it, what's in it for you?'

'Why, commission, of course.'

'Don't you normally press-gang men for this kind of thing?'

'Not men of your calibre, Mr Kenway. Not men we might consider *officer material*.'

'All because I showed promise in a fight?'

'Because of the way you *conducted* yourself in that fight, Mr Kenway, in all aspects of it.'

I nodded. 'If I promise to think about it does that mean I don't need to return the favour of an ale?'

8

I went to bed that night knowing I had to tell Father my destiny lay not in sheep farming, but in swashbuckling adventure as a privateer.

He'd be disappointed, of course, but maybe somewhat relieved also. Yes, on the one hand, I had been an asset, and had developed trading skills and put them to good use for the benefit of the family. But, on the other hand, there was the drinking, the brawling and, of course, the rift with the Cobleighs.

Shortly after the two dead carcasses had been deposited in our front yard there'd been another incident where we'd woken to find the flock had been let out in the night. Father thought fences had been deliberately damaged. I didn't tell Father about what had happened at the quayside but it was obvious Tom Cobleigh still harboured a grudge – a grudge that wasn't likely to go away any time soon.

That I had brought down on Father's head. And without me in the picture, then perhaps the vendetta would end.

And so as I laid my head down that night, my only decision was how to break the news to my father. And how my father might break the news to my mother.

And then I heard something from the window. A tapping.

I looked out with no little trepidation. What did I expect to see? I wasn't sure, but the memories of the Cobleighs were still fresh in my mind. Instead, what I saw, sitting astride her horse in the pale moonlight of the yard, as though God himself was shining his lantern upon her beauty, was Caroline Scott.

She was dressed as if for riding school. Her clothes were dark. She wore a tall hat and a white shirt and black jacket. With one hand she held the reins and the other was raised, about to throw a second fistful of gravel at my window.

I myself had been known to use the very same trick to attract the attention of a lady friend, and I remembered well the terror of waking up the whole household. So when I threw stones at a casement window, I usually did it from behind the safety of a stone wall. Not Caroline. That was the difference in our social standing. She had no fears of being run off the property with a boot in her behind and a flea in her ear. She was Caroline Scott of Hawkins Lane in Bristol. She herself was being courted by the son of an East India Company executive. Clandestine assignation or not – and there was no doubt this was clandestine – hiding behind stone walls was not for her.

'Well . . .' she whispered. I saw her eyes dance in the moonlight. 'Are you going to leave me sitting out here all night?'

No. In moments I was in the yard by her side, taking the reins of the horse and walking her away from the property as we spoke.

'Your actions the other day,' she said. 'You put yourself in great danger in order to protect that young thief.'

(Yes, yes, I know what you're thinking. And, yes, yes, I did feel a little guilt at that.)

(But not too much guilt.)

'There is nothing I hate so much as a bully, Miss Scott,' I said. Which did at least have the benefit of being true.

'So I thought. This is twice now I have been most impressed by the gallantry of your actions.'

'Then it is on two occasions that I have been pleased you were there to witness it.'

'You interest me, Mr Kenway. And your own interest in me has not gone unremarked.'

I stayed silent. And we walked for a while. And even though no words were spoken there was meaning in our silence. As though we acknowledged our feelings for each other. I felt the closeness of her riding boot. Above the heat and scent of the horse, I thought I could smell the powder she wore. Never before had I been so aware of a person, of the nearness of a person.

'I expect you have been told that I am betrothed to another,' she said.

We stopped along the lane. There were stone walls on either side of us, the green pastures beyond interrupted by clusters of white sheep. The air was warm and dry around us, not even a breeze to disturb the trees that rose to make the skyline. From somewhere came the cry of an animal, lovelorn or hurt, but certainly feral, and a sudden disturbance in the bushes startled us. We felt like interlopers. Uninvited guests to nature's household.

'Why, I don't think –'

'Mr Kenway –'

'You can call me Edward, Miss Scott.'

'Well, you can continue calling me Miss Scott.'

'Really?'

'Oh go on then, you can call me Caroline.'

'Thank you, Miss Scott.'

She gave me a sideways look, as though to check whether or not I was mocking her.

'Well, Edward,' she continued, 'I know full well you have been making enquiries about me. And though I do not pretend to know exactly what you've been told, I think I know the gist: that Caroline Scott is betrothed to Matthew Hague; that Matthew Hague bombards her with love poems, that the union has the blessing of his father and, of course, her father. Am I right?'

I admitted I had heard as much.

'Perhaps in the short dealings we have had together you might understand how I would feel about this particular arrangement?'

'I wouldn't like to say.'

'Then I shall spell it out for you. The thought of marriage to Matthew Hague turns my stomach. Do you think I want to live my life in the household of the Hagues? Expected to treat my husband like a king, turn a blind eye to his affairs, run the household, shout at the staff, choose flowers and pick out doilies, go visiting, take tea, trade gossip with other wives?

'Do you think I want to hide myself so deeply beneath the petty concerns of manners and etiquette that I can no longer find myself? At the moment I live between two worlds, Edward, able to see them both. The world I see on my visits to the harbour is the world that is most real to me, Edward. The one that is most alive. And as for Matthew Hague himself, I despise him almost as much as his poetry.

'Do not think me a helpless damsel in distress, Edward, because I am not that. But I'm not here for your help. I have come to help myself.'

'You've come to help yourself to *me*?'

'If you wish. Your next move is yours to make, but if you make it do so knowing this: any relationship between you and me would not have the blessing of my father, but it would have mine.'

'Excuse me, but it's not so much your father who concerns me, as his choice for you.'

'And the thought of making an enemy of the Hagues, does that put you off?'

I knew at that moment nothing would put me off. 'No, Caroline, it doesn't.'

'I hoped as much.'

We parted, with arrangements made to meet again.

And after that, our relationship began in earnest. We were able to keep it a secret. For some months, in fact, our meetings were held entirely in private: snatched moments spent wandering the lanes between Bristol and Hatherton, riding in the pastures.

Until one day she announced that Matthew Hague planned to ask for her hand in marriage the following morning, and my heart stopped.

I was determined not to lose her. Because of my love for her, because I could think of nothing but her, because when we were together I savoured every moment. Every word, every gesture that Caroline made was like nectar to me – everything about her, every curve and contour, her scent, her laugh, her refined manners, her intelligence.

And all of this ran through my mind as I dropped to one knee and took her hand, because what she was telling me, perhaps it wasn't an invitation but a farewell, and if it was, well, at least my humiliation would not be known far and wide, confined to the birds in the trees and the cows that stood in the fields watching us with sleepy eyes and chewing ruminatively.

'Caroline, will you marry me?' I said.

I held my breath. During our courtship every meeting we'd had, every stolen kiss we'd shared, I'd been haunted by a feeling of not believing my luck. It was as though a great joke was being played on me – I half expected Tom Cobleigh to come leaping out of the shadows snorting with laughter. And if not that – if not some vengeful practical joke at my expense – then perhaps I was merely a diversion for Caroline, a final fling, before she applied herself to her familial duty.

'Ah, Edward,' she smiled, 'I thought you'd never ask.'

9

I couldn't accept it, though, and I found myself travelling into town the next day, my journey taking me to Hawkins Lane. All I knew was that Matthew Hague planned to pay her a visit in the morning, and as I sidled up the highway and passed the row of houses among which was hers, I wondered if he was in there now, perhaps making his proposal.

One thing I knew of Caroline, she was a brave woman, but even so the bravest I'd ever known, but even so, she was passing up the opportunity to live the rest of her days in pampered luxury; and, worse, she was going to scandalize her mother and father. I knew only too well the pressures of trying to please a parent, how tempting it was to go down that route. An unfulfilled soul, or a soul troubled with guilt – which was the hardest cross to bear?

With me standing before her – and she loved me I'm sure of that – perhaps the decision was easier to make. But what about at night, when misgivings made their rounds and doubt came visiting? Perhaps she might simply have changed her mind and she was, at this very moment, blushing in her acceptance of Matthew Hague's proposal, and mentally writing a letter to me.

And if that happened, well, there was always Dylan Wallace, I supposed.

But then from the corner of my eye I saw the front door open and Wilson appear, quickly followed by the draughtsman and behind them Matthew Hague, who offered his arm for Caroline, Rose taking up the rear as they began their perambulations.

Staying some distance behind, I followed them all the way to the harbour, puzzling over his intentions. Not the harbour, surely? The dirty, smelly, crowded harbour, with its stench of manure and burning pitch and just-caught fish and men who had returned from months away at sea without so much as a bath during that time.

They were making their way towards what looked like a schooner moored at the dock, around which were gathered some men. It was difficult to tell, though, because hanging from the back of the ship was some kind of canvas, obscuring the name of the vessel. However, as the group drew closer to it I thought I knew what it was. I thought I knew his plan.

Sure enough, they stopped before it and still out of sight I watched as Caroline's eyes flicked nervously from Matthew Hague to the schooner, guessing that she, too, had worked out the purpose of their visit.

Next thing I knew, Hague was down on one knee, and the staff of the schooner, Wilson and the draughtsman, were all standing with their hands behind their backs, ready for the round of applause as Matthew

Hague popped his question, 'My darling, would you do me the honour of becoming my wife?'

Caroline swallowed and stammered. 'Matthew, m-must we do this here?'

He shot her a patronizing look, then with an expansive gesture of his hand ordered the canvas come off the rear of the schooner. There etched in a gold leaf was the vessel's name: *Caroline.*

'Where better place, my dear?'

And if it hadn't been for the situation I might even have slightly enjoyed the sight of Caroline at a loss. Usually she was nothing if not sure of herself. The doubt and near-panic I saw in her eyes was, I suspect, as new to her as it was to me.

'Matthew, I must say, you're embarrassing me.'

'My dear, dear Caroline, my precious flower . . .' he said, and made a small gesture to his draughtsman, who immediately began rooting around for his quill in order to record his master's poetic words.

'But how else would I have unveiled my marital gift to you? Now, I must press you for an answer. Please, with all these people watching . . .'

And, yes, I realized looking around, the entire harbour seemed to have halted, everybody hanging on Caroline's next words, which were . . .

'No, Matthew.'

Hague stood up so sharply that his draughtsman was forced to scurry backwards and almost lost his footing. Hague's face darkened and his lips pursed as he fought to retain composure and force a smile. 'One of your little jokes, perhaps?'

'I fear not, Matthew, I am betrothed to another.'

Hague drew himself up to his full height as though to intimidate Caroline. Standing back in the crowd I felt my blood rising and began to make my way forward.

'*To another*,' he croaked. 'And just who is this *other* man?'

'Me, sir,' I announced, having reached the front of the crowd and presented myself to him.

He looked at me with narrowed eyes. '*You*,' he spat.

From behind him Wilson was already moving forward, and in his eyes I could see his fury that I'd failed to heed his warning. And how that became his failure.

With an outstretched arm Hague stopped him. 'No, Wilson,' he said, adding pointedly, 'not here. Not now. I'm sure my lady may want to reconsider . . .'

A ripple of surprise and, I guess, not a little humour had travelled through the crowd and it rose again as Caroline said, 'No, Matthew, Edward and I are to be married.'

He rounded on her. 'And does your father know about this?'

'Not yet,' she said, then added, 'I've a feeling he soon will, though.'

For a moment Hague simply stood and trembled with rage, and for the first but not, as it would turn out, the last time, I actually felt sympathy for him. In the next instant he was barking at bystanders to get back to their work, then shouting at the schooner crew to replace the canvas, then calling to Wilson and his draughtsman to leave the harbour, turning his back pointedly on Caroline and offering me a look of hate as he exited. At his rear was Wilson and our eyes locked. Slowly, he drew a finger across his throat.

I shouldn't have done it really; Wilson was not a man to provoke, but I couldn't help myself, returning his death threat with a cheeky wink.

10

And that was how Bristol came to know that Edward Kenway, a sheep farmer worth a mere seventy-five pounds a year, was to marry Caroline Scott.

And what a scandal it was: Caroline Scott marrying beneath her would have been cause for gossip enough. That she had spurned Matthew Hague in the process constituted quite a stir, and I wonder if that scandal might ultimately have worked in our favour, because while I steeled myself for retribution – and for a while I looked for Wilson round every corner, and my first glance from the window to the yard each morning was filled with trepidation – none came. I saw nothing of Wilson, heard nothing of Matthew Hague.

In the end, the threat to our marriage came not from outside – not from the Cobleighs, Emmett Scott, Matthew Hague or Wilson. It came from the inside. It came from me.

I've had plenty of time to think about the reasons why, of course. And the problem was that I kept returning to my meeting with Dylan Wallace and his promises of riches in the West Indies. I wanted to go and return to Caroline a rich man. I had begun to see it as my only chance of making a success of myself. My only chance of being worthy of her. For, of course, yes, there was the immediate glory, or perhaps you might say *stature*, of having made Caroline Scott my wife, taking her from beneath the nose of Matthew Hague, but that was soon followed by a kind of . . . well, I can only describe it as *stagnation*.

Emmett Scott had delivered his cutting blow at the wedding. We should have been grateful, I suppose, that he and Caroline's mother had deigned to attend. Although for my own part I was not at all grateful. I would have preferred it if the pair of them had stayed away. I hated to see my father, cap in hand, bowing and scraping to Emmett Scott, hardly a noble man after all, just a merchant, separated from us not by any aristocratic leanings but by money alone.

For Caroline, though, I was glad they came. It wasn't as if they approved of the marriage, far from it, but at the very least they weren't prepared to lose their daughter over it.

I overheard her mother say, 'We just want you to be happy, Caroline,' and knew that she was speaking for herself alone. In the eyes of Emmett Scott I saw no such desire. I saw the look of a man who had been denied his chance to clamber higher up the social ladder, a man whose dreams of great influence had been dashed. He came to the wedding under sufferance, or perhaps for the pleasure of delivering his pronouncement in the churchyard after the vows had been made.

Emmett Scott had black hair brushed forward, dark

sunken cheeks and a mouth pinched permanently into a shape like a cat's anus. His face, in fact, wore the permanent expression of a man biting deep into the flesh of a lemon.

Except for this one occasion, when his lips pressed into a thin smile and he said, 'There will be no dowry.'

His wife, Caroline's mother, closed her eyes tightly as though it was a moment she'd dreaded, had hoped might not happen. Words had been exchanged, I could guess, and the last of them had belonged to Emmett Scott.

So we moved into an outhouse on my father's farm. We had appointed it as best we could, but it was still, at the end of the day, an outhouse: packed mud and sticks for the walls, our roof thatch badly in need of repair.

Our union had begun in the summer, of course, when our home was a cool sanctuary away from the blazing sun, but in winter, in the wet and wind, it was no kind of sanctuary at all. Caroline had been used to a brick-built townhouse with the life of Bristol all around, with servants to boot, her washing, her cooking, every whim attended to. Here she was not rich. She was poor. And her husband was poor. With no prospects.

I began visiting the inns once more, but I was not the same man as before, not as I'd been in the days when I was a single man, the cheerful, boisterous drunk, the jester. Now I had the weight of the world on my shoulders, and I sat with my back to the room, hunched, brooding over my ale, feeling as though they were all talking about me, like they were all saying, 'There's Edward Kenway, who can't provide for his wife.'

I had suggested it to Caroline, of course. Me becoming a privateer. And while she hadn't said no – she was still my wife, after all – she hadn't said yes, and in her eyes were doubt and worry.

'I don't want to leave you alone, but I can leave here poor and come back rich,' I told her.

Now, if I was to go, I went without her blessing. I went without her blessing and I left her alone in a farmyard shack, and her father would say I had deserted her, and her mother would despise me for making Caroline unhappy.

I couldn't win.

'Is it dangerous?' she asked one night when I spoke about privateering.

'It wouldn't be so highly paid if it wasn't,' I told her, and, of course, she reluctantly agreed that I could go. What choice did she have? But I didn't want to leave her behind with a broken heart.

One morning, I awoke from a drunken stupor, blinking in the morning light, only to find Caroline already dressed for the day ahead.

'I don't want you to go,' she said, and turned and left the room.

Another night I sat in the Livid Brews. I'd like to say I was not my usual self as I sat with my back to the rest of the tavern, hunched over my tankard, taking great big gulps in between dark thoughts and watching the level fall. Always watching the level of my ale fall.

But the sad fact of the matter was that I *was* my usual self. That younger man, always ready with a quip and a smile had disappeared. In his place, still a young man, but one who now had the cares of the world on his shoulders.

On the farm Caroline helped Mother, who at first had been horrified by the idea, saying Caroline was too much of a lady to work on the farm. Caroline had just laughed and insisted. When I had watched her stride across the same yard where I had first seen her sitting astride her horse, now wearing a crisp white bonnet, work boots, a smock and apron, I'd had a proud feeling. Now when I saw her in workclothes it reminded me of my own failings as a man.

What made it worse somehow was that Caroline didn't seem to mind; it was as though she was the only person in the area who did not see her current position as a descent down the social ladder. Everybody else did, and none felt it more keenly than me.

'Can I get you another ale?' I recognized the voice that came from behind me and turned to see him there: Emmett Scott, Caroline's father. I'd last seen him at the wedding when he refused his daughter her dowry. Now he was offering his hated son-in-law a drink. That's the thing about the drink, though. When you're into the drink like I was – when you watch the level of your ale fall and wonder where your next one is coming from – you'll take a fresh mug from anyone. Even Emmett Scott. Your sworn enemy. A man who hated you almost as much as you hated him.

So I accepted his offer of an ale, and he bought his own, and pulled up a stool, which scraped on the flagstones as he sat down.

You remember Emmett Scott's expression? That of a man sucking a lemon. Now, talking to me, the hated Edward Kenway, you'd have to say he looked even more pained. The tavern was somewhere I felt completely at home, an environment in which I could lose myself, but it didn't suit him at all. Every now and then he would glance over one shoulder, then the other, like he was frightened of being suddenly attacked from behind.

'I don't think we've ever had a chance to talk,' he said. And I made a short scoffing laugh in reply.

'Your appearance at the wedding put paid to that, did it not?'

Of course the booze had loosened my tongue, made me brave. That and the fact that in the battle to win his daughter I had won. Her heart, after all, belonged to me. And there was no greater evidence of her devotion to me than the fact that she had given up so much to be with me. Even he must have seen that.

'We're both men of the world, Edward,' he said simply, and you could see he was trying to make himself seem in charge. But I saw through him. I saw what he really was: a frightened nasty man, browbeaten in business, who kicked downwards, who probably beat his servants and his wife, who assumed the likes of me ought to be bowing and scraping to him as my mother and father had (and I had a twinge of rage to remember it) at the wedding.

'How about we do a deal like businessmen?'

I took a long slug of my ale and held his eyes. 'What did you have in mind, father-in-law of mine?'

His face hardened. 'You walk out on her. You throw her out. Whatever you want. You set her free. Send her back to me.'

'And if I do?'

'I'll make you a rich man.'

I drained the rest of my ale. He nodded towards it with questioning eyes and I said yes, waited while he fetched another one, then drank it down, almost in one go. The room was beginning to spin.

'Well, you know what you can do with your offer, don't you?'

'Edward,' he said, leaning forward, 'you and I both know you can't provide for my daughter. You and I both know you sit here *in despair* because you can't provide for my daughter. You love her, I know that, because I was once like you, a man of no qualities.'

I looked at him with my teeth clenched. 'No qualities?'

'Oh, it's true,' he spat, sitting back. 'You're a sheep farmer, boy.'

'What happened to "Edward"? I thought you were talking to me like an equal.'

'An equal? There will never be a day when you will be equal to me and you know it.'

'You're wrong. I have plans.'

'I've heard about your plans. Privateering. Becoming a man of substance on the high seas. You don't have it in you, Edward Kenway.'

'I do.'

'You don't have the moral fibre. I am offering you a way out of the hole you have dug for yourself, boy, I suggest you think about it very hard.'

I sank the rest of my ale. 'How about I think about it over another drink?'

'As you wish.'

A fresh tankard materialized on the table in front of me and I set to making it a thing of history, my mind reeling at the same time. He was right. This was the most devastating thing about the whole conversation. Emmett Scott was right. I loved Caroline yet could not provide for her. And if I truly was a dutiful husband then I would accept his offer.

'She doesn't want me to go away,' I said.

'And you want to?'

'I want for her to support my plans.'

'She never will.'

'I can but hope.'

'If she loves you as she says, she never will.'

Even in my drunken state I could not fault his logic. I knew he was right. He knew he was right.

'You have made enemies, Edward Kenway. Many

enemies. Some of them powerful. Why do you think those enemies haven't taken their revenge on you?'

'They're frightened?' A drunken arrogance in my voice.

He scoffed. 'Of course they're not frightened. They leave you alone because of Caroline.'

'Then if I was to accept your offer there would be nothing to stop my enemies from attacking me?'

'Nothing but my protection.'

I wasn't sure about that.

I sank another ale; he sank deeper into despondency. He was still there at the end of the night, his very presence reminding me how far my choices had shrunk.

When I tried to stand to leave my legs almost gave way and I had to grab the side of the table just to remain on my feet. Caroline's father, a disgusted look on his face, came to help me and before I knew it he was taking me home, though not because he wanted to see me safe, but because he wanted to make sure Caroline saw me in my drunken state, which indeed she did as I rolled in laughing. Emmett Scott puffed up and told her, 'This tosspot is a ruined man, Caroline. Unfit for life on land, much less at sea. If he goes to the West Indies, it's you who will suffer.'

'Father . . . Father.'

She was sobbing, so upset and then as I lay on the bed I saw his boots move off and he was gone.

'That old muck worm,' I managed. 'He's wrong about me.'

'I hope it so,' she replied.

I let my drunken imagination carry me away. 'You believe me, don't you? Can you not see me, standing out there on the deck of a ship sliding into port. And there I am, a man of quality . . . With a thousand doubloons spilling from my pockets like drops of rain. I can see it.'

When I looked at her she was shaking her head. She couldn't see it.

And when I sobered up the next day, neither could I.

It was only a matter of time, I suppose. My lack of prospects became like another person in the marriage. I reviewed my options. Emmett Scott offering me money in return for having his daughter back. My dreams of sailing away.

Both of them involved breaking Caroline's heart.

11

The next day I went back to see Emmett Scott, returning to Hawkins Lane, where I knocked on the door to request an audience. Who should answer, but Rose?

'Mr Kenway,' she said, surprised and going slightly red. There was a moment of awkwardness, and then I was being asked to wait, and then, shortly after that, was led to Emmett Scott's study, a room dominated by a desk in its centre, wood panelling giving it a dark, serious atmosphere. He stood in front of his desk, and, in the gloom, with his dark hair, his cadaverous look and dark, hollowed-out cheeks he looked like a crow.

'You have thought my offer over, then?' he said.

'I have,' I replied, 'and felt it best to tell you my decision as soon as possible.'

He folded his arms and his face cracked into a triumphant smirk, 'You come to make your demands, then? How much is my daughter worth?'

'How much were you willing to pay?'

'*Were?*'

It was my turn to smile, though I was careful not to overdo it. He was dangerous, Emmett Scott. I was playing a dangerous game with a dangerous man.

'That's right. I have decided to go to the West Indies.'

I knew where I could reach Dylan Wallace. I had given Caroline the news.

'I see.'

He seemed to think, tapping his fingertips together.

'But you don't intend to stay away permanently?'

'No.'

'This was not the terms of my offer.'

'Not quite the terms of your offer, no,' I said. 'In effect, a counter-offer. A measure I hope will find your favour. I am a Kenway, Mr Scott; I have my pride. That I hope you will understand. Understand too that I love your daughter, however much that fact may ail you, and I wish nothing but the best for her. I aim to return from my travels a rich man and with my fortune give Caroline the life she deserves. A life, I'm sure, you would wish for her.'

He was nodding, though the purse of his lips betrayed his utter contempt for the notion.

'And?'

'I give you my word I will not return to these shores until I am a rich man.'

'I see.'

'And I give you my word I will not tell Caroline that you attempted to buy her back.'

He darkened. 'I see.'

'I ask only to be given the opportunity to make my fortune – to provide for Caroline in the manner to which she has become accustomed.'

'You will still be her husband – it is not what I wanted.'

'You think me a good-for-nothing, not fit to be her husband. I hope to prove you wrong. While I am away you will no doubt see more of Caroline. Perhaps if your hatred of me runs so deeply you might use the opportunity to poison her against me. The point is, you would have ample opportunity. Moreover, I might die while at sea, in which case she is returned to you for ever: a young widow, still at an eligible age. That is my deal. In return I ask only that you allow me to try to make something of myself unhindered.'

He nodded, considering the idea, perhaps savouring the thought of me dying while at sea.

12

Dylan Wallace assigned me to the crew of the *Emperor*, which was docked in Bristol harbour and leaving in two days. I returned home and told my mother, father and Caroline.

There were tears, of course, and recriminations and pleas to stay, but I was firm in my resolve, and after I had broken my news, Caroline, distraught, left. She needed time to think, she said, and we stood in the yard and watched her gallop away – to her family, where at least she would give the news to Emmett Scott, who would know I was fulfilling my part of the deal. I could only hope – or, should I say, I hoped at the time – that he would fulfil his part of the deal, too.

Sitting here talking to you now, all these years later, well, it has to be said that I don't know whether he did. But I will. Shortly, I will. And there will be a day of reckoning . . .

But not then. Then I was young, stupid, arrogant and boastful. I was so boastful that once Caroline was away I took to the taverns again, and perhaps found that some of my old liveliness had returned as I told all who would listen that I was to sail away, and that Mr and Mrs Edward Kenway would soon be a rich couple thanks to my endeavours on the high seas. I took great delight in their sneering looks, their rejoinders that I was too big for my boots or did not have enough character for the task; that I would soon return with my tail between my legs; that I was letting down my father.

Not once did I let my grin slip. My knowing grin. My grin that said, 'You'll see.'

But even with the booze inside me and my departure a day or so away – or maybe even *because* of those things – I still took their words to heart. I asked myself, *Did I really have enough of a man inside me to survive the life of the privateer. Was I going to return with my tail between my legs?* And, yes, I knew that I might die.

And, also, they were right: I was letting my father down. I'd seen the disappointment in his eyes the moment I delivered the news and it had remained there since. It was a sadness, perhaps that his dream of running the farm together – fading as it must have been – had finally been dashed for good. I was not just leaving to embrace a new life but wholeheartedly rejecting my old one. The life he had built for himself, my mother and me. I was rejecting it. I'd decided I was too good for it.

Perhaps I never gave enough thought to the effect that all of this might have on Caroline's relationship with my mother and father, but, looking back now, it is ludicrous to me to have expected her to simply remain at the farm.

One night, I returned home to find her dressed up.

'Where are you going?' I slurred, having spent most of the evening in a tavern.

She was unable to meet my gaze. By her feet was a bedsheet tied into a bulging parcel, somehow at odds with her attire, which as I focused on her I realized was more smart than usual.

'No, I . . .' Finally her eyes met mine. 'My parents have asked me to go and live with them. And I'd like to.'

'What do you mean, "live with them"? You live here. With me.'

She told me that I shouldn't have given up work with Father. I should have been happy with what I had.

I should have been happy with her.

Through a fog of ale I tried to tell her that I *was* happy with her. That everything I was doing I was doing for her. She had been talking to her parents while she was away, of course, and while I had expected her father to begin poisoning her against me, that muck worm, I hadn't expected him to start quite so soon.

'Decent wage?' I raged. 'That job was near as dammit to robbery. You want to be married to a peasant the whole of your life?'

I had spoken too loudly. A look passed between us and I cringed to think of my father hearing. And then she was leaving. And I was calling after her, still trying to persuade her to stay.

To no avail, and the next morning, when I'd sobered up and recalled the events of the night before, Mother and Father were brooding, staring at me with recriminatory looks. Not only had they liked – I'd go as far as saying *loved* – Caroline, because Mother had lost a daughter many years ago, so to her Caroline was the daughter she never had, but she was also a help around the farm, and did it for minimal wages. To help out, so she said . . .

'Maybe before the baby arrives?' my mother would say and give my grinning father a nudge in the ribs, to which Caroline would blush to her roots and reply, 'Maybe.'

Well, we were trying. And there'd be an end to that when I was away on my travels, of course. And apart from being well-liked and a help on the farm, another female to have around the place, she'd also been helping my mother with her numbers and letters.

Now she was gone – gone because I had not been content with my lot. Gone because I wanted adventure. Because the drink was no longer doing anything to stave off boredom.

Why couldn't I be happy with her? she'd asked. I *was* happy with her.

Why couldn't I be happy with my life? she'd asked. But I wasn't happy with my life.

I went to see her, to try to persuade her to change her mind. As far as I was concerned she was still my wife, I was still her husband, and what I was doing was for the good of the marriage, for the good of *both of us*, not just me.

(And I think I kidded myself that was true. And maybe to some small degree it was true. But I knew, and probably she knew, too, that while of course I wanted to provide for her, I also wanted to see the world beyond Bristol.)

It did no good. She told me she was worried about me being hurt. I replied that I would be careful; that I would return with coin or send for her. I told her I needed her faith, but my appeals fell on deaf ears.

It was the day I was due to leave, and I left them and I packed my bags, slung them over my horse and went, with those very same recriminatory looks boring into my back, stabbing at me like arrows. And I rode into the dark as evening fell with a heavy heart, and there found the *Emperor*. But instead of the expected industry, the ship due to sail the following morning, I found it near deserted. The only people present were a group of six men who I took to be deckhands, who sat gambling with leather flasks of rum close at hand, casks for chairs, a crate for a dice table.

I looked from them to the *Emperor*. A refitted merchant ship, she was riding high in the water. The decks were empty, none of the lamps were lit and the railings shone in the moonlight. A sleeping giant, she was, and despite feeling perplexed at the lack of activity I was still in awe of her size and stature. On those decks I would serve. On hammocks in quarters below decks I would sleep. The masts I would climb. I was looking at my new home.

One of the men eyed me carefully. 'Now, what can I do for you?' he said.

I swallowed, feeling very young and inexperienced

and suddenly, tragically wondering if everything they said about me — Caroline's father, the drinkers in the taverns, even Caroline herself — might be true. That, actually, I might not be cut out for life at sea.

'I'm here to join up,' I said. 'Sent here by Dylan Wallace.'

A snicker ran through the group of four and each of them looked at me with an even greater interest. 'Dylan Wallace, the recruitment man, eh?' said the first. 'He's sent one or two to us before. What is it you can do, boy?'

'Mr Wallace thought I would be material enough to serve,' I said, hoping I sounded more confident and able than I felt.

'How's your eyesight?' said one.

'My eyesight is fine.'

'Do you have a head for heights?'

I knew what they meant now, as they pointed up to the highest point of the *Emperor*'s rigging, the crow's-nest, home to the lookout.

'Mr Wallace had me more in mind as a deckhand, I think.'

Officer material was what he'd actually said, but I wasn't about to tell this lot. I was young and nervous. Not stupid.

'Well, can you sew, lad?' came the reply.

They were mocking me, surely. 'What does sewing have to do with privateering, then?' I asked, feeling a little impudent despite the circumstances.

'The deckhand needs to be able to sew, boy,' said one

of the other men. Like all the others he had a tarred pigtail and tattoos that crept from the sleeves and neck of his shirt. 'Needs to be good with knots, too. Are you good with knots, boy?'

'These are things I can learn,' I replied.

I stared at the ship with its furled sails, rigging hanging in tidy loops from the masts and the hull studded with brass barrels peeking from its gun deck. I saw myself like the men who sat on the casks before me, their faces leathery and tanned from their time at sea, eyes that gleamed with menace and adventure. Custodians of the ship.

'You have to get used to a lot else as well besides,' said one man, 'scraping barnacles off the hull, caulking the boat with tar.'

'You got your sea legs, son?' asked another. They were laughing at me now. 'Can you keep your stomach when she's lashed with waves and hurricane winds?'

'I reckon I can,' I replied, adding with a surge of impetuous anger, 'either way, that's not why Mr Wallace thought I might make a good crewmate.'

A look passed between them. The atmosphere changed a little.

'Oh yes?' said one of them, swinging his legs round. He wore dirty canvas trousers. 'And why is it that the recruiting officer thought you might make a good crewmate, then?'

'Having seen me in action, he thought I might be useful in a battle.'

He stood. 'A fighter, eh?'

'That's right.'

'Well, you have ample opportunity to prove your abilities in that area, boy, starting tomorrow. Perhaps I'll put myself down for a bout, shall I?'

'What do you mean, "tomorrow"?' I asked.

He had sat down, returning his attention to the game. 'Tomorrow, when we sail.'

'I was told we sailed tonight.'

'Sail tomorrow, lad. Captain isn't even here yet. We sail first thing.'

I left them, knowing I might well have made my first enemies on ship; still, I had some time – time to put things right. I retrieved my horse. And headed for home.

13

I galloped towards Hatherton, towards home. Why was I going back? Perhaps to tell them I was sorry. Perhaps to explain what was going through my mind. After all, I was their son. Maybe Father would recognize in me some vestige of himself. And maybe if he did, he would forgive me.

Because as I travelled back along the highway, what I realized more than anything was that I wanted him to forgive me. Both of them.

Is it any wonder that I was distracted, that my guard was down?

I was near to home, where the trees formed a narrow avenue, when I sensed a movement in the hedgerow. I drew to a halt and listened. When you live in the country side you sense the changes, and something was different now. From above came a sharp whistle that could only have been a warning and at the same time I saw more movement ahead of me, except this was in the yard of our farmhouse.

My heart hammered as I spurred my horse and galloped towards the yard. At the same time I saw the unmistakable flare of a torch. Not a lamp, but a torch. The kind of torch you might use if you were intending to set something ablaze. At the same time I saw running figures and in the glare of torchlight saw that they wore hoods.

'Hey,' I shouted, as much to try to wake Mother and Father as to frighten off our attackers.

'Hey,' I yelled again.

A torch arced through the air, twirling end over end, leaving an orange trail in the night sky before landing in a shower of sparks on the thatch of our home. It was dry – *tinder dry*. We tried to keep it doused in the summer because the risk of fire was so great, but there was always something more important to do and, at a guess, it hadn't been done for a week because it went up like, *Whoompf.*

I saw more figures. Three, perhaps four. And then just as I came into the yard and pulled up, a shape flew at me from the side, hands grabbed my tunic and I was dragged from the back of my horse.

The breath was driven from me as I thumped hard to the ground. Nearby were rocks for a stone wall. *Weapons.* Then above me loomed a figure that blocked out the moon, hooded, like the others. Before I could react he stooped and I caught a brief impression of the hood fabric pulsing at his mouth as he breathed hard, and then his fist smashed into my face. I twisted and his second blow landed on my neck. Beside him appeared another figure, and I saw a glint of steel and knew I was powerless to do anything and prepared to die. But the first man stopped the new arrival with a simple barked,

'*No*,' and I was saved from the blade at least, but not from the beating, and a boot in my midriff doubled me up.

That boot – I recognized that boot.

Again it came, again and again, until at last it stopped and my attacker ran off. My hands went to my wounded belly and I rolled on to my front and coughed, the blackness threatening to engulf me. Maybe I'd let it. The idea of sinking into oblivion seemed tempting. Let unconsciousness take the pain. Deliver me into the future.

The sound of running feet as my attackers escaped. Some indistinct shouting. The cries of the disturbed ewes.

But no. I was still alive, wasn't I? About to kiss steel I'd been given a second chance and that was too good a chance to pass up. I had my parents to save. And even then I knew that I was going to make these people pay. The owner of those boots would regret not killing me when he had the chance. Of that I was sure.

I pulled myself up. Smoke drifted across the yard like a bank of incoming fog. One of the barns was already alight. The house, too. I needed to wake them, needed to wake my mother and father.

The dirt around me was bathed in the orange glow of the fire. As I stood I was aware of horse's hooves and swung about to see several riders retreating – riding away from the farmhouse, their job done, the place well alight now. I snatched up a rock and considered hurling it at one of the riders, but there were more important matters to worry about, and instead with a grunt that was part effort and part pain, I launched it at the top window of the farmhouse.

My aim was true and I prayed it would be enough to rouse my parents. The smoke thick in the yard now, the roar of the flames like an escaped hell. Ewes were screaming in the barns as they burned alive.

At the door they appeared: Father battling his way out of the flames with Mother in his arms. His face was set, his eyes blank. All he could think about was making sure she was safe. After he'd taken Mother out of the reach of the flames, and laid her carefully down in the yard near where I stood, he straightened and like me gaped helplessly at the burning building. We hurried over to the barn where the screams of the ewes had died down – our livestock, father's livelihood, gone. And then, his face hot and glowing in the light of the flames, my father did something I'd never seen. He began to cry.

'Father . . .' I reached for him, and he pulled his shoulder away with an angry shrug, and when he turned to me, his face blackened with smoke and streaked by tears, he shook with restrained violence, as though it was taking every ounce of his self-control to stop himself from lashing out. From lashing out at me.

'Poison. That's what you are,' he said through clenched teeth, 'poison. The ruin of our lives.'

'Father . . .'

'Get out of here,' he spat. 'Get out of here. I never want to see you again.'

Mother stirred as though she was about to protest, and rather than face more upset – rather than be the *cause* of more upset – I mounted my horse and left.

It would be the last time I saw either of them.

14

I flew through the night with heartbreak and fury my companions, riding the highway into town and stopping at the Auld Shillelagh, where all this had begun. I staggered inside, one arm still clutching my hurt chest, face throbbing from the beating.

Conversation in the tavern died down. I had their attention.

'I'm looking for Tom Cobleigh and his weasel son,' I managed, breathing hard, glaring at them from beneath my brow. 'Have they been in here?'

Backs were turned to me. Shoulders hunched.

'We'll not have any trouble in here,' said Jack the landlord from behind the bar. 'We've had enough trouble from you to last us a lifetime, thank you very much, Edward Kenway.' He pronounced 'thank you very much' as though it was all one word. *Thankyouverymuch.*

'You know the full meaning of trouble if you're sheltering the Cobleighs,' I warned, and I strode to the bar where he reached for something I knew to be there, a sword that hung on a nail out of sight. I got there first, and stretched with a movement that set the pain in my stomach off, but grabbed it and snatched it from its scabbard in one swift movement.

It all happened too quickly for Jack to react. One second he'd been considering reaching for the sword, the next instant that very same sword was being held to his throat, *thankyouverymuch*.

The light in the inn was low. A fire bimbled in the grate, dark shadows pranced on the walls, and drinkers regarded me with narrowed, watchful eyes.

'Now tell me,' I said, angling the sword at Jack's throat, making him wince, 'have the Cobleighs been in here tonight?'

'Weren't you supposed to be leaving on the *Emperor* tonight?'

It wasn't Jack; it was somebody else who spoke. Someone I couldn't see in the gloom. Didn't recognize the voice.

'Aye, well my plans changed and it's lucky they did, otherwise my mother and father would have burned in their beds.' My voice rose. 'Is that what you wanted all of you? Because that's what would have happened. Did you know about this?'

You could have heard a pin drop in that tavern. From the darkness they regarded me: the eyes of men I'd drunk and fought with, women I'd taken to bed. They kept their secrets. They would continue to keep them.

From outside came the rattle and clank of a cart arriving. Everybody else heard it, too. The tension in the tavern seemed to increase. It could be the Cobleighs. Here to establish their alibi, perhaps. Still with the sword to his throat, I dragged Jack from behind the bar and to the door of the inn.

'Nobody say a word,' I warned. 'Nobody say a bloody word and Jack's throat stays closed. The only person who needs to be hurt here tonight is whoever took a torch to my father's farm.'

Voices from outside now. I heard Tom Cobleigh. I positioned myself behind the door just as it opened, with Jack held as a shield, the point of the sword digging into his neck. The silence was deathly, and instantly noticeable to the three men who were a fraction too slow to realize something was wrong.

What I heard as they came in was Cobleigh's throaty chuckle dying on his lips, and what I saw was a pair of boots I recognized, boots that belonged to Julian. So I stepped out from behind the door and ran him through with the sword.

You should have killed me when you had the chance. I'll have it on my gravestone.

Arrested in the door frame Julian simply stood and gawped, his eyes wide as he stared, first down at the sword embedded in his chest, then into my eyes. His final sight was of his killer. His final insult to cough gobbets of blood into my face as he died. Not the last man I ever killed. Not by any means. But the first.

'Tom! It's Kenway!' came a shout from within the tavern, but it was hardly necessary, even for someone as stupid as Tom Cobleigh.

Julian's eyes went glassy and the light went out of them as he slid off my sword and slumped in the door frame like a bloodied drunk. Behind him stood Tom Cobleigh and his son Seth, mouths agape like men seeing a ghost. Then all thoughts of a refreshing tankard and a satisfying boast about the night's entertainment were forgotten as they turned tail and ran.

Julian's body was in the way and they gained precious seconds as I clambered over him, emerging into the dark on the highway. Seth had tripped and was just picking himself up from the dirt, while Tom, not waiting, not stopping to help his son, had hared across the highway heading for the farmhouse opposite. In a moment I was upon Seth, the blood-streaked sword still in my hand, and it crossed my mind to make him the second man I killed. My blood was up and, after all, they say the first is the hardest. And wouldn't I be doing the world a favour, ridding it of Seth Cobleigh?

But no. There was mercy. And as well as mercy there was doubt. The chance – slim, but still a chance – that Seth hadn't been there.

Instead as I passed I brought the hilt of the sword down hard on the back of his head and was rewarded with an outraged, pained scream and the sound of him sprawling, hopefully unconscious, back to the dirt, as I dashed past him, arms and legs pumping as I crossed the road in pursuit of Tom.

I know what you're thinking. I had no proof Tom had been there either. But I just knew. I just knew.

Across the roadway, he risked a quick glance over his shoulder before placing both hands on the top of the stone wall and heaving himself over. Seeing me, he let out a small, frightened whimper and I had time to think that though he was sprightly for a man of his years – his speed aided by his fear, no doubt – I was catching up with him, and tossed the sword from one hand to the other in order to vault the wall, land on two feet on the other side and sprint off in pursuit.

I was close enough to smell his stink, but he'd reached an outhouse and disappeared from view. I heard the scrape of boot on stone nearby, as though a third person was in the yard, and dimly wondered if it was Seth. Or perhaps the farm owner. Perhaps one of the drinkers from the Auld Shillelagh. Focused on finding Tom Cobleigh, I gave it no mind.

By the wall of the outhouse I crouched, listening hard. Wherever Cobleigh was, he'd stopped moving. I glanced to my left and right, and saw only farm buildings, black blocks against the grey night, and heard only the occasional bleating of a goat and the sound of insects. On the other side of the highway lights burned at the window but otherwise the tavern was quiet.

Then, in the almost oppressive quiet I heard a crunch of gravel from the other side of the building. He was there waiting for me.

I thought about our positions. He'd be expecting me to come running recklessly from round the side of the outhouse. So, very slowly, and as quietly as I could,

I crept towards the opposite corner. I winced as my boots disturbed the stones and hoped the noise wouldn't carry. Then I began to edge quietly along the side of the building and at the end stopped and listened. If I was right Tom Cobleigh would be lying in wait at the other side. If I was wrong I could expect a knife in my belly.

I held my breath then risked a peek round the side of the outhouse.

I'd judged right. There was Cobleigh at the far corner. His back was to me and in his fist was a raised knife. Waiting for me to appear, he was a sitting duck. I could have reached him in three quick strides and slipped my blade into his spine before he had a chance to fart.

But no. I wanted him alive. I wanted to know who his companions had been. Who the tall ring-wearing man able to stop Julian from killing me had been.

So instead I disarmed him. Literally. I darted forward and I cut his arm off.

Or, that was the intention, at least. But my inexperience as a swordsman was all too obvious, or was it simply because the sword was too blunt? Either way as I brought it down two-handed on Tom Cobleigh's forearm, it cut his sleeve and burrowed into the flesh, but didn't sever the arm. At least he dropped the knife.

Cobleigh screamed and pulled away. He grabbed at his wounded arm that jetted blood across the wall of the outhouse and on to the dirt. At the same time I saw a movement in the darkness and remembered the noise

I had heard, that possible other presence. Too late. The shadows delivered a figure into the moonlight, and I saw blank eyes behind the hood, and workclothes and boots that were somehow too clean.

Poor Tom Cobleigh. He never saw it coming and virtually backed on to the stranger's sword, pinned as the new arrival thrust his blade into his back and through the front of his ribcage so that it emerged dripping blood. He looked down at it, a grunt his final worldly utterance before the stranger flicked his sword to one side and the corpse span from the blade and thumped heavily to the dirt.

There is a saying, isn't there? *My enemy's enemy is my friend.* Something like that. But there's always an exception that proves the rule and in my case he was a man in a hood with a bloodstained sword. My neck was still stinging from the mark of his ring. My face still throbbed from his fists. Why he'd killed Tom Cobleigh, I had no idea and didn't care; instead with a warrior roar I lunged forward and the shafts of our swords rang like bells in the quiet night.

He parried easily. One. Two. From going forward I was already being driven back, forced to defend messily and sloppily. Inexperienced swordsman? I wasn't a swordsman at all. I might as well have been wielding a club or a cosh for all the skill I had with the blade. With a swish of his sword point he opened a gash in my arm and I felt warm blood wash down my bicep and soak my sleeve, before the strength seemed to leak out of my sword arm. We weren't fighting. Not any more. He was playing with me. Playing with me before he killed me.

'Show me your face,' I gasped, but he made no reply. The only sign he'd even heard was a slight smiling of the eyes. Then the arc of his sword fooled me and I was too slow – not just a little too slow, but *far too slow* – to stop him opening a second gash in my arm.

Again he struck. Again. I've since realized he cut me with the precision of a medical man, enough to hurt but not permanently injure me. Certainly enough to disarm me. And in the end I didn't feel the sword drop from my fingertips. I just heard it hit the dirt and looked down to see it on the ground with the blood from my wounded arm dripping on to the blade.

Perhaps I expected him to remove his hood. But he did not. Instead he levelled the point of his sword just below my chin and with his other hand indicated for me to drop to my knees.

'You don't know me well enough if you think I'm going to meet my end on my knees, stranger,' I told him, feeling oddly calm in the face of defeat and death. 'If it's all the same to you I'll stay standing.'

He spoke in tones deep and flat, possibly disguised. 'You'll not meet your end tonight, Edward Kenway. More's the pity. But I tell you this. Unless the *Emperor* sails with you on it tomorrow this night is only the beginning for anyone bearing the Kenway name. Leave at first light and no more harm will come to your mother or father.

But if that ship sails without you they will suffer. You *all* will. Do I make myself clear?'

'And do I get to know the identity of my gracious enemies?' I asked.

'You do not. You should know only that there are forces in this world more powerful than you could possibly comprehend, Edward Kenway. Tonight you have seen them in action. You have suffered at their hands. Let this be an end to it. Never return to these shores. And now, Edward Kenway, *you will kneel.*'

His sword came up and the hilt smashed into my temple.

When I woke up I was on the *Emperor*.

15

At least I thought I was on the *Emperor*. I hoped so anyway. And with my head throbbing, I pulled myself out of my hammock, put my boots to the deck and was sent flying forward.

My fall was broken – by my face. I lay groaning on the planks for a moment or so, wondering why I felt so drunk when I didn't remember doing any actual drinking. Except, of course, I wasn't drunk.

But if I wasn't drunk why was the floor moving? It tipped this way and that, and I spent a moment or so waiting for it to settle until I realized that the constant rocking was exactly that. Constant. It wasn't going to stop.

On unsteady feet that shuffled and danced in the sawdust I straightened, hands out like a man trying to negotiate a balancing beam. My body still hurt from the beating I'd taken but I was on the mend, my wounds a day or so old.

What hit me next was the air thick with a smell. No, not a smell. *A stench*.

Oh my days it stank. A mix of shit, piss, sweat and seawater. A smell I came to learn was unique to the below decks of a ship. Just as every butcher's shop and every tavern has its own smell, so does every below decks. The frightening thing was how quickly you got used to it.

The smell was of men, and on the *Emperor* there were one hundred and fifty of the blighters, who when they weren't manning their positions, hanging from the rigging or crowded into the galleys, would sleep cuddled up to carriages on the gun decks, or in hammocks much like the one I'd woken up in.

I could hear one of the crew now, sniggering in the shadows as the ship lurched and I was thrown against a wooden support, then just as violently slammed into a column opposite. Sea legs. That was what they called it. I had to get my sea legs.

'Is this the *Emperor*?' I said into the murk.

The creak of the ship. Like the smell and the sea legs it was something I'd get used to.

'Aye, you're on the *Emperor*,' came the reply.

'I'm new on the ship,' I called into the darkness, clinging on for dear life.

There was a rasping chuckle. 'You don't say.'

'How far are we from land?'

'A day. You were brought on asleep or unconscious. Too much booze, I'd say.'

'Something like that,' I replied, still hanging on to the support for dear life. My mind went to the events of the last day or so, but it was like worrying at an open wound. Too soon, too painful. I'd need to try to make sense of what had happened. I'd need to face the guilt, and I'd have letters to write. (Letters I wouldn't have been able to write without Caroline's tuition, I reminded myself, with a fresh feeling of regret). But all that would have to wait until later.

From behind me came a grating, wrenching sound. I swung round and squinted in the half-light, and when my eyes adjusted I could see a capstan. From above I could hear feet and the raised voices of men at work on the deck above. The capstan groaned and creaked and turned.

'*Heave*,' came the shout from above. '*Heave*.' Despite everything the sound of it made me a wide-eyed little boy again.

I cast my gaze around. Either side of me were the rounded shapes of the carriage guns. Their barrels shone dully in the dark. At the other end of the deck I could see where a rope ladder hung from a square of daylight. I headed there, climbed to the quarterdeck above.

I soon discovered how my shipmates had earned their sea legs. Not only did they sport a different style of dress to men of the land – short jackets, checked shirts, long, canvas breeches – but they had a different style of walking, too. Their entire bodies seemed to move with the ship, something that happened entirely by instinct. I spent my first couple of days on board being tossed from pillar to post by the heaving waves beneath us, and had to grow accustomed to the sound of laughter as I sprawled on the deck time after time.

But soon, just as I got used to the smell below decks, and the constant creak of the hull, and the sense that the whole sea was kept at bay by a few puny planks of wood and coats of caulking, so I learnt to move with the motion of the water, with the *Emperor*. Soon I, too, walked like every other man on board.

My shipmates were nut-brown, every single one of them. Most wore scarves or handkerchiefs tied loosely round the neck, had tattoos, beards and wore gold earrings. There were older crewmates aboard, their brown, weather-worn faces like melted candles, their eyes hooded and cautious, but most were about ten years older than I was.

They came from all over I soon discovered: London, Scotland, Wales, the West Country. Many of our number, around a third, were black; some of them runaway slaves who'd found freedom on the seas, treated as an equal by their captain and shipmates – or should that be, treated as the same level of scum by their captain and shipmates. There were also men from the American colonies, from Boston, Charleston, Newport, New York and Salem. Most seemed to wear weapons constantly: cutlasses, daggers, flintlock pistols. Always more than one pistol, it seemed, which I soon found out was due to the danger of the first one failing to fire because of a damp charge.

They liked to drink rum, were almost unbelievably coarse in their language and the way they spoke about women, and liked nothing better than a roaring argument. But what bonded them all were the captain's articles.

He was a Scotsman. Captain Alexander Dolzell. A big man, he rarely smiled. He adhered to the articles of the ship, and liked nothing more than reminding us of them. Standing on the sterncastle deck, his hands on the rail as we stood assembled on the quarterdeck, main deck and forecastle, warning us that any man who fell asleep on duty would be tarred and feathered. Any man found with another man would be punished with castration. No smoking below decks. No pissing in the ballast. (And, of course, as I've already told you, that particular article was something I carried over to my own commands.)

I was fresh, though, and new on board ship. At that stage of my career I don't think it would even have occurred to me to break the rules.

I soon began to settle into the rhythm of life at sea. I found my sea legs, learnt which side of the ship to use depending on the wind and to eat with my elbows on the table to stop my plate from sliding away. My days consisted of being posted as lookout or on watch. I learnt how to take soundings in shallow waters and picked up the basics of the navigation. And I learnt from listening to the crew, who when not exaggerating tales of going into battle against the Spanish, liked nothing better than to impart nuggets of nautical wisdom: *'Red at night, sailor's delight. Red in the morning, sailors take warning.'*

The weather. The winds. What slaves we were to them. When it was bad the usual cheery atmosphere would be replaced by one of grim industry as the day-to-day business of keeping the ship afloat became a matter of simple survival in hurricane winds, when we would snatch food in between maintaining sail, patching the hull and pumping out. All done with the quiet, concentrated desperation of men working to save their own lives.

Those times were exhausting, physically draining. I'd be kept awake, told to climb the ratlines or man pumps below decks, and any sleep would be snatched below decks, curled up against the hull.

And then the weather would abate and life would resume. I watched the activities of the older crewmates, their drinking, gambling and womanizing, understanding how relatively tame my own exploits in Bristol had been. Some of those I used to encounter in the taverns of the West Country, how they thought of themselves as hardened drinkers and brawlers, if only they could have been here to see my shipmates in action. Fights would break out over nothing. At the drop of a hat. Knives pulled. Blood drawn. In my first month at sea I heard more bones crunch than I had in the previous seventeen years of my life. And don't forget: I grew up in Swansea and Bristol.

And yet the violence would dissipate as quickly as it had flared up; men who moments before had been holding blades to each other's throats would make up with a round of bear hugs that looked almost as painful as the fighting, but which seemed to have the desired effect. The articles stated that any man's quarrels should be ended on shore by sword or pistol in a duel. Nobody really wanted that, of course. A quarrel was one thing, possibility of death quite another. So fights tended to be over as quickly as they'd begun. Tempers would flare, then die down.

Because of this genuine grievances on board were few and far between. So it was just my luck to be on the receiving end of one.

I first became aware of it on my second or third day aboard, because I turned, feeling a penetrating stare upon me and returned it with a smile. A friendly smile, or so I thought. But one's man's friendly smile is another man's cocky grin and all it seemed to do was infuriate him even more. Back came a glare.

The next day as I made my way along the quarter-deck I was struck by an elbow so hard that I fell to my knees, and when I looked up, expecting to see a grinning face – 'Gotcha!'– saw only the smirking face of the same man as he glanced over his shoulder on his way to his station. He was a big man. Not the sort you'd want to be on the wrong side of. Looked like I was on the wrong side of him, though.

Later I spoke to Friday, a black deckhand who often had the hammock near mine. When I described the man who had knocked me down, he knew who I was talking about straight away.

'That'll be Blaney.'

Blaney. That was all I ever heard anybody call him. And unfortunately – by which I mean, unfortunately for *me* – Blaney hated me. He hated the guts of me.

There was probably a reason. Since we'd never spoken it couldn't have been an especially good reason; the important thing was it existed in Blaney's head, which at the end of the day was all that mattered. That and the fact that Blaney was big and, according to Friday, skilled with a sword.

Blaney, you might have guessed by now, was one of the gentlemen I first met the evening that I arrived early for the departure of the *Emperor*. Now, I know what you're thinking: he was the one to whom I'd spoken, who was all ready to teach me a lesson or two for my impudence.

Well, no, if you thought that you'd be wrong. Blaney was one of the other men sitting at the cask playing cards. A simple, brutish man, with what you might call a prominent forehead, thick eyebrows that were permanently bunched together as though he was always confused about something. I hardly noticed him on the night and, thinking about it now, perhaps that was why he was so infuriated; perhaps that's why the grudge was born: he'd felt ignored by me.

'Why might he have taken against me?' I asked, to which Friday could only reply with a shrug and a mumble of 'Ignore him', and then he closed his eyes to indicate our conversation was at an end.

So I did. I ignored him.

This obviously infuriated Blaney even more. Blaney didn't want to be ignored. Blaney wanted to be taken notice of. He wanted to be feared. My failure to be frightened of Blaney, well, it – yes, it stoked his hatred of me.

16

Meantime, there were other things to think about. For example, a rumour going round the crew that the captain was feeling left out of spoils. There had been no raids for two months; we'd not earned so much as a half-penny and there were rumblings of discontent, most of which were coming from his cabin. It became common knowledge that our captain felt as though he was holding up his end of the bargain, but getting little in return.

What bargain, you might ask? Well, as privateers, we provided a presence for Her Majesty; it was as though we were unenlisted soldiers in her war against the Spanish. In return, of course, we were allowed to raid Spanish ships with impunity, which means as much as we bloody well wanted, and for as long as anyone could remember that's exactly what had happened.

There were fewer and fewer Spanish ships at sea, however. At port, we'd begun to hear rumours that the war might be coming to an end; that a treaty might soon be signed.

Captain Dolzell, though, well, you'd have to give him credit for being able to look ahead of times and see which way the wind was blowing, and what with us being left out of spoils, he decided to take us on a course of action that was outside the remit of our letters of marque.

Trafford, the mate, stood next to Captain Dolzell, who removed his tricorne and wiped sweat from his brow, before replacing it and addressing us all.

'This raid will make us rich, lads; your pockets will split. But I've got to warn ye, and I would be failing my duty as your captain if I did not, that it is indeed a risky venture.'

Risky. Yes. The risk of capture, punishment and death by the drop of the hangman's scaffold.

A hanged man's bowels open, I'd been told. A pirate's breeches would be tied at the ankles to stop the shit escaping. It was the indignity of that which scared me more than anything. It wasn't how I wanted Caroline to remember me, dangling from a rope, reeking of shit.

I had not left Bristol in order to become a fugitive from the law, a pirate. And if I stayed with the ship and we went through with the captain's plan then that is what I would be. We would have the combined forces of the East India Company's own Marines, plus no doubt Her Majesty's navy, after us.

No, I hadn't joined up as a privateer in order to become a pirate, but all the same if I was ever going home I couldn't do it penniless. I had this idea that if I returned with riches I could pay the price on my head, that my enemies might be appeased.

So, no, I hadn't joined up to be a pirate. The money I earned would be earned legally.

And please cease your sniggering. I know how quaint I sound now. But back then, I still had fervour in my belly and dreams in my head. So when the captain made his offer, when he said he knew not all on board would want a part of any badness, and that anybody not wanting a part of the badness should say now, or for ever hold their peace, so that he could organize passage off the ship, I went to step forward.

Friday stopped me with a surreptitious hand. Not looking at me. Just stopping me moving forward and staring straight ahead. From the side of his mouth he said, 'Wait' and I didn't have to wait long to find out why. Five of the crew had shuffled up the deck, good men who wanted no part of any piracy. At a word from the captain the first mate had these five good men thrown overboard.

I decided there and then to keep my trap shut. And what I decided instead was this: I would follow the captain, but only up to a point. I'd follow him, reap my share of the money we made and then jump ship. After I'd jumped ship, I'd join up with other privateers – after all, I was an experienced jack tar now – and deny ever having been on the *Emperor* when this terrible crime was committed.

As plans go, it wasn't especially sophisticated. It had its flaws, I had to admit, but yet again I found myself stuck between a rock and a hard place, with neither of my options particularly appealing.

As the appeals of the men thrown overboard receded behind us, the captain went on to outline his plans for piracy. He didn't go so far as suggesting we attack the Royal Navy, that would have been suicide; instead, he knew of a target to be found along the west coast of Africa. So there, in January 1713, was where the *Emperor* headed.

17

As we sailed among the islands we would drop anchor in a sheltered bay or river estuary and men would be sent ashore to find supplies: wood, water, beer, wine, rum. We could be there for days and we'd pass the time catching turtles to eat or taking potshots at birds, or hunting cattle, goats or pigs if we could.

Once we had to careen the *Emperor*, which involved beaching her then using block and tackle to turn her over. We used lit torches to burn off seaweed and barnacles, caulk her and replace any rotten planks, all under the direction of the ship's carpenter, who used to look forward to such occasions. Hardly surprising, really, because we also took the opportunity to make repairs to the masts and sails, so he had the pleasure of ordering around the quartermaster, as well as the first and second mates, who had no choice but to keep their mouths shut and carry on with the task.

They were happy days: fishing, hunting, enjoying the discomfort of our superiors. It was almost a disappointment having to set sail again. But set sail we did.

The ship we were after was a merchant ship run by

the East India Company and we came across her off the coast of west Africa. There'd been many rumblings below decks regarding the wisdom of the enterprise. We knew that by attacking such a prestigious vessel we were making ourselves wanted men. But the captain had said there were only three naval warships and two naval sloops patrolling the entire Caribbean Sea, and that the East India Company's ship, the *Amazon Galley*, was said to be carrying treasure, and that providing we brought the *Galley* to a halt in open water, out of sight of land, we should be able to plunder the ship at our leisure, escape and be out of it.

Wouldn't the crew of the *Galley* be able to identify us, though? I wondered aloud. Wouldn't they tell the navy they'd been attacked by the *Emperor*? Friday had just looked at me. I didn't care for that look he gave me.

We found it on the third day of hunting.

'Sail ho!' came the cry from above. We'd been used to hearing it, so we didn't get our hopes raised. Just watched as the captain and quartermaster conferred. Moments later they'd confirmed it was the *Galley* and we set off across the water towards it.

As we approached we raised a red ensign, the British flag, and sure enough the *Galley* remained where she was, thinking us an English privateer on her side.

Which we were. *In theory.*

Men primed their pistols and checked the action of their swords. Boarding hooks were taken up and the guns manned. As we came up alongside and the *Galley* crew realized we were primed for battle, we were close enough to see their faces fall and panic gallop through the ship like a startled mare.

We forced her to heave to. Our men raced to the gunwales, where they stood ready for action, aiming pistols, manning the swivel guns or with cutlasses drawn and teeth bared. I had no pistol and my sword was a rusty old thing the quartermaster had found at the bottom of a chest, but even so. Squeezed in between men twice my age but ten times as fierce, I did my utmost to scowl with as much ferocity as they did. To look just as savage.

The guns below were trained on the *Galley* opposite. One word and we'd open fire with a volley of shot, enough to break their vessel in half, send them all to the bottom of the sea. On the faces of their crew was the same sick, terrified expression. The look of men caught out, who now had to face the terrible consequences.

'Let your captain identify himself,' our first mate called across the gap between our two vessels. He produced a timer and banged it down on the gunwale rail. 'Send out your captain before the sands run out, or we shall open fire.'

It took them until their time was almost up, but he appeared on deck at last, dressed in all his finery and fixing us with what he hoped was an expression of defiance – which couldn't disguise the trepidation in his eyes.

He did as he was told. He followed instructions,

ordered a boat to be launched, then clambered aboard and was rowed across to our ship. Secretly I couldn't help but feel sympathy for him. He put himself at our mercy in order to protect his crew, which was admirable, and his head was held high when, as he ascended the Jacob's ladder from his boat, he was jeered at by the men manning the mounted guns on the deck below, before being grabbed roughly by the shoulders and hauled over the rail of the gunwale to the quarterdeck.

When he was dragged to his feet he pulled away from the men's clutching hands, threw his shoulders back and, after adjusting his jacket and cuffs, demanded to see our captain.

'Aye, I'm here,' called Dolzell, who came down from the sterncastle with Trafford, the first mate, at his heels. The captain wore his tricorne with a bandanna tied beneath it, and his cutlass was drawn.

'And what's your name, captain?' he said.

'My name is Captain Benjamin Pritchard,' replied the merchant captain sourly, 'and I demand to know the meaning of this.'

He drew himself up to full height but was no match for the stature of Dolzell. Few men were.

'The *meaning* of this,' repeated Dolzell. The captain wore a thin smile, possibly the first time I had ever seen him smile. He cast an arch look around at his men gathered on the deck, and a cruel titter ran through our crew.

'Yes,' said Captain Pritchard primly. He spoke with an upper-class accent. Oddly, I was reminded of Caroline.

'I mean exactly that. You are aware, are you not, that my ship is owned and operated by the British East India Company and that we enjoy the full protection of Her Majesty's navy?'

'As do we,' replied Dolzell. At the same time he indicated the red ensign that fluttered from the topsail.

'I rather think you forfeited that privilege the moment you commanded us to stop at gunpoint. Unless, of course, you have an excellent reason for doing so?'

'I do.'

I glanced across to where the crew of the *Galley* were pinned down by our guns but just as enthralled by the events on deck as we were. You could have heard a pin drop. The only sound was the slapping of the sea on the hulls of our ships and the whisper of the breeze in our masts and rigging.

Captain Pritchard was surprised. 'You do have a good reason?'

'I do.'

'I see. Then perhaps we should hear it.'

'Yes, Captain Pritchard. I have forced your vessel to heave to in order that my men might plunder it of all its valuables. You see, pickings on the seas have been awfully slim of late. My men are getting restless. They are wondering how they will be paid on this trip.'

'You are a privateer, sir,' retorted Captain Pritchard. 'If you continue along this course of action you will be a *pirate*, a wanted man.' He addressed the entire crew. 'You *all* will be wanted men. Her Majesty's navy will hunt you down, and arrest you. You'll be hanged at Execution Dock then your bodies displayed in chains at Wapping. Is that really what you want?'

Pissing yourself as you died. Stinking of shit, I thought.

'Way I hear it, Her Majesty is on the verge of signing treaties with the Spanish and the Portuguese. My services as a privateer will no longer be required. What do you think my course of action will be then?'

Captain Pritchard swallowed, for there was no real answer to that. And now, for the first time ever, I saw Captain Dolzell really smile, enough to reveal a mouth full of broken and blackened teeth, like a plundered graveyard. 'Now, sir, how about we retire to discuss the whereabouts of whatever treasure you might happen to have on board?'

Captain Pritchard was about to complain, but Trafford was already moving forward to grab him and he was propelled up the steps and into the navigation room. The men, meanwhile, turned their attention to the crew of the ship opposite, and an uneasy, threatening silence reigned.

And then we began to hear the screams.

I jumped, my eyes going to the door of the cabin to which they had gone. Darting a look at Friday I saw that he, too, was staring at the navigation-room door, an unreadable look on his face.

'What's going on?' I asked.

'Hush. Keep your voice down. What do you think is going on?'

'They're torturing him?'

He rolled his eyes. 'What did you expect, rum and pickles?'

The screams continued. Over on the other ship the men's expressions had changed. A moment ago they had stared at us resentfully, balefully, as though biding their time before they might launch a cunning counter-attack. Like we were scoundrels and knaves and would soon be whipped like the scurvy dogs we were. Now in their eyes was sheer terror – that they might be next.

It was strange. I felt both ashamed and emboldened by what was happening. I've caused my fair share of pain, and left sorrow in my wake, but I've never been able to abide cruelty for its own sake. Dolzell would have said, 'Not for its own sake, boy; to find out where the treasure was hid.' But he would have been telling a half-truth. For the fact was that as soon as our men swarmed their vessel they'd quickly locate whatever booty was aboard. No, the real purpose of torturing the captain was the changing faces of the men who stood opposite. It was to strike terror into their crew.

Then, after I don't know how long, perhaps a quarter of an hour or so, when the screams had reached a peak, when the heartless sniggering of the deckhands had been exhausted, and even the most pitiless man had begun to wonder if, perhaps, enough pain had been inflicted for one day, the door to the navigation room was thrown open. And Dolzell and Trafford appeared.

Wearing a look of grim satisfaction the captain surveyed the men of our own ship and then the apprehensive faces of the other crew, before pointing and saying, 'You, boy.'

He was pointing at me.

'Y-yes, sir,' I stammered.

'Into the cabin, boy. Guard the captain, while we find out what his information is worth. You too.' He was pointing at somebody else. I didn't see who as I hurried to the front of the quarterdeck, barging against the tide of a surge towards the gunwales as men readied themselves to board the other ship.

And then I had the first of two shocks as I entered the navigation room and saw Captain Pritchard.

The cabin had a large dining table that had been set to one side. As too was the quartermaster's table, on which were laid his navigation instruments, maps and chart.

In the middle of the cabin Captain Pritchard sat tied to a chair, his hands bound behind him. Lingering in the cabin was a brackish smell I couldn't place.

Captain Pritchard's head hung, chin on his chest. At the sound of the door he lifted it and focused bleary, pain-wracked eyes on me.

'My hands,' he croaked. 'What have they done to my hands?' Before I could find out I had my second surprise, when my fellow jailer entered the room and it was none other than Blaney.

Oh shit. He pulled the door to behind him. His eyes

slid from me to the wounded Captain Pritchard and back to me again.

From outside came the cries of our crew as they prepared to board the other ship, but it felt as though we were cut off from it, as though it was happening far away and involved people not known to us. I held Blaney's gaze as I walked round to the back of the captain, where his hands were tied behind his back. And I realized what the smell had been. It was the smell of burnt flesh.

18

Dolzell and Trafford had pushed lit fuses between Captain Pritchard's fingers in order to make him talk. There was a scattering of them on the boards, as well a jug of something that when I put my nose to it I thought was brine they'd used to pour on his wounds, to make them more painful.

His hands were blistered, charred black in some places, raw and bleeding in others, like tenderized meat.

I looked for a flask of water, still cautious of Blaney, wondering why he hadn't moved. Why he hadn't spoken.

He put me out of my misery. 'Well, well, well,' he rasped, 'we find ourselves together.'

'Yes,' I replied drily. 'Aren't we lucky, mate?'

I saw a jug of water on the long table and moved towards it.

He ignored my sarcasm. 'And what would you be up to exactly?'

'I'm fetching water to put on this man's wounds.'

'Captain didn't say nothing about attending to the prisoner's wounds.'

'He's in pain, man, can't you see?'

'Don't you talk to me like that, you little whelp,' snapped Blaney with a ferocity that chilled my blood.

Still, I wasn't going to show it. Full of bravado. Always tough on the outside.

'You sound like you're fixing up for a fight, Blaney.'

I hoped I came across more confident than I felt.

'Aye, maybe I am at that.'

He had a brace of pistols in his belt and a cutlass at his waist, but the silver that seemed to appear in his hand, almost from nowhere, was a curved dagger.

I swallowed.

'And what do you plan on doing, Blaney, with the ship about to mount a raid, us in charge of guarding the captain here? Now, I don't know what it is you have against me, what measure of grudge it is you're nursing, but it'll have to be settled another time, I'm afraid, unless you've got a better idea.'

When Blaney grinned, a gold tooth flashed. 'Oh, I've got other ideas, boy. An idea that maybe the captain here tried to escape and ran you through in the process. Or how about another idea altogether? An idea that it was *you* who helped the captain. That you untied the prisoner and tried to make good your escape, and it was me who stopped you, running you both through in the process. I think I like that idea even better. How's about that?'

He was serious, I could tell. Blaney had been biding his time. No doubt he wanted to avoid the flogging he would have received for giving me a beating. But now he had me where he wanted.

Then something happened that directed me. I'd

knelt down to see to the captain and something caught my eye. The ring he was wearing. A thick signet ring, it bore a symbol I recognized.

The day I'd woken up on the *Emperor* I'd found a looking glass below decks and inspected my wounds. I had cuts, bruises and scrapes; I looked like what I was: a man who'd been beaten up. One of the marks was from where I'd been punched by the man in the hood. His ring had left its imprint on my skin. A symbol of a cross.

I saw that very same symbol now on Captain Pritchard's ring.

Despite the poor man's discomfort I couldn't help myself. 'What's this?'

My voice, a little too sharp and a little too loud, was enough to arouse the suspicions of Blaney, and he pushed himself away from the closed cabin door and moved further into the room to see.

'What is what?' Pritchard was saying, but by now Blaney had reached us. And he too had seen the ring, only his interest in it was less to do with its meaning, more to do with its value, and without hesitation, and heedless to Pritchard's pain, he reached and yanked it off, flaying the finger of burnt and charred skin at the same time.

The captain's screams took some time to die down, and when they had, his head lolled forward on to his chest and a long rope of saliva dripped to the cabin floor.

'Give me that back,' I said to Blaney.

'Why should I give it to you?'

'Now come on, Blaney –' I started. And then we heard something. A shout from outside.

'Sail ho!'

It wasn't as though our feud was forgotten, more like it was placed to one side for a moment as Blaney said, 'Wait there.' And pointing with his dagger he left the room to see what was going on.

The open door framed a scene of panic outside and as the ship lurched it slammed shut. I looked from that to Captain Pritchard, now groaning in pain. I'd never wanted to be a pirate. I was a sheep farmer from Bristol. A man in search of adventure, it's true. But by fair means not foul. I wasn't a criminal, an outlaw. I'd never wanted to be party to the torture of innocent men.

'Untie me,' said the captain, his voice dry and pained. 'I can help you. I can guarantee you a pardon.'

'If you tell me about the ring.'

Captain Pritchard was moving his head slowly from side to side as though to shake away the pain. 'The ring, what ring . . . ?' he was saying, confused, trying to work out why on earth this young deckhand should be asking him about such an irrelevance.

'A mysterious man I consider my enemy wore a ring just like yours. I need to know its significance.'

He gathered himself. His voice parched but measured. 'Its significance is great power, my friend, great power that can be used to help you.'

'What if that great power was being used against me?'

'That can be arranged as well.'

'I feel it already has been used against me.'

'Set me free and I can use my influence to find out for you. Whatever wrong has been done to you I can see it put right.'

'It involves the woman I love. Some powerful men.'

His next words reminded me of something the man in the hood had said that night in the farmyard. 'There are powerful men and powerful men. I swear on the Bible, boy, that whatever ails you can be solved. Whatever wrong has been done to you can be put right.'

Already my fingers were fiddling with his knots but just as the ropes came away and slithered to the cabin floor the door burst open. Standing in the doorway was Captain Dolzell. His eyes were wild. His sword was drawn. Behind him was a great commotion. Men who moments before had been ready to board the *Amazon Galley*, as organized a fighting unit as privateers could be, were suddenly in disarray.

Captain Dolzell said one word, but it was enough. The word was. *'Privateers.'*

19

'Sir?' I said.

And thankfully, Dolzell was too preoccupied with developments to wonder what I was doing standing behind Captain Pritchard's chair. 'Privateers are coming,' he cried.

In terror I looked from Dolzell to where I'd just untied Captain Pritchard's hands.

Pritchard revived. And though he had the presence of mind to keep his hands behind his back, he couldn't resist taunting Dolzell. 'It's Edward Thatch, come to our rescue. You'd better run, captain. Unlike you, Edward Thatch is a privateer loyal to the Crown and when I tell him what has taken place here —'

In two long strides Dolzell darted forward and thrust the point of his sword into Pritchard's belly. Pritchard tautened in his seat, impaled on the blade. His head shot back and upside-down eyes fixed on mine for a second before his body went limp and he slumped in the chair.

'You'll tell your friend nothing,' snarled Dolzell as he removed his blade.

Pritchard's hands fell to hang limply by his sides.

'His hands are untied.' Dolzell's accusing eyes went from Pritchard to me.

'Your blade, sir, it sliced the rope,' I said, which seemed to satisfy him, and with that he turned and ran from the cabin. At the same time the *Emperor* shook – I later found out that Thatch's ship had hit us side-on. There were some who said the captain had been rushing towards the fight and that the impact of the privateers' ship had knocked him off the deck, over the gunwale and into the water. There are others who said that the captain, with images of Execution Dock in his mind, had plunged off the side in order to escape capture.

From the navigation room I took a cutlass and a pistol that I thrust into my belt, then dashed out of the cabin and on to the deck.

What I found was a ship at war. The privateers had boarded from the starboard, while on the port side the crew of the *Amazon Galley* had taken their opportunity to fight back. We were hopelessly outnumbered and, even as I ran into the fray with my sword swinging, I could see that the battle was lost. Sluicing across the deck was what looked like a river of blood, while everywhere I could see men I had been serving with dead, draped over the gunwales, their bodies lined with bleeding slashes. Others were fighting on. There was the roar of musket and pistol, the day torn apart by the constant ring of steel, the agonized screams of the dying, the warrior yells of the attacking buccaneers.

And yet, even so, I found myself strangely on the outside of the battle. Cowardice has never been a problem with me, but I am not sure I exchanged more than two sword strokes with one of the enemy, before it seemed the battle was over. Many of our men were dead. The rest began to drop to their knees and let their swords fall to the deck, hoping, no doubt, for the clemency of our invaders. Some still fought on, including the first mate, Trafford – by his side another man I didn't know. Melling, I think his name was – and, as I watched, two of the attacking buccaneers came at him at once, swinging their swords with such force that no amount of fighting skill could have stopped them and he was driven back to the rail, slashes and cuts opening up in his face, screaming as they both stabbed into him.

Blaney was there I saw. Also, not far away, was the third captain, a man I would come to know as Edward Thatch, and who years later the world would know as Blackbeard. He was just as the legend would describe him, though his beard was not so long back then: tall and thin, with thick dark hair. He had been in the fray, his clothes were splattered with blood and it dripped from the blade of his sword. He and one of his men had advanced up the deck and I found myself standing with two of my shipmates, Trafford and Blaney.

Blaney. It would have to be him.

And now the battle was over. I saw Blaney look from me to Trafford, then to Thatch. A plan formed and in the next instant he'd called to Thatch. 'Sir, shall I finish them for you?' And he swept his sword around to point at me and Trafford. For me he reserved an especially evil grin.

We both stared at him in absolute disbelief. *How could he do this?*

'Why, you scurvy bilge-sucking bastard!' yelled Trafford, outraged at the treachery, and he leapt towards Blaney, jabbing his cutlass more in hope than expectation – unless his expectation was to die, for that's exactly what happened.

Blaney stepped easily to one side and at the same time whipped his sword in an underhand slash across Trafford's chest. The first mate's shirt split and blood drenched his front. He grunted in pain and surprise, but that didn't stop him launching a second, yet sadly for him, even wilder attack. Blaney punished him for it, slashing again with the cutlass, landing blow after blow, catching Trafford again and again across the face and chest, even after Trafford had dropped his own blade, fallen to his knees and with a wretched whimper and blood bubbling at his lips pitched forward to the deck and lay still. I snatched up a sword and launched myself at Blaney, but my attack was just as haphazard as poor old Trafford, and Blaney hardly broke a sweat disarming me.

The rest of the deck had fallen silent, each man left alive was now looking over to where we stood near the entrance to the captain's cabin – just Blaney and I between the invaders and the doorway.

'Shall I finish him, sir?' said Blaney. The point of his sword was at my throat. Again, the grin.

The crowd of men seemed to part round Edward Thatch as he stepped forward.

'Now –' he waved at Blaney with his cutlass, which still dripped with the blood of our crew – 'why would you be calling me, "sir", lad?'

The point of Blaney's sword tickled my throat. 'I hope to join you, sir,' he replied, 'and prove my loyalty to you.'

Thatch turned his attention to me. 'And you, young 'un, what did you have in mind, besides dying at your shipmate's sword, that is? Would you like to join my crew as a privateer or die a pirate, either at the hands of your crewmate here, or back home in Blighty?'

'I never wanted to be a pirate, sir,' I said quickly. (Stop yer grinning.) 'I merely wanted to earn some money for my wife, sir, honest money to take back to Bristol.'

(A Bristol from which I was banished and a wife I was prevented from seeing. But I decided not to bother Thatch with the little details.)

'Aye,' laughed Thatch, and threw out an arm to indicate the mass of captured men behind him, 'and I suppose I could say this for every one of your crew left alive. Every man will swear he never intended a career in piracy. Ordered to do it by the captain, they'll say. Forced into it against their will.'

'He ruled with a rod of iron, sir,' I said. 'Any man who said as much would be telling you the truth.'

'And how did your captain manage to persuade you to enter into this act of piracy, pray tell?' demanded Thatch.

'By telling us we would soon be pirates anyway, sir, when a treaty was signed.'

'Well, he's right most likely,' sighed Thatch thoughtfully. 'No denying it. Still, that's no excuse.' He grinned. 'Not while I remain a privateer that is, sworn to protect and assist Her Majesty's navy, which includes watching over the likes of the *Amazon Galley*. Now, you're not a swordsman, are you, boy?'

I shook my head.

Thatch chuckled. 'Aye, that is apparent. Didn't stop you throwing yourself at this man here, though, did it? Knowing that you would meet your end at the point of his sword. Why was that then?'

I bristled. 'Blaney had turned traitor, sir; I saw red.'

Thatch jammed the point of his cutlass into the deck, rested both hands on the hilt and looked from me to Blaney, who had added wariness to his usual expression of angry incomprehension. I knew how he felt. It was impossible to say from Thatch's demeanour where his sympathies lay. He simply looked from me to Blaney, then back again. From me to Blaney, then back again.

'I have an idea,' he roared at last, and every man on the deck seemed to relax at once. 'Let's settle this with a duel. What do you say, lads?'

Like a set of scales, the crew's spirits rose as mine sank. I had barely used a blade. Blaney, on the other hand, was an experienced swordsman. Settling the matter would be the work of a heartbeat for him.

Thatch chuckled. 'Ah, but not with swords, lads, because we've already seen how this one here has certain skills with the blade. No, I suggest a straight fight. No weapons, not even knives. Does that suit you, boy?'

I nodded my head, thinking what would suit me most was no fight at all, but a straight fight was the best I could hope for.

'Good.' Thatch clapped his hands and his sword juddered in the wood. 'Come on, lads, form a ring; let these two gentlemen get to it.

The year was 1713, and I was about to die, I was sure of it.

Thinking about it – that was twelve years ago, wasn't it? It would have been the year you were born.

20

'Then let us begin,' Thatch commanded.

Men had shimmied up the rigging and clung to the masts. Men were in the ratlines, on the rails and the top decks of all three ships – every man-jack of them craning to get a better view. Playing to the crowd, Blaney stripped off his shirt so that he was down to his breeches. Conscious of my puny torso I did the same. Then we dropped our elbows, raised our fists, eyed each other up.

My opponent grinned behind raised forearms – his fists were as big as hams and twice as hard. His knuckles like statues' noses. No, this probably wasn't quite the sword fight Blaney wanted, but it was the next best thing. The chance to pulverize me with the captain's consent. To beat me to death without risking the taste of a cat-o'-nine-tails.

From the decks and rigging came the shouts of the crew, keen to witness a good bout. By which I mean a bloody bout. Just from the catcalls it was difficult to make out if they had a favourite, but I put myself in their position: what would I want to see if I were them? I'd want to see *sport*.

So let's give it to them, I thought. I brought my own fists up higher and what I thought about was how Blaney had been a huge pain in the arse from the moment I had set foot on board. Nobody else. Just him. This thick-as-pigshit cretin. All my time on ship I'd spent dodging Blaney and wondering why he hated me, because I wasn't snot-nosed and arrogant then, not like I'd been back home. Life on board had tamed that side of me. I dare say I'd grown up a bit. What I'm saying is, he had no real *reason* to hate me.

But right then it came to me. The reason why. He hated me *because*. Just because. And if I hadn't been around to hate he would have found someone else to fill my shoes. One of the cabin boys, perhaps. One of the blacks. He just liked hating.

And for that I hated him in return, and I channelled that feeling, that hate. Perplexed at his hostility? I turned it into hate. Staying out of his way day after day? I turned it into hate. Having to look at his stupid, thick face day after day? Turned it into hate.

And because of that the first strike was mine. I stepped in and it seemed to explode out of me, using my speed and my size to my advantage, ducking beneath his protecting fists and smashing him in the solar plexus. He let out an oof and staggered back, the surprise more than the pain making him drop his guard, enough for me to dance quickly to my left and drive forward with my left fist, finding a spot above his right eye that, just for one delicious second, I thought might have been good enough to finish him off.

A roar of approval and bloodlust from the men. It

had been a good punch. Enough to open a cut that began to leak a steady stream of blood down his face. But, no, it wasn't enough to stop him for good. Instead the look of angry incomprehension he always wore became even more uncomprehending. Even angrier. I'd landed two punches, he precisely none. He hadn't even moved from his spot.

I flitted back. I've never been one for fancy foot-work, but compared to Blaney I was nimble. Plus I had the advantage. First blood to me and with the crowd on my side. David versus Goliath.

'Come on, you fat bastard,' I taunted him. 'Come on, this is what you've wanted to do the minute I came aboard the ship. Let's see what you got, Blaney.'

The crew had heard me and shouted their approval, perhaps for my sheer gumption. From the corner of my eye I saw Thatch throw back his head and laugh, with his hand at his belly. To save face, Blaney had to act. You have to give it to him. He acted.

Friday had told me that Blaney was skilled with his blade, and was an essential member of the *Emperor*'s boarding party. He hadn't mentioned that Blaney was also good with his fists. He'd left that bit out. And I, for some reason, never assumed he had much in the way of boxing skills. But one bit of nautical wisdom I had learnt was 'never assume' and, on this occasion at least, I ignored it. Once again my arrogance had got me into trouble.

And how quick the crowd was to turn as Blaney struck. Never go down in the fight. It's the one golden rule. Never go down in a fight. But I had no choice as his fist made contact and bells rang in my head as I went to the deck on my hands and knees, and spat out teeth on a string of blood and phlegm. My vision jarred and blurred. I'd been hit before, of course, many times, but never – *never* – as hard as that.

Amid the rushing of my pain and the roaring of the spectators – roaring for blood, which Blaney was going to give to them, with pleasure – he bent to me, putting his face close enough for me to smell his rancid breath, which spilled like fog over black and rotted teeth.

'"Fat bastard", eh?' he said and hawked up a green. I felt the wet slap of phlegm on my face. One thing you have to say about a 'fat bastard' taunt. It always gets them going.

And then he straightened, and I could see his boot so near to my face I saw the spider-cracks in the leather, and still trying to shake off the pain I lifted one pathetic hand as though to ward off the inevitable kick.

The kick, though, when it came was aimed not at my face but squarely at my belly, and was so hard that it lifted me into the air and I was deposited back on the deck. From the corner of my eye I saw Thatch, and perhaps I had allowed myself to believe that he favoured me in the bout, but he was laughing just as heartily at my misfortune as he had been when Blaney was rocked. I rolled weakly to my side as I saw Blaney coming towards me. He lifted his boot to stamp on me and looked up to Thatch. 'Sir?' he asked.

To hell with that; I wasn't waiting. With a grunt I grabbed his foot, twisted it and sent him sprawling back to the deck. A tremor of renewed interest ran through the spectators. Whistles and shouts. Cheers and boos.

They didn't care who won. They just wanted the spectacle. But now Blaney was down and with a fresh surge of strength I threw myself on top of him, pummelling him with my fists at the same time as I drove my knees into his groin and midriff, attacking him like a child in the throes of a temper tantrum, hoping against hope that I might lay him out with a lucky blow.

I didn't. There were no lucky blows today. Just Blaney grabbing my fists, wrenching me to the side, slamming the flat of his hand into my face and sending me flying backwards. I heard my nose break and felt blood gush over my top lip. Blaney lumbered over and this time he wasn't waiting for Thatch's permission. This time he was coming in for the kill. In his fist shone a blade . . .

There was the crack of a pistol and a hole appeared on his forehead. His mouth dropped open, and the fat bastard fell to his knees – dead to the deck.

When my vision cleared I saw Thatch reaching to help me from the deck with one hand. In the other, a flintlock pistol, still warm.

'I got a vacancy on my crew, lad,' he said. 'Do you want to fill it?'

I nodded as I stood and looked down at Blaney's body. A wisp of smoke rose from the bloody hole in his forehead. *Should have killed me when you had the chance*, I thought.

21

March, 1713

Miles away in a place I'd never visited and never would –
although, after all, it's never too late – a bunch of
representatives of England, Spain, France, Portugal
and Holland were sitting down to draft a series of treaties that would end up changing all our lives, forcing us
to take a new direction, shattering our dreams.

But that was to come. First, I found myself adjusting
to a new life – a life I liked very much.

I was lucky, I suppose, because Edward Thatch took
to me. A scrapper, was what he called me. And I think
he liked having me around. He used to say that in me he
had a trusted hand, and he was right, he did; for Edward
Thatch had saved me from embarking on a life of crime
under Captain Dolzell – well, either that or be thrown
overboard like those other poor fellows. It was thanks
to his intervention, and thanks to being taken under his
wing that I could make something of myself, return to
Bristol and to Caroline as a man of quality, head held
high.

And, yes, just because you and I know that it didn't
work out that way doesn't make it any less true.

Life at sea was very much the same as it had been before, but with certain attractive differences. There was no Blaney, of course. The last I'd seen of that particular barnacle on my life was him slipping into the sea like a dead whale. And there was no Captain Alexander Dolzell. He ended up being condemned to death by the British in 1715. Without those two life on ship immediately improved; it was the life of a privateer. And so we engaged the Spanish and Portuguese when we could, and took prizes when we could, and along with the skills of a sailor I began to refine the craft of combat. Thatch took me under his wing. From him I learnt better sword skills, and I learnt how to use pistols.

And, also from Edward Thatch, I learnt a certain philosophy of life, a philosophy that he in turn had learnt from another older buccaneer, a man under who Edward served, who would also be my mentor. A man named Benjamin Hornigold.

And where else should I meet Benjamin but at Nassau?

I'm not sure we ever thought of the port of Nassau on New Providence Island as ever really 'belonging' to us, because that wasn't our way. But it was a kind of heaven for us, with its steep cliffs on one side, its long sloping beach that swept down to a shallow sea – too shallow for His Majesty's men-of-war – its quayside where we offloaded booty and supplies, and its hillside fortress on the hill, overlooking a raggle-taggle collection of shanty houses, huts and crumbling wooden terraces. And of course, it had a wonderful harbour, where vessels enjoyed shelter from the elements and from our enemies. Making an attack even more difficult was the ships' graveyard, where the skeletal remains of burnt and grounded ships were a warning to the unwary. There were the palms, the smell of seawater and tar in the air, taverns and plentiful run. And Edward Thatch was there. And Benjamin Hornigold was there.

I liked Benjamin. He had been Blackbeard's mentor, just as Blackbeard was mine, and there was never a better sailor than Benjamin Hornigold.

And yet, although you may think I'm only saying this because of what subsequently happened, you're going to have to believe me when I swear it's true. I always thought there was something apart about him. Not only did he have a more military bearing and a hawk nose like a toff English general, but he dressed differently as well, more like a soldier than a buccaneer.

But still, I liked him, and if I didn't like him as much as I liked Edward, well, then I respected him as much, if not more. After all, Benjamin was the one who had helped establish Nassau in the first place. For that, if nothing else, I liked him.

I was sailing with Edward in July 1713 when the quartermaster was killed on a trip ashore. Two weeks after that we received a message and I was called to the captain's quarters.

'Can you read, son?'

'Yes, sir,' I said, and I thought briefly of my wife back home.

Edward sat at one side of his navigation table rather than behind it. His legs were crossed and he wore long black boots, a red sash at his waist and four pistols in a thick leather shoulder belt. Maps and charts were laid out beside him but something told me it wasn't those he needed reading.

'I need a new quartermaster,' he said.

'Oh, sir, I don't think —'

He roared with laughter and slapped his thighs. 'No, son, I don't "think" either. You're too young and you don't have the experience to be a quartermaster. Isn't that right?'

I looked at my boots.

'Come here,' he said, 'read this.'

I did as I was asked, reading aloud a short communication with news of a treaty between the English, the Spanish, Portuguese . . .

'Does it mean . . . ?' I said when I had finished.

'Indeed it does, Edward,' he said (and it was the first time he'd ever called me by my name rather than 'son' or 'lad' — in fact, I don't think he ever called me 'son' or 'lad' again). 'It means your Captain Alexander Dolzell was right, and that the days of privateers filling their boots are over. I'll be making an announcement to the crew later. Will you follow me yourself?'

I would have followed him to the ends of the Earth

but I didn't say so. Just nodded, as though I had a lot of options.

He looked at me. All that black hair and beard lent his eyes an extra penetrating shine. 'You will be a pirate, Edward, a wanted man. Are you sure you want that?'

To tell you the truth, I wasn't, but what choice did I have? I couldn't go back to Bristol. I didn't dare go back without a pot of money, and the only way of making money was to become a pirate.

'We shall set sail for Nassau,' said Thatch. 'We pledged to meet Benjamin should this ever happen. I dare say we shall join forces, for we'll both lose crew in the wake of this announcement.

'I'd like you by my side, Edward. You've got courage and heart and skill in battle, and I can always use a man with letters.'

I nodded, flattered.

When I went back to my hammock, though, and was alone, I closed my eyes for fear that tears might squeeze out. I had not come to sea to be a pirate. Oh, of course, I saw I had no other choice but to follow that path. Others were doing it, including Edward Thatch. But even so, it was not what I had wanted for myself. I'd never wanted to be an outlaw.

Like I say, though, I didn't feel I had much choice. And from that moment on, I abandoned any plans I had of returning to Bristol as a man of quality. The best I could hope for was to return to Bristol as a man of means. From that moment on my quest became one of acquiring riches. From that moment on I was a pirate.

PART TWO

PART TWO

22

June, 1715

There is nothing quite so loud as the sound of a carriage-gun blast. Especially when it goes off in your ear.

It's like being pummelled by nothing. A nothing that seems to want to crush you. And you're not sure whether it's a trick of your eyesight, shocked and dazzled by the blast, or whether the world really is shaking. Probably it doesn't even matter.

Somewhere the shot impacts. Boat planks splinter. Men with their arms and legs torn off, and men who look down and in the few seconds they have before dying realize half their body has been shot away, begin shrieking. All you hear in the immediate aftermath is the shrieking of the damaged hull, the screams of the dead and dying.

I wouldn't say you ever get used to it, the blast of a carriage gun, the way it tears a hole in your world, but the trick is to recover swiftly. The trick is to recover from it more swiftly than your enemy. That's how you stay alive.

We'd been off the coast of Cape Buena Vista in Cuba when the English had attacked. We called them the English upon the brigantine, even though English made up the core of our crew and I myself was English by birth, English in my heart. But it counted for nothing as a pirate. You were an enemy of His Majesty (Queen Anne had been succeeded by King George), an enemy of the Crown. Which made you an enemy of His Majesty's navy. And so when, 'Sail ho!', we saw the red ensign on the horizon, the sight of a frigate foaming across the ocean towards us and the figures running to and fro on her decks, what we said was, 'The English are attacking! The English are attacking!' with no regard for the small details of our actual nationalities.

And this one, she came at us fast. We were trying to turn and put distance between us and her six-pounders, but she bore down upon us, slicing across our bows, so close we could see the whites of the crew's eyes, the flash of their gold teeth, the glint of sun on the steel in their hands.

Flame bloomed along her sides as her carriage guns thundered. Steel tore the air. Our hull shrieked and cracked as the shots found their mark. The day had been full of rain. The powder smoke turned it into a night full of rain. It filled our lungs and made us cough, choke and splutter, throwing us into even more disarray and panic.

And then that feeling of the world crashing in, that shock, and those moments of wondering if you'd been hit and if maybe you were dead, and perhaps this was what it felt like in heaven. Or most likely – in my case at least – in hell. Which of course it must do, because hell is smoke and fire and pain and screaming. So in actual fact whether you were dead or not, it made no difference. Either way you were in hell.

At the first crash-bang I'd raised my arms to protect myself. Luckily. I felt shards of splintered wood that would otherwise have punctured my face and eyes embed themselves into my arm, and the force was enough to send me staggering back, tripping and falling.

They'd used bar shot. Big iron bars that would blast a hole in virtually anything provided they were close enough. In this case, they'd done their job. The English had no interest in boarding us. As pirates we would inflict as little damage upon our target as possible. Our aim was to board and to loot, over a period of days if needs be. It was difficult to loot a sinking ship. But the English – or this particular command, at least – either knew we had no treasure aboard or didn't care – they simply wanted to destroy us. And they were doing a bloody good job of it.

I dragged myself to my feet, felt something warm running down my arm and looked to see blood from a splinter blob to the planks of the deck. With a grimace I reached to tear the wood from my arm and tossed it to the deck, barely registering the pain as I squinted through a fog of powder smoke and lashing rain.

A cheer went up from the crew of the English

frigate as she churned past our starboard side. There was the pop and fizz of musket and flintlock pistol shot. Stinkpots and grenadoes came sailing over, exploding on deck and adding to the chaos, the damage and the choking smoke that hung over us like a death shroud. The stinkpots in particular let out a vicious sulphur gas that sent men to their knees, making the air so dense and black that it became difficult to see, to judge distance.

Even so, I saw him: the hooded figure who stood on their forecastle deck. His arms were folded, and he stood still in his robes, his entire demeanour emanating unconcern at the events that were unfolding around him. This I could tell from his posture and his eyes that gleamed from beneath the cowl of his robes. Eyes that for a second were fixed on me.

And then our attackers were swallowed up by smoke. A ghost ship amid a fug of powder belch, sizzling rain and choking stinkpot fumes.

All around me was the sound of shattering wood and screaming men. The dead were everywhere, littering torn planks awash with their blood. Through a gash in the main deck I saw water on the decks below and from above heard the complaint of wood and the tearing of the smoky shroud, and looked up to see our mainsail half destroyed by chain shot. A dead lookout with most of his head shorn away hung by his feet from the crow's-nest and men were already scaling the ratlines to try to cut the broken mast free, but they were too late. She was already listing, wallowing in the water like a fat woman taking a bath.

At last enough of the smoke cleared to see that the British frigate was coming round in order to use its starboard guns. But now she ran into a spot of bad luck. Before the ship could be brought to bear, the same wind that had dispersed the smoke dropped, and her plump sails flattened and she slowed. We had been given our second chance.

'Man the guns!' I shouted.

Those members of our crew still on their feet were scrambling to the mounted guns. I manned a swivel gun and we delivered a broadside that the attacking frigate could do nothing about, our shot inflicting almost as much damage to them as they had to us. And now it was our turn to cheer. Defeat had turned if not quite to victory, then at least to a lucky escape. Perhaps there were those of us who were even wondering what treasures might be on board the British vessel, and I saw one or two of our men, the optimistic few, with boarding hooks, axes and marlinspikes, ready to lash the ship close and take them on man on man.

But any plans were dashed by what happened next.

'*The magazine*,' came the cry.

'She's going up.'

The news was followed by screams, and as I looked from my post at the swivel gun towards the bow, I saw flames around the breach in the hull. Meanwhile, from the stern came the cries of our captain, Captain Bramah, while on the poop deck of the ship opposite, the man in the robes leapt into action. Literally. He unfolded his arms and in one short jump was on the rail of the deck, then in the next instant had jumped across to our ship.

For a moment the impression I had of him in the air was like an eagle, his robes spread out behind him, his arms outstretched like wings.

Next I saw Captain Bramah fall. Crouched over him the hooded man's arm pulled back and a hidden blade sprang from within his sleeve.

That blade. I was transfixed by it for a second. The flames from the burning deck made it alive. And then the hooded man drove it deep into Captain Bramah.

I stood and stared, my own cutlass in my hand. From behind I vaguely heard the cries of the crew as they tried in vain to stop the fire spreading to the magazine.

It will go up, I thought distractedly. *The magazine will explode.* Thinking of the barrels of gunpowder stored there. The English ship close enough so that the explosion would surely blast a hole in the hull of both ships. All of this I knew, but only as distant distracted thoughts. I was spellbound by the hooded man at work. Mesmerized by this agent of death, who had ignored the carnage around him by biding his time and waiting to strike.

The kill was over, Captain Bramah dead. The assassin looked up from the dead body of the captain, and once again our eyes met, only this time something flared within his features and in the next instant he had bounded to his feet, a single lithe jump that took him over the corpse, and he was bearing down upon me.

I raised my cutlass, determined not to go easily into the great unknown. And then from the stern – in fact, from the magazine, where our men had obviously failed to douse the fire whose fingers had found the stores of gunpowder – came a great explosion.

In a thunderclap I was blasted off the deck, describing a circle in the air and finding a moment of perfect peace, not knowing whether I was alive or dead, whether I still had all of my limbs and in that moment not caring anyway. Not knowing where I'd come to rest: whether I'd slam to the deck of a ship and break my back or land impaled on a snapped mast or be tossed into the eye of the magazine inferno.

Or what I did, which was slap into the sea.

Maybe alive, maybe dead, maybe conscious, maybe not. Either way I seemed to drift not far below the surface, watching the sea above: a shifting mottle of blacks, greys and the flaming orange of burning ships. Past me sank dead bodies, eyes wide open as though surprised in death. They discoloured the water in which they sank and trailed guts and stringy sinew like tentacles. I saw a smashed mizzen mast twirling in the water, bodies snared in rigging dragged to the depths.

I thought of Caroline. Of my father. Then of my

adventures on the *Emperor*. I thought about Nassau, where there was only one law: pirate law. And, of course, I thought about how I had been mentored from privateer to pirate by Edward – Edward Thatch.

23

All of this I thought as I sank, eyes open, aware of everything happening around me: the bodies, the wreckage ... Aware of it, yet uncaring. As though it was happening to somebody else. Looking back, I know it for what it was, that brief moment – and it was brief – as I sank in the water. I had, in those moments, lost the will to live.

After all, this expedition – Edward had warned against it. He'd told me not to go. 'That Captain Bramah's bad news,' he'd said. 'You mark my words.'

And he was right. And I was going to pay for my greed and stupidity with my life.

And then I found it again. The will to go on. I found it. I grasped it. I shook it. I held it close to my bosom and from that moment to this I never let it go again. My legs kicked, my arms arrowed, and I streaked towards the surface, breaking the water and gasping – for air, and in shock at the carnage around me, watching as the last of the English frigate slipped below the water, still ablaze. All across the ocean were small blazes soon to be doused by the water, floating debris everywhere, and men, of course – survivors.

And then, just as I had feared, the sharks started to

attack, and the screams began – screams of terror at first and then, as the sharks began to investigate more insistently, screams of agony that only intensified as more predators gathered and they began to feed. The screams I'd heard during the battle, agonized as they were, were nothing compared to the shrieks that tore that soot-filled afternoon apart.

I was one of the lucky ones, whose wounds were not enough to attract the sharks' attention, and I swam for shore. At one point I was knocked by a shark gliding past, thankfully too concerned with joining the feeding frenzy to stop. My foot seemed to snag what felt like a fin in the water and I prayed that whatever blood I was leaking was not enough to tempt the shark away from the more plentiful chum elsewhere. It was a cruel irony that those more heavily wounded were the ones who were attacked first.

I say 'attacked'. You know what I mean. They were eaten. Devoured. How many survivors there were from the battle, I have no way of knowing. All I can say is that I saw that most survivors ended up as food for the sharks. Me, I swam to the safety of the beach at Cape Buena Vista and there I collapsed with sheer relief and exhaustion, and if the dry land hadn't been made up entirely of sand I probably would have kissed it.

My hat was gone. My beloved three-pointer, which had sat upon my head as man and boy. What I didn't know at the time, of course, was that it was the first step in me shedding the past, saying goodbye to my old life. What's more, I still had my cutlass, and given the choice between losing my hat or cutlass . . .

And so, after some time thanking my lucky stars, listening out for other survivors but hearing just faint screams in the distance, I rolled on to my back, then heard something to my left.

It was a groan. And looking over I saw its source was the robed assassin. He'd come to rest just a short distance away from me and he was lucky, very lucky, not to be eaten by the sharks, because when he rolled over to his back he left behind a patch of crimson-stained sand. And as he lay there with his chest rising and falling, his breath coming in short, jagged gasps, his hands went to his stomach. His obviously wounded stomach.

'Was it good for you as well?' I asked, laughing. Something about the situation struck me as funny. Even after these few years at sea, there was still something of the Bristol brawler about me, who couldn't help but make light of the situation, no matter how dark it seemed. He ignored me. Or ignored the quip at least.

'Havana,' he groaned, 'I must get to Havana.'

That produced another smile from me. 'Well, I'll just build us another ship, will I?'

'I can pay you,' he said through gritted teeth. 'Isn't that the sound you pirates like best? A thousand escudos.'

That had aroused my interest. 'Keep talking.'

'Will you or won't you?' he demanded to know.

One of us was badly wounded, and it wasn't me. I

stood to look over him, seeing the robes, hidden in which, presumably, was his blade. I had liked the look of that blade. I had the feeling that the man in possession of that particular blade might go far. Especially in my chosen trade. Let's not forget that before my ship's magazine had exploded this very man was about to use that very blade on me. You may think me callous. You may think me cruel and ruthless. But, please understand, in such situations a man must do what is necessary to survive, and a good lesson to learn if you're standing on the deck of a burning ship about to move in for the kill: finish the job.

Lesson two: if you don't manage to finish the job, it's probably best not to expect help from your intended target.

And lesson three: if you ask your intended target for help anyway, probably best not to start getting angry with them.

For all those reasons I ask you not to judge me. I ask you to understand why I gazed down at him so dispassionately.

'You don't have that gold on you now, do you?'

He looked back at me, and his eyes blazed briefly and then in a second, more quickly than I could possibly have anticipated – imagined even, he'd drawn a pocket pistol and shoved it into my stomach. The shock more than the impact of the gun barrel sent me staggering back, only to fall on my behind some feet away.

With one hand clutching at his wound, the other with the pistol trained on me, he pulled himself to his feet.

'Bloody pirates,' he snarled through clenched teeth.

I saw his finger whiten on the trigger. I heard the hammer on the pistol snap forward and closed my eyes expecting the shot to come.

But it never did. And of course it didn't. There was indeed something unearthly about this man – his grace, his speed, his garb, his choice of weaponry – but he was still just a man, and no man can command the sea. Even he couldn't prevent his powder getting wet.

Lesson four: if you're going to ignore lessons one, two and three, it's probably best not to pull out a gun filled with wet powder.

His advantage lost, the killer turned and headed straight for the tree line, one arm still clutching his wounded stomach and the other warding off undergrowth as he crashed into it and out of sight. For a second I simply sat there, unable to believe my luck: if I was a cat then I'd have used up at least three of my nine lives, and that was just today.

And then without a second thought – well, maybe perhaps a *single* second thought, because, after all, I'd seen him in action and wound or no wound he was dangerous – I took off in pursuit. He had something I wanted. That hidden blade.

I heard him crashing through the jungle ahead of me so, heedless of the branches whipping my face and dancing over roots underfoot, I gave chase. I reached out to prevent myself being slapped in the face by a thick green leaf the size of a banjo and saw a bloody handprint on it. Good. I was on the right track. From further ahead came the sound of disturbed birds crashing through the canopy of trees, and I reflected that I hardly needed to worry about losing him – the whole jungle shook to the sound of his clumsy progress. His grace, it seemed, was no more, lost in the blundering fight for survival.

'Follow me, and I'll kill you,' I heard from ahead.

I doubted that. As far as I could see, his killing days were over.

And so it proved. I reached a clearing where he stood, bent over with the pain of his stomach wound. He'd been trying to decide which route to take but at the sound of me crashing out of the undergrowth turned to face me. A slow, painful turn, like an old man crippled with bellyache.

Something of his old pride returned, and a little fight crept into his eyes as there was a sliding noise and from his right sleeve sprouted the blade, which gleamed in the duskiness of the clearing.

It struck me that the blade must have inspired fear in his enemies, and that to inspire fear in your enemy was half the battle won. Make someone frightened of you, that was the key. Unfortunately, just as his killing days were over, so too was his ability to inspire dread in his foes. Exhausted and hunched over with pain as he was, his robes, hood and even the blade looked like the trinkets they were. I took no pleasure in killing him, and possibly he didn't even deserve to die. Our captain had been a cruel, ruthless man, fond of a flogging. So fond, in fact, that he was apt to let the cat out of the bag and administer them himself. And he'd enjoyed doing what he called 'making a man a governor of his own island', which in other words was marooning him. Nobody but his own mother was going to mourn our captain's passing. To all intents and purposes, the man with the robes had done us a favour.

But the man with the robes had been about to kill me as well. And the first lesson was that if you set out to kill someone you'd better finish the job.

He knew that, I'm sure, as he died.

Afterwards I rifled through his things. And yes, the body was still warm. And no, I'm not proud of it, but please don't forget, I was – *I am* – a pirate. So I rifled through his things. From inside his robes I retrieved a satchel.

Hmm, I thought. *Hidden treasure.*

But when I upended it on to the ground so the sun could dry the contents what I saw was . . . well, not treasure. An odd cube made of crystal, with an opening on one side – an ornament, perhaps? (Later I'd find out what it was, of course, then I'd laugh at myself for ever thinking it a mere *ornament*.) And some maps I laid to one side, as well as a letter with a broken seal that as I began reading I realized held the key to everything I wanted from this mysterious killer . . .

Señor Duncan Walpole,

I accept your most generous offer, and await your arrival with eagerness.

If you truly possess the information we desire, we have the means to reward you handsomely.

Though I do not know your face by sight, I believe I can recognize the costume made infamous by your secret order.

Therefore, come to Havana in haste. And trust that you shall be welcomed as a brother. It will be a great honour to meet you at last, señor; to put a face to your name and shake your hand as I call you friend. Your support for our secret and most noble cause is warming.

Your most humble servant,
Governor Laureano Torres y Ayala

I read the letter twice. Then a third time for good measure.

Governor Torres of Havana, eh? I thought.

'Reward you handsomely', eh?

A plan had begun to form.

I buried Señor Duncan Walpole. I owed him that much at least. He went out of this world the way he'd arrived – naked – because I needed his clothes in order to begin my deception and, though I do say so myself, they were a perfect fit. I looked good in his robes. I looked the part.

Acting the part, though, would be another matter entirely. The man I was impersonating? Well, I've already told you of the aura that seemed to surround him. When I secured his hidden blade to my own forearm and tried to eject it as he had, well – it just wasn't happening. I cast my mind back to seeing him do it and tried imitating him. A *flick* of the wrist. Something special, obviously, to stop the blade engaging by accident. I flicked my wrist. I twisted my arm. I wriggled my fingers. All to no avail. The blade sat stubbornly in its housing. It looked both beautiful and fearsome but if it wouldn't engage it was no good to man nor beast.

What was I to do? Carry it around and keep trying? Hope I'd eventually chance upon its secret? Somehow I thought not. I had the feeling there was arcane knowledge attached to this blade. Found upon me, it could betray me.

With a heavy heart I cast it away then addressed the graveside I had prepared for my victim.

'Mr Walpole . . .' I said, 'let's collect your reward.'

24

I came upon them at Cape Buena Vista beach the next morning: a schooner anchored in the harbour, boats brought ashore and crates offloaded and dragged on to the beach, where they'd been stacked, either by the dejected-looking men who sat on the sand with their hands bound, or perhaps by the bored English soldiers who stood guard over them. As I arrived a third boat was arriving, more soldiers disembarking and casting their eyes over the prisoners.

Why the men were tied up, I wasn't sure. They certainly didn't appear to be pirates. Merchants by the looks of them. Either way, as another rowing boat approached I was about to find out.

'The commodore's gone ahead to Kingston,' announced one of the soldiers. In common with the others he wore a tricorne and waistcoat, carried a musket. 'We are to commandeer this lubber's ship and follow.'

So that was it. The English wanted their ship. They were as bad as pirates themselves.

Merchants like to eat almost as much as they like to drink. Thus they tend towards the stout side. One of the captives, however, was even more florid-faced and plump than his companions. This was the 'lubber' the

English were talking about, the man I came to know as Stede Bonnet, and at the sound of the word 'Kingston' he'd seemed to perk up, and he raised his head, which before had been contemplating the sand with the look of a man wondering how he'd got into this position and how he was going to get out.

'No, no,' he was saying, 'our destination is Havana. I'm just a merchant –'

'Quiet, you bleeding pirate!' an irate soldier responded by toeing sand into the wretched man's face.

'Sir,' he cringed, 'my crew and I have merely anchored to water and resupply.'

And then, for some reason known only to them, Stede Bonnet's companions chose that moment to make their escape. Or *try* to make their escape. Hands still tied, they scrambled to their feet and began a lurching run towards the tree line where I hid watching the scene. At the same time the soldiers, seeing the escape, raised their muskets.

Shot began zinging into the trees around me and I saw one of the merchants fall in a spray of blood and brain matter. Another went down heavily with a scream. Meanwhile one of the soldiers had placed the muzzle of his rifle at Bonnet's head.

'Give me one reason I shouldn't vent your skull,' he snarled.

Poor old Bonnet, accused of being a pirate, about to lose his ship, and now seconds away from a steel ball in the brain. He did the only thing a man in his position could do. He stammered. He spluttered. Possibly even wet himself.

'Um . . . um . . .'

And now I drew my cutlass and emerged from the tree line with the sun behind me. The soldier gaped. What I must have looked like as I stepped out of the glare of the sunshine with my robes flowing and cutlass swinging I don't know, but it was enough to give the rifleman pause. A second in which he hesitated. A second that cost him his life.

I slashed upwards, opening his waistcoat and spilling his guts to the sand, spinning around in the same movement and dragging my blade across the throat of another soldier who stood nearby. Two men dead in the blink of an eye and a third about to join them as I ran him through with my cutlass and he slid from my blade and died writhing on the beach. I snatched my dagger from my belt with my other hand, jammed it into the eye of a fourth, and he fell back with a shocked yell, blood gushing from the hilt embedded in his face, staining the teeth of his screaming mouth.

The soldiers had all loosed their shot at the escaping merchants, and though they weren't slow to reload they were still no match for a swordsman. That's the thing with soldiers of the Crown. They rely too much on their muskets: great for frightening native women, not so effective at close quarters with a scrapper who'd learnt his trade in the taverns of Bristol.

The next man was still bringing his musket to bear

when I despatched him with two decisive strokes. The last of the soldiers was the first to get a second shot off. I heard it part the air by my nose and reacted with shock, hacking at his arm wildly until his musket dropped and he fell to his knees, pleading for his life with a raised hand until I silenced him with the point of my cutlass into his throat. He dropped with a gurgle, his blood flooded the sand around him, and I stood over his body with my shoulders heaving as I caught my breath, hot in my robes but knowing I had handled myself well. And when Bonnet thanked me, saying, 'By God's grace, sir, you saved me. A profusion of thanks!' it wasn't Edward Kenway the farmboy from Bristol he was thanking. I had started again. I was Duncan Walpole.

Stede Bonnet, it turned out, had not only lost his crew but had no skill for sailing. I had saved him from having his ship commandeered by the English, but to all intents and purposes I had commandeered it myself. We had one thing in common. We were both heading for Havana, and his ship was fast and he was talkative but good company, so we sailed together in what was a mutually beneficial partnership – for the time being at least.

As I steered I asked him about himself. What I found was a rich but fretful man, evidently attracted to more, shall we say, *questionable* ways of making money. For one thing, he constantly asked about pirates.

'Most hunt the Windward Passage between Cuba

and Hispaniola,' I told him, suppressing a smile as I steered his schooner.

He added, 'I shouldn't worry about being waylaid by pirates, truth be told. My ship is small and I have nothing of immense value. Sugar cane and its yields. Molasses, rum, that sort of thing.'

I laughed, thinking of my own crew. 'There's not a pirate living who'd turn his back on a keg of rum.'

Havana was a low port surrounded by forest and tall palm trees, their fronds a lush green that wafted gently in the breeze, waving us in as our schooner sailed into dock. In the busy town white stone buildings with red-slate roofs looked dilapidated and weather-beaten, bleached by the sun and blasted by the wind.

We moored and Bonnet set about his business, the business being helping to maintain amicable links with our former enemies the Spanish, and doing it using that age-old diplomacy technique – selling them things.

He seemed to know the city, so rather than strike out alone I waited for his diplomacy mission to end then agreed to accompany him to an inn. As we made our way there it occurred to me that the old me, the Edward Kenway me, would have been looking forward to reaching the tavern. He'd have been getting thirsty right now.

But I had no urge to drink – and I mulled that over as we made our way through Havana, weaving through townsfolk who hurried along the sun-drenched streets, and watched by suspicious old folk who squinted at us from doorways. All I'd done was assume a different name and clothes, but it was as though I had been given a second chance at becoming . . . well . . . *a man.* As if Edward Kenway was a rehearsal from which I could learn my mistakes. But Duncan Walpole would be the man I'd always wanted to be.

We reached the inn, and where the taverns of Edward past's had been dark places with low ceilings and shadows that leapt and danced on the walls; where men hunched over tankards and spoke from the sides of their mouths, here, beneath the Cuban sun, twinkled an outdoor tavern crowded with sailors who were leathery-faced and sinewy from months at sea, as well as portly merchants – friends of Bonnet, of course – and locals: men and children with handfuls of fruit for sale, women trying to sell themselves.

A dirty, drunken deckhand gave me the evil eye as I took a seat while Bonnet disappeared to meet his contact. Perhaps this sailor didn't like the look of me – after the Blaney business I was used to that kind of thing – or maybe he was a righteous man and didn't approve of the fact that I had swiped the ale of a sleeping drunk.

'Can I help you, friend?' I said over the lip of my newly acquired beaker.

The jack tar made a smacking sound with his mouth. 'Fancy meeting a Taffy deep in Dago country,' he slurred, 'I'm English meself, biding me time till the next war calls me to service.'

I curled my lip. 'Lucky old King George, eh? Having a pisspot like you flying his flag.'

That made him spit. 'Oi, skulk,' he said. The saliva gleamed on his lips as he leaned forward and huffed the sour smell of week-old booze over me. 'I've seen your face before, haven't I? You's mates with those pirates down in Nassau, ain't yer?'

I froze and my eyes darted to where Bonnet stood with his back to me, then around the rest of the inn. Didn't look like anybody had heard. I ignored the piss-head next to me.

He leaned forward, insinuating himself even further into my face. 'It is you, isn't it? It is . . .'

His voice had begun to rise. A couple of sailors at a table nearby glanced our way.

'It *is* you, isn't it?' Almost shouting now.

I stood, grabbed him, writhing from his seat, and slammed him against a wall. 'Shut your gob before I fill it with shot. You hear me?'

The sailor looked blearily at me. If he'd heard a word I'd said he showed no sign.

Instead he squinted, focused and said, 'Edward, isn't it?'

Shit.

The most effective way to silence a blabbermouth jack tar in a Havana tavern is a knife across the throat. Other ways include a knee in the groin and the method I chose. The headbutt.

I slammed my forehead into his face and his next

words died on a bed of broken teeth as he slipped to the floor and lay still.

'You bastard,' I heard from behind me, and turned to find a second red-faced sailor. I spread out my hands. *Hey, I don't want trouble.*

But it wasn't enough to prevent the right-hander across my face. And next I was trying to peer through a thick crimson curtain of pain shooting across the back of my eyes as two more crewmates arrived. I swung and made contact and it gave me precious seconds to recover. That Edward Kenway side of me, buried so deep? I exhumed him now. Because wherever you go in the world, whether it's Bristol or Havana, a pub brawl is a pub brawl. They say practice makes perfect and while I'd never claim to be perfect, the fighting skills honed during my misspent youth prevailed and soon the three sailors lay in a groaning heap of arms and legs and broken furniture fit only for kindling.

I was still dusting myself off when the cry went up. 'Soldiers!' And in the next moment I found myself doing two things: first, running full pelt through the streets of Havana in order to escape the beetroot-faced men with muskets; second, trying not to get lost.

I managed both and later rejoined Bonnet at the tavern, only to discover that not only had the soldiers taken his sugar but the satchel I'd taken from Duncan Walpole as well. The satchel I was taking to Torres. *Shit.*

The loss of Bonnet's sugar I could live with. But not the satchel.

25

Havana's the kind of place where you can loiter without attracting much attention. And that's on a normal day. On a day they're hanging pirates, in the very square the executions are due to take place, then loitering's not only expected, it's bloody well encouraged. The alliance between England and Spain may well have been an uneasy one, but there were certain matters on which both countries agreed. One of them being: they both hated pirates. Another one: they both liked to see pirates hanged.

So on the scaffold in front of us three buccaneers stood with their hands tied, staring with wide, frightened eyes through the nooses before them.

Not far away was the Spaniard they called El Tiburón, a big man with a beard and dead eyes. A man who never spoke because he couldn't: a mute. I looked from him to the condemned men. Then found I couldn't look at them, thinking, *There but for the grace of God go I . . .*

We weren't here for them anyway. Bonnet and I stood with our backs to a weather-bleached stone wall, looking for all the world as though we were idly watching the world go by and awaiting the execution, and not at all interested in the conversation of the Spanish soldiers gossiping nearby. Oh no, not at all.

'Are you still keen to look over the cargo we confiscated last night? I hear there were some crates of English sugar.'

'Aye, taken from the Barbadian merchant.'

'Duncan,' said Bonnet from the side of his mouth, 'they're talking about my sugar.'

I looked down at him and nodded, grateful for the translation.

The soldiers went on to discuss last evening's brawl at the tavern. Meanwhile, from the stage a Spanish officer was announcing the execution of the first man, stating his crimes and ending by intoning, 'You are hereby sentenced to be hanged by the neck until dead.'

At his signal El Tiburón pulled the lever, the trapdoor opened, the bodies fell and the crowd went, 'Ooh'.

I forced myself to look at the three swinging corpses, finding that I held my breath just in case what I'd been told about the loose bowels was true. Those bodies would be displayed in gibbets around the city. Bonnet and I had already seen such things on our travels. They had little tolerance for pirates here and wanted the world to know it.

I was hot in my robes but right now I was glad of the disguise.

We left, our expedition to the scaffold having given us the information we needed. The cargo was in the *castillo*. That, then, was where we needed to be.

26

The vast grey stone wall rose way above us. Did it really block out the sun or was it just an illusion? Either way we felt cold and lost in its shadow, like two abandoned children. I'll say this for the Cubans, or the Spanish, or whoever you'd say was responsible for building the grand Castillo de los Tres Reyes del Morro, they knew how to build an intimidating fortress. Around one hundred and fifty years old, it was built to last, too, and looked as though it would still be there in one hundred and fifty years' time. I looked from its walls out to sea and pictured it bombarded by the broadsides of a man-of-war. What impression would the steel balls of mounted guns make? I wondered. Not much.

Either way, I didn't have a man-of-war. I had a sugar merchant. So what I needed was a more covert way of gaining entry. The advantage I had was that nobody in their right mind actually *wanted* to be on the inside of those dark, brooding walls, for in there was where the Spanish soldiers tortured confessions from their prisoners and perhaps even performed summary executions. Only a fool would want to go in there, where the sun didn't shine, where nobody could hear you scream. Even so, you couldn't just walk right in. '*Oi, mate, you*

couldn't tell us where the loot room is, could you? I've lost a satchel
full of important documents and a weird-looking crystal.'

Thank God, then, for prostitutes. Not because I was
feeling randy, but because I'd seen a way to get inside –
inside the fortress, I mean. Those ladies of the night,
who sat on a fortune, well, they had good reason to
be on the other side of those walls, so who better to get
us in?

'You need a friend, gringo? You need a woman?' said
one, sidling up with a flurry of tits, ruby-red lips and
smoky eyes full of promise.

I ushered her away from the castle walls.

'What's your name?' I asked.

'Name, señor?'

'Do you speak English?'

'No, no English.'

I smiled. 'But gold is a language we all speak, no?'

Yes, as it turned out, Ruth did speak gold. She was
almost fluent in gold. And so was her friend, Jacqueline.

Bonnet had been hanging around, looking shifty.
Introductions were made and a few minutes later we were
walking, bold as brass, to the front gate of the castle.

At the top of the approach I looked back to where
the hustle, bustle and heat of Havana seemed to recede,
kept at bay by the forbidding stone and tall watch-
towers of the *castillo*, which radiated a kind of malignancy,
like the mythical monsters sailors said lived in the
uncharted depths of the deepest oceans: fat and deadly.

Stop it, I told myself. I was giving myself the heebie-jeebies. We had a plan. Now to see if it played out.

In the role of burly minder, I banged my fist on the wicket door and we waited for it to open. Two Spanish soldiers carrying bayoneted muskets stepped outside and gave us the long look up and down: me and Bonnet, with especially lascivious looks reserved for Ruth and Jacqueline.

I played my part. I looked tough. Ruth and Jacqueline played their parts. They looked sexy. Bonnet's job was to speak the lingo, some of which I could understand, the rest he filled me in on later.

'Hello,' he said. 'I'm afraid neither of my two lady friends speaks Spanish, thus I've been asked to speak for them, and my colleague here –' he indicated me – 'he is here to ensure the ladies' safety.'

(*Lie!* I held my breath, feeling as though there was a sign above our heads advertising our dishonesty. *Lie!*)

The two soldiers looked at the girls who, fortified with gold, not to mention several glasses of rum, preened and pouted so professionally that anybody would think they did it for a living. It wasn't enough to convince the guards, though, who were about to wave us away and let themselves be swallowed up once again by the squatting grey beast when Bonnet said the magic words: El Tiburón. The girls had been called for by El Tiburón, the executioner himself, he explained, and the guards paled, sharing a nervous look.

We'd seen him at work earlier, of course. It takes no

skill whatsoever to pull a lever, but it does require a certain – how shall we say? – *darkness of character* to pull the lever that opens the trap and sends three men plummeting to their deaths. So it was that El Tiburón's name alone was enough to inspire fear.

With a wink Bonnet added that El Tiburón liked the girls from Portugal. And Ruth and Jacqueline, continuing to play their parts well, giggled and blew mock kisses and adjusted their bosoms flirtatiously.

'El Tiburón is the governor's right-hand man, his enforcer,' said one of the soldiers suspiciously. 'What makes you think he will be in the *castillo*?'

I swallowed. My heart nudged up against my ribcage and I cast Bonnet a sideways look. *So much for his information.*

'My dear man,' he smiled, 'do you really think this assignation would meet the approval of Governor Torres? El Tiburón would need new employment if the governor were to discover him consorting with prostitutes. And as for doing it on the governor's own property . . .'

Now Bonnet looked from side to side and the two soldiers craned to hear more secrets.

Bonnet continued. 'I need hardly say, gentlemen, that being in possession of this information puts you in a most *delicate* position. On the one hand, you now know things about El Tiburón – Havana's most dangerous man, let's not forget – which he would pay, or perhaps kill –' here he paused just enough to let this information sink in — 'in order to protect. Depending on how you want to conduct yourselves in possession of this information would no doubt dictate the level of El Tiburón's gratitude. Do I make myself clear, gentlemen?'

To me it sounded as though he was spouting twaddle, but it seemed to have the desired effect on the two sentries, who at last stood aside and let us in.

And in we went.

'The mess hall,' said one of the guards, indicating walkways that looked down upon the courtyard in which we now stood. 'Tell them you're looking for El Tiburón; they'll point you in the right direction. And tell these ladies to behave themselves lest you inadvertently reveal the true nature of your business here.'

Bonnet gave his best greasy smile, bowing as we moved past and giving me a sly nod at the same time. We left two thoroughly hoodwinked guards in our wake.

I left them to it as I climbed steps, hoping for all the world that I looked like I belonged in the fortress. At least it was quiet: apart from the sentries there were very few troops about. Most seemed to have congregated in the mess room.

Me, I headed straight for the loot room where I almost cheered to find the satchel with all the documents and the crystal present and correct. I pocketed it and glanced around. Bloody hell. For a loot room it was woefully empty of any actual loot. All there was, apart from a pouch containing a few gold coins (which went into my pocket), were crates of Bonnet's sugar. I looked at them. It occurred to me we had no contingency for their rescue. *Sorry, Bonnet, it will have to wait for another time.*

A few minutes later and I'd rejoined them; they'd decided not to risk the mess room and instead had been loitering on the walkways nervously awaiting my return. Bonnet was too relieved to see me back to ask about the sugar – that particular pleasure would have to wait until later – and wiping nervous sweat from his brow he ushered us back along the passage and down the steps to the courtyard, where our friends the sentries shared a look as we approached.

'I see. Back so soon . . .'

Bonnet shrugged. 'We asked at the mess hall, but of El Tiburón there was no sign. Possibly there has been some mistake. Perhaps his desires have been satisfied elsewhere . . .'

'We will tell El Tiburón that you were here, then,' said one of the guards.

Bonnet nodded approvingly, 'Yes, please do that, but remember, be discreet.'

The two guards nodded, and one even tapped the side of his nose. Our secret would be safe with them.

Later we stood on the port with Bonnet's ship nearby.

I handed him the bag I'd filched from the loot room at the *castillo*. Seemed the decent thing to do – to make up for his lost sugar. I wasn't all bad, you know.

'Oh, it's no great loss,' he said, but took it anyway.

'Will you stay long?' I asked him.

'For a few weeks, yes. Then back to Barbados, to the tedium of domesticity.'

'Don't settle for tedium,' I told him. 'Sail to Nassau. Live life as you see fit.'

By now he was halfway up the gangplank, his newly acquired crew readying themselves to set sail.

'Haven't I heard that Nassau is crawling with pirates?' he laughed. 'Seems a very tawdry place.'

I thought of it. I thought of Nassau.

'No, not tawdry,' I told him. 'Liberated.'

He smiled. 'Oh, God, that would be an adventure. But no, no. I'm a husband and a father. I have responsibilities. Life can't be all pleasure and distraction, Duncan.'

For a moment I'd forgotten my assumed identity and felt the tremor of guilt. Bonnet had done nothing but help me. Quite what had possessed me, I wasn't sure. Guilt, I suppose. But I told him.

'Hey, Bonnet. The name's Edward in truth. Duncan is only a handle.'

'Ah . . .' He smiled. 'A secret name for your secret meeting with the governor . . .'

'Yes, the governor,' I said. 'Right. I think I've kept him waiting long enough.'

27

I went straight to Governor Torres's residence, a vast mansion set behind steep walls and metal gates, well away from Havana's hubbub. There I told the sentries, 'Good afternoon. Mr Duncan Walpole of England to see the governor. I believe he is expecting me.'

'Yes, Mr Walpole, please enter.'

That was easy.

The gates squeaked, a hot summer's day sound, and I stepped through to be awarded with my first glance of how the other half lived. Everywhere were palm trees and short statues on plinths, and from somewhere the sound of running water – a marked contrast to the fortress: opulent where that had been grimy, gaudy where that had been forbidding.

As we walked the two sentries stayed a respectful but still watchful distance behind, and my limited Spanish picked up fragments of their gossip: apparently I was a couple of days late; apparently I was an *asesino*, an assassin, and there was something about the way they said the word that was odd. The way they stressed it.

I kept my shoulders back, chin held high, thinking only that I needed to continue the subterfuge for a short while longer. I'd enjoyed being Duncan Walpole – it had felt liberating to leave Edward Kenway behind, and there were times I'd considered saying goodbye for good. Certainly there were parts of Duncan I wanted to keep, souvenirs, keepsakes: his robes, for one, his fighting style. His bearing.

Right now, though, what I wanted most was his reward.

We came into a courtyard, which was vaguely reminiscent of the fortress, except while that was a stony drill square overlooked by shadowed walkways, this was an oasis of sculpture, lush-leaved plants and the ornate galleries of the *palacio* framing a sky of deep blue and a sun that smouldered in the distance.

There were two men already there. Both well dressed, men of class and distinction, I could tell. *More difficult to fool.* Close by them was a rack of weapons. One of them stood aiming a pistol at a target. The other cleaning another pistol.

At the sound of myself and the sentries entering the courtyard the shooter looked over, annoyed at the interruption, and then with a little shake of his shoulders composed himself, squinted along the line of the pistol and squeezed off a shot.

The sound rang around the courtyard. Applause came from startled birds. A tiny wisp of smoke rose from the dead centre of the target, which had rocked slightly on its tripod. The shooter looked to his companion with a wry smile, received an impressed eyebrow-raise in return, this the vocabulary of the well-to-do. And then they turned their attention to me.

You're Duncan Walpole, I told myself and tried not to wilt beneath their scrutiny. *You're Duncan Walpole. A man of danger. An equal. Here at the invitation of the governor.*

'Good afternoon, sir!' The man who had been cleaning the gun smiled broadly. He had long greying hair tied back, and a face that had spent many an hour in the sea breeze. 'Would I be correct in thinking you are Duncan Walpole?'

Remembering how Walpole had spoken. Cultured tones.

'I am indeed,' I replied, and I sounded so phony to my own ears that I half expected the gun-cleaner to point his pistol straight at me and order the guards to arrest me on the spot.

Instead he said, 'I thought as much,' and still beaming strode across the courtyard to offer me a hand that was as hard as oak. 'Woodes Rogers. A pleasure.'

Woodes Rogers. I'd heard of him, and the pirate in me paled, because Woodes Rogers was the scourge of my kind. A former privateer, he'd since declared a hatred of those who turned to piracy and pledged to lead expeditions aimed at rooting them out. A pirate such as Edward Kenway he'd like to see hanged.

But you're Duncan Walpole, I told myself, and met his eye as I shook his hand firmly. Not a pirate, oh no. Perish the thought. An equal. Here at the invitation of the governor.

The thought, comforting as it had been, faded in my mind as I realized that he'd fixed me with a curious gaze. At the same time he wore a quizzical half-smile, as though he'd had a thought and wasn't sure whether to let it go free.

'I must say, my wife has a terrible eye for description,' he said, evidently letting his curiosity get the better of him.

'I'm sorry?'

'My wife. You met her some years ago at the Percys' masquerade ball.'

'Ah, quite . . .'

'She called you "devilishly handsome". Obviously a lie to stoke my jealousy.'

I laughed as though in on the joke. Should I be offended he didn't think me devilishly handsome? Or just pleased the conversation had moved on?

Eyes on his gun I plumped for the latter.

Now I was being introduced to the second man, a dark Frenchman with a guarded look called Julien DuCasse, who was calling me the 'guest of honour' and talking about some 'order' I was supposed to join. Again I was referred to as an 'assassin'. Again it was with an odd emphasis I couldn't quite decode.

Asesino – assassin – *Assassin*.

He was querying the honesty of my 'conversion' to the 'order', and my mind returned to the wording of Walpole's letter: *Your support for our secret and most noble cause is warming.*

What secret and noble cause would that be, then? I wondered.

'I have not come to disappoint,' I said uncertainly. Tell the truth, I didn't have the foggiest what he was on about. What I wanted was to give the satchel with one hand and receive a bulging bag of gold with the other.

Failing that, I wanted to move on, because right now I felt as though my deception was likely to crumble at any second. In the end it was a relief when Woodes Rogers's face broke into a grin – the same grin he no doubt grinned at the thought of pirates' heads in hangmen's nooses – and he clapped me on the back and insisted I take part in the shooting.

Happy to oblige, anything to take their minds off me, I engaged them in conversation at the same time. 'How is your wife these days, Captain Rogers? Is she here in Havana?'

I held my breath, steeling myself against his next words, *'Yes! Here she is right now! Darling, you remember Duncan Walpole, don't you?'*

Instead he said, 'Oh, no. No, we've been separated these two years past.'

'Sorry to hear that,' I said, thinking what excellent news it was.

'I trust she is well,' he went on, a touch of wistfulness in his voice that sparked a brief thought of my own lost love, 'but . . . I wouldn't know. I have been in Madagascar some fourteen months, hunting pirates.'

So I had heard. 'You mean Libertalia, the pirate town?'

That was Libertalia in Madagascar. According to

legend, Captain William Kidd had stopped there in 1697 and ended up leaving with only half his crew, the rest of them seduced by the lifestyle of a pirate utopia where the motto was 'for God and liberty', with the emphasis on liberty. Where they spared the lives of prisoners, kept killing to a minimum, shared all the spoils fairly, no matter your rank or standing.

It sounded too good to be true, and there were plenty who thought it was a mythical place, but I'd been assured it existed.

Rogers was laughing. 'What I saw in Madagascar was little more than the aftermath of a sad orgy. A ruffians' squat. Even the feral dogs seemed ashamed of its condition. As for the twenty or thirty men living there, I cannot say they were ragged, since most wore no clothes at all. They had gone *native*, as the saying goes . . .'

I thought of Nassau, where such low standards wouldn't be tolerated – not before nightfall at least.

'And how did you deal with their kind?' I asked, the picture of innocence.

'Very simply. Most pirates are as ignorant as apes. I merely offered them a choice . . . Take a pardon and return to England penniless but free men, or be hanged by the neck until dead. It took some work to dislodge the criminals there, but we managed it. In future, I hope to use the same tactics throughout the West Indies.'

'Ah,' I said, 'I imagine Nassau will be your next target.'

'Very astute, Duncan. Indeed. Point of fact . . . the moment I return to England I intend to petition King George with the hope of becoming his emissary in the Bahamas. As governor, no less.'

So that was it. Nassau *was* the next step. A place I had come to think of as my spiritual home was under threat – from the carriage gun, the musket ball or maybe just the scratch of a quill. But under threat all the same.

I managed to distinguish myself in the shooting and was feeling pretty pleased with myself all told. So once again my thoughts returned to the reward. As soon as I had my money I could return to Nassau, and once there warn Edward and Benjamin that the infamous Woodes Rogers had a Bahamas-shaped bee in his bonnet for our little pirate republic. That he was coming for us.

And then a box was opened, and I heard Rogers say, 'Wonderful. You're a crack shot, Duncan. As good with a pistol as with your wrist blade, I imagine.'

Wrist blade, I thought distantly. *Wrist blade?*

'If only he had one,' DuCasse was saying as I peered at several sets of hidden blades displayed in the box – blades like the one I had reluctantly discarded on the beach at Cape Buena Vista. 'Duncan, where is your wrist blade? I have never seen an Assassin so ill-equipped.'

Again: assassin. As in: *Assassin.*

'Ah, damaged, sadly, beyond repair,' I replied.

DuCasse indicated the selection in the box. 'Then

have your choice,' he purred. And was it his thick French accent or did he mean to make it sound more like a threat than an offer?

I wondered where the blades were from. Other assassins, of course. (But assassins or *Assassins*?) Walpole had been one, but had been meaning to convert. A traitor? But what was this 'order' which he'd been planning to join?

'These are souvenirs,' Julien was saying.

Dead men's blades. I reached into the box and drew one out. The blade shone and its fixings trailed against my arm. At which point it dawned on me. They wanted me to use it. They wanted to see me in action. Whether as a test or for sport it didn't matter. Either way they wanted a display of proficiency in a weapon I'd never used before.

Immediately I went up from congratulating myself on having discarded the bloody thing (it would have given me away!) to cursing myself for not having kept it (I could have practised and been competent with it by now!).

I squared my shoulders in Duncan Walpole's robes. An impostor. Now I had to be him. I had to really *be* him.

They watched as I strapped on the blade. A weak joke about being out of practice elicited polite but humourless chuckles. With it on I let my sleeve drop down over my hand and as we walked began to flex my fingers, adjusting my wrist and feeling for the tell-tale catch of the blade engaging.

Walpole's blade had been wet that day we fought. Who knows – perhaps it really had been damaged. This one, greased and shined, would surely be more cooperative?

I prayed it would be. Imagined the looks on their faces if I simply failed to make it work.

'Are you sure you are who you say you are?'

'Guards!'

Instinctively I found myself seeking out the nearest escape route. And not only that, but wishing I'd just left the bloody satchel of documents where I'd found it, wishing I'd left Walpole well alone. What was wrong with life as Edward Kenway anyway? I was poor but at least I was alive. I could have been back in Nassau right now, planning raids with Edward and eyeing up Anne Bonny at the Old Avery.

Edward had warned me not to join Captain Bramah. From the moment I'd suggested it he'd told me Bramah was bad news. Why didn't I bloody listen?

The voice of Julien DuCasse interrupted my thoughts.

'Duncan –' he pronounced it *dern-kern* – 'would you indulge us with a demonstration of your techniques?'

I was being tested. Every question, every challenge they threw my way – it was all an attempt to force me to prove my mettle. So far I'd passed. Not with flying colours, but I'd passed.

But now we'd stepped outside the confines of the courtyard and I was greeted with what looked like a newly constructed practice area, tall palms lining either side of a grassed avenue, with targets at one end and just beyond that what looked like an ornamental lake, shimmering like a plateful of blue sunshine.

Behind the tree line, shadows moved among the scaly trunks of the palm trees. More guards, in case I made a break for it.

'We put together a small training course in anticipation of your arrival,' said Rogers.

I swallowed.

My hosts stood to one side: expectant. Rogers still carried the pistol, held loosely in one hand, but his finger was on the trigger, and Julien rested his right palm on the hilt of his sword. Behind the trees the figures of the guards stood motionless, waiting. Even the chirruping of insects and birds seemed to drop away.

'It would be a shame to leave here without seeing you in action.'

Woodes Rogers smiled but his eyes were cold.

And just my luck, the only weapon I had I couldn't bloody use.

Doesn't matter. I can take them anyway.

To the old Bristolian scrapper in me they were just another pair of lairy twats outside a tavern. I thought of how I'd watched Walpole fight, with perfect awareness of his surroundings. How he could lay these two out, and then be upon the nearest guards before they had a chance to even raise their muskets. Yes, I could do that, catch them unawares . . .

Now was the time, I thought. *Now*.

I braced and drew back my arm to throw the first punch.

And the blade engaged.

28

'Oh well done, Duncan,' said Rogers, clapping, and I looked from him and DuCasse to my shadow cast on the grass. I had struck quite a pose with the blade engaged. What's more, I thought I knew how I had done it. A tensing of muscle that came as much from the upper arm as the forearm . . .

'Very impressive,' said DuCasse. He stepped forward, held my arm with one hand that he used to release a catch, and then, very carefully, used the flat of his other palm to ease the blade back into its housing.

'Now, let's see you do it again.'

Without taking my eyes off him, I took a step back and assumed the same position. This time there was no luck involved, and even though I didn't know quite what I was doing I had perfect confidence it would work. Don't ask me how I knew. I just did. Sure enough: *snick*. The blade sprang from the support and glinted evilly in the afternoon sun.

'A little noisy,' I smiled, getting cocky now. 'Ideally, you'd not hear a thing. Otherwise it's fine.'

Their challenges were interminable but by the end I felt I was performing for the pleasure rather than their reassurance. Any tests were over. The guards had drifted away, and even DuCasse, who wore his wariness like a favoured old frock coat, seemed to have relaxed. By the time we left the makeshift training area he was talking to me like an old friend.

'The Assassins have trained you well, Duncan,' he said.

The Assassins, I thought. So that's what this group were called. Walpole had been a member but intended to betray his brothers, lowdown scum-sucker that he obviously was.

Betray them for what? is the question.

'You chose the perfect time to leave them behind.'

'At great risk,' enthused Rogers. 'Betraying the Assassins is never good for one's health.'

'Well,' I said, somewhat pompously, 'neither is drinking liquor, but I am drawn to its dangers all the same.'

He chuckled as I turned my attention to DuCasse. 'And what is your business here, sir? Are you an associate of the governor's? Or an impending acquaintance like me?'

'Ah, I am . . . How do you say? Weapons dealer. I deal in pilfered guns and armaments.'

'A smuggler of sorts,' piped up Rogers.

'Guns, blades, grenadoes. Anything that may kill a man, I am happy to provide,' clarified the Frenchman.

By now we had reached the terrace, where I first clapped eyes on Governor Torres.

He was about seventy years old, but not fat the way rich men get. Apart from a clipped goatee beard his face was brown and lined and topped with brushed-forward thinning white hair, and with one hand on the bowl of a long-stemmed pipe he peered through round spectacles at correspondence he held in his other hand.

He didn't look up, not at first. All the looking was taken care of by the big bearded man who stood patiently at his right shoulder, his arms folded, as still as one of the courtyard statues and ten times as stony.

I recognized him at once, of course. The previous day I'd seen him send three pirates to their death. Why, that very morning I'd pretended to procure prostitutes in his name. It was the Spaniard, El Tiburón, and although by now I should have been accustomed to intense examination by my hosts, his eyes seemed to drill right through me. For a while, as his stare bore into me, I was absolutely certain that not only had he spoken to the guards at the *castillo* but that they had given him my detailed description, and that any second now he would raise a trembling finger, point at me and demand to know why I'd been at the fortress.

'Grand Master Torres.'

It was Rogers who broke the silence.

'Mr Duncan Walpole has arrived.'

Torres looked up and regarded me over the top of his spectacles. He nodded, then handed his letter to El Tiburón, and thank God he did, for it meant that at last El Tiburón tore his eyes away from me.

'You were expected one week ago,' said Torres, but without much irritation.

'Apologies, governor,' I replied. 'My ship was set upon by pirates and we were scuttled. I arrived only yesterday.'

He nodded thoughtfully. 'Unfortunate. But were you able to salvage from these pirates the items you promised me?'

I nodded, thinking, *One hand to give you the satchel, the other hand to take the money,* and from my robes I took the bag and dropped it on a low table by Torres's knees. He puffed on his pipe then opened the satchel and took out the maps. I'd seen the maps before, of course, and they didn't mean anything to me. Nor did the crystal for that matter. But they meant something to Torres all right. No doubt about it.

'Incredible,' he said in tones of wonderment, 'the Assassins have more resources than I had imagined . . .'

And now he reached for the crystal, squinting at it through his spectacles and turning it over in his fingers. This *ornament* or whatever it was . . . well – to him it was no ornament.

He placed the papers and crystal back into the satchel and crooked a hand for El Tiburón who stepped forward and took the satchel. With that, Torres reached for my hand to shake, pumping it vigorously as he spoke. 'It is a pleasure to meet you at last, Duncan,' he said. 'You are most welcome. Come, gentlemen.' He motioned to the others. 'We have much to discuss. Come . . .'

We began to move away from the terrace, all friends together.

Still no word about the bloody reward. *Shit*. I was getting deeper and deeper into something I wanted no part of.

29

We stood around a large table in a private room inside the main building: me, Torres, El Tiburón, DuCasse and Rogers.

El Tiburón, who remained at his master's shoulder, held a long, thin box, like a cigar box. Did I imagine it, though, or were his eyes constantly on me? Had he somehow seen through me, or been alerted? *'Sir, a strange man in robes was looking for you at the fortress earlier.'*

I didn't think so, though. Apart from him, everybody else in the room seemed relaxed, accepting drinks from Torres and chatting amiably while he made his own. Like any good host, he'd ensured his guests were holding full glasses first, but I wondered why he didn't have staff to serve them, and then thought I knew the answer: it was the nature of our business in this room. The atmosphere might well have been relaxed – at least it was for the time being – but Torres had been sure to post a sentry then close the door with a gesture that seemed to say *Anything said in this room is for our ears only*, the kind of gesture that was making me feel less reassured with each passing moment, wishing I'd taken note of the line in the letter about my support for their 'secret and most noble cause'.

I must remember that next time I'm considering becoming an impostor, I thought, *give noble causes a wide berth. Especially if they're* secret *noble causes.*

But now we all had our drinks so a toast was raised, Torres saying, 'Convened at last. And in such continental company . . . England, France, Spain . . . Citizens of sad and corrupted empires.'

At a wave from Torres El Tiburón moved across, opened the box he held and placed it on the table. I saw red-velvet lining and the gleam of metal from inside. Whatever it was, it looked significant and indeed it proved as Torres, his smile fading, the natural gleam of his eyes replaced by something altogether more serious, began what was obviously a ceremony of some importance.

'But you are Templars now,' he was saying, 'the secret and true legislators of the world. Please hold out your hands.'

The convivial atmosphere was suddenly solemn. Drinks were set down. I shuffled quickly to my side, seeing that the others had placed themselves at intervals around the table. Next I did as I was asked and proffered my hand, thinking, *Templars* – so that's what they were.

And it seems odd to say now, but I relaxed – I relaxed in the belief that they were nothing more sinister than a secret society. A silly club like any other silly club, full of deluded, pompous fools, whose grandiose aims ('the secret and true legislators of the world' no less!) were hot air, just an excuse for bickering about meaningless titles and trinkets.

What were their petty concerns? I wondered. And found I didn't care. After all, why would I? As a pirate I'd renounced all law but pirate law. My freedom absolute. I was governed by rules, of course I was, but they were the rules of the sea and adhering to them was a matter of *need*, for survival, rather than the acquisition of status and the peacocking of sashes and baubles. What were their squabbles with the Assassins, I wondered, and found I couldn't give a fig about that either.

So yes, I relaxed. I didn't take them seriously.

Torres placed the first ring on DuCasse's finger. 'Mark and remember our purpose. To guide all wayward souls till they reach a quiet road.'

A second ring was placed on Rogers's finger. 'To guide all wayward desire till impassioned hearts are cooled.'

Hot air, I thought. Nothing but empty, meaningless statements. No purpose other than to award their speaker unearned authority. Look at them all, lapping it up, like it meant something. Silly men so deluded by a sense of their own importance that they were unable to see that it extended no further than the walls of the mansion.

Nobody cares, my friends. Nobody cares about your secret society.

Now Torres was addressing me, and he placed on my finger a third ring, saying 'To guide all wayward minds to safe and sober thought.'

Sober, I thought. That was a laugh.

And then I looked down at the ring he'd put on my finger and suddenly I was no longer amused. Suddenly I was no longer thinking of these Templars as a silly secret society with no influence outside their own homes, because on my finger was the same ring as worn by the East India Company's ship captain Benjamin Pritchard; the same ring worn by the man in the hood, the leader of the group who had burned my father's farmhouse, both of whom had warned me of great and terrible powers at work. And suddenly I was thinking that whatever squabbles these people had with the Assassins, then, well, I was on the side of the Assassins.

For now, I would bide my time.

Torres stood back. 'By the father of understanding's light let our work now begin,' he said. 'Decades ago the council entrusted me with the task of locating in the West Indies a forgotten place our precursors once called the Observatory. See here . . .'

On the table before him were spread out the documents from the satchel, placed there by El Tiburón.

'Look upon these images and commit them to memory,' added Torres. 'They tell a very old and important story. For two decades now I have endeavoured to locate this Observatory . . . The place is rumoured to contain a tool of incredible utility and power. It houses a kind of armillary sphere, if you like. A device that would grant us the power to locate and monitor *every man and woman on earth*, whatever their location.

'Only imagine what it would mean to have such

power. With this device there would be no secrets among men. No lies. No trickery. Only justice. Pure justice. This is the Observatory's promise. And we must take it for our own.'

So that, then, was when I first learnt of the Observatory.

'Do we know its whereabouts?' asked Rogers.

'We will soon,' replied Torres, 'for in our custody is the one man who does. A man named Roberts. Once called a Sage.'

DuCasse gave a small scoffing laugh. 'It has been forty-five years since anyone has seen an actual Sage. Can you be sure this one is authentic?'

'We are confident he is,' replied Torres.

'The Assassins will come for him,' said Rogers.

I looked at the documents spread out before us. Drawings of what looked like an ancient race of people building something – the Observatory presumably. Slaves breaking rocks and carrying huge stone blocks. They looked human, but not quite human.

One thing I did know – a plan was beginning to form. This Observatory, which meant so much to the Templars. What would it be worth? More to the point, what would it be worth to a man planning revenge on the people who had helped torch his childhood home?

The small crystal cube was still on the table. I puzzled over it, just as I had on the beach at Cape Buena Vista. Now I watched as Torres reached and picked it up, replying to Rogers at the same time. 'Indeed, the

Assassins will come for us but, thanks to Duncan and the information he has delivered, the Assassins won't be a problem for much longer. All will be made clear tomorrow, gentlemen, when you meet the Sage for yourselves. Until then . . . let us drink.'

Our host indicated a drinks table, and while backs were turned I reached to the documents and pocketed a page of manuscript – a picture of the Observatory.

Just in time. Torres turned, handing glasses to the men.

'Let us find the Observatory together, for with its power kings will fall, clergy will cower, and the hearts and minds of the world will be ours.'

We drank.

We drank together, though I know for sure we drank in honour of very different things indeed.

30

The next day I had been asked to meet my 'fellow Templars' at the city's northern ports, where it was said the treasure fleet would be arriving with my reward, and we could discuss further schemes.

I nodded, keen to give the impression that I was an eager Templar, plotting with my new firm friends to do whatever it was that Templars plot to do – the small matter of being able to influence 'every man and woman on earth'. In fact, what I intended to do, just between me and you, was pocket the money, make my excuses, whatever those excuses needed to be, and leave. I was looking forward to spending my money and sharing my newfound information with my confederates at Nassau, then finding the Observatory, reaping the rewards, helping the downfall of these Templars.

But first I had to collect my money.

'Good morning, Duncan.' I heard Woodes Rogers hailing me from the docks. It was a fresh morning in Havana, the sun yet to reach full temperature and a light breeze blowing in from the Gulf of Mexico.

I began following Rogers, then I heard a voice shout, *'Edward! Hello, Edward!'*

For a second or so I thought it was a case of

mistaken identity, even found myself looking over my shoulder to see this 'Edward'. Until I remembered. Edward was me. I was Edward. Stupid Edward. Who, from a misplaced sense of guilt, had admitted my secret to Havana's biggest blabbermouth, Stede Bonnet.

'I found a man to purchase my remaining sugar. Quite a coup I must say,' he called across the harbour.

I waved back – *excellent news* – aware of Rogers's eyes upon me.

'He just called you Edward,' said my companion. That same curious smile I'd seen yesterday played about his lips again.

'Oh, that's the merchant who sailed me here,' I explained, with a conspiratorial wink. 'Out of caution, I gave him a false name.'

'Ah . . . Well done,' said Rogers. But not convinced.

I was thankful to leave the main harbour behind when Rogers and I joined the same group of Templars who'd met at Torres's mansion the day before. Hands were shaken, the rings of our brotherhood, still fresh on our fingers, glinted, and we gave each other short nods. Brothers. Brothers in a secret society.

And then Torres led us to a line of small fishermen's huts, with rowing boats tethered in the water nearby. There was no one about, not yet. We had this small area of the harbour to ourselves, which was the intention, no doubt, as Torres guided us to the end, where guards waited at a small hut and inside, sitting on an upturned crate, with a beard and ragged clothes, in his eyes a dejected but defiant look, was the Sage.

I watched the faces of my companions change. Just as the conflict between defeat and belligerence seemed to play out on the face of the Sage, so the Templars appeared to struggle, too, and they returned his glare with a look that was a mix of pity and awe.

'Here he is,' said Torres, speaking quietly, almost reverently, whether he knew it or not, 'A man both Templars and Assassins have sought for over a decade.'

He addressed the Sage. 'I am told your name is Bartholomew Roberts. Is this so?'

Roberts, or the Sage, or whatever we were calling him today, said nothing. Merely stared balefully at Torres.

Without taking his eyes off the Sage, Torres opened a hand at shoulder level. Into his palm El Tiburón placed the crystal cube. The same crystal cube I'd wondered about. I was going to find out what it was now.

Torres, speaking to the Sage again, said, 'You recognize this, I think?'

Silence from Bartholomew Roberts – the Sage was saying nothing. Perhaps he knew what was coming next. For now Torres indicated again, and a second upturned crate was brought to him on to which he sat so that he faced the Sage, man to man, except that one of the men was governor of Havana and the other man was ragged and had wild hermit eyes and his hands were bound.

It was to those bound hands that Torres reached, bringing the crystal cube to bear, and then inserting it over the Sage's thumb.

The two men stared at each other for a moment or so. Torres's fingers seemed to be manipulating the Sage's thumb somehow, before a single droplet of blood filled the vial.

I watched, not quite sure what I was witnessing. The Sage seemed to feel no pain and yet his eyes went from one man to the next as though cursing each of us in turn, me included, and he fixed me with a stare of such ferocity that I found myself having to resist the impulse to shrink away.

Why on earth did they need this poor man's blood? What did it have to do with the Observatory?

'According to the old tales, the blood of a Sage is required to enter the Observatory,' said DuCasse in a whisper, as though reading my thoughts.

The operation was over and Torres stood up from his crate, a little shaky, with one hand holding the vial for all to see. Caught by the light the blood-filled crystal gave his hand a red glow.

'We have the key,' he announced. 'Now we need only its location. Perhaps Mr Roberts will be eager to provide it.'

He waved guards forward. 'Transfer him to my residence.'

And that was it. The ghastly procedure was over, and I was pleased to leave the strange scene behind as we began making our way back to the main harbour, where a vessel had arrived. The one containing the treasure, I hoped. I *sorely* hoped.

'Such a fuss over one man,' I said to Torres as we walked, trying to sound more casual than I felt. 'Is the Observatory *really* such a grand prize?'

'Yes, indeed,' replied Torres, 'the Observatory was a tool built by the precursor race. Its worth is without measure.'

I thought of the ancients I had seen in the pictures at the mansion. Torres's precursor race?

'I do wish I could remain to see our drama done,' said Rogers, 'but I must avail myself of these winds and sail for England.'

Torres nodded. That familiar twinkle had returned to his eyes. 'By all means, captain. Speed and fortune to you.'

The two men shook hands. Brothers. Brothers in a secret society. And then Rogers and I did the same, before the legendary pirate-hunter turned and left, off to continue being the scourge of buccaneers everywhere. We would meet again, I knew. Though I hoped the day would come later rather than sooner.

By now one of the ship's deckhands had arrived and handed Torres something that looked suspiciously like it might contain my money. Not that the bag seemed quite as hefty as I'd hoped.

'I consider this the first payment in a long-term investment,' said Torres, handing me the pouch – the suspiciously *light* pouch. 'Thank you.'

I took it cautiously, knowing by the weight that there was more to come, and by more to come I mean more money as well as more challenges for me to face.

'I would like you to be present for the interrogation tomorrow. Call around noon,' said Torres.

So that was it. In order to collect the rest of my fee I needed to see the Sage terrorized further.

Torres left me and I stood there for a moment on the dock, deep in thought, before leaving to prepare. I had decided I was going to rescue the Sage.

And I wonder *why* I decided to rescue the Sage. I mean, why didn't I simply take what money I'd been given, show a clean pair of heels and fill the sails on a passage to Nassau in the north-east? Back to Edward, Benjamin and the delights of the Old Avery?

I'd like to say it was a noble desire to free the Sage, but there was a bit more to it than that. After all, he could help find this Observatory, this device to follow people around. And what would a thing like that be worth? Sell it to the right person and I would be rich, the richest pirate in the West Indies. Return to Caroline a rich man. So perhaps it was merely greed that made me decide to rescue him. Looking back, probably a mixture of the two.

Either way, it was a decision I'd shortly regret.

31

Night-time, and the walls of Torres's mansion formed a black border beneath a grey starless night. The chirping insects were at their loudest, almost drowning out the trickle of running water and the soft rattle of the palm trees.

With a quick look left and right – my approach had been timed to make sure no sentries were present – I flexed my fingers and jumped, pulled myself up to the top of the wall, then lay there for a second to control my breath and listen out for running feet, cries of 'hey!' and the swish of swords being drawn . . .

And then, when there was nothing – nothing apart from the insects, the water and the whisper of night wind among the trees, I dropped down to the other side and into the grounds of the governor of Havana's mansion.

Like a ghost I made my way across the gardens and into the main building, where I hugged the walls along the perimeter of the courtyard. On my right forearm I felt the comforting presence of my hidden blade and strapped across my chest were my pistols. A short sword hung from my belt beneath my robes and I wore my cowl over my head. I felt invisible. I felt lethal. I felt as though I was about to deliver a blow against the Templars and even though, no, freeing the Sage wasn't equal to the harm their brothers had done me, and it wasn't like this was going to even the score, it was a start. It was a first strike.

What's more, I'd have the location of the Observatory and could reach it before they did. And that was a far, far bigger blow. That would hurt. I'd think of how much it hurt while I was counting my money.

I'd had to make an informed guess as to where the governor kept his state prisons, but I'm pleased to say I was right. It was a small compound, separate from the mansion, where I found a high wall and . . .

That's odd. Why is the door hanging open?

I slid through. Flaming torches bracketed on the walls illuminated a scene of carnage. Four or five soldiers were dead in the dirt, gaping holes at their throats, pulverized meat at their chests.

Where the Sage had been kept, I had no idea. But one thing was beyond doubt: he wasn't here now.

I heard a sound behind me too late to stop the blow but in time to prevent it knocking me out, and I pitched forward, landing badly on the dirt, but having the presence of mind to roll at the same time. A pikestaff with my name on it was driven into the ground where I'd been. At the other end of it was a surprised soldier. I kicked myself up, grabbed his shoulders and span. At the same time I booted the shaft of the pikestaff and snapped it, then rammed his body on to it at the same time.

He flopped like a landed fish, impaled on the broken shaft of his own pikestaff, but I didn't stick around to admire his death throes. The second soldier was upon me, angry, the way you get when you see your friend die.

Now, I thought, *let's see if this works every time.*

Snick.

The hidden blade engaged and I met the steel of his blade with steel of my own, knocking his sword away and slashing open his throat with the backswipe. I drew the sword at my belt in time to meet a third attacker. Behind him were two soldiers with muskets. Close by was El Tiburón, his sword drawn but held at his hip as he watched the fight. I saw one of the soldiers grimace and it was a look I recognized, a look I've seen before from men on the deck of a ship lashed to mine.

He fired just as I drove both my sword and hidden blade into the soldier in front of me, pinning him with the blades and swinging him round at the same time. His body, already dead, jerked as the musket ball slammed into him.

I let my human shield go, plucking a dagger from his belt as he dropped and praying that my aim would be as good as it always had been, after countless hours at home spent tormenting tree trunks with throwing knives.

It was. I took out, not the first musketeer – he was already making a panicky attempt to reload – but the second, who fell with the knife embedded between his ribs.

In a bound I was over to the first one and punched him in the stomach with my blade hand, so that he coughed and died on the shaft. Blood beads described an arc in the night as I pulled the blade free and span to meet the attack of El Tiburón.

There was no attack, though.

Instead El Tiburón calmed the tempo of the fight, and rather than begin his attack straight away, simply stood and very casually tossed his sword from one hand to the other before addressing me with it.

Fine. At least there wouldn't be a lot of chat during this bout.

I snarled and went forward, blades cutting half-circles in the air, hoping to daze him, disorientate him. His expression hardly changed, and with fast movements of his elbow and forearm he met my attack easily. He was concentrating on my left hand, the hand that held the sword, and before I even realized he was doing it, my cutlass went spinning from my bloody fingers to the dirt.

My blade now. He concentrated on it, seeming to know it was new to me. Behind him more guards had gathered in the courtyard and though I couldn't understand what they were saying it was obvious: that I was no match for El Tiburón; that my end was but a heartbeat away.

And so it proved. The last of his attacks ended with a smash of the knuckle guard across my chin, and I felt teeth loosen and my head spin as I sank, first to my knees, before pitching forward. Beneath my robes, blood sluiced my sides like sweat, and what little fight was left in me was leeched away by the pain.

El Tiburón came forward. A boot stepped on to my blade and held my arm in place, and dimly I wondered if the blade had a quick-release buckle, even though it would do me no good, as the tip of his sword nudged my neck ready for the final lethal strike . . .

'*Enough*,' came the cry from the compound door. Squinting through a veil of blood I saw the guards part and Torres step through, followed closely by DuCasse. The two Templars shouldered El Tiburón aside, and with the merest flicker of irritation in his eyes – the hunter denied his kill – the enforcer stepped away. I'll be honest. I wasn't sad to see him go.

I gasped ragged breath. My mouth filled with blood and I spat as Torres and DuCasse crouched, studying me like two medical men examining a patient. When the Frenchman reached for my forearm I half expected him to feel for my pulse but instead he disengaged the hidden blade, unclipped it with practised fingers then tossed it away. Torres looked at me, and I wondered if he really was as disappointed as he looked, or whether it was theatrics. He took hold of my other hand, removed my Templar ring and pocketed it.

'What is your true name, rogue?' said Torres.

Disarmed as I was, they let me pull myself to a sitting position. 'It's, ah . . . Captain Piss Off.'

Again I spat, this time close to DuCasse's shoe, and

he looked from the gobbet of blood to me with a sneer. 'Nothing but a filthy peasant.' He moved to strike me, but Torres held him back. He had been looking around the courtyard at the bodies, as though trying to assess the situation.

'Where is the Sage?' he asked. 'Did you set him free?'

'I had nothing to do with that, much as I wish I did,' I managed.

As far as I was concerned the Sage had either been sprung by Assassin friends or staged a breakout himself. Either way, he was out – out of harm's way and in possession of the one secret we all wanted: the Observatory location. And my trip was a wasted one.

Torres looked at me and must have seen the truth in my eyes. His Templar affiliations made him my enemy, but there was something in the old man I liked, or respected at least. Perhaps he saw something in me, a sense that maybe we weren't so different. Certainly one thing I knew: if the decision had been left to DuCasse I'd have been watching my guts drop to the compound floor. Instead, Torres stood up and signalled to his men. 'Take him to the ports. Send him to Seville with the treasure fleet.'

'To Seville?' queried DuCasse.

'Yes,' replied Torres.

'But we can interrogate him ourselves,' said DuCasse. I heard the cruel smile in his voice. 'Indeed . . . it would be a pleasure.'

'Which is *exactly* why I intend to entrust the job to

our colleagues in Spain,' said Torres firmly. 'I hope this is not a problem for you, Julien?'

Even fogged by pain I could hear the irritation in the Frenchman's voice.

'*Non, monsieur,*' he replied.

Still, he took a great pleasure in knocking my lights out.

32

When I awoke I was on the floor of what looked like the lower deck of a galleon. A large galleon it was, the kind that looked like it was used to transport ... people. My legs were gripped by iron bilboes – big, immovable manacles that were scattered all around the deck, some empty, some not.

Not far away I could make out more bodies in the gloom. More men back there, at a guess maybe a dozen or so, shackled just as I was, but in what sort of shape it was difficult to tell from the low groans and mumblings that reached my ears. At the other end of the deck was piled what I took to be the captives' possessions – clothes, boots, hats, leather belts, backpacks and chests. In among them I thought I saw my robes, still dirty and bloody from the fight in the prison compound.

You remember me saying how lower decks had their own smell? Well, this one had a different smell altogether. The smell of misery. The smell of fear.

A voice said, 'Eat it fast,' and a wooden bowl landed with a dull thump by my bare feet before the black leather boots of a guard retreated, and I saw sunlight from a hatch and heard the clip-clop of a ladder being climbed.

Inside the bowl: a dry flour biscuit and a splodge of oatmeal. Not far away sat a black man, and, like me, he was eyeing the food dubiously.

'You hungry?' I asked him.

He said nothing, made no move to reach for the food. Instead he reached to the manacles at his feet and began to work at them, on his face an expression of profound concentration.

At first I thought he was wasting his time, but as his fingers worked, sliding between his feet and the irons, his eyes went to me, and though he said nothing I thought I saw in them the ghost of painful experience. His hands went to his mouth and for a moment he looked like a cat cleaning itself, until the same hand dipped into the oatmeal, mixing the goo inside with saliva and then using it to lubricate his foot in the manacle.

I knew what he was doing now, and could only watch in admiration and hope as he continued to do it, making the foot more and more greasy until it was slippery enough to . . .

Try. He looked at me, silenced any encouragement before it even left my lips, then twisted and pulled at the same time.

He would have yelled in pain if he wasn't concentrating on keeping so quiet, and his foot when it came free of the leg iron was covered in a revolting mixture of blood and spit and oatmeal. But it was free. And neither of us wanted to eat the oatmeal anyway.

He glanced back up the deck towards the ladder and both of us steeled ourselves against the appearance of a guard, then he began working at the other foot and was soon free. Crouched on the wood with his head cocked, he listened as footsteps from above us seemed to move towards the hatch, then, thankfully, moved away again.

There was a moment in which I wondered if he might simply leave me there. After all, we were strangers; he owed me nothing. Why should he waste time and endanger his own bid for freedom by helping me?

But in the next instant, after a moment's hesitation – perhaps he wondered himself about the wisdom of helping me – he scrambled over towards me, checked the shackles, then hurried over to an unseen section of the deck behind me, returning with keys.

His name was Adewalé he told me as he opened the shackles. I thanked him quietly, rubbing my ankles and whispering, 'Now, what's your plan, mate?'

'Steal a ship,' he said simply.

I liked the sound of that. First, though, I retrieved my robes and hidden blade, as well as adding a pair of leather braces and a leather jacket to my ensemble.

Meanwhile my new friend Adewalé was using the keys to release the other prisoners. I snatched another set from a nail on the wall and joined him.

'There's a catch to this favour,' I told the first man I came to as my fingers worked at the key in his restraints, 'you're sailing with me.'

'I'd follow you to hell for this, mate . . .'

Now there were more men standing on the deck and free of shackles than there were still restrained, and perhaps those above had heard something because suddenly the hatch was flung open and the first of the guards thundered down the steps with his sword drawn.

'Hey,' he said, but 'hey' turned out to be his final word. I'd already fitted my hidden blade (and had a moment's reflection that though I had only been wearing it for such a short space of time, it still felt somehow familiar to me, almost as though I had been wearing it for years) and with a flick of my forearm had engaged the blade, then stepped forward and introduced the blade to the guard, driving it deep into his sternum.

It wasn't exactly stealthy or subtle. And I stabbed him so hard that the blade punctured his back and pinned him to the steps until I wrenched him free. Now I saw the boots of a second soldier and the tip of his sword as reinforcements arrived and for this one I didn't wait. Backhanded I sliced the blade just below his knees and he screamed and toppled, losing his sword, losing his balance, one of his lower legs cut to the bone and pumping blood to the deck as he joined his mate on the wood.

By now it was a full-scale mutiny, and the freed men ran to the piles of confiscated goods and liberated their own gear, arming themselves with cutlasses and pistols, pulling boots on. I saw squabbles breaking out – already! – over whose items were whose, but there was no time to play arbitrator. A clip around the ear was what it took and then our new team was ready to go into action. Above us we heard the sound of rushing feet and panicked shouting in Spanish as the guards prepared themselves for the uprising.

Just then, something else. The ship suddenly rocked by what I knew was a gust of wind. Across the deck I caught Adewalé's eye and he mouthed something to me. One word: hurricane.

Again it was as though the ship had been rammed as a second gust of wind hit us. Now time was against us; the battle needed to be won fast, and we had to take our own ship, because these winds, furious as they were, were nothing – *nothing* – compared to the force of a full-scale hurricane.

You could time its arrival by counting the delay between the first gusts. You could see the direction the hurricane was coming from. And if you were an experienced seaman, which I was by now, then you could use the hurricane to your advantage. So as long as we set sail soon, we could outrun any pursuers.

Yes, that was it. The terror of the hurricane had been replaced by the notion that we could make it work in our favour. Use the hurricane; outrun the Spanish. A few words in Adewalé's ear and my new friend nodded and began to spread news of the plan throughout the rest of the men.

They would be expecting us out of the main hatch.

They'd be expecting an uncoordinated, haphazard attack through the hatch of the quarterdeck.

So let's make them pay for underestimating us.

Directing some of the men to stay near the foot of the steps and make the noise of men preparing to attack, I led the rest to the stern, where we broke through into the infirmary, then stealthily climbed the steps to the galley.

In the next instant we poured out on to the main deck, and sure enough the Spanish soldiers stood unaware, their backs turned and their muskets trained on the quarterdeck hatch.

They were idiots. They were careless idiots, who had not only turned their backs on us, but brought muskets to a sword fight, and they paid for it with steel in their guts, and across their throats, and for a moment the quarterdeck was a battlefield as we ruthlessly pressed home the advantage our surprise attack gave us, until at our feet lay dead or dying Spaniards, while the last of them threw themselves overboard in panic, and we stood and caught our breath.

Though the sails were furled the ship rocked as it was punched by another gust of wind. The hurricane would be upon us any minute. Now on other ships along the harbour belonging to the treasure fleet we saw soldiers handing out pikes and muskets as they began to prepare themselves for our attack.

We needed a faster ship than this one and Adewalé

had his eye on one, already leading a group of our men across the gangplank and to the quay. Soldiers on the harbour died by their blade. There was a crack of muskets and some of our men fell, but already we were rushing the next galleon beside us, a beautiful-looking ship – the ship I was soon to make my own.

And then we were up on it just as the sky darkened, a suitable backdrop for the battle and a terrifying augur of what was to come.

Wind whipped at us. Growing stronger now, hammering us in repeated gusts. The Spanish soldiers, you could see they were in disarray, as terrified of the oncoming storm as they were of the escaped prisoners, unable to avoid the onslaught of either.

The battle was bloody and vicious, but over quickly and the galleon was ours. For a moment I wondered if Adewalé would want to assume command; indeed he had every right to do so – this man had not only set me free, but led the charge that helped win us this boat. And if he did decide to captain his own ship I would have to respect that, find my own command and go my own way.

But no. Adewalé wanted to sail with me as quarter-master.

And I was more than grateful, not only that he was willing to serve under me, but that he chose not to take his skills elsewhere. In Adewalé I had a loyal quarter-master, a man who would never rise up against me in mutiny, provided I was a just and fair captain.

I knew that then at the beginning of our friendship, just as I know it now with all those years of comradeship between us.

(Ah, but the Observatory. The Observatory came between us.)

We set sail just as the masts unfurled and the first tendrils of the coming storm fattened our sails. Crosswinds battered us as we left the harbour and I glanced behind from my place at the tiller to see the remaining ships of the treasure fleet being assaulted by wind and rain. At first their masts swung crazily from side to side like out-of-control pendulums, then they were clashing as the storm hit. Without ready sails they were sitting ducks and it gladdened my heart to see them knocked into matchwood by the oncoming hurricane.

Now the air seemed to grow colder and colder around us. Above I saw clouds gathering, scudding fast across the sky and blocking out the sun. Next we were lashed with wind and rain and sea spray. Around us the waves seemed to grow and grow: towering mountains of water with foaming peaks, every one of them about to drown us, tossing us from one huge canyon of sea to another.

The poultry were washed overboard. Men hung on to cabin doors. I heard screams as unlucky deckhands were snatched off the ship. The galley fire was extinguished. All hatches and cabin doors battened down. Only the bravest and most skilful men dared scale the ratlines to try to manage the canvas.

The foremast snapped and I feared for the main mast and the mizzen, but they held, thank God, and I gave silent praise for this fast, plucky ship that had been brought to us by fate.

The sky was a patchwork of black cloud that every now and then parted to allow rays of sunshine through, as if the sun was being kept prisoner behind them, as though the weather was taunting us. Still we kept going, with three men at the tiller and men hanging on to the rigging as though trying to fly a huge, abominable kite, desperately trying to keep us ahead of the storm. To slow down would be to surrender to it. To surrender to it would be to die.

But we didn't die, not that day. Behind us the rest of the treasure fleet was smashed at port, but the one ship — just the one ship containing the freed prisoners — managed to escape and the men we had — a skeleton crew — pledged their allegiance to myself and Adewalé, and agreed with my proposal that we set sail immediately for Nassau. At last I was going back to Nassau, to see Edward and Benjamin, and rejoin the republic of pirates I had missed so much.

I was looking forward to showing them my ship. My new ship. I had christened it the *Jackdaw*.

33

September, 1715

'You've named your new brig after a poxy bird?'

Any other man and I would have drawn my pistol or perhaps engaged my hidden blade and made him eat his words. But this was Edward Thatch. Not Blackbeard yet, oh no. He had yet to grow the face fur, which would give him his more famous moniker, but he still had all that braggadocio that was as much his trademark as the plaited beard and the lit fuses he would wear in it.

Benjamin was there too. He sat with Edward beneath the sailcloth awnings of the Old Avery, a tavern on the hill overlooking the harbour, one of my very favourite places in the world, and my first port of call on entering Nassau – a Nassau I was pleased to see had hardly changed: the stretch of purest blue ocean across the harbour, the captured ships that littered the shores, English flags flying from their masts, the palms, the shanty houses, the huge Fort Nassau that towered above us, its death's head flag flapping in the easterly breeze. I tell a lie; it had changed. It was busier than it had been before. Some nine hundred men and women now made it their base, I discovered – seven hundred of them pirates. And that included Edward and Benjamin – planning raids and drinking, drinking and planning raids, six of one, half a dozen of the other.

Nearby was another pirate I recognized as James Kidd, who some said was the son of William Kidd, who sat by himself. But for now my attention went to my old shipmates, who both rose to greet me. Here, there were none of the formalities, the insistence on politeness and decorum that shackles the rest of society. No, I was given a proper pirate greeting, embraced in huge hugs by Benjamin and Edward, the pirate scourges of the Bahamas, but really soft old bears, with grateful tears in their eyes to see an old friend.

'By God, you're a sight for salty eyes,' said Benjamin, 'come you in and have a drink.'

Edward gave Adewalé a look. 'Ahoy, Kenway. Who's this?'

'Adewalé, the *Jackdaw*'s quartermaster.'

And that was when Edward made his crack about the *Jackdaw*'s name. Neither of them had yet made mention of the robes I wore, but perhaps I had that pleasure to come. Certainly there was a moment, after the greeting, when they both gave me long, hard looks and I wondered whether those looks were as much to gawp at my clothes as to see the change in me, because the fact was that I had been but a boy when I first met them, but I had grown from a feckless, arrogant teenager, an errant son, a lovelorn but unreliable husband, into something else – a man scarred and made hard by battle, who was not quite so careless with his feelings, not so liberal with his emotions, a cold man in many respects, a man whose true passions were buried deep.

Perhaps they saw that, my two old friends. Perhaps they took note of that hardening of boy to man.

I was looking for men to crew my ship, I told them.

'Well,' said Edward, 'there's scores of capable men about, but use caution. A shipload of the king's sailors showed up a fortnight back, causing trouble and knocking about like they own the place.'

I didn't like the sound of that. Was it Woodes Rogers's work? Had he sent out an advance party? Or was there another explanation? The Templars. Looking for me maybe? Looking for something else? The stakes were high now. I should know. I'd done more than my fair share to increase them.

As it turned out, in recruiting more men for my ship I was to learn a little more about the presence of the English in the Bahamas. Men that Adewalé and I spoke to talked of seeing soldiers prancing around in the king's colours. The British wanted us out, well, of course they did, we were a thorn in His Majesty's side, a dirty great stain on the red ensign, but it felt as though there was, if anything, an increase in British interest. So it was that when I next met Edward, Ben and, joining us, James Kidd in the Old Avery, I was extra wary of unfamiliar faces and sure to speak out of earshot.

'Have you ever heard of a place called the Observatory?' I asked them.

I'd been thinking about it a lot. At its mention there was a flicker in James Kidd's eyes. I shot him a glance. He was young – about nineteen or twenty years old, I'd say, so a bit younger than I was, and, just like me, a bit of a hothead. So as Thatch and Hornigold shook their heads, it was he who spoke up.

'Aye,' he said, 'I've heard of the Observatory. An old legend, like Eldorado or the Fountain of Youth.'

I ushered them to a table where, with a look left and right, a check to see if any of the king's spies were in residence, I smoothed out the picture purloined from Torres's mansion and placed it on the table. A bit dog-eared but, still, there in front of us was an image of the Observatory and all three men looked at it with interest, some with more interest than others. Some who pretended they were less interested than they really were.

'What have you heard?' I asked James.

'It is meant to be a temple or a tomb. Hiding a treasure of some kind.'

'Ah, rocks,' bellowed Edward. 'It's fairy stories you prefer to gold, is it?'

Edward – he'd have no part in trying to find the Observatory. I knew that from the start. Hell, I'd known that before I'd even opened my mouth. He wanted treasure he could weigh on scales; chests filled with pieces of eight, rusted with the blood of their previous owners.

'It's worth more than gold, Thatch. Ten thousand times above what we could pull off any Spanish ship.'

Ben was looking doubtful, too – matter-of-fact, the only ear I seemed to have belonged to James Kidd.

'Robbing the king to pay his paupers is how we earn our keep here, lad,' said Ben with an admonishing tone. He jabbed a grimy weather-beaten finger at my stolen picture. 'That ain't a fortune; it's a fantasy.'

'But this is a prize that could set us up for life.'

My two old shipmates, they were salt of the earth, the two very best men I'd ever sailed with, but I cursed their lack of vision. They spoke of two or three scores to set us up for months, but I had in mind a prize that would set us up for life! Not to mention making me a gentleman: a man of property and promise.

'Are you still dreaming on that strumpet back in Bristol?' jeered Ben when I mentioned Caroline. 'Jaysus, let go, lad. Nassau is the place to be, not England.'

And for a while I tried to convince myself that it was true, and that they were right, and that I should set my sights on more tangible treasures. During days spent drinking, planning raids, then carrying out those raids, drinking to their success and planning more raids, I had plenty of time to reflect on the irony of it all, how standing around the table with my Templar 'friends' I'd thought them deluded and silly and yearned for my pirate mates with their straight talking and free thinking. Yet here on Nassau, I found men who had closed their minds, despite appearances to the contrary, despite what they said and even the symbolism of the black flag, with which I was presented one afternoon when the sun beat down upon us.

'We fly no colours out here, but praise the lack of them,' said Edward as we looked out towards the *Jackdaw*, where Adewalé stood by the flagpole. 'So let the black flag signal nothing but your allegiance to man's natural freedoms. This one is yours. Fly it proud.'

The flag flapped gently in the wind and I was proud – I *was* proud. I was proud of what it represented and of my part in it. I had helped build something worthwhile, struck a blow for freedom – *true freedom*. And yet there was still a hole deep in my heart, where I thought of Caroline, and of the wrong that had been done to me. You see, my sweet, I had returned to Nassau a different man. Those passions buried deep? I was waiting for the day to act upon them.

In the meantime there were other things to think about, specifically the threat to our way of life. One night found us sitting around a campfire on the beach, our ships, the *Benjamin* and the *Jackdaw*, moored offshore.

'Here's to a pirate republic, lads,' said Thatch. 'We are prosperous and free, and out of the reach of the king's clergy and debt collectors.'

'Near five hundred men now pledge their allegiance to the brethren of the coast in Nassau. Not a bad number,' said James Kidd. He cast me a brief sideways glance I pretended not to notice.

'True,' burped Thatch, 'yet we lack sturdy defences. If the king were to attack the town he'd trample us.'

I grasped the bottle of rum he handed to me, held it up to the moonlight to examine it for bits of floating sediment and then, satisfied, took a swig.

'Then let us find the Observatory,' I offered, 'if it does what these Templars claim, we'll be unbeatable.'

Edward sighed and reached for the bottle. They'd heard this from me a lot. 'Not that *twaddle* again, Kenway. That's a story for schoolboys. I mean *proper* defences. Steal a galleon, shift all the guns to one side. It would make a nice ornament for one of our harbours.'

Now Adewalé spoke up. 'It will not be easy to steal a full Spanish galleon.' His voice was slow, clear, thoughtful. 'Have you one in mind?'

'I do, sir,' retorted Thatch drunkenly. 'And I'll show you. She's a fussock she is. Fat and slow.'

Which was how we came to be launching an attack on the Spanish galleon. Not that I knew it then, of course, but I was about to run into my old friends the Templars again.

34

March, 1716

We set course south-east or thereabouts. Edward said he'd seen this particular galleon lurking around the lower reaches of the Bahamas. We took the *Jackdaw*, and as we sailed we found ourselves talking to James Kidd and quizzing him on his parentage.

'The bastard son of the late William Kidd, eh?' Edward Thatch was most amused to relate. 'Is that a true yarn you like spinning?'

The three of us stood on the poop deck and shared a spyglass like it was a blackjack of rum, trading it in order to peer through a wall of early-evening fog so thick it was like trying to stare through milk.

'So my mother told me,' replied Kidd primly. 'I'm the result of a night of passion just before William left London . . .'

It was difficult to tell from his voice if he was vexed by the question. He was different like that. Edward Thatch, for example, wore his heart on his sleeve. He'd be angry one second, cheerful the next. Didn't matter whether he was throwing punches or doling out drunken, rib-crushing bear hugs, you knew what you were getting with Edward.

Whatever cards Kidd was holding, he kept them close to his chest. I remembered a conversation we'd had a while back. 'Did you steal that costume from a dandy in Havana?' he'd asked me.

'No, sir,' I replied. 'Found this on a corpse . . . one that was walking about and talking shite to my face only moments before.'

'Ah . . .' he'd said, and a look had crossed his face, impossible to decipher . . .

Still, there was no hiding his enthusiasm when we finally saw the galleon we were looking for. 'That ship's a monster; look at the size of her,' said Kidd as Edward preened himself as though to say, *I told you so.*

'Aye,' he warned, 'and we cannot last long face-to-face with her. You hear that, Kenway? Keep your distance, and we'll strike when fortune favours us.'

'Under cover of darkness, most likely,' I said with my eye to the spyglass. Thatch was right. She was a beauty. A fine ornament for our harbour indeed, and an imposing line of defence in its own right.

We let the galleon draw away towards a disruption of horizon in the distance that I took to be an island. Inagua Island, if my memory of the charts was correct, where a cove provided the perfect place for our vessels to moor, and the abundant plant and animal life made it ideal for re-stocking supplies.

Edward confirmed it. 'I know the place. A natural stronghold used by a French captain named DuCasse.'

'*Julien DuCasse?*' I said, unable to keep the surprise out of my voice. 'The Templar?'

'Name's right,' replied Edward, distracted. 'I didn't know he had a title.'

Grimly I said, 'I know the man. And if he sees my ship, he'll know it from his time in Havana. Meaning he may wonder who's sailing her now. I can't risk that.'

'And I don't want to lose that galleon,' said Edward. 'Let's think on it . . . and maybe wait till it's darker before hopping aboard.'

Later I took the opportunity to address the men, climbing the rigging and gazing down upon them gathered on the main deck, Edward Thatch and James Kidd among them. I wondered, as I hung there for a moment, waiting for silence to fall, whether Edward looked at me and felt proud of his young protégé, a man he had mentored in the ways of piracy. I hoped so.

'Gentlemen! As is custom among our kind we do not plunge headlong into folly on the orders of a single madman, but act according to our own collective madness!'

They roared with laughter.

'The object of our attention is a square-rigged galleon, and we want her for the advantage she shall bring Nassau. So I'll put it to the vote . . . All those in favour of storming this cove and taking the ship stomp and shout "Aye!"'

The men roared their approval, not a single voice of dissent among them, and it gladdened the heart to hear it.

'And those who oppose, whimper "Nay!"'

There was not a nay to be heard.

'Never was the king's council this unified!' I roared and the men joined in, and I looked down at James Kidd, and especially at Edward Thatch, and they beamed their approval.

Shortly after as we sailed into the cove I had a thought: I needed to be sure that Julien DuCasse was taken care of. If he saw the *Jackdaw*, and more to the point, if he saw me and then escaped, he could tell his Templar confederates where I was, and I didn't want that. Not if I still held out hope of locating the Observatory, which, despite what my pals were saying, I did. I gave the matter some thought, mulling over the various possibilities, and in the end decided to do what had to be done: I jumped overboard.

Well, not straight away, I didn't. First I told Edward and James of my plans and then, when my friends had been told that I planned to go on ahead and surprise DuCasse before the main attack started, I jumped overboard.

I swam to shore, where I moved like a wraith in the night, thinking of Duncan Walpole as I did it, my mind going back to the evening I'd broken into Torres's mansion and dearly hoping that tonight didn't turn out the same way.

I passed clusters of DuCasse's guards, my limited Spanish picking up snippets of conversation as they moaned about having to hunt down supplies for the boat. Night was falling by the time I came to an encampment and crouched in the undergrowth, where I listened to a conversation from within the canvas of a lean-to. One voice I recognized in particular: Julien DuCasse.

I already knew DuCasse kept a manor house on the island, where he no doubt liked to relax after returning from his endeavours to control the world. The fact that he wasn't returning there now meant that this was but a fleeting visit to collect supplies.

Now just one problem. Inside the lean-to my former Templar associate was surrounded by guards. They were truculent, probably uncooperative guards, who were hacked off at having to collect stocks for the ship, not to mention feeling the sharp edge of Julien DuCasse's tongue. But they were guards all the same. I looked around at the encampment. On the opposite side was a fire that had burned down almost to the embers. Close to me were crates and barrels, and looking from them to the fire I could see that they had been placed there deliberately. Sure enough, when I crabbed over and had a better look what I saw were kegs of gunpowder. I reached behind my neck, where I'd stowed my pistol to keep it dry. My powder was wet, of course, but access to powder was no longer a problem.

In the middle of the encampment stood three soldiers. On guard, supposedly, but in actual fact mumbling something I couldn't hear. Cursing DuCasse probably. Other troops were coming and going and adding to the pile of supplies: firewood mainly, kindling, as well as scuttlebuts that slopped with water drawn from a watering hole nearby. Not exactly the feast of wild boar and fresh spring water DuCasse was hoping for I'd wager.

Staying in the shadows, and with one eye on the movement of the troops, I crept close to the kegs and gouged a hole in the bottom one, big enough to fill my hands with gunpowder and create a little trail as I crept round the edge of the compound until I was as close to the fire as I dared. My line of gunpowder led in a half-circle from where I crouched back to the kegs. At the other side of that circle was the lean-to where Julien DuCasse sat, drinking and dreaming of grand Templar plans to take over the world – and shouting abuse at his recalcitrant men.

Right. I had fire. I had a trail of gunpowder leading from the fire through the undergrowth and to the kegs. I had men waiting to be blown up and I had Julien DuCasse awaiting our moment of reckoning. Now all I needed to do was time things so that none of the clod-hopping troops would see my makeshift fuse before it could detonate the powder.

Crouching I moved to the fire then flicked a glowing ember on to the tail of the gunpowder fuse. I steeled myself for the sound it made – it seemed so loud in the night – and thanked God the soldiers were making so much noise. And then, as the fuse fizzed away from me,

I hoped I hadn't inadvertently broken the line of the fuse; hoped I hadn't accidentally trickled the gunpowder into anything wet; hoped none of the soldiers would arrive back just at the very instant that . . .

And then one did. He carried a bowl full of something. Fruit, perhaps. But either the smell or the noise alerted him and he stopped at the edge of the clearing and looked down at his boots just as the sizzle-burn of gunpowder trail ran past his feet.

He looked up and his mouth formed an O to shout for help as I snatched a dagger out of my belt, pulled my arm back and threw it. I was grateful once again for those wasted afternoons vandalizing trees back home at Bristol and thanked God as the knife hit him somewhere just above the collarbone – not an especially accurate shot, but it did the job. So instead of shouting the alarm he made a muted, strangulated sound and slumped forward to his knees, with his hands scrabbling at his neck.

The men in the clearing heard the noise of his body falling, his bowl of fruit tumbling, the fruit rolling, and turned to see its source. All of a sudden they were alert, but it didn't matter, because even as they pulled their muskets from their shoulders and a shout went up they had no idea what was about to happen.

I don't suppose they knew what hit them. I'd turned my back, put my hands over my ears and curled up into a ball as the explosion tore across the clearing. Something hit my back. Something that was soft and wet, which I didn't particularly want to think about. From further away I heard shouts and knew there would be more men arriving at any moment, so I turned and ran into the clearing, past blown-up bodies of soldiers in various states of mutilation and dismemberment, most of them dead, one of them pleading for death, and through thick black smoke that filled the clearing, embers floating in the air.

DuCasse emerged from the tent, swearing in French, shouting for someone, anyone, to put out the fire. Coughing, spluttering, he waved his hand in front of his face to clear smoke and choking particles of flaming soot and peered into the fog.

And standing in front of him he saw me.

And I know that he recognized me because he said so. 'You' was the only word he said before I drove my blade into him.

My blade hadn't made a sound.

'You remember the gift you gave me?' It made a slight sucking noise as I pulled it from his chest. 'Well, it answers just fine.'

'You son of a whore.' He coughed and blood speckled his face. Around us rained the flaming shot like satanic snow.

'As bold as a musket ball, and still half as sharp,' he managed as the life drained from him.

'I'm sorry about this, mate. But I can't risk you telling your Templar friends about me still kicking around.'

'I pity you, buccaneer. After all you have seen, after

all we showed you of our Order, still you embrace the life of an ignorant and aimless rogue.'

Round his neck I saw something I hadn't seen before. A key on a chain. I yanked it and it came away easily in my fingers.

'Is petty larceny the extent of your ambition?' he mocked. 'Have you no mind to comprehend the scope of ours? All the empires on earth, abolished! A free and opened world, without parasites like you.'

He closed his eyes, dying. His last words were, 'May the hell you find be of your own making.'

Behind me I heard men crashing into the clearing and knew it was time to leave. In the distance I could hear more shouts and the sounds of battle and knew that my shipmates had arrived and that the cove and galleon would soon be ours and that the night's work would soon be over. And as I disappeared into the undergrowth I thought about DuCasse's final words: *May the hell you find be of your own making.*

We would see about that, I thought. We would see.

PART THREE

35

May, 1716

It was two months later, and I was in Tulum on the eastern coast of the Yucatán Peninsula. My reason for being there? The ever-mysterious James Kidd, and what he had showed me in San Inagua Island.

He had been waiting, I now realize. Waiting for his moment to get me alone. After the death of DuCasse, the theft of his galleon and the . . . well, let's just say 'disposal' of the rest of the Frenchman's men, an operation that boiled down to either 'join us and become a pirate' or 'enjoy your swim', Thatch had sailed for Nassau with the Spanish galleon, taking most of the men with him.

Myself, Adewalé and Kidd had remained behind with some vague idea of how we might utilize the cove. What I had in mind, of course, was relaxing on its beaches and drinking until the supplies of rum were dry, and then returning to Nassau. *Oh, you constructed the fortified harbour without me. What a shame I missed the opportunity to help.* Something like that.

What Kidd had in mind – well, who could tell? At least until he approached me that day, told me he had something to show me, led me to the Mayan stones.

'Odd-looking things, aren't they?' he said.

He wasn't wrong. From a distance they'd looked like a collection of rubble, but up close were actually a carefully arranged formation of strangely carved blocks.

'Is this what they call Mayan?' I asked him, staring at the rock closely. 'Or is it Aztec?'

He looked at me. He wore that same penetrating, quizzical look he always seemed to when we spoke. It made me feel uncomfortable, if I'm honest. Why did I always get the feeling he had something to say, something to tell me? Those cards he held close to his chest, there were times I wanted to wrench his hands away and look at them for myself.

Some instinct, though, had told me that I'd find out in good time. That instinct would be proved right, it would turn out.

'Are you good with riddles, Edward?' he asked me. 'Puzzles and ponderings and the like?'

'I'm no worse than the next man,' I said carefully. 'Why?'

'I think you have a natural gift for it. I've sensed it for some time, in the way you work and think. The way you understand the world.'

Now we were getting to it. 'I'm not so sure about that. You're talking in riddles now, and I don't understand a word.'

He nodded. Whatever he had to tell me it wasn't going to appear all at once. 'Clamber on top of this thing here, will you? Help me solve something.'

Together we scrambled to the top of the rocks where we crouched. When James put a hand to my leg I looked down at it, just as tanned, weathered and worn as that of any pirate, with the same latticework of tiny cuts and scars earned at sea. But smaller, the fingers slightly tapered, and I wondered what it was doing there. If . . . *But no. Surely not.*

And now he was speaking, and he sounded more serious than before, like a holy man in contemplation.

'Concentrate and focus all your senses. Look past shadow and sound, deep into matter, until you see and hear a kind of shimmering.'

What was he going on about? His hand gripped my leg harder. He urged me to concentrate, to focus. His grip, in fact, his whole manner, brooked no disbelief, banishing my reluctance, my resistance . . .

And then – then I saw it. No, I didn't *see* it. How can I explain this? I *felt it – felt it* with my eyes.

'Shimmering,' I said quietly. It was in the air around me – all around me – a more vivid version of something I had experienced before, sitting in the farmyard at home in Hatherton, late at night when, in a dream, my mind roaming free, it was as if the world had suddenly become that bit brighter and more clear. I had been able to hear things with extra clarity, see things ahead I hadn't been able to see before, and here was the funny thing: as though there was contained within me a huge bank, a huge vault of knowledge awaiting my access, and all I needed to open it was the key.

And that was it, sitting there, with Kidd's hand gripping my leg.

It was as though I had found the key.

I knew why I'd felt different all those years ago.

'You understand?' hissed Kidd.

'I think so. I've seen its like before. Glowing, like moonlight on the ocean. It's like using every sense at once to see sounds and hear shapes. Quite a combination.'

'Every man and woman on earth has in them a kind of intuition hidden away,' Kidd was saying as I gazed about myself, like a man suddenly transported to another world. A blind man who could suddenly see.

'I've had this sense most of my life,' I told him, 'only I thought it related in some way to my dreaming, or the like.'

'Most never find it,' said Kidd, 'others it takes years to tease out. But for a rare few it comes as natural as breathing. What you feel is the light of life. Of living things past and present. The residue of vitality come and gone. Practice. Intuition. Any man's senses can be tuned well past what he is born with. If he tries.'

After that, we'd parted, with arrangements to meet in Tulum, which is why I found myself standing in the baking heat trying to talk to a native woman who stood by what looked like a pigeon coop and who squinted up at me when I arrived.

'You keep these things as pets?' I asked.

'Messengers,' she replied in faltering English. 'This is

how we communicate between these islands. How we share information . . . and contracts.'

'Contracts?' I asked, thinking, *assassins. Assassins' contracts?*

She told me Kidd was waiting for me at a temple and I moved on. How did she know? And why, as I walked, did I get the feeling that they were awaiting my arrival? Why, as I passed through a village made up mainly of low huts, did I feel as though the villagers were all talking about me, gaping blankly at me when I looked their way? Some wore colourful flowing robes and jewellery, and carried spears and sticks. Some had bare chests and wore breechcloths, were daubed with markings and wore strange adornments, bracelets made of silver and gold and beaded necklaces with bones for pendants.

I wondered if they were like the people from my world, bound by notions of rank and social class. And just as back in England a high-class gentleman might be recognized by the cut of his clothes and quality of his walking cane, here those at the top of the scale simply wore finer robes, more ornate jewellery and had more intricate daubing.

Perhaps Nassau really was the only place that was truly free. Or perhaps I was fooling myself about that.

And then it was as if the jungle fell away and rising high, high above me in a pyramid shape was a vast tiered Mayan temple, with huge flights of steps rising through the centre of the layers of stone.

Standing gulping in the undergrowth I noticed the

freshly cut branches and stems around me. A path had been recently cleared and I followed it until I reached a doorway in the foot of the temple.

In there? Yes. In there.

I felt along its sides and with effort dragged it across until I was able to squeeze inside, into what looked like an entrance chamber, but not as dark as I'd expected. As though somebody had already lit . . .

'Captain Kenway,' said a voice from the shadows. It was a voice I didn't recognize, and in the next instant my pistol was drawn as I span and peered into the dark. My new enemies had the advantage of surprise, though, and the pistol was knocked from my hand at the same moment as I was grabbed and pinned from behind. The flickering torch lit hooded, shadowy figures holding me in place, while in front of me two men had appeared from the shadows. One of them was James Kidd. The other, a native, hooded like the others, his face indistinct in the shadows. And for a second he simply stood and stared at me. He stared at me until I stopped struggling and cursing James Kidd, and had calmed down, and then he said, 'Where is the assassin Duncan Walpole?'

I threw a glance at Kidd. With his eyes he assured me everything was all right, that I was in no danger. Why I trusted him, I didn't know. He'd tricked me into this meeting, after all. But I relaxed, nevertheless.

'Dead and buried,' I said of Walpole, and I didn't see the native man in front of me bridle with anger so much as sense it. Quickly I added, 'After he tried to kill me.'

The native gave a short, thoughtful nod. 'We are not sorry to see him gone. But it is you who carried out his final betrayal. Why?'

'Money was my only aim,' I said impudently.

He moved in closer, giving me a good look at him. A native man, he had dark hair and piercing serious eyes within a brown lined face adorned with paint. He was also very angry.

'Money?' he said tightly. 'Should I find comfort in that?'

'He has the sense, mentor,' said James, stepping in.

The sense. That much I understood. But now this: *mentor*. How was this native chief *mentor* to James?

Mention of my sense seemed to calm the native chief – the man I would later come to know as Ah Tabai.

'James tells me you met the Templars in Havana,' he said. 'Did you see the man they call the Sage?'

I nodded.

'Would you recognize his face if you saw it again?' asked Ah Tabai.

'I reckon so,' I said.

He thought and then seemed to reach a decision. 'I must be certain,' he said quickly, and then he and his men dissolved into the shadows, leaving me alone with James, who gave me a sharp look and raised a don't-say-a-word finger before I could remonstrate with him.

Instead he took a torch, grimacing at the dwindling,

meagre light it provided, then bent to move into a narrow passageway that went further into the temple. There the ceiling was so low that we were almost bent double as we made our way along, both conscious of what might be lurking within this thousands-of-years-old structure, what surprises might lie in store. Whereas in the chamber our words had echoed, now they were deadened by the walls – damp rock that seemed to crowd in on us.

'You walked me blind and backwards into this mess, Kidd! Who the bloody hell was that jester back there?'

He called over his shoulder. 'Ah Tabai, an Assassin, and my mentor.'

'So you're all part of some daffy religion?'

'We are Assassins and we follow a creed. But it does not command us to act or submit . . . Only to be wise.'

He came out of the low tunnel into another passageway, but one that did at least let us stand upright.

'A creed,' I said as he walked. 'Oh do tell. I'd love to hear it.'

'"Nothing is true, everything is permitted." This is the world's only certainty.'

'"Everything is permitted?" I like that – I like the sound of that. Thinking what I like and acting how I please –'

'You parrot the words, Edward, but you do not understand them.'

I gave a short laugh. 'Don't get all haughty with me, Kidd. I followed you as a friend and you tricked me.'

'I saved your skin bringing you here, man. These men wanted you dead for consorting with Templars. I talked them out of it.'

'Well, cheers for that.'

'Aye, cheers.'

'So it's you lot them Templars have been chasing, then?'

James Kidd chuckled. 'Until you came along and mucked things up, it was us chasing them. We had them running scared. But they have the upper hand now.'

Ah . . .

As we kept walking along passageways I could hear strange sounds around us.

'Is someone in here with us?'

'It's possible. We're trespassing.'

'Someone's watching us?'

'I don't doubt it.'

Our words dropped like a stone, echoing around the walls of the temple. Had Kidd been in here before? He didn't say, but seemed to know how to operate the doors that we came to, then the stairways and bridges, climbing up and up, until we reached the final door.

'Whatever's waiting at the end of this path had better be worth my time,' I said, irritated.

'That'll depend on you,' he replied mysteriously.

Next thing we knew, the stones beneath our feet gave way and we plunged to water below.

36

The way was blocked by rubble – another challenge – so we swam underwater until at last, just when I had begun to wonder if I could hold my breath a second longer, we broke the surface of water and found ourselves in a pool at one end of another large chamber.

We moved on, out of this chamber and through into the next where we came upon a bust displaying a face. A face I recognized.

'Jesus,' I exclaimed. 'That's him. The Sage. But this thing must be hundreds of years old.'

'Older still,' said Kidd. He looked from me to the bust. 'You're certain it's him?'

'Aye, it's the eyes that mark him.'

'Did the Templars say why they wanted this Sage?'

With distaste I remembered. 'They drew some of his blood into a little glass cube.'

The cube you gave them, I recalled, but felt no guilt. Why should I?

'Like this one?' Kidd was saying. In his hands was another vial.

'Yes. They meant to ask him about the Observatory, too, but he escaped.'

The vial had disappeared back into the depths of

Kidd's pouch. He seemed to consider something before turning away from the bust of the Sage. 'We've finished here.'

We returned, finding a new set of steps through the temple's innards until we were heading towards what looked like a door. As it slid away I saw sunlight for the first time in what felt like hours, and in the next moment was gulping down fresh air, and instead of cursing the heat of the sun as usual, was thankful for it after the clammy cold of the temple's interior.

Ahead Kidd had stopped and was listening. He threw a look back and motioned me to hush my noise and stay out of sight. What was going on I couldn't tell, but I did as I was told, then followed him. Slowly and quietly we inched forward to where we found Ah Tabai crouched out of sight behind a rock – out of sight because in the distance we could hear the unmistakable Cockney bray of English soldiers at work.

Behind the boulder we waited in silence and Ah Tabai turned his penetrating stare upon me. 'The statue in the temple,' he whispered, 'was that the man you saw in Havana?'

'Spitting likeness, aye,' I whispered back.

Ah Tabai turned back to watch the soldiers over the edge of the boulder. 'And it seems another Sage has been found,' he said to himself. 'The race for the Observatory begins anew.'

Was it wrong of me to feel a thrill? I was part of this now.

'Is that why we're whispering?' I said.

'This is your doing, Captain Kenway,' said Ah Tabai quietly. 'The maps you sold the Templars have led them straight to us. And now the agents of two empires know exactly where we operate.'

Kidd was about to step forward to engage the soldiers. No doubt he felt more comfortable hacking down English soldiers than natives, but Ah Tabai was already stopping him. With one hand restraining Kidd his eyes went to me. 'They have taken Edward's crew as well,' he said. I started. *Not the crew. Not Adewalé and my men.* But Ah Tabai, with a final reproachful look my way, slipped away. Behind him he'd left what was unmistakably a blowpipe that Kidd picked up.

'Take this,' he said, handing it to me. 'You'll attract no attention and take fewer lives.' And as he gave me a few tips on how to use it I wondered, Was this part of some new challenge? Or was it something new? Was I being trained? Evaluated?

Let them try, I thought darkly. *I'm nobody's man but my own. Answerable only to myself and to my conscience. Rules and baubles? Not for me, thanks.*

They could stuff their creed where the sun don't shine as far as I was concerned. Besides, why would they even want me? This *sense*, perhaps? My skill in battle!

Doesn't come cheap, gentlemen, I thought as I came to the perimeter of the clearing where my crew had been deposited, sitting back-to-back with their hands bound.

Good lads, they were giving the English soldiers all kinds of grief: 'Let me up, tosspot, and face me like a soldier!'

'If only you knew what was coming to you . . . I think you'd pack your kits and run.'

I fitted the first of my darts into the blowpipe. I could see what needed to be done: take out the English soldiers one by one, try to even up the numbers a little. A poor unfortunate native gave me just the diversion I needed. Howling outrage he staggered to his feet and tried to run. With him went the attention of the soldiers, grateful for the sport, gleefully fitting their muskets to their shoulders and firing. *Crack. Crack.* Like snapping branches in the forest. There was laughter as he crashed down in a haze of crimson, but they didn't notice that one of their number folded silently into the undergrowth, too, his hand clutching at the blowpipe dart protruding from his neck.

As the guards returned to the clearing I crossed the path behind them and at the same time spat a second dart at the soldier bringing up the rear. I span on my heel and caught him as he fell, and as I dragged his body into the bush, I thanked God for my rowdy men. They had no idea of my presence but couldn't have been more helpful if I'd primed them.

A soldier swung round. 'Hey,' he said, his friend nowhere to be seen. 'Where's Thompson?'

Hidden in the undergrowth I fitted the next dart and raised the pipe to my lips. Took a quick breath and puffed out my cheeks just as Kidd had shown me. The dart pierced him below the jawbone and he probably thought he'd been bitten by a mosquito – right up until the second he lost consciousness.

Now we were in business. From my vantage point in the bushes I counted. Three men dead, six still alive, and if I could take out a couple more before the remaining guards worked out they were being picked off, well, then I thought I could take the rest myself. Me and my hidden blade.

Did this make me an Assassin now? Now that I was behaving and thinking like one? After all, hadn't I pledged to fight the Templars for what happened in Hatherton?

My enemy's enemy is my friend.

No. I'm my own man. Answer to no one but myself. No creed for me. I'd had years of wanting to be free of convention. I wasn't about to give all that up.

By now the soldiers were looking around themselves. They'd begun to wonder where their comrades were. And I realized I didn't have the luxury of picking another one off. I had to take them all out myself.

Six against one. But I had the advantage of surprise, and as I leapt from within the undergrowth I made it my first order of business to swipe my blade across the ropes that bound Adewalé. Behind me he scrambled to find a weapon of his own. My blade was in my right hand, my pistol held in my left. Positioned between two men with my arms out straight, I pulled the trigger of the pistol and slashed with my right hand at the same time, bringing my arms to cross in front of me. One man died with a metal ball ploughing through his chest, the other with a gaping throat wound.

I dropped the empty pistol, pivoted, snatched a new pistol from my belt and uncrossed my arms at the same time. Two new targets, and this time the blade's back-swipe sliced open a man's chest, while I shot a fourth man in the mouth. I met a sword blow with a parry from the blade, and then a soldier came forward with bared teeth giving me no time to snatch my third pistol. For a moment we traded blows, and he was better than I had expected, better than I had dared hope he would be, because while I wasted precious seconds bettering him, his comrade was looking along the barrel of his musket at me, ready to pull the trigger. I dropped to one knee, jabbed upwards with the blade and sliced into the swordsman's side.

Dirty trick. Nasty trick.

There was even something of the outraged English sense of honour in his agonized howl of anguish and pain as his legs gave way beneath him and he came thumping to the ground, his sword swinging uselessly and not enough to prevent my blade punching up underneath his jaw and through the roof of his mouth.

A dirty trick. A nasty trick. And a stupid one. Now I was on the ground (never go down in a fight) with my blade wedged in my opponent. A sitting duck. My left hand scrabbled to find my third pistol, but unless his musket misfired because the powder was wet I was dead.

I looked over to him, saw him do the about-to-fire face.

A blade appeared from his chest as Adewalé ran him through.

I breathed a sigh of relief as he helped me up, knowing I'd been close – *this close* – to death.

'Thank you, Adé.'

He smiled, waved my thanks away, and together our gaze went to the soldier. His body rose and fell with his last breaths, and one hand twitched before it went still, and we wondered what might have been.

37

Not long later the men were free, and James and I stood on the beach at Tulum – a Tulum once again in the hands of natives, rather than soldiers or slavers – looking out to sea. With a curse he handed me his spyglass.

'Who's out there?' I asked. A huge galley cruised along the horizon, getting more and more distant with each passing second. I could just about make out men on deck, and one in particular seemed to be ordering the others around.

'See that mangy old codger?' he said. 'He's a Dutch slaver called Laurens Prins. Living now like a king in Jamaica. Bastard's been a target for years. Bloody hell, we nearly had him!'

Kidd was right. This slave trader had been in Tulum but was now well on his way to safety. He considered his mission a failure, no doubt. But at least he'd escaped with his liberty.

Another Assassin none too pleased was Ah Tabai, who joined us wearing a face so serious I couldn't help but laugh.

'By God, you Assassins are a cheery bunch, eh? All frowns and furrowed brows.'

He glared at me. 'Captain Kenway. You have remarkable skill.'

'Ah, thanks, mate. It comes natural.'

He pursed his lips. 'But you are churlish and arrogant, prancing around in a uniform that you have not earned.'

'Everything is permitted,' I laughed. 'Isn't that your motto?'

The native man might have been old but his body was sinewy and he moved like a man much younger. But his face could have been carved from wood, and in his eyes was something truly dark, something both ancient and ageless. I found myself unnerved as he gave me the full benefit of his stare, and for a moment I thought he might say nothing, simply make me wilt in the heat of his contempt.

Until at last he broke the ghastly silence. 'I absolve you of your errors in Havana and elsewhere,' he said, 'but you are not welcome here.'

And with that he left, and in his wake James shot me a look. 'Sorry, mate, wish it were otherwise,' he said, then left me alone to ponder.

Bloody Assassins, I thought. They were just as bad as the other lot. The self-righteous sanctimonious attitude they had. We're this, we're that. Like the priests back home who used to wait outside taverns and curse you for being a sinner and called on you to repent. Who wanted you to feel *guilty* all the time.

But the Assassins didn't burn your father's farm, did they? I thought. *It was the Templars who did that.*

And it's the Assassins who showed you how to use the sense.

With a sigh I decided I wanted to smooth things over with Kidd. I wasn't interested in the path he wanted me to take. But being asked. Being considered suitable. There was something to be said for that.

I found him by the same pigeon coop where I'd met the native woman earlier. There he stood, tinkering with his hidden blade.

'Cheery bunch of mates you've got,' I offered.

Though he frowned, a light in his eyes betrayed that he was pleased to see me.

Nevertheless, he said, 'You deserve scorn, Edward, prancing about like one of us, bringing shame to our cause.'

'What's that, your cause?'

'He tested his blade — in and out, in and out — and then turned his eyes on me.

'To be blunt . . . we kill people. Templars and their associates. Folks who'd like to control all the empires on earth . . . Claiming they do it in the name of peace and order.'

Yes, I'd come across those sort of people before. These people who wanted jurisdiction of everyone on earth — I had broken bread with them.

'Sounds like DuCasse's dying words,' I said.

'You see? It's about power really. About lording over people. Robbing us of liberty.'

And that — liberty — was something I held very, very dear indeed.

'How long have you been one of these Assassins?' I asked him.

'A couple of years now. I met Ah Tabai in Spanish Town and there was something about him I trusted, a sort of wisdom.'

'And is all of this his idea? This clan?'

Kidd chuckled. 'Oh no, the Assassins and Templars have been at war for thousands of years, all over the world. The natives of this new world had similar philosophies for as long as they've been here and when Europeans arrived our groups sort of . . . matched up. Cultures and religions and languages keep folks divided . . . but there's something in the Assassin's Creed that crosses all boundaries. A fondness for life and liberty.'

'Sounds a bit like Nassau, don't it?'

'Close. But not quite.'

I knew when we parted that I'd not seen the last of Kidd.

38

July, 1716

As the pirates of Nassau finished their rout of Porto Guarico's guards, I stepped into the fort's treasure room and the sound of clashing swords, the crackle of musket fire and the screams of the dead and dying faded behind me.

I shook blood from my blade, enjoying the look of surprise my presence brought to the face of its only occupant.

Its only occupant being Governor Laureano Torres.

He was just as I remembered him. Spectacles perched on his nose. Neatly clipped beard and twinkling, intelligent eyes that recovered easily from the shock of seeing me.

And behind him, the money. Just as had been promised by Charles Vane . . .

The plan had been hatched two days ago. I'd been at the Old Avery. There were other taverns in Nassau, of course, and other brothels, too, and I'd be lying if I said I didn't avail myself of both, but it was to the Old Avery that I returned, where Anne Bonny the barmaid would serve drinks (and there was no one prettier who ever bent to a bung hole with a tankard in her hand than Anne Bonny), where I'd spent so many happy hours in appreciation of that fine posterior, roaring with laughter with Edward and Benjamin, where for the hours we spent drinking there it was as though the world could not touch us and where, since returning to Nassau from Tulum, I found I'd rediscovered my thirst.

Oh yes. Just like those old days back in Bristol, the more dissatisfied I was, the thirstier I became. Not that I realized it at the time, of course, not being as prone to putting two and two together as I should have been. No, instead I just drank to quench that thirst and work up an even bigger one, brooding on the Observatory, and how it figured in my plans to get rich and strike at the Templars; brooding on James Kidd and Caroline. And I must have looked as though I was deep in a brown study that particular day, for the first thing that the pirate known as Calico Jack Rackham said to me was, 'Oi, you, why the long look? Are you falling in love?'

I looked at him with bleary eyes. I was drunk enough to want to fight him; too drunk to do anything about it. And, anyway, Calico Jack stood by the side of Charles Vane, the two of them having just arrived on Nassau, and their reputation preceded them. It came on the lips of every pirate who passed through Nassau. Charles Vane was captain of the *Ranger*, and Calico Jack his quartermaster. Jack was English but had been brought up in Cuba, so he had a hint of the swarthy South

American about him. As well as the bright calico gear that had given him his nickname, he wore big hoop earrings and a headscarf that seemed to emphasize his long brow. It might sound like the pot calling the kettle black, but he drank constantly. His breath was always foul with it; his dark eyes heavy and sleepy with it.

Vane, meanwhile, was the sharper of the two, in mind and in tongue, if not in appearance. His hair was long and unkempt and he wore a beard and looked haggard. Both were armed with pistols on belts across their chests, and cutlasses, and were smelly from months at sea. Neither was the type you'd hurry to trust: Calico Jack, as dippy as he was tipsy; Vane on a knife edge, like you were always one slip of the tongue away from sudden violence. And not averse to ripping off his own crew either.

Still, they were pirates, both of them. Our kind.

'You're welcome to Nassau, gents,' I told them. 'Everyone is who does his fair share.'

Now, one thing you'd have to say about Nassau, specifically about the upkeep of Nassau, was that as housekeepers we made good pirates.

After all, you have enough of that when you're at sea, when having your ship spick and span is a question of immediate survival. They don't call it shipshape for nothing. So on dry land, when it's not really a question of survival – not immediate survival anyway – but more the sort of thing you feel you *should* do . . . What I'm saying is, the place was a pit: our grand Nassau Fort crumbled, great cracks along its walls; our shanty houses were falling down; our stocks and stores were badly kept and in disarray, and as for our privies – well, I know I've not exactly spared you the gory details of my life so far, but that's where I draw the line.

By far the worst of it was the smell. No, not from the privies, though that was bad enough, let me tell you, but a stench hung over the whole place, emanating from the stacks of rotting animal hides pirates had left on the shore. When the wind was blowing the right way – oh my days.

So you can hardly blame Charles Vane when he looked around and, though it was rich coming from a man who smelled like a man who'd spent the last month at sea, which is exactly what he was, said, 'So this is the new Libertalia? Stinks the same as every squat I've robbed in the past year.'

It's one thing being rude about your own hovel; it's a different kettle of fish when someone else does it. You suddenly feel defensive of the old place. Even so, I let it ride.

'We was led to believe Nassau was a place where men did as they please,' snorted Calico Jack. But before I could answer salvation arrived in the form of Edward Thatch, who with a bellow that might have been greeting but could just as well have been a war cry, appeared at the top of the steps and burst on to the terrace, as though the Old Avery was a prize and he was about to pillage it.

A very different-looking Edward Thatch it was, too, because to his already impressive head of hair he had added a huge black beard.

Ever the showman, he stood before us with his hands spread. *Behold.* Then tipped me a wink and moved into the centre of the terrace, taking command without even trying. (Which is funny, when you think on it, because for all our talk of being a republic, a place of ultimate freedom, we did still conform to our own forms of hierarchy, and with Blackbeard around there was never any doubt who was in charge.)

Vane grinned. Away with his scowl went the tension on the terrace. 'Captain Thatch, as I live and breathe. And what is this magnificent muzzle you've cultivated?'

He rubbed a hand over his own growth as Blackbeard preened.

'Why fly a black flag when a black beard will do?' laughed Thatch.

That was the moment, in fact, that his legend was born. The moment he took the name Blackbeard. He'd go on to plait his face fuzz. When he boarded ships he inserted lit fuses into it, striking terror in all who saw him. It helped make him the most infamous pirate, not just in the Bahamas, not just in the Caribbean, but in the whole wide world.

He was never a cruel man, Edward, though he had a fearsome reputation. But like Assassins, with their robes and vicious blades springing from secret places, like Templars and their sinister symbols and their constant insinuations about powerful forces, Edward Thatch, Blackbeard as he came to be known, knew full well the value of making your enemies shit their breeches.

Now, it turned out that the ale, the sanctuary and the good company weren't the only reasons we'd been graced with the presence of Charles Vane and Calico Jack.

'The word is the Cuban governor himself is fixing to receive a mess of gold from a nearby fort,' said Vane when we'd availed ourselves of tankards and lit our pipes. 'Until then, it's just sitting there, itching to be took.'

And *that* was how we found ourselves laying siege to Porto Guarico . . .

Well, the fight had been bloody, but short. With every man tooled up and our black flags flying we brought four galleons to the bay and hammered the fortress with shot, just to say we'd arrived.

Then we dropped anchor, launched yawls then waded through the shallows, snarling and shouting battle cries, our teeth bared. I got my first look at Blackbeard in full flight, and he was indeed a fearsome sight. For battle he dressed entirely in black, and the fuses in his beard coughed and spluttered so that he seemed to be alive with snakes and wreathed in a terrifying fog.

There's not many soldiers who won't turn tail and run at the sight of that charging up the beach towards them, which is what a lot of them did. Those brave souls who remained behind to fight or die, they did the latter.

I took my fair share of lives, the blade on my right

hand as much a part of me as my fingers and thumbs, my pistol blasting in my left. When my pistols were empty I drew my cutlass. There were some of our men who had never seen me in action before, and you'll forgive me for admitting there was an element of showmanship in my combat, as I span from man to man, cutting down guards with one hand, blasting with the other, felling two, sometimes three, at a time; driven, not by ferocity or bloodlust – I was no animal, there was little savagery or cruelty to what I did – but by skill, grace and dexterity. There was a kind of artistry to my killing.

And then, when the fort was ours, I entered the room where Laureano Torres sat smoking his pipe, overseeing the money count, two soldiers his bodyguards.

It was the work of a moment for his two soldiers to become two dead soldiers. He gave me a look of scorn and distaste as I stood in my Assassin's robes – slightly tatty by now but still a sight to see – and my blade clicked back into place beneath my fist. The blood of his guards leaked through the sleeve.

'Well hello, Your Excellency,' I said. 'I had word you might be here.'

He chuckled. 'I know your face, pirate. But your name was borrowed the last time we spoke.'

Duncan Walpole. I missed him.

By now Adewalé had joined us in the treasure room, and as his gaze went from the corpses of the soldiers to Torres, his eyes hardened, perhaps as he remembered being shackled in one of the governor's vessels.

'So,' I continued, 'what's a Templar Grand Master doing so far from his *castillo*?'

Torres assumed a haughty look. 'I'd rather not say.'

'And I'd rather not cut yer lips off and feed 'em to ya,' I said cheerily.

It did the trick. He rolled his eyes but some of his smugness had evaporated. 'After his escape from Havana we offered a reward for the Sage's recapture. Today someone claims to have found him. This gold is his ransom.'

'Who found him?' I asked.

Torres hesitated. Adewalé put his hand to the hilt of his sword and his eyes burned hatefully at the Templar.

'A slaver by the name of Laurens Prins,' sighed Torres. 'He lives in Kingston.'

I nodded. 'We like this story, Torres. And we want to help you finish it. But we're going to do it *our* way. Using you and your gold.'

He had no choice, and he knew it. Our next stop was Kingston.

39

So it was that some days later myself and Adewalé found ourselves roasting in the heat of Kingston as we shadowed the governor on his way to his meeting with Prins.

Prins, it was said, had a sugar plantation in Kingston. The Sage had been working for him but Prins had got wind of the bounty and thought he could make the sale.

Storm the plantation, then? *No*. Too many guards. Too high a risk of alerting the Sage. Besides, we didn't even know for certain he was there.

Instead we wanted to use Torres to buy the man: Torres would meet Prins, give him half the gold and offer the other half in return for the deliverance of the Sage; Adewalé and I would swoop in, take the Sage, whisk him off and then prise out of him the location of the Observatory. Then, we would be rich.

Simple, eh? What could go wrong with such a well-wrought plan?

The answer, when it came, came in the shape of my old friend James Kidd.

At the port Torres was greeted by Prins, who was old and overweight and sweating in the sun, and the two of them walked together, talking, with two bodyguards slightly in front of them, two behind.

Would Torres raise the alarm? Perhaps. And if he did, then Prins surely had enough men at his command to overpower us easily. But if that happened, Torres knew that my first sword slash would be across his throat. And if that happened, none of us would see the Sage again.

The funny thing is, I didn't *see* him. Not at first. It was as though I sensed him or that I became *aware* of him. I found myself looking around, the way you do if you smell burning when you shouldn't. *What's that smell? Where's that coming from?*

Only then did I see him. A figure who loitered in a crowd at the other end of the pier, part of the background but visible to me. A figure who, when he turned his face, I saw who it was. James Kidd. Not here to take the air and see the sights by the look of him. Here on Assassin business. Here to kill . . . who? Prins? Torres?

Jesus. We kept close to the harbour wall as I led Adewalé over, grabbed Kidd and dragged him into a narrow alleyway between two fishing huts.

'Edward, what the hell are you doing here?' He writhed in my grip but I held him easily. (And I'd think back to that later – how easily I was able to pin him to the hut wall.)

'I'm tailing these men to the Sage,' I told him. 'Can you hold off until he appears?'

Kidd's eyebrows shot up. 'The Sage is here?'

266

'Aye, mate, he is, and Prins is leading us straight to him.'

'Jaysus.' He pulled a frustrated face but I wasn't offering him a choice. 'I'll stay my blade for a time – but not long.'

Torres and Prins had moved off now and we had no choice but to go after them. I followed Kidd's lead and got some on-the-spot Assassin training in the art of stealth. And it worked, too. Like a dream. By staying at a certain distance we were able to remain out of sight and pick up on snippets of conversation, like Torres getting peeved at being made to hang on.

'I grow tired of this walk, Prins,' he was saying, 'we must be close by now.'

As it turned out we were. But close to what? Not to Prins's plantation, that much was certain. Ahead was the dilapidated wooden fencing and odd, incongruous arched entrance of what looked like a graveyard.

'Yes, just here,' Prins answered. 'We must be on equal footing you see? I'm afraid I don't trust Templars any more than you must trust me.'

'Well, if I'd known you were so skittish, Prins, I'd have brought you a bouquet of flowers,' Torres said with forced humour, and with a last look around he entered the graveyard.

Prins laughed. 'Ah, I don't know why I bother . . . For the money, I suppose. Vast sums of money . . .' His voice had tailed off. With a nod we slipped inside the cemetery behind them, keeping low and using the crooked markers as cover, one eye on the centre where Torres, Prins and his four minders had congregated.

'Now is the time,' Kidd told me as we gathered.

'No. Not until we see the Sage,' I replied firmly.

By now the Templar and the slaver were doing their deal. From a pouch hanging at his waist, Torres produced a bag that clinked with gold and dropped it into Prins's outstretched hand. Greasing his palm not with silver but gold. Prins weighed it, his eyes never leaving Torres.

'This is but a portion of the ransom,' said Torres. A twitch of his mouth was the only clue he was not his usual composed self. 'The rest is close at hand.'

By now the Dutchman had opened the bag. 'It pains me to traffic someone of my own race for profit, Mr Torres. Tell me again . . . What has this Roberts fellow done to upset you?'

'Is this some form of Protestant piety I am not familiar with?'

'Perhaps another day,' Prins said, then unexpectedly tossed the bag back to Torres, who caught it.

'*What?*'

But Prins was already beginning to walk away. He motioned to his guards at the same time, calling to Torres, 'Next time, see that you are not followed!'

And then to his men, 'Deal with this.'

But it wasn't towards Torres that the men rushed. It was towards us.

Blade engaged, I stood from behind my grave marker, braced, and met the first attack with a quick upwards slash across the flank of the first man. It was enough to stop him in his tracks, and I span round him and drove the blade-edge into the other side of his neck, slicing the carotid artery, painting the day red.

He sank and died. I wiped his blood from my face then wheeled and punched through the breastplate of another. A third man I misdirected by leaping to a grave marker. Then made him pay for his mistake with hot steel. Adewalé's pistol cracked, and the fourth man fell and the attack was over. But Kidd had already taken to his heels in pursuit of Prins. With a final glance back at where Torres stood, dazed and unable to take in the sudden turn of events, I gave a yell to Adewalé then set off in pursuit.

'You lost your chance, Kenway,' called Kidd over his shoulder as we both raced through the sun-bleached streets.

'Kidd, no. Come on, man, we can work this together.'

'You had your chance.'

By now Prins had worked out what had gone wrong: his four men, his best bodyguards, lay dead in a graveyard – how apt – and he was alone, pursued through the streets of Kingston by an Assassin.

Little did he know it, but his only chance of survival was me. You had to feel sorry for him. Nobody in their right mind wants Edward Kenway as their only hope.

And then I caught Kidd, grabbed him by the waist and pulled him to the ground.

(And I swear to God – and I'm not just saying this

because of what would happen later – but I thought to myself how light he was, how slender was the waist that I grabbed.)

'I can't let you kill him, Kidd,' I gasped, 'not until I've found the Sage.'

'I've been stalking that pig for a week now, charting his moves,' said Kidd angrily, 'and here I find not one but two of my targets – and you rob me of both.'

Our faces were so close together I could feel the heat of his rage.

'Patience,' I said, 'and you'll have your kills.'

Furious now he pulled away. 'All right, then,' he agreed, 'but when we locate the Sage, you're going to help me take Prins. Got that?'

We spat and shook. The volcano had erupted but now seemed to settle, and we made our way to Prins's plantation. So we would have to break in after all. How's about that for being made to eat your words?

On a low hill overlooking the sugar plantation we found a platform and sat awhile. I watched the work below. The male slaves sang sadly as they hacked at cane, the constant rustle of which seemed to float on the breeze, and women stumbled past bent double beneath heavy baskets of sugar harvest.

Adewalé had told me about life on a plantation, how when the cane was cut and harvested it was run between two metal rollers, and how it was common for a man's arm to be dragged into the rollers. And when that happened, the only way 'to separate the man from his plight' was to hack off the arm. And how after collecting the sugar juice it was time to boil away the waters from the sugar and how the boiling sugar would stick like birdlime and burn on, leaving a terrible scar. 'I had friends lose eyes,' he said, 'and fingers, and arms. And as slaves believe that we never heard a word of praise, nor an apology of any kind.'

I thought of something he'd told me. 'With this skin and with this voice, where can I go in the world and feel at ease?'

Men like Prins, I realized, were the architects of misery for his people, their ideology the opposite of everything I believed in and everything we stood for at Nassau. We believed in life and liberty. Not this . . . *subjugation*. This torture. This slow death.

My fists clenched.

Kidd took a pipe from his pocket and smoked a little as we observed the comings and goings below us.

'There's guards patrolling that property from end to end,' he said. 'Looks to me like they use the bells to signal trouble. See? There.'

'We'll want to disable those before pushing too far,' I said thoughtfully.

From the corner of my eye I saw something odd: Kidd licking his thumb then pressing it into the bowl of his pipe to put it out. Well, that wasn't odd, but what he did next was. He began dabbing his thumb in the bowl and rubbing ash on his eyelids.

'With so many men about we can't rely on stealth

alone,' he said, 'so I'll do what I can to distract and draw their attention, giving you a chance to cut them down.'

I watched, wondering what the hell he was playing at, as he cut his finger with a tiny pocket knife, and then squeezed out a drop of blood which he put to his lips. Next he removed his tricorne. He pulled the tie from his hair, pulled at his hair and ruffled it, so that it fell across his face. He licked the back of one thumb then, like a cat, used it to clean his face. And then he pushed his fingers into his gums, removed bits of wet wadding that had fattened his cheeks and dropped them to the ground.

Next he pulled up his shirt and began unlacing a corset that he pulled out from beneath his shirt and tossed to the ground, revealing, as he then opened the top buttons of his shirt and pulled the collar wider what were, unmistakably, his tits.

My head span. *His* tits? No. *Her* tits. Because when I eventually tore my eyes off the tits and to his face – no, *her* face – I could see that this man was not a man at all.

'Your name is not James, is it?' I said, slightly unnecessarily.

She smiled. 'Not most days. Come on.'

And when she stood, her posture had changed so that where before she'd seemed to walk and move like a man, now there was no doubt. It was as plain as the tits on her chest. She was a woman.

Already beginning to clamber down the hill towards the plantation fence, I skidded to catch up with her.

'Damn it, man. How is it you're a woman?'

'Christ, Edward, is it something that needs explaining? Now, I'm here to do a job. I'll let you be amused later.'

In the end, though, I wasn't really amused. To tell the truth it made perfect sense that she should resort to dressing like a man. Sailors hated having a woman on board ship. They were superstitious about it. If the mystery woman wanted to live the life of a seaman, then that's what she had to be – a sea*man*.

And when I thought about it I goggled at the sheer bloody guts of it. The courage it must have taken for her to do what she did. And I tell you, my sweet, I've met a lot of extraordinary people. Some bad. Some good. Most a mix of good *and* bad, because that's the way most people are. Of all of them the example I'd most like you to follow is hers. Her name was Mary Read. I know you won't forget it. Bravest woman I ever met, bar none.

40

As I waited for Mary by the gates I overheard guards chatting. So Torres had managed to slip away. *Interesting.* And Prins was holed up in his plantation in fear of his life. Good. I hope the fear gripped icy hands at his stomach. I hope the terror kept him awake at nights. I'd look forward to seeing it in his eyes when I killed him.

First, though, to gain entry. And for that I needed . . .

Here she is now. And you had to hand it to her, she was a superb actor. For God knows how long she'd convinced all of us that she was a man, and now here she was in a new role, not changing sex this time but convincing the guards she was ill. And, yes, doing a bloody good job of it.

'Stand your ground!' ordered a soldier at the gate.

'Please, I've been shot,' she rasped, 'I need aid.'

'Christ, Phillips, look at her. She's hurt.'

The more sympathetic of the two soldiers stepped forward and the gate to the plantation opened in front of her.

'Sir,' she said weakly, 'I'm poorly and faint.'

Sympathetic Soldier offered her his arm to help her inside.

'Bless you, lads,' she said and limped through the

gate that closed behind them. I didn't see it from my vantage point, of course, but I heard it: the swish of a blade, the muffled punching sound it made as she drove it into them, the low moan as the last of life escaped them and then the thump of their bodies on the dirt.

And now we were both inside and darting across the compound towards his manor. Probably we were seen by slaves, but we had to hope they wouldn't raise the alarm. Our prayers were answered because moments after that we were creeping into the manor, using hand signals to move stealthily around the rooms – until we came across him standing in a gazebo in a rear yard off the house. Crouched on either side of an archway we pecked round and saw him there, standing with his back to us, his hands across his stomach, looking out over his grounds, pleased with his lot in life – a fat slaver, his fortune built on the suffering of others. You remember me saying I'd met some who were all bad? Laurens Prins was top of that list.

We looked at one another. The kill belonged to her and yet, for some reason (because they were trying to recruit me?), she waved me onwards, then left on a scout of the rest of the mansion. I got to my feet, went through to the yard, crept beneath the gazebo and stood behind Laurens Prins.

And engaged my blade.

Oh, I kept it well greased; the one thing you can be sure of when it comes to pirates is that while we may not be a particularly domesticated breed, not at all house-proud, with the general state of Nassau a testament to that, we kept our weapons in good nick. Same philosophy as keeping a galleon shipshape. A question of need. A question of survival.

So it was with my blade. When it got wet I cleaned it thoroughly, and I kept it greased to within an inch of its life, and so these days it barely made a noise when I ejected it. It was so quiet, in fact, that Prins didn't hear it.

I cursed, and at last he turned in surprise, perhaps expecting to see one of his guards there, about to shout at the man for his impudence, for creeping up on him like that. Instead I thrust the blade into him and his eyes opened wide and were frozen like that as I let him down to the floor, keeping the blade in him, holding him there as blood filled his lungs and the life began to leave him.

'Why hang over me like a leering crow?' he coughed. 'To see an old man suffer.'

'You've caused no small portion of suffering yourself, Mr Prins,' I told him dispassionately. 'This is retribution, I suppose.'

'You absurd cutthroats and your precious philosophy,' he jeered, the final pathetic contempt of a dying man. 'You live in the world, but you cannot make it move.'

I smiled down at him. 'You mistake my motive, old man. I'm only after a bit of coin.'

'As was I, lad,' he said. 'As was I . . .'

He died.

I was stepping out of the gazebo, leaving his body behind, when I heard a noise from above. Looking up

I saw the Sage Roberts, just as I remembered him, on a balcony. He held Mary hostage, with a flintlock pistol aimed at the side of her head and – clever lad – he held her wrist to stop her engaging her blade.

'I found your man,' she called down, seemingly unconcerned about the pistol at her head. He'd use it, too. The heat in his eyes said so. They blazed. *Remember me, do you, mate?* I thought. *The man who stood by while they took your blood?*

He did. 'The Templar from Havana,' he said, nodding.

'I'm no Templar, mate,' I called back. 'That was just a ruse. We've come here to save your arse.'

(By which of course I meant, 'Torture you until you tell us where the Observatory is.')

'Save me? I work for Mr Prins.'

'Well then, he's a poor man to call master. He meant to sell you out to the Templars.'

He rolled his eyes. 'You can't trust anyone, it seems.'

Perhaps he relaxed, for she chose that moment to make her move. She dragged the heel of her boot down his shin and he cried out in pain as she twisted to one side and from underneath his grasp. She flailed for his gun arm but he whipped it away, aimed the gun and fired but missed. Now she was off balance and he saw his chance, pivoting on the rail of the balcony and kicking her with both feet. With a yell she flipped over the rail and I was already starting forward to try to catch her when she caught herself and swung into the balcony below.

Meanwhile, the Sage had drawn another pistol, but guards were arriving, alerted by the gunfire.

'Roberts,' I shouted, but instead of shooting at the guards he aimed his second shot at the bell.

Clang.

He couldn't miss, and it had the desired effect: as Mary dropped lithely down from the second balcony to join me, engaging her blade at the same time, guards came pouring from the archways into the courtyard. Back to back we stood, but there was no time to appraise our enemy at leisure. Muskets and pistols were being produced, so into action we sprang.

Six each, I think, was the tally. Twelve men who died with varying degrees of bravery and skill, and at least one case of dubious suitability for any kind of combat. It was the way he screwed up his eyes and whimpered as he came running into battle.

We heard the running feet of more men arriving and knew that was our cue to escape, dashing from the courtyard then across the compound, urging the slaves to *run, run,* free themselves, as we went. And if there had not been scores of soldiers on our tails, then we would have stopped and forced them to escape. As it is, I don't know whether they pressed home the advantage we'd given them.

Later we stopped and when I was done cursing my luck at losing Roberts, I asked her real name.

'Mary Read to my mum,' she answered, and at the

same time I felt something press into my crotch and when I looked down, saw that it was the point of Mary's hidden blade.

She was smiling, thank God.

'But not a word of it to anyone,' she said, 'or I'll unman you as well.'

And I never did tell anyone. After all, this was a woman who knew how to piss standing up. I wasn't about to underestimate her.

41

January, 1718

Dear Edward,

*I write with sad news of your father, who passed away one
month ago, taken by pleurisy. His passing was not painful,
and he died in my arms I am pleased to say. So at least we
were together until the very end.*

*We were poor at the time of his passing and so I have
taken a job at a local tavern where you may reach me if you
wish to correspond. News of your exploits has found my ears.
They say you are a pirate of some infamy. I wish that you
could write to me and allay my fears on this matter. I regret to
say I have not seen Caroline since you left, and so I am unable
to pass you any details regarding her health.*

Mother

I looked at the return address. I wasn't sure whether to
laugh or cry.

42

Well, I know I was in Nassau during that early part of 1718 – where else would I be, it was my home – but to be honest I remember only fragments. Why? That's a question you need to direct to him in there. Him, that little voice inside who tells you you need one more drink when you know you've had enough. That was the little voice who started hooting and wouldn't let me pass the Old Avery without a trip inside to while away the day, then wake up the next, rough as arseholes, knowing there was only one thing that would make me feel better, and it was served by Anne Bonny, barmaid at the Old Avery. And then, what do you know? The whole circle a *vicious* bloody circle – would begin again.

And yes I've since worked out I drank to drown my discontent, but that's the thing with drinking, you often don't know why at the time. You don't realize that the drinking is a symptom, not a cure. So I sat and watched as Nassau fell to rack and ruin. And being so drunk I forgot to feel disgusted about it. Instead I spent day after day at the same table of the Old Avery, either staring at my filched picture of the Observatory or attempting to etch out a letter to Mother or to Caroline. Thinking of Father. Wondering if the fire at the farmhouse had hastened his death. Wondering if I was to blame for that, too, and knowing the answer was the reason why my letters to Mother ended up crumpled bits of paper on the floor of the terrace.

Mind you, I wasn't so wrapped up in my problems that I forgot to eye up the delicious behind of Anne Bonny, even if she was off-limits (*officially*, that was. But Anne, let's just say she liked the company of pirates, if you know what I mean).

Anne had arrived in Nassau with her husband, James, a buccaneer and lucky bleeder for being married to her. Having said that, she had a way about her did Anne, like she wasn't afraid to give a fellow the glad eye, which did make you wonder if old James Bonny had his hands full with that one. I'd wager that serving ales at the Old Avery wasn't *his* idea.

'There's precious little in this town but piss and insects,' she used to complain, blowing strands of hair off her face. She was right, but still she stayed, fending off the advances of most, accepting the advances of a lucky few.

It was around that time, as I wallowed in my own misery, days spent chasing away hangovers and working on new ones, that we first heard about the king's pardon.

'It's a bag of shite!'

Charles Vane had said that. His words penetrating that mid-morning booze buzz I'd been working on.

What was?

'It's a ruse,' he thundered to keep us soft before they attack Nassau! You'll see. Mark me.'

What was a ruse?

'It's no ruse, Vane,' said Blackbeard, his voice betraying an unusual seriousness. 'I heard it straight from the mouth of the greasy Bermudan captain. There's a pardon on offer for any pirate that wants it.'

A pardon. I let the words sink in.

Hornigold was there, too. 'Ruse or not, I think it's plain the British may return to Nassau,' he said. 'With arms no doubt. In the absence of any clear ideas, I say we lay low. No piracy and no violence. Do nothing to ruffle the king's feathers for now.'

'Preserving the king's plumage is no concern of mine, Ben,' Blackbeard rebuked him.

Benjamin turned on him. 'It will be when he sends his soldiers to scrub this island clean of our residue. Look around you man, is this cesspool worth dying for?'

He was right, of course. It stank, and more so every day: a vomitous mixture of shit and bilge water and rotting carcasses. But even so, difficult though it might be for you to believe, it was *our* vomitous mixture of shit and bilge water and rotting carcasses, and we were prepared to fight for it. Besides, it didn't smell so bad when you were drunk.

'Aye, it's our republic. Our idea,' insisted Blackbeard. 'A free land for free men, remember? So maybe it's filthy to look at. But ain't it still an idea worth fighting for?'

Benjamin averted his eyes. *Had he already decided? Had he made his choice?*

'I can't be sure,' he said. 'For when I look on fruits of our years of labour, all I see is sickness . . . idleness . . . idiocy.'

Remember what I said about Benjamin? How he dressed differently, had a more military bearing. Looking back now I think he never really wanted to be a pirate; that his ambitions lay on the other side, with His Majesty's navy. He was never especially keen on attacking ships, for one thing, which was a rarity among us. Blackbeard told the story of how a vessel under his command had once laid siege to a sloop, only for Benjamin to steal the passengers' hats. That's all, just their hats. And yes, you might think it was because he was an old softy and didn't want to terrorize the passengers too much, and maybe you'd be right. But the fact is, out of all of us, Benjamin Hornigold was the least like a pirate, almost as though he wasn't willing to accept that he was one.

All that being the case, I don't suppose I should have been surprised by what happened next.

43

July, 1718

Dearest Caroline . . .

And that, on that particular occasion (location: the Old Avery, as if you needed telling), was as far as I got.

'Putting some shape to your sentiments?' Anne stood over me, brown and beautiful. A treat for the eyes.

'Just a short letter home. I reckon she's past caring anyway.'

I crumpled up the letter and tossed it away.

'Ah, you've got a hard heart,' said Anne as she moved off behind the bar, 'it should be softer.'

Aye, I thought. Yer right, lass. And that soft heart felt like it was melting. In the months since we'd heard about the king's pardon, Nassau was riven, divided into those who took the pardon, those who planned to take the pardon (after one final score), and those who were dead against the pardon and cursed all others, led by Charles Vane, and . . .

Blackbeard? My old friend was keeping his powder

dry, but looking back I think he'd decided that a life of piracy was no longer for him. He was away for Nassau on the lookout for prizes. News of big scores and strange allegiances were reaching our ears. I began to think that when Blackbeard had left Nassau he never had any intention of returning. (And he never did, as far as I know.)

And me? Well, on the one hand, I was wary being mates with Vane. On the other, I didn't want to take the pardon, which made me mates with Vane whether I liked it or not. Vane had been waiting for Jacobite reinforcements to arrive but they never had. Instead he began making plans to leave, maybe establish another pirate republic elsewhere. I would take the *Jackdaw* and leave with him. What other choice did I have?

And then came that morning, a few days before we were due to depart, as I sat on the terrace of the Old Avery, trying to write my letter to Caroline and passing the time of day with Anne Bonny, when we heard the sound of carriage-gun fire from the harbour. An eleven-gun salute, it was, and we knew exactly what was up. We'd been forewarned about it. The British were coming to take control of the island.

And here they were. A blockade that bottles up both entrances to the harbour. HMS *Milford* and HMS *Rose* were the muscle. Two warships escorting a fleet of five other vessels, on which were soldiers, craftsmen, supplies, building materials, an entire colony come to flush out the Pirates, drag Nassau up by its bootstraps and return it to respectability.

They were led by the flagship *Delicia*, which despatched rowing boats to negotiate the graveyard of ships and land on our beach. As we arrived there, along with every other jack tar in Nassau, its occupants were just landing. None other than my old friend Woodes Rogers. He was helped out of his rowing boat looking as tanned and well-kept as ever, though more careworn. You remember his promise to be governor of Havana? He'd delivered on that. Remember him telling me how he planned to rout the pirates from Nassau? Looked as though he planned on delivering on that one, too.

Never had I longed for Blackbeard more. One thing I knew was that my old friend Edward Thatch would have known which way to turn. A mix of instinct and cunning would have powered him like the wind.

'Well I'll be hanged,' Calico Jack said by my side (*tempting fate there, Jack*), 'King George has grown tired of our shenanigans. Who's the grim fella?'

'That's Captain Woodes Rogers,' I replied, and as I was in no hurry to reacquaint myself with him, I shrank into the crowd, but still close enough to hear as Rogers was handed a roll of parchment that he consulted, before saying, 'we desire a parley with the men who call themselves governors of this island. Charles Vane, Ben Hornigold and Edward Thatch. Come forth, if you please?'

Benjamin stepped forward.

'Lily-livered punk,' cursed Jack. And never was a truer word spoken. For if there was a moment that Nassau came to an end and our hopes for the republic were dashed, then that was it.

44

It wasn't until I found him that I really realized how much I had missed him.

Little did I know I was soon to lose him for good.

It was on a North Carolina beach, Ocracoke Bay, just before dawn and he was having a party – of course – and had been up all night – of course.

There were campfires dotted all over the beach, men dancing a jig to the sound of a fiddle further along, other men passing a blackjack of rum between them and guffawing loudly. Wild boar cooked on a spit and the delicious scent of it made my stomach do hungry flips. Perhaps here, on Ocracoke Beach, Blackbeard had established his own pirate republic. Perhaps he had no interest whatsoever in returning to Nassau and making things right.

Charles Vane was already there, and as I approached, trudging up the sand towards them and already anticipating the liquor on my lips and the wild boar in my belly, he was standing, his conversation with Blackbeard evidently just ending.

'A great disappointment you are, Thatch!' he bellowed

nastily, then on seeing me said, 'His mind is made up to stay here, he says. So sod him and hang all you that follow this sorry bastard into obscurity.'

Anybody else but Blackbeard and Vane would have slit his throat for being a traitor to the cause. But he didn't, because it was Blackbeard.

Anybody else but Vane and Blackbeard would have had him put in leg irons for his insolence. But he didn't. Why? Maybe out of guilt, because Blackbeard had turned his back on piracy. Maybe because no matter what you thought of Charles, you had to admire his guts, his devotion to the cause. None had fought harder against the pardon than Charles. None had been a bigger thorn in Rogers's side than he. He'd launched a fireship against their blockade and escaped, then continued to orchestrate raids on New Providence, doing anything he could to disrupt Rogers's governorship while he waited for reinforcements to arrive. The particular reinforcements he hoped for wore black in battle and went by the name Blackbeard. But as I arrived on the beach that balmy morning, it looked as though the last of Charles Vane's hopes had been dashed.

He left, his feet kicking up clouds of sand as he stomped back along the beach, away from the flickering warmth of the campfires, shaking with rage.

We watched him go. I looked down at Blackbeard. His belts were unbuckled, his coat unbuttoned and his newly acquired belly thrust at the buttons of his shirt. He said nothing, simply ushered me to take a seat on the sand beside him, handed me a bottle of wine and waited for me to take a drink.

'That man is a prick,' he said slightly drunkenly, waving a hand in the direction of where Charles Vane had been.

Ah, I thought, *but the irony is your old mucker Edward Kenway wants the same thing as the prick.*

Vane might have been devoted to the cause, but he didn't have the faith of the brethren. Always a cruel man, he'd lately become even more ruthless and savage. I'd been told that his new trick was to torture captives by tying them to the bowsprit, inserting matches beneath their eyelids – and then lighting them. Even the men who followed him had begun to question him. Perhaps Vane knew it as well as I did – that Nassau needed a leader who could inspire the men. Nassau needed Blackbeard.

He stood now, Blackbeard, Charles Vane a distant dot on the horizon, and beckoned me to follow.

'I know you've come to call me home, Kenway.' He looked touched. 'Your faith in me is kind. But with Nassau done in, I feel I'm finished.'

I was telling the truth when I said, 'I'm not of the same mind, mate. But I won't begrudge you the state of yours.'

He nodded. 'Jaysus, Edward. Living like this is like living with a large hole in your gut, and every time your innards spill over the ground, you're obliged to scoop 'em up and shove 'em back in. When Ben and me first set down in Nassau, I undervalued the needs for folks of character to shape and guide the place to its full purpose. But I was not wrong about the corruption that comes with that course.'

For a moment as we walked we listened to the tide on the sand, the soft rushing, receding noise of the sea. Perhaps he, like me, when he thought of corruption, thought of Benjamin.

'Once a man gets a taste of leadership, it's hard for him not to wonder why he ain't in charge of the whole world.'

He gestured behind. 'I know these men think me a fine captain, but I bloody hate the taste of it. I'm arrogant. I lack the balance needed to lead from behind the crowd.'

I thought I knew what he meant. I thought I understood. But I didn't like it – I didn't like the fact that Blackbeard was drifting away from us.

We walked.

'You still looking for that Sage fellow?' he asked me. I told him I was, but said nothing of how the search for the Sage had consisted mainly of sitting in the Old Avery drinking and thinking of Caroline.

'Ah, well, taking a prize a month back I heard a man named Roberts was working a slave ship called the *Princess*. Might want to see about it?'

So – the carpenter with the dead eyes, the man with the ageless knowledge, had moved on from plantations to slave ships. That made sense.

'The *Princess*. Cheers, Thatch.'

45

The British were coming after Blackbeard, of course. I later found out it was a force led by Lieutenant Maynard of HMS *Pearl*. A reward had been put on Blackbeard's head by the governor of Virginia after merchants made a noise about Blackbeard's habit of sailing from Ocracoke Bay and taking the odd prize here and there; the governor worried that Ocracoke inlet would soon become another Nassau. The governor didn't like having the world's most infamous pirate in his back yard. So the governor put a bounty on his head. And so they came, the British did.

The first we heard of it was a whispered alarm. 'The English are coming. The English are coming,' and looking through the gun hatches of Blackbeard's sloop the *Adventure* we saw that they'd launched a small boat and were trying to sneak up on us. We would have completely destroyed them, of course, but for one thing. One crucial thing. You know that party I was talking about? The wine and the wild boar? It had gone on. And on.

We were very, very, catastrophically hungover.

And so the best response we could manage was warning the rowing boat off with some shot.

There were very few us aboard the Blackbeard's ship that morning. Perhaps twenty at the most. But I was one of them, little knowing I was to play a part in what happened next: the fate of the world's most famous pirate.

And give him his due, he may have been hungover – just as we all were – but Blackbeard knew the waterways around Ocracoke Bay and so off we went, weighing anchor and making haste for the sandbanks.

Behind us came Maynard's men. They flew the red ensign and left us in no doubt as to what they intended. I saw it in Blackbeard's eyes. My old friend Edward Thatch. All of us aboard the *Adventure* that day knew the English were after him and him alone. The governor of Virginia's declaration had named only one pirate, and that pirate was Edward Thatch. I think we all knew we weren't the real targets of these dogged English, it was Blackbeard. Nevertheless, not one man gave himself up or threw himself overboard. There was not a man among us who was not willing to die for him – that was the devotion and loyalty he inspired. If only he could have used those qualities in service of Nassau.

The day was calm, there was no wind in our sails and we had to use our sweepers to make progress. We could see the whites of our pursuers' eyes, and they could see ours. Blackbeard ran to our stern, where he leaned over the gunwale and shouted across the still channel at Maynard.

'Damn you, villains, who are you? And where did you come from?'

Those on the ship behind gave no answer, just stared at us blank-eyed. Probably they wanted to unsettle us.

'You may see by our colours we are no pirates,' bellowed Blackbeard waving around himself, his voice echoing strangely from the steep sandbanks on both sides of the narrow channel. 'Launch a boat to board us. You'll see we are no pirates.'

'I cannot spare a boat to launch,' called Maynard back. There was a pause. 'I'll board you with my sloop soon enough.'

Blackbeard cursed and raised a glass of rum to toast him. 'I drink *damnation* to you and your men, who are cowardly puppies! I shall give nor take no quarter.'

'And in return I expect no quarter from you, Edward Thatch, and nor will I give any in return.'

The two sloops under Maynard's command came on, and for the first time ever, I saw my friend Edward Thatch at a loss for what to do. For the first time ever, I thought I saw fear in those eyes.

'Edward . . .' I tried to say, wanting to take him to one side, wanting us to sit together, as we had so many times at the Old Avery, to plot and plan and scheme, but not for the taking of a prize this time, no. To escape the English. To get to safety. Around us the crew worked in a kind of booze-soaked daze. Blackbeard himself was swigging rum, his voice rising along with his inebriation. And of course the more drunk he became, the less open to reason, the more reckless and rash his actions, such as when he ordered the guns be primed, and because we had no shot, filled with nails and pieces of old iron.

'Edward, no . . .'

I tried to stop him, knowing there had to be a better, more tactful way to escape the English. Knowing that to fire upon them would be to sign our own death warrants. We were outnumbered, outgunned. Their men were not drunk or hungover and they had the burning light of zealotry in their eyes. They wanted one thing and that thing was Blackbeard – drunk, angry, raging and probably, secretly, terrified Blackbeard.

Boom.

The spread of the gun shot was wide, but we saw nothing beyond a shroud of smoke and sand, which obscured our vision. For long moments we waited with bated breath to see what damage our broadside had inflicted, and all we heard were screams and the sound of splintering wood. Whatever damage we'd done, it sounded grievous, and as the fog cleared we saw that one of the pursuing ships had veered off to the side and beached, while the other seemed to have been hit as well, with no sign of any crew aboard and parts of its hull shredded and splintered. From the mouths of the crew came a weak if heartfelt cheer and we began to wonder if all was not lost after all.

Blackbeard looked at me, next to him at the gunwale, and winked.

'The other one's still coming though, Edward,' I warned. 'They'll return fire.'

Return fire they did. They used chain shot, which destroyed our jib, and in the next moment victorious cheers had turned to shouts as our ship was no longer seaworthy, lurching to the side of the channel and listing, its splintered masts grazing the steep-sided banks. Meantime, as we bobbed uselessly in the swell, the chasing sloop nosed up on our starboard side, giving us a good opportunity to see what strength they had remaining. Precious little, it looked like. We could see a man at the tiller, with Maynard by his side gesturing as he cried, 'Pull alongside, pull alongside . . .'

Which is when Edward decided attack was the best form of defence. He gave word for the men to arm themselves and prepare to board, and we waited with our pistols primed and cutlasses drawn, a final stand in a deserted back channel in the West Indies.

Powder smoke shrouded us, thick layers of it hanging like hammocks in the air. It stung our eyes and gave the scene an eerie feel, as though the English sloop was a ghost ship, appearing from within the folds of a spirit-mist. To add to the effect, its decks remained empty. Just Maynard and the mate at the helm, Maynard shouting, 'Pull alongside, pull alongside . . .' his eyes wild and rolling like a madman. The look of him, not to mention the state of his ship, gave us hope – it gave us hope that maybe they were in even worse shape than we'd at first thought; that this wasn't the final stand after all; that maybe we'd live to fight another day.

A false hope, as it would turn out.

All was quiet, just Maynard's increasingly hysterical shrieking as we crouched hidden behind the gunwale. How many men were still left alive on the sloop, we had no real way of telling, but one of us was confident at least.

'We've knocked them on their heads except three or four,' shouted Blackbeard. He was wearing his black hat, I noticed, and he'd lit the fuses in his beard, was shrouded in smoke, his hangover cast off, he glowed like a devil. 'Let's jump aboard and cut them to pieces.'

Only three or four? There had to be more of them left alive than that, surely?

But by then the two hulls had bumped, and with a shout, Blackbeard led us over the side of the *Adventure* and on to the British sloop, roaring a brutal warrior roar as the men flooded towards Maynard and the first mate at the tiller.

But Maynard, he was as good a performer as my friend Mary Read. For as soon as our dozen pirates boarded his ship, that wild hysterical look left his face, he shouted, '*Now, men, now!*' and a hatch in the quarterdeck opened and the trap was sprung.

They'd been hiding from us, playing possum, pretending to be dead, luring us on board. And now out they came, like rats escaping bilge water, two dozen of them to meet our plucky twelve, and straight away the clashing of steel, the popping of gunshot and the screams filled the air.

A man was upon me. I punched him in the face and engaged my blade at the same time, dodging to the side to avoid a fountain of blood and snot that erupted from his nose. In my other hand was my pistol, but I heard Blackbeard calling me, '*Kenway.*'

He was down, with a leg bleeding badly, defending himself with his sword and calling for a gun. I tossed him mine and he caught it, using it to fell a man coming at him with raised cutlass.

He was dead, though. We both knew it. We all knew it.

'In a world without gold, we could have been heroes!' he shouted as they teemed over him.

Maynard led a renewed attack upon him and Blackbeard, seeing his nemesis up close, bared his teeth and swung his sword. Maynard screeched, his hand gushing crimson as he pulled away and his sword fell, its guard broken. From his belt he snatched a pistol, fired it, catching Edward on the shoulder and sending him back to his knees where he grunted and swung his sword as the enemy moved in on him remorselessly.

Around us I could see more of our men falling. I drew my second pistol, fired, and gave one of their men a third eye, but now they were upon me, swarming over me. I cut men down. I cut them ruthlessly. And the knowledge that my next attacker would die the same way kept a few of them at bay, giving me the chance to glance over and see Edward dying by a thousand cuts, on his knees but fighting still, surrounded by vultures who hacked and chopped at him with their blades.

With a shout of frustration and anger I stood and whirled with outstretched hands, my blade forming a perimeter of death that sent men flailing backwards. I snatched the initiative, shooting forward and drop-kicking the man in front of me so that his chest and face became my springboard and I broke through the barrier of men surrounding me. In the air my blade flashed and two men fell away with open veins, blood hitting the deck with an audible slap. I landed then sprang across the deck to help my friend.

But never made it. From my left came a sailor who stopped my progress, a huge brute of a man who thumped into me, the two of us moving at such speed that neither of us could stop the momentum that took us over the side of the gunwale and into the water below.

I saw one thing before I fell. I saw my friend's throat open and blood sheet down his front, his eyes rolling to the top of his head as Blackbeard fell for a final time.

46

December, 1718

You've not heard a man screaming in pain until you've heard a man who's just had his kneecap blown off screaming in pain.

That was the punishment dealt by Charles Vane to the captain of the British slave ship we'd boarded. The same British slave ship had virtually scuttled Vane's own vessel, so we'd had to sail the *Jackdaw* nearby and allow his men on board. Vane had been furious about that, but even so that was no excuse to lose his temper. After all, this whole expedition had been his idea.

He'd hatched his plan soon after Edward's death.

'So Thatch has been topped?' he said as we sat in the captain's quarters of the *Jackdaw*, with Calico Jack drunk and asleep nearby, lying straight-legged in the chair in a way that seemed to defy gravity. He was another who had refused to take the king's pardon, so we were stuck with him.

'He was outnumbered,' I said of Blackbeard. The image was an unwelcome new arrival in my mind. 'I couldn't reach him.'

I remembered falling, seeing him die, blood pouring

from his throat, hacked down like a rabid dog. I took another long swig of rum to banish the image.

They'd hung his head from the bowsprit as a trophy, so I'd heard.

And they called *us* scum.

'Devil damn the man, he was fierce, but his heart was divided,' said Charles. He'd been worrying at my tabletop with the point of his knife. Any other guest I'd have told to stop but not Charles Vane. A Charles Vane defeated by Woodes Rogers. A Charles Vane mourning the death of Blackbeard. Most of all, a Charles Vane with a knife in his hand.

He was right, though, with what he said. Even if Blackbeard had lived there was little doubt he intended to leave the life behind. To stand at our head and lead us out of the wilderness was not something that had appealed to Edward Thatch.

We lapsed into silence. Perhaps we were both thinking of Nassau and how it belonged in the past. Or perhaps we were both wondering what to do in the future, because after some moments, Vane took a deep breath, seemed to pull himself together and slapped his fists to his thighs.

'Right, Kenway,' he announced, 'I've been musing on this plan of yours . . . This . . . Observatory you was going on about. How do we know it exists?'

I shot him a sideways look to see if he was joking. After all, he wouldn't have been the first. I'd been much mocked for my tales of the Observatory and wasn't in the mood for any more, not now anyway. But he wasn't, he was deadly serious, leaning forward in his chair, awaiting my answer. Calico Jack slumbered on.

'We find a slave ship called the *Princess*. Aboard should be a man called Roberts. He can lead us to it.'

Charles seemed to think. 'All them slavers work for the Royal African Company. Let's find any one of their ships and start asking some questions.'

But unfortunately for us all, the first Royal African Company ship we encountered blew holes in Vane's ship, the *Ranger*, meaning he needed to be rescued. At last we boarded the slave ship, where our men had already quietened down the slaver's crew. There we found the captain.

'This captain claims the *Princess* sails out of Kingston every few months,' I told Vane.

'All right. We'll set a course,' said Vane, and the decision was made: we were heading for Kingston, and no doubt the slave captain would have been okay and left unharmed, had he not called out angrily, 'You made a hash of my sails and rigging, you jackanapes. You owe me a share.'

Every man there who knew Charles Vane could have told you what would happen next. Not exactly. But the kind of thing: terrible violence, no remorse. So it was at that moment, when he swung round, drew his gun and strode over to the captain in one quick and furious movement. Then he put the muzzle of the gun to the captain's knee, his other hand held to stop himself being splashed with blood. And pulled the trigger.

It happened quickly. Matter-of-factly. And in the aftermath Charles Vane walked away, about to move past me.

'Dammit, Vane!'

'Oh, Charles, what a surly devil you are,' said Calico Jack, and it was a rare moment of sobriety from Calico Jack, a fact that was almost as shocking as the captain's piercing screams, but then the old drunkard was seemingly in the mood to challenge Charles Vane.

Vane turned on his quartermaster. 'Don't fuck with me, Jack.'

'It is my mandate to fuck with you, Charles,' snapped Calico Jack, normally laid out drunk, but today in a mood to challenge Vane's authority, it seemed. 'Lads,' he commanded, and as if on cue – as though they had been awaiting their chance – several men loyal to Calico Jack stepped forward with drawn weapons. We were outnumbered, but that didn't stop Adewalé, about to draw his cutlass, only to feel the full weight of a guard across his face, which sent him crumpling to the deck.

I found myself with a face full of pistol barrels when I moved forward to help.

'See . . . The boys and I had a bit of a council while you were wasting time with this lot,' said Calico Jack, indicating the captured slaver. 'And they figured I'd be a fitter captain than you reckless dogs.'

He gestured towards Adewalé, and my blood rose as he said, 'This one I figure I may sell for a tenner in Kingston. But with you two, I can't take any chances.'

Surrounded, me, Charles, and our men were helpless to do anything. My mind reeled, wondering where it had all gone so wrong. Had we needed Blackbeard that much? Did we rely on him so heavily that things could go so terribly awry in his absence? It seems so. It seems so.

'You'll regret this day, Rackham,' I hissed.

'I regret most of them already,' sighed the mutineer Calico Jack. His colourful Indian shirt was the last thing I saw as another man came forward clutching a black bag that he pulled over my head.

47

And that was how we found ourselves marooned on Providencia. After a month adrift on the damaged *Ranger*, that was.

Jack had left us food and weapons but we had no means of steering or sailing the ship, so it was a month at sea in which we tried and failed to repair the broken rigging and masts and spent most of the day manning the pumps in order to stay afloat; a month in which I'd had to listen to Vane ranting and raving all hours of the day and night. Shaking his fist at thin air, he was. 'I'll get ya Jack Rackham! I'll open y'up. I'll tear out your organs and string a bloody lute with them.'

We spent Christmas 1718 on the *Ranger*, bobbing around like a discarded liquor bottle on the waves, praying for mercy from the weather. Just me and him. And of course we had no calendars or such, so it was impossible to say when Christmas fell or which day 1718 became 1719, but I'm prepared to wager I spent them listening to Charles Vane rage at the sea, at the sky, at me, and especially at his old mucker Calico Jack Rackham.

'I'll get ya! You see if I don't, y'scurvy bastid!'

And when I tried to remonstrate with him, hinting

that perhaps his constant shouting was doing more harm to our morale than good, he turned on me.

'Well, well, the fearsome Edward Kenway speaks!' he'd bawl. 'Pray tell us, cap'n, how to quit this predicament and tell us what genius you have for sailing a boat with no sails and no rudder.'

How we didn't kill each other during that time, I'll never know, but by God we were glad to see land. We hooted with pleasure, clasped each other, jumped up and down. We launched a yawl from the stricken *Ranger*, and as night fell we rowed ashore then collapsed on the beach, exhausted but ecstatic that after a month drifting at sea we'd finally found land.

The next morning we awoke to find the *Ranger* wrecked against the beach and cursed one another for failing to drop anchor.

And then cursed our luck as we realized just how small it was, the island on which we were now marooned.

Providencia, it was called, a small island with its fair share of history. A bloody history, at that. English colonists, pirates and the Spanish had done nothing but fight over it for the best part of a century. Forty years ago, the great pirate Captain Henry Morgan had set his cap at it, recaptured it from the Spanish and used it as his base for a while.

By the time Vane and I set down upon the island, it was home to a few colonists, escaped slaves and convicts and the remnants of the Mosquito Indians who were native to it. You could explore the abandoned fort, but there was nothing much left. Nothing you could eat or drink anyway. And you could swim across to Santa Catalina, but then, that was even smaller. So mainly we spent the days fishing and finding frond oysters in small pools, and occasionally having a kind of snarling stand-off with groups of passing natives, ragged, wandering colonists or turtle fishermen. The colonists, in particular, always wore a wild, frightened look, as though they weren't sure whether to attack or run away, and could just as well do either. Their eyes seemed to swivel in their sockets in different directions at once and they made odd, twitchy movements with dry, sun-parched lips.

I turned to Charles Vane after one particular encounter, about to comment, and saw that he, too, was wearing a wild look, and his eyes seemed to swivel in their sockets, and he made odd, twitchy movements with his dry, sun-parched lips.

Until whatever fragile cord holding Charles Vane together snapped one day, and off he went to start a new Providencia tribe. A tribe of one. I should have tried to talk him out of it. *'Charles we must stick together.'* But I was sick to the back teeth of Charles Vane, and, anyway, it wasn't like I'd seen the last of him. He took to stealing my oysters for a start, scuttling out of the jungle, hairy and unshaven, his clothes ragged and with a look of the madman in his eyes. He'd scoop up my just-caught frond oysters, curse me for a bastard then scuttle back into the undergrowth from which he would curse me some more. My days were spent on the beach, swimming, fishing or scanning the horizon for vessels, all the time knowing full well he was tracking me from within the undergrowth.

On one occasion I tried to remonstrate with him. 'Will you talk with me, Vane? Are you fixed on this madness?'

'Madness?' he responded. 'Ain't nothing mad about a man fighting to survive, is there?'

'I mean you no harm, you corker. Let's work this out like gentlemen.'

'Ah. God, I've a bleedin' headache on account of our jabbering. Now stay back and let me live in peace!'

'I would if you'd stop filching the food I gather, and the water I find.'

'I'll stop nothing till you paid me back in blood. You was the reason we were out looking for slavers. You was the reason Jack Rackham took my ship!'

You see what I had to contend with? He was losing his mind. He blamed me for things that were plainly his own fault. It was he who had suggested we go after the Observatory. It was he who'd caused our current predicament by killing the slaver captain. I had as much reason to hate him as he had to despise me. The difference between us was that I hadn't lost my mind. At least not yet anyway. He was doing his best to remedy that, it seemed. He got crazier and crazier.

'You and your fairy stories got us into this mess, Kenway!'

He stayed in the bushes, like a rodent in the darkened undergrowth, curled up in roots, with his arms round tree trunks, crouched in his own stink and watching me with craven eyes. It began to occur to me that Vane might try to kill me. I kept my blades clean and though I didn't wear them – I'd become accustomed to wearing very little – I kept them close at hand.

Before I knew it he graduated from being a madman ranting at me from within the undergrowth to leaving traps for me.

Until one day I decided I'd had enough. I had to kill Charles Vane.

The morning that I set out to do it, it was with a heavy heart. I wondered whether it was better to have a madman as a companion than no companion at all. But he was a madman who hated me, and who probably wanted to kill me. It was either him or me.

I found him in a water hole, sitting crouched with his hands between his legs, trying to make a fire and singing to himself, some nonsense song.

His back was to me, offering me an easy kill, and I tried to tell myself I was being humane by putting him out of his misery, as I approached stealthily and activated my blade.

But I couldn't help myself. I hesitated, and in that moment he sprang his trap, flinging out one arm and tossing hot ashes into my face. As I reeled back he jumped to his feet, cutlass in hand, and the battle was on.

Attack. Parry. Attack. I used my blade as a sword, meeting his steel and replying with my own.

And I wondered: did he think of me as *betraying* him? Probably. His hatred gave him strength and for some moments he was no longer the pathetic troglodyte he had become, the fight returned to his eye. But it was not enough to turn the battle. The weeks spent crouching in the undergrowth and feeding off what he could steal had weakened him and I disarmed him easily. Instead of killing him then I sheathed my blade, unstrapped it and tossed it away, tearing off my shirt at the same time, and we fought with fists, stripped to the waist.

Then when I had him down and pummelled him, I caught myself and stopped. I stood, breathing heavily, with blood dripping from my fists. Below me on the ground, Charles Vane. This unkempt, hermit-looking man – and of course I stank myself, but I wasn't as bad as him. I could smell the shit I saw dried on his thighs as he half rolled on the ground and spat out a tooth on a thin string of saliva, chuckling to himself. *Chuckling to himself like a madman.*

'You nancy boy,' he said, 'you've only done half the job.'

I shook my head. 'Is this my reward for believing the best about men? For thinking a bilge rat like you could muster up some sense once in a while? Maybe Hornigold was right. Maybe the world does need men of ambition, to stop the likes of you from messing it all up.'

Charles laughed. 'Or maybe you just don't have the stones to live with no regrets.'

I spat. 'Don't save me a spot in hell, shanker. I ain't coming soon.'

And then I left him there, and when later I was able to help myself to a fisherman's boat I wondered whether to go and fetch him, but decided against.

God forgive me, but I'd had just about all I could take of Charles bloody Vane.

48

May, 1719

I arrived home to Inagua after months away, thankful to be alive and glad to see my crew. Even more when I saw how pleased they were to see me. *He is alive! The cap'n is alive!* They celebrated for days, drank the bay dry, and it gladdened the heart to see.

Mary was there too, but dressed as James Kidd, so I banished all thoughts of her bosoms, called her James when others were present, even Adewalé, who rarely left my side when I first returned, as though not wanting to let me out of his sight.

Meanwhile Mary had news of my confederates: Stede Bonnet had been hanged at White Point.

Poor old Stede. My merchant friend who evidently changed his mind where pirates were concerned – so much so he'd taken up the life himself. 'The gentleman pirate' they had called him. He'd worn a dressing gown and worked the routes further north for a while, before meeting Blackbeard on his travels. The pair had teamed up, but because Bonnet was as bad a pirate captain as he was a sailor, which is to say a very bad pirate captain, his crew had mutinied and joined Blackbeard. For

Bonnet the final insult was that he had to remain as a 'guest' on Blackbeard's ship, the *Queen Anne's Revenge*. Well, not the 'final insult' obviously. The final insult was being caught and hanged.

Meanwhile on Nassau – poor, ailing Nassau – James Bonny was spying for Woodes Rogers, bringing more shame upon Anne than her roving eye ever had upon him, while Rogers had struck a mortal blow to the pirates. In a show of strength he'd ordered eight of them be hanged on Nassau harbour, and since then his opposition had crumbled. Even a plot to kill him had been half-hearted and easily overthrown.

And – joy of joys – Calico Jack had been captured and the *Jackdaw* recovered. Turned out the liquor had got the better of Jack. Privateers commissioned by Jamaica's governor had caught up with him south of Cuba. Jack and his men had gone ashore and were sleeping off the booze under tents when the privateers arrived, so they fled into the jungle and the *Jackdaw* was recovered. Since then the scurvy dog had crawled back to Nassau where he'd persuaded Rogers to give him a pardon and was hanging around the taverns selling stolen watches and stockings.

'So what now?' said Mary, having delivered her news. 'Still chasing your elusive fortune?'

'Aye, and I'm close. I've heard the Sage is sailing out of Kingston on a ship called the *Princess*.'

James had stood and was beginning to walk away,

headed for the port. 'Put your ambition to better use, Kenway. Find the Sage with *us*.'

The Assassins she meant, of course. There was silence when I thought about them.

'I've no stomach for you and your mystics . . . Mary. I want a taste of the good life. An easy life.'

She shook her head and began to walk away. Over her shoulder she said, 'No one honest has an easy life, Edward. It's aching for one that causes the most pain.'

If the *Princess* was sailing out of Kingston then Kingston was where I needed to be.

And, my God, Kingston was beautiful. It had grown from a refugee camp into the largest town in Jamaica, which isn't to say it was an especially large town, just the largest in Jamaica, the buildings new yet ramshackle-looking, overlooked by hills populated by beautiful greenery and caressed by a cool sea breeze that rolled off Port Royal and took some of the sting out of a blistering sun – just some of it, mind, just some of it. I loved it. In Kingston, I'd look around and wonder if Nassau could have been this way, if we'd stuck at it. If we hadn't allowed ourselves to be so easily corrupted.

The sea was the clearest blue and it seemed to glitter and hold aloft the ships that were anchored in the bay. For a moment, as I gasped at the beauty of the sea and was reminded of the treasures it held, I thought of Bristol. How I'd stood on the harbour there and looked out to the ocean, dreaming of riches and adventure. The adventure I'd found. The riches? Well, the *Jackdaw* hadn't lain completely dormant during my time on Providencia. They'd taken some prizes. Added to what I already had in my coffers, I wasn't rich, exactly, but neither was I poor. Perhaps I was, finally, a man of means.

But if I could just find the Observatory.

(Greed, you see, my sweet, it's the undoing of many a man.)

Tethered at the quay were rowing boats, dandies and yawls, but it wasn't those I was interested in. I stopped and held a spyglass to my eye, scanning the horizon for signs of a slaver – the *Princess* – stopping to relish the glorious sight of the *Jackdaw*, then continued. Citizens and traders bustled past, all wares for sale. And soldiers, too. Spaniards, with their blue tunics and tricornes, muskets over their shoulders. A pair of them passed, looking bored and gossiping.

'What's all this fuss about here? Everyone's got sticks shoved well up their arses today.'

'Aye, we're on alert because of some visiting Spaniard. Toreador or Torres or something.'

So he was here. Him and Rogers. Did they know about the Sage on the Princess, *too?*

And then something that struck me as very interesting indeed, when I overheard a soldier say, 'Do you know what I heard? Governor Rogers and Captain Hornigold are part of a secret society. A secret order made up of Frenchies and Spaniards and Italians and even some Turks.'

Templars, I was thinking, even as I caught sight of Adewalé beckoning to me. He stood with a sweaty, nervous-looking sailor, who was introduced as working for the Royal Africa Company. A jack tar persuaded to talk with a surreptitious dagger in his ribs.

'Tell him what you told me,' said Adewalé.

The merchant looked uncomfortable. As you would, I suppose. 'I haven't seen the *Princess* for eight weeks or more,' he said. 'Meaning she may soon be back.'

We let him go and I mulled over the news. The *Princess* wasn't here . . . yet. We could stay, I decided. Bring the men ashore, make sure they behaved themselves, try not to attract too much attention . . .

Adewalé pulled me to one side. 'I grow tired of chasing these fantasies of yours, Edward. As does the crew.'

And that's all I need. Unrest in the bloody crew.

'Hang in there, man,' I reassured him, 'we're getting close.'

Meanwhile, I had an idea. Find Rogers and Benjamin . . .

By sticking close to the harbour I found them, and began tailing them, remembering what I'd been taught by Mary. Staying out of sight and using the sense to listen to their conversation.

'Have you alerted the men?' Woodes Rogers was saying, 'We're short on time.'

'Aye,' replied Hornigold, 'there'll be two soldiers waiting for us at the crossroads.'

'Very good.'

Ah, a bodyguard. Now where might they be lurking?

Not wanting to be taken by surprise I glanced around. But by now Hornigold was speaking again. 'If you don't mind me asking, sir. What's the meaning behind these blood samples we're taking?'

'Torres tells me that blood is required for the Observatory to properly function.'

'How do you mean, sir?'

'If one wishes to use the Observatory to, say . . . spy on King George, then one would require a drop of the king's blood to do so. In other words, a small sample of blood gives us access to a man's everyday life.'

Mumbo-jumbo. I paid it little mind at the time, but I'd regret that later.

'Does Torres mean to spy on me, then?' Benjamin was saying. 'For I have just given him a sample of my own blood.'

'As have I, Captain Hornigold. As will all Templars. As a measure of insurance.'

'And trust, I reckon.'

'Yes, but fear not. Torres has shipped our samples to a Templar safe house in Rio de Janeiro. We will not be the Observatory's first subjects, I assure you.'

'Aye, sir. I suppose it's a small price to pay for what the Templars have given me in return.'

'Precisely . . .'

And that is when I met the bodyguards: let's call them brute number one and brute number two.

'And what can we do for you?'

Ah, I thought, so these are the two soldiers you were talking about.

49

Brute number one is left-handed but wants me to think he'll lead with his right. Brute number two is not quite as combat-proficient. Too relaxed. Thinks I'm easily beaten.

'Now where would you be going?' said number one. 'Because my friend and I have been watching you, and you'll have to forgive me for saying, chief, but it looks awfully like you're following Mr Rogers and Mr Hornigold and listening in on their conversation . . . ?'

The Mr Rogers and Mr Hornigold in question were oblivious to the work their guards were doing on their behalf. That was good. What wasn't quite so good was that they were moving off, and I still had much to learn.

So get rid of these guys.

The advantage I had was my hidden blade. It was strapped to my right hand. My sword hung on that side, too, so I would reach for it with my left. An experienced swordsman would expect my attack to come from that side and would defend himself accordingly. Big brute number one, he was an experienced swordsman. I could see by the way he'd planted one foot slightly in front of the other and angled his body side-on (and yet, when the time came, would quickly switch feet, feinting to take me from a different side – I knew that too) and that's because big brute number one was expecting my sword to be drawn with my left hand. Neither knew I had a hidden blade, which would sprout from my right.

So we stared at one another. Mainly me and big brute number one. And then I made my move. Right hand outstretched as though in protection, but then – *engage blade, strike* – and brute number two was still reaching for his own sword when my blade pierced his neck. At the same time I'd snatched my sword from my belt with my left hand and was able to defend big brute number one's first attack, our swords clashing with the force of first impact.

Big brute number two gurgled and died, the blood pumping through fingers he held to his own throat, and now we were on equal footing. I brandished blade and sword at big brute number one and saw that the look he'd worn, a look of confidence – you might even say arrogance – had been replaced by fear.

He should have run. I probably would have caught him, but he should have run anyway. Should have tried to warn his lords and masters that a man was following them. A dangerous man. A man with the skills of an Assassin.

But he didn't run. He stood and stayed to fight, and though he was a man of skill, and he fought with more intelligence and more bravery than I was used to, it was that pride, on the streets of Kingston with a crowd of people looking on, a pride he could not bear to sacrifice that ultimately was his undoing. And when the end came, which it did, but only after a hard-fought battle, I made sure that for him the end was swift, his pain kept to a minimum.

The bystanders shrank back as I made my escape, swallowed up by the docks, hoping to catch Rogers and Hornigold. I made it, arriving at a quayside and crouching beside two drunks at the harbour wall as they met another man. Laureano Torres. They greeted each other with nods of the head. Supremely aware of their own importance. I ducked my head – *groan, had too much rum* – as his gaze swept past where I sat, and then he delivered his news.

'The *Princess* was taken by pirates six weeks ago,' he said. 'And insofar as we know the Sage Roberts was still aboard.'

I cursed to myself. If only the men knew how close they'd been to a short holiday in Kingston. Now, though, we were going to have to hunt pirates.

They started walking and I stood and joined the crowds, following, invisible. Using the sense. Hearing everything they said. 'What of the Sage's present location? Do we know?' asked Torres.

'Africa, Your Excellency,' said Rogers.

'Africa . . . By God, the winds do not favour that route.'

'I concur, Grand Master. I should have sailed there myself. One of my slave galleys would be more than capable of making a swift journey.'

'Slave galley?' said Torres, not happy, 'Captain, I asked you to divest yourself of that sick institution.'

'I fail to see the difference between enslaving some men and all men,' said Rogers. 'Our aim is to steer the entire course of civilization, is it not?'

'A body enslaved inspires the mind to revolt,' said Torres curtly, 'but enslave a man's mind and his body will trot along naturally.'

Rogers conceded. 'A fair point, Grand Master.'

Now they had reached the perimeter of the docks where they stopped at the entrance to a dilapidated warehouse, watching the activities inside the open door. Men seemed to be disposing of bodies, either clearing them from the warehouse or putting them to one side, perhaps for loading on to a cart or ship. Or, what was more likely, tipping them straight into the sea.

Torres asked the question I wanted answered myself. 'What has happened here?'

Rogers smiled thinly. 'These were men who resisted our generous requests for blood. Pirates and privateers mostly.'

Torres nodded. 'I see.'

I tightened at the thought, looked at the bodies, crooked arms and crooked legs, unseeing eyes. Men no different to me.

'I have been using my king's pardon as an excuse to collect samples from as many men as possible,' said Rogers. 'And when they refuse, I hang them. All within the boundaries of my mandate, of course.'

'Good. For if we cannot keep watch on all the world scoundrels, then the seas should be rid of them entirely.'

Now they moved on, heading towards the gangplank of a ship moored nearby. I followed, darting behind a stack of crates to listen.

'Remind me,' said Torres, 'where in Africa are we looking?'

'Príncipé, sir. A small island,' said Hornigold.

Torres and Rogers strode up the gangplank but Hornigold hung back. Why? Why was he hanging back? And now I saw. With squinted eyes, the practised look of a seafarer, he scanned the horizon and studied the ships anchored like sentinels in the glittering ocean, and his eyes alighted on one ship in particular. And then with a lurch of shock, I realized where we were – and where we were was within sight of the *Jackdaw*.

Hornigold tensed, his hand went to the hilt of his sword and he turned round slowly. He was looking for me, I knew, guessing that wherever the *Jackdaw* was, I wouldn't be far away.

'Edward Kenway,' he called out, as his gaze passed around the docks. 'Imagine my surprise at seeing your *Jackdaw* anchored here. Have you heard all you came to hear? Will you now go and rescue the poor Sage from our clutching hands?'

In retrospect it was a bit rash, what I did next. But I was unable to think of anything but the fact that Benjamin had been one of us. One of my mentors. A friend of Edward Thatch. And now he worked to try to destroy us. All of that bubbled to the surface in a rage as I emerged from behind the crates to face him.

'A pox on you traitor. You sold us down the river!'

'Because I found a better path,' said Hornigold. Instead of drawing his weapon he signalled with his hand. From the warehouse behind I heard the sound of swords being drawn.

Hornigold continued. 'The Templars know order, discipline, structure. But you never could fathom these subtleties. Goodbye old friend! You were a soldier once! When you fought for something real. Something beyond yourself!'

He left, almost breaking into a run. From the warehouse came his reinforcements and the men closed in behind him, forming a crescent around me.

Taking them by surprise I started quickly forward, grabbed a sailor who waved his sword to no particular effect and span him, using him as a shield and pushing him forward so that his boots skidded on the harbour stone.

At the same time there was the crack of a pistol and my human shield took a musket ball that was meant for me before I shoved him into the line of men and with my left hand snatched out my first pistol. I shot a heavy in the mouth, holstered it and snatched my second at the same time as I engaged the blade and sliced open a third man's chest. Discharged the pistol. A wayward shot it nevertheless did the job and stopped a man bearing a cutlass and sent him falling to the ground with his hands at his stomach.

I crouched and whirled, taking the legs from beneath the next man, finished him with a quick and ruthless blade-punch to the chest. Then I was on my feet, scattering the last two men, their faces portraits in terror, not wishing to join their comrades dead or bleeding on the harbour floor, and ran for my rowing boat and to get back to the *Jackdaw*.

And as I worked the oars to where my ship was moored I could imagine the conversation with my quartermaster; how he'd remind me that the men didn't approve of my quest.

They'd approve, though, once we found the Observatory. Once we found the Sage.

And it took me a month, but I did.

50

July, 1719

I found him on Principé, one afternoon, in a camp full of corpses.

Now, here's what learnt about the Sage, Bartholomew Roberts, some of which was later told to me by him, some by others.

Firstly, we had something in common: we were both Welsh, me from Swansea, him from Casnewydd Bach, and that he had changed his name from John to Bartholomew. That he had gone to sea when he was just thirteen, as a carpenter, before finding himself an object of interest for this secret society known as the Templars.

At the beginning of 1719, with the Templars *and* the Assassins on his tail, the Sage had found himself serving as a third mate on the *Princess*, just as I'd been told, under Captain Abraham Plumb.

As I'd learnt in Kingston, in early June the *Princess* had been attacked by pirates in *The Royal Rover* and *The Royal James*, led by captain Howell Davis. Somehow, Roberts, wily operator that he was, had inveigled himself in with Captain Howell Davis. He'd convinced the pirate captain, also a Welshman, as it happens, that he was a superb navigator, which he may well have been, but he was also able to talk to Captain Davis in Welsh, which created a further bond between the two men.

It was said that Bart Roberts was not keen on becoming a pirate at first. But as you'll see, he took to his new job like a duck to water.

And then they landed on Principé. The *Royal Rover*, this was, what with the *Royal James* having to be abandoned with worm damage. So, the *Royal Rover* headed for Principé, and by hoisting British colours, was allowed to dock, where the crew played the part of visiting English sailors.

Now, according to what I heard, Captain Davis came up with a plan. His plan was to invite the governor of Principé on board the *Rover* on the pretext of giving him lunch, and then as soon as he was aboard take him hostage and demand a huge ransom for his release.

Perfect. Couldn't fail.

But when Davis took men to meet the governor, they were ambushed at a camp along the way.

Which was where I came in.

I crept into the camp, into the deserted scene of the ambush, where the fire had burned down to red embers, one man actually lying in the dying embers, his corpse slowly cooking. Scattered around were more bodies. Some were soldiers, some were pirates.

'Captain Kenway?' came a voice and I span round to see him there: the Sage. Perhaps I would have been pleased to see him; perhaps I would have thought my journey was at an end. If he hadn't been pointing a gun at me.

At the insistence of his gun barrel I put my hands in the air.

'Another dire situation, Roberts. We must stop meeting like this.'

He smiled grimly. Does he bear me any ill will? I wondered. He had no idea of my plans, after all. A crazy part of me realized that I wouldn't have been surprised if he could read minds.

'Stop tailing me and your wish would come true,' he said.

'There's no need for this. You know I'm as good as my word.'

Around us the jungle was silent. Bartholomew Roberts seemed to be thinking. It was odd, I mused. Neither of us really had the measure of the other. Neither of us really knew what the other one wanted. I knew what I wanted from him, of course. But what about him? What did he want? I sensed that whatever it was, it would be more dark and more mysterious than I could possibly imagine. All I knew for sure was that death followed Bart Roberts and I wasn't ready to die. Not yet.

He spoke. 'Our Captain Howell was killed today in a Portuguese ambush. Headstrong fool. I warned him not to come ashore.'

It was to the recently deceased captain that

Bartholomew Roberts went now. Evidently deciding I was not a threat as he holstered his pistol.

And of course. The attack. I thought I knew who was behind it.

'It was orchestrated by the Templars,' I told him. 'The same sort who took you to Havana.'

His long hair shook as he nodded, seeming to think at the same time. 'I see now there is no escaping the Templars' attention, is there? I suppose it is time to fight back?'

Now you're talking, I thought.

As we'd been speaking I'd watched him peel off his sailor's rags and pull on first the breeches of the dead captain and then the shirt. The shirt was bloodstained so he discarded it, put his own back on, then hunched his shoulders into the captain's coat. He pulled the tie from his hair and shook it free. He popped the captain's tricorne on his head and its feather wafted as he turned to face me. This was a different Bartholomew Roberts. His time aboard ship had put health back in his cheeks. His dark, curly locks shone in the sun and he stood resplendent in a red jacket and breeches, white stockings, with a hat to match. He looked every inch the buccaneer. He looked every inch the pirate captain.

'Now,' he said, 'we must go before Portuguese reinforcements arrive. We must get back to the *Rover*. I have an announcement to make there, that I'd like you to witness.'

I thought I knew what it was, and I was surprised in

one way – he was but a lowly deckhand, after all – but unsurprised also, because this was Roberts. The Sage. And the tricks up his sleeve were never-ending. (Watch yourself, Kenway. He's dangerous.) And sure enough when we arrived at the *Rover*, where the men waited nervously for news of the expedition, he leapt up to a crate to command their attention. They goggled at him up there: the lowly deckhand, a new arrival on board to boot, now resplendent in the captain's clothes.

'In honest service there are thin commons, low wages, and hard labour. Yet as gentlemen of fortune we enjoy plenty and satisfaction, pleasure and ease, liberty and power . . . so what man with a sensible mind would choose the former life, when the only hazard we pirates run is a sour look from those without strength or splendour.

'Now, I have been among you six weeks, and in that time have adopted your outlook as my own, and with so fierce a conviction, that it may frighten you to see your passions reflected from me in so stark a light. But . . . if it's a captain you see in me now, aye then . . . I'll be your bloody captain!'

You had to hand it to him, it was a rousing speech. In a few short sentences proclaiming his kinship, he had these men eating out of the palm of his hand. As the meeting broke up I approached, deciding now was the time to make my play.

'I'm looking for the Observatory,' I told him. 'Folks say you're the only man that can find it.'

'Folks are correct.'

He looked me up and down as if to confirm his impressions. 'Despite my distaste for your eagerness, I see in you a touch of untested genius.' He held out his hand to shake. 'I'm Bartholomew Roberts.'

'Edward.'

'I've no secrets to share with you now,' he told me.

I stared at him, unable to believe what I was hearing. He was going to make me wait.

51

September, 1719

Damn the man. Damn Roberts.

He wanted me to wait two months. *Two whole months.*
Then meet him west of the Leeward islands, east of
Puerto Rico. With only his word to take for that, I sailed
the *Jackdaw* back to San Inagua. There I rested the crew
for a while, and we took prizes when we could, and my
coffers swelled, and it was during that period, I think,
that I cut off the nose of the ship's cook.

And when we weren't taking prizes and when I
wasn't slicing off noses, I brooded at my homestead. I
wrote letters to Caroline in which I assured her I would
soon be returning as a man of wealth, and I fretted
over the Observatory, only too aware that with it lay all
my hopes of a fortune. And it was built on nothing
more than a promise from Bartholomew Roberts.

And then what? To my one-track mind, the Observatory was a place of enormous potential wealth. But
even if I found it – even if Bart Roberts came good on
his word – it remained a source of *potential* wealth.
Wasn't it Edward who had scoffed at the very idea? Gold
doubloons was what we wanted, he'd said. Perhaps he

was right. Even if I found this amazing machine, how the bloody hell was I going to convert it into the wealth I hoped to acquire? After all, if there were riches to be made, then why hadn't Roberts made them?

Because he has some other purpose.

And I thought of my parents. My mind went back to the burning of our farmhouse and I thought anew of striking a blow at the Templars, this secret society who used their influence and power to grind down anyone who displeased them; to exercise a grudge. I still had no idea exactly who was behind the burning of my farmhouse. Or why. Was it a grudge against me for marrying Caroline and humiliating Matthew Hague? Or against my father, mere business rivalry? Probably both, was my suspicion. Perhaps the Kenways, these arrivals from Wales, who had shamed them so, simply deserved to be taken down a peg or two.

I would find out for sure, I decided. I would return to Bristol one day, and exact my revenge.

And on that I brooded, too. Until the day came in September when I gathered the crew and we readied the *Jackdaw*, newly caulked, its masts and rigging repaired, its shrouds ready, its galley stocked and the munitions at capacity, and we set sail for our appointment with Bartholomew Roberts.

As I say, I don't think I ever truly knew what was on his mind. He had his own agenda, and wasn't about to share it with me. What he did like to do, however, was keep me guessing. Keep me hanging on. When we'd parted he'd told me he had business to attend to, which I later found out involved taking his own crew back to Principé and exacting his revenge for the death of Captain Howell Davis on the people of the island.

They'd attacked at night, put to the sword as many men as they could, and made off, not only with as much treasure as they could carry but the beginnings of Black Bart's fearsome reputation: unknowable, brave and ruthless, and apt to carry off daring raids. The one we were about to carry out, for example. The one that began with Roberts insisting the *Jackdaw* join him on a jaunt around the coast of Brazil to the Todos os Santos Bay.

We didn't have long to find out the reason why. A fleet of no fewer than forty-two Portuguese merchant ships. What's more with no navy escorts. Roberts lost no time in capturing one of the outlying vessels to 'hold talks' with the captain. It wasn't something I got involved with, but from the bruised Portuguese naval officer he'd learnt that the flagship had on it a chest, a coffer that, he told me, contained 'crystal vials filled with blood. You may remember.'

Vials of blood. How could I forget?

We anchored the *Jackdaw* and I took Adewalé and a skeleton crew to join Roberts on his purloined Portuguese vessel. Up to now we'd remained at the fringes of the fleet, but now it seemed to split up, and we saw our chance. The flagship was testing her guns.

Anchored some distance away we watched, and Bartholomew looked at me.

'Are you stealthy, Edward Kenway?'

'That I am,' I said.

He looked over to the Portuguese galleon. It was anchored not far away from land with most of the crew on the gun deck firing inland, carrying out exercises. Never was there a better time to steal aboard, so at a nod from Bart Roberts I dived overboard and swam to the galleon, on a mission of death.

Shinning up a Jacob's ladder I found myself on deck, where I moved quietly along the planks to the first man, engaged my blade, swept it quickly across his throat then helped him to the deck and held my hand over his mouth while he died.

All the time I kept my eyes on the lookouts and crow's-nest above.

I disposed of a second sentry the same way then began scaling the rigging to the crow's-nest. There a lookout scanned the horizon, his spyglass moving from left to right, past Roberts's ship and then back again.

He focused on Roberts's vessel, his gaze lingered on it, and I wondered if his suspicions were churning. Perhaps so. Perhaps he was wondering why the men on board didn't *look* like Portuguese merchants. He seemed to decide. He lowered the spyglass and I could see his chest inflate as though he were about to call out, just as I sprang into the lookout position, grabbed his arm and slid my blade into his armpit.

I swept my other arm across his neck to silence any cries as blood gushed from beneath his arm and he breathed his last as I let him fold to the well of the crow's-nest.

Now Bart's ship came alongside, and as I descended the ratlines the two ships bumped and his men began pouring over the sides.

A hatch in the quarterdeck opened and the Portuguese appeared, but they stood no chance. Their throats were cut, their bodies thrown overboard. And in a matter of a few bloody moments the galleon was controlled by Bart Roberts's men. Fat lot of good their gun training had done.

Everything that could be pillaged was pillaged. A deckhand who dragged the coffer on deck and grinned at his captain, hoping for some words of praise got none, Roberts ignoring him and indicating for the chest to be loaded on his stolen ship.

Then, suddenly, came a shout from the lookouts, 'Sail ho!' and in the next instant we were piling back to the stolen ship, some of the slow men even falling to the sea as Roberts's ship pulled away from the flagship and we set sail, two Portuguese naval warships bearing down upon us.

There was the pop of muskets but they were too far away to do any damage. Thank God we were in a stolen Portuguese ship; they had no desire to fire their carriage guns at us. Not yet. Probably they hadn't worked it out yet. Probably they were still wondering what the bloody hell was going on.

We came around the bay, sails pregnant with wind, men dashing below decks to man the guns. Ahead of us was anchored the *Jackdaw*, and I prayed that Adewalé had ordered lookouts. I thanked God my quartermaster was an Adewalé and not a Calico Jack, and so would have made sure the lookouts were posted. And I prayed that those lookouts would at this very moment be relaying the news that Roberts's vessel was speeding towards them with the Portuguese navy in pursuit and that they would be manning their positions and weighing anchor.

They were.

Even though we were being pursued I still had time to admire what to my eyes is one of the most beautiful sights of the sea. The *Jackdaw*, men on its rigging, its sails unfurling gracefully, being secured, then blooming with a noise I could hear even from my vantage point far away.

Still, our speed meant we caught them smartly, just as the *Jackdaw* was gaining speed herself, and after exchanging quick words with Roberts I stood on the poop deck and my mind returned to the sight of Duncan Walpole, he who had begun this whole journey, as I leapt from the poop of Roberts's ship back on to the *Jackdaw*.

'Ah, there's nothing like the hot winds of hell blowing in your face!' I heard Roberts cry as I crouched and watched as our two vessels peeled apart. I gave orders to man the stern guns below. The Portuguese reluctance to open fire was over, but their hesitancy had cost them dear, for it was the *Jackdaw* who took first blood.

I heard our stern guns boom then spin back across the deck below. I saw hot metal speed over the face of the ocean and slam into the leading ship, saw splinters fly from jagged holes in the bow and along the hull, men and bits of men joining the debris already littering the sea. The bow gained wings of foam as it dipped and I could imagine the scene below decks, men at the pumps, but the vessel already shipping too much water and soon . . .

She turned in the water, listing, her sails flattening. A cheer went up from my men but from around her came the second ship, and that was when Bartholomew Roberts decided to test his own guns.

His shot found its mark, just as mine had, and once more we were treated to the sight of the Portuguese vessel ploughing on, even as the bowstring dipped and the bows sunk, her hull looking as though they had been the victim of a giant shark attack.

Soon both ships were seriously floundering, the second one more badly damaged than the first and boats were being launched, men were jumping over the side and the Portuguese navy had, for the time being at least, forgotten about us.

We sailed, celebrating for some hours until Roberts commanded both vessels drop anchor and I stood alert on the quarterdeck wondering, What now?

I'd primed my pistols and my blade was at the ready, and via Adewalé I'd told the crew that if there were any signs of a double-cross they were to fight to save themselves, don't surrender to Roberts, no matter what. I'd seen how he treated those he considered his enemy. I'd seen how he treated his prisoners.

Now, though, he called me across, having his men on the rack lines swing me a line so that first I, then Adewalé could cross to his ship. I stood on the deck and faced him, a tension in the air so thick you could almost taste it, because if Roberts did plan to betray us, then now was the time. My hand flexed at my blade mechanism.

Roberts, though, whatever he was planning, and it was safe to say that he was planning *something*, it wasn't for now. At a word from him, two of his crewmates came forward with the chest we had liberated from the Portuguese flagship.

'Here's my prize,' said Roberts, with his eyes on me. It was a coffer full of blood. That was what he had promised. Hardly the grand prize I was after. But we would see. We would see.

The two hands set down the chest and opened it. As the crew gathered round to watch us. I was reminded of the day I had fought Blaney on the deck of Edward Thatch's galleon. They did the same now. They clambered on the mast and in the rigging and stood on the gunwales in order to get a better look as their captain reached into the chest, picked out one of the vials and examined it in the light.

A murmur of disappointment ran around those watching. No gold for you, lads. No silver pieces of eight. Sorry. Just vials that probably to the untrained eye might have been wine but that I knew were blood.

Oblivious to his crew's disappointment and no doubt uncaring of it anyway, Roberts was examining the vials, one by one.

'Ah, the Templars have been busy I see . . .' he replaced a vial with nimble fingers that danced over the glittering crystals as he picked out another one, held it up to the light and examined it. Around us the men, disconsolate with the turn of events, descended the ratlines, jumped down from the gunwales and returned to their business.

Roberts squinted as he held up yet another crystal.

'Laurens Prins's blood,' he said, then tossed it to me. 'Useless now.'

I stared carefully at it as Robert cycled quickly through the contents of the coffer, calling out names, 'Woodes Rogers. Ben Hornigold. Even Torres himself. Small quantities, kept for a special purpose.'

Something to do with the Observatory. But what? The time for taunting me with promises was over. I felt anger beginning to rise. Most of his men had gone back to work, the quartermaster and first mate stood nearby, but I had Adewalé. Maybe, just maybe, it was time to show Bartholomew Roberts how serious I was. Maybe it was time to show him that I was sick and tired of being messed around. Maybe it was time to use my blade to *insist* he told me what I wanted.

'You must take me to the Observatory, Roberts,' I said firmly, 'I need to know what it is.'

Roberts twinkled. 'To what end, hey? Will you sell it from under my nose? Or work with me and use it to bolster our gains?'

'Whatever improves my lot in life,' I said guardedly.

He closed the chest with a snap and placed both hands on the curved lid. 'How ridiculous. A merry life and a short life that's my motto. It's all the optimism I can muster.'

He seemed to consider. I held my breath. Again that thought, *What now?* And then he looked at me and the mischievous look in his eyes had departed, in its place a blank stare. 'All right, Captain Kenway. You've earned a look.'

I smiled.

At last.

52

'Can you feel it, Adewalé,' I said to him, as we followed the *Rover* around the coast of Brazil. 'We're moments away from the grandest prize of all.'

'I feel nothing but hot wind in my ears, captain,' he said enigmatically, face in the wind, sipping at the breeze.

I looked at him. Once again I felt almost overpowered with admiration for him. Here was a man who had probably saved my life on hundreds of occasions and definitely saved my life on at least three. Here was the most loyal, committed and talented quartermaster a captain could ever have; who had escaped slavery yet still had to deal with the jibes of common mutineers like Calico Jack, who thought themselves above him because of his colour. Here was a man who had overcome all the bilge life had thrown at him, and it was a lot of bilge, the kind that only a man sold as a slave will ever know. A man who stood by my side on the *Jackdaw* day after day and demanded no great prizes, no rich-making haul, demanded little but the respect he deserved, enough of the shares to live on, a place to rest his head, and a meal made by a cook without a nose.

And how had I repaid this man?

By going on and on and on about the Observatory. And still going on about it.

'Come on, man. When we take this treasure, we'll be set for life. All of us. Ten times over.'

He nodded. 'As you wish.'

By now the *Jackdaw* was not far from the *Rover* and I looked across the deck to see their captain, just as he looked over to see me.

'Ahoy Roberts!' I called. 'We'll cast anchor and meet ashore.'

'You were followed, Captain Kenway. How long for? I wonder.'

I snatched the spyglass from Adewalé and scuttled up the ratlines, shouldering aside the lookout in the crow's-nest and putting the spyglass to my eye.

'What do you think that is, lad?' I snarled at the lookout.

He was young – as young as I was when I first joined the crew of the *Emperor*. 'It's a ship, sir, but there are plenty of vessels in these waters, and I didn't think it close enough to raise the alarm.'

I snapped the glass shut and glared at him. 'You didn't think at all, did you? That ship out there isn't any other ship, son, it's the *Benjamin*.'

The lad paled.

'Aye, that's right, the *Benjamin*. Captained by one Benjamin Hornigold. If they've not caught up with us, then it's because they haven't wanted to catch up with us.'

I began to make my way down the ratlines.

'Call it then, lad,' I shouted up to the lookout. 'Sound the alarm, late as it is.'

'Sail ho!

The Cuban coastline was to our starboard, the *Benjamin* behind us. But now I was at the tiller, and I hauled her over, the rudder complaining as she turned, the men reaching for a handhold as our masts swung, our port side dipped and we began to come around, until the manoeuvre was complete and the men were bitching and moaning as the oars were deployed, the sails reefed and we began a trudge aimed at meeting the *Benjamin* head on. *You won't be expecting that, will you, Benjamins?*

'Captain, think carefully about what you mean to do here,' said Adewalé.

'What are you grousing about, Adewalé? It's Ben Hornigold come to kill us out there.'

'Aye, and that traitor needs to die. But what then? Can you say with certainty that you deserve the Observatory more than he and his Templars?'

'No, I can't. And I don't care to try. But if you've a better idea, by all means tell me.'

'Forget working with Roberts,' he said with a sudden surge of passion, something I'd rarely seen from him, such a cool head usually. 'Tell the Assassins. Bring them here, and let them protect the Observatory.'

'Aye, I'll bring them here. If they're willing to pay me a good sum for it, I will.'

He made a disgusted noise and walked away.

Ahead of us the *Benjamin* had turned – Hornigold with no stomach for a fight, it seemed – and we saw the men in her masts securing the sails. Oars appeared and were soon spanking the water, our two ships in a rowing race now. For long moments all I could hear was the shout of the coxswain, the creak of the ship, the splash of the sweepers in the water, as I stood at the bow of the *Jackdaw* and Hornigold stood at the stern of the *Benjamin*, and we stared at one another.

As we raced, the sun dipped below the horizon, flickering orange, the last of its light as night fell and brought with it a wind from the north west that dragged fog inland. The *Benjamin* anticipated the wind with more success than we did. The first we knew of it was seeing her sails unfurl, and she put distance between them and us.

Some fifteen minutes later, it was dark and fog billowed in towards that part of the Cuban coastline they call the Devil's Backbone, crags that look like the spine of a giant behemoth, a moon giving the mist a ghostly glow.

'We'll have a hard fight if Hornigold draws us any deeper into this fog,' warned Adewalé.

That was Hornigold's plan, though, but he'd made a mistake, and a big mistake for such an experienced sailor. He found himself being hustled by the wind. It rushed in from the open sea, it charged at cross-purposes along the coast, turning the sandbanks of the

Devil's Backbone into a haze of impenetrable layers of fog and sand.

'The winds are tossing them about like a toy,' said Adewalé.

I pulled up the cowl of my robes against the chill wind which had just begun to assault us as we came within its range.

'We can use that to get close.'

He looked at me. 'If we are not dashed to pieces as well.'

Now the sails were rolled up again, but on the *Benjamin* they weren't so quick. They were being buffeted by the wind. I saw men trying to reef the sails but finding it tough in the conditions. One fell, his scream carried to us by the gusts.

The *Benjamin* was in trouble. It bobbled on an increasingly choppy sea, buffeted by the wind that snatched at its sails, turning it first one way then another. It veered close towards the banks of the Backbone. Men scurried about the decks. Another was blown off board. They'd lost control. At the mercy of the elements now.

I stood on the forecastle deck, one hand braced and the other held out, feeling the wind on my palm. I felt the pressure of the hidden blade on my forearm and knew it would taste the blood of Hornigold before the night was old.

'Can you do this, breddah? Is your heart up for it?'

Benjamin Hornigold, who had taught me so much about the ways of the sea. Benjamin Hornigold, the man who had established, who had mentored my greatest friend Edward Thatch, who in turn had mentored me. Actually, I didn't know if I could.

'Truth be told, I was hoping the sea would swallow him up, and see the job done for me,' I told him. 'But I'll do what I must.'

My quartermaster. God bless my quartermaster. He knew the fate of the *Benjamin* before even the Fates knew of the fate of the *Benjamin*. And as it crashed sidelong into a high bankside, seemingly wrenched from the sea by a gust of wind and spirited into a cloud of sand and fog, he saw to it that we drew alongside.

We saw the shapes of crewmen tumbling from her top decks, figures indistinct in the murk. I stepped up to the gunwale of the forecastle deck braced with one hand on the bow strip then used the sense, just as James Kidd had shown me. And among those falling bodies of men who slipped from the deck of the ship on to the boggy sandbanks and into the water, I was able to make out the form of Benjamin Hornigold. Over my shoulder I said, 'I'll be coming back.'

And then I jumped.

53

The snap of muskets from the *Jackdaw* began behind me as a one-sided battle between my ship and the crew of the now-beached *Benjamin*. My senses had returned to normal, but Hornigold was doing me a favour, shouting encouragement and curses to his men.

'Some mighty piss-poor sailing back there, lads. And if we live out this day, by God, I'm flaying every last bitch of you. Hold your ground and be ready for anything.'

And then I appeared from the mist on the bank nearby, and rather than heed his own words he took to his heels, scrambling along to the top of the incline and then across it.

My men had started to use mortars on the fleeing crew of the *Benjamin*, though, and I found myself placed in danger as they began raining on to the sand around me. Until one exploded near Benjamin and the next thing I knew he was disappearing out of sight over the other side of the sandbank in a spray of blood and sand.

I scrambled over the top made hasty by my desire to see his fate, and paid for it with a sword swipe across my arm, opening a cut that bled. In a single movement I span, engaged the blade and met his next attack, our steel sparking as it met. The force of his attack was enough to send me tumbling down the bank and he came after me, launching himself from the slope with his cutlass swinging. I caught him on my boots and kicked him away, his sword point parting the air before my nose. Rolling I pulled myself to my feet and scrambled after him, and again our blades met. For some moments we traded blows, and he was good, but he was hurt and I was the younger man, and I was lit by vengeful fire and so, I cut his arm, his elbow, his shoulder – until he could hardly stand or raise his sword and I finished him.

'You could have been a man who stood for something true,' he said as he died. His lips worked over the words carefully. His teeth were bloodstained. 'But you've a killer's heart now.'

'Well, it's a damn sight better than what you have, Ben,' I told him. 'The heart of a traitor, who thinks himself better than his mates.'

'Aye, and proven true. What have you done since Nassau fell? Nothing but murder and mayhem.'

I lost my temper, rounded on him. 'You threw in with the very kind we once hated!' I shouted.

'No,' he said. He reached to grab at me and make his point, but I angrily batted his hands away. 'These Templars are different. I wish you could see that. But if you continue on your present course, you'll find you're the only one left walking it. With the gallows at the end.'

'That may be,' I said, 'but now the world has one less snake in it. And that's enough for me.'

But he didn't hear me. He was already dead.

54

'Is the pirate hunter dead?' said Bartholomew Roberts.

I looked at him, Bartholomew Roberts, this unknowable character, a Sage, a carpenter who had turned to a life of piracy. Was this the first time he'd visited the Observatory? Why did he need me here? So many questions – questions to which I knew I would never be given answers.

We were at Long Bay, on the northern shores of Jamaica. He had been loading his pistols as I arrived. Then he asked his question to which I replied, 'Aye, by my own hand.'

He nodded and went back to cleaning his pistols. I looked at him and found a sudden rage gripped me. 'Why is it you alone can find what so many want?'

He chuckled. 'I was born with memories of this place. Memories of another time entirely, I think. Like . . . Like another life I have already led.'

I shook my head, and wondered whether I would ever be free of this mumbo-jumbo.

'Curse you for a lurch, man, and speak some sense.'

'Not today.'

Nor any other day, I thought angrily, but before I could find a reply there came a noise from the jungle.

Natives? Perhaps they had been disturbed by the battle between the *Jackdaw* and the *Benjamin*. Remained of Hornigold's crew was being herded aboard the *Jackdaw* and I had left my men to it. *Deal with the prisoners and await my return shortly*. I had embarked on this meeting with Bartholomew Roberts alone.

He gestured to me. 'After you, captain. The path ahead is dangerous.'

With around a dozen of his men we began to move through the jungle, beating a path through the undergrowth as we began to head upwards. I wondered whether I should be able to see it by now, this Observatory? Weren't they great constructs, built on high peaks? All around the hillsides greenery waved at us. Bushes and palm trees. Nothing as far as the eye can see, unless you counted our ships in the bay.

We had been going only a few hundred yards when we heard a sound from the undergrowth and something streaked from the bushes to one side of us and one of Roberts's men fell with a glistening, gore-filled hole where the back of his head had been. I know a club strike when I see one. But it was gone as quickly as it had come.

A tremor of fear ran through the crew who drew their swords, pulled muskets from their backs and snatched pistols from their belts. Crouched. Ready.

'The men native to this land will put up a fight, Edward,' said Roberts quietly, eyes scanning the undergrowth, which was silent, keeping its secrets.

'You willing to push back if necessary? To kill, if needed?'

I engaged my hidden blade.

'You'll hear from me soon.'

And then I crouched, rolled sideways into the jungle and became a part of it.

55

The natives, they knew their land well, but I was doing something they simply would not expect, I was taking the fight to them. And so, the first man I came across was surprised to see me, and that surprise was his undoing. He wore nothing but a breech cloth, his black hair tied up on his head, a club still gleaming with the blood of a buccaneer upon it, and eyes wide with shock. The natives were only protecting what was theirs. It gave me no pleasure to slide my blade between his ribs and I hoped his end was quick, but I did it anyway, and then moved on. The jungle began to resound to the noise of screams and gunshots, but I found more natives and dealt more death until at last the battle was over and I returned to the main party.

Eight had been killed in the battle. Most of the natives had fallen under my blade.

'The guardians of the Observatory,' Bartholomew Roberts told me.

'How long have their kind being here?' I asked him.

'Oh . . . At least a thousand years or more. Very dedicated men. Very deadly.'

I looked around at what remained of his group, his

terrified, traumatized men, who had watched their shipmates picked off one by one. Then we continued our journey, climbing still, going up and up until we came upon it, grey stone walls a dark contrast with the vibrant jungle colours, a monolithic building rising way, way above us.

The Observatory.

How had it not been seen? I wondered. How had it remained invisible?

'This is it, then?'

'Aye, an almost sacred place. All it needs is a drop of my blood . . .'

In his hand appeared a small dagger and he never took his eyes from mine as he used it to prick his thumb then placed the red-beaded finger into a tiny recess by the side of the door. It began to open.

All six of us looked at one another. Only Bart Roberts seemed to be enjoying himself.

'And the door opens,' he said with the voice of a showman, 'after almost eighty thousand years.'

He stepped to one side and ushered his men through. The nervous crew members looked at one another then did as their captain ordered and began to move towards the door . . .

And then, for some reason known only to himself, Roberts killed them, all four of them. With one hand he buried his dagger into the eye socket of the leading man, pushing his body aside at the same time as he drew his pistol and fired into the face of the second man.

The last two crew members had no time to react as Black Bart drew his second pistol and fired point-blank into the chest of a third man, pulled his sword and ran the final survivor through.

It was the same man who had brought the chest on deck, who'd looked to Roberts for some words of praise. He made an odd, choking sound and Roberts held him there a second then slid the cutlass home to the hilt and twisted it. The body on his blade went taut and the deckhand looked at his captain with imploring, uncomprehending eyes until his body relaxed, slid off the steel and thumped to the ground, chest rising once, twice, then staying still.

So much death. *So much death.*

'Jesus, Roberts, have you gone mad?'

He shook blood from his cutlass then fussily cleaned it with a handkerchief.

'Quite the contrary, Edward. These wags would have gone mad at seeing what lies beyond this gate. But you, I suspect, are made of sterner stuff. Now pick up that chest and carry it hither.'

I did as he asked. Knowing that to follow Roberts was a bad idea. *A terrible bloody idea.* But unable to prevent myself doing it. I'd come too far to back out now.

Inside it was like an ancient temple. 'Dirty and decrepit,' said Roberts, 'not quite as I remember. But it has been over eighty millennia.'

I shot him a glare. *More mumbo-jumbo.* 'Oh rot, that's impossible.'

His look in return was unknowable. 'Step as if on thin ice, captain.'

On stone steps we descended through the centre of the Observatory, moving into a large bridge chamber. All my senses were alive as I looked around and took in the vast openness of the space.

'Beautiful, isn't it?' said Roberts in a hushed voice.

'Aye,' I replied and found I was whispering, 'like something out of a fairy tale, one of them old poems.'

'There were many stories about this place once. Tales that turned into rumours, and again into legend. The inevitable process of facts becoming fictions, before fading away entirely.'

And now we entered a new room altogether, what could only be described as an archive, a huge space lined with low shelves on which were stacked hundreds of small vials of blood, just like the ones in the coffer – just like the one I had seen Torres use on Bartholomew Roberts.

'More blood vials.'

'Yes. These cubes contain the blood of an old and ancient people. A wonderful race, in their time.'

'The more you talk, man, the less I understand,' I said irritably.

'Only remember this; the blood in these vials is not worth a single reale to anyone any more. It may be again, one day. But not in this epoch.'

We were deep within the bowels of the earth now, and walked through the archives into what was the main theatre of the Observatory. Again it was astounding and we stood for a second, craning our necks to gaze from one side of the vast domed chamber to the other.

At one side of the chamber was what looked like a pit, with just a sloshing sound from far below to indicate water somewhere, while in the middle was a raised dais with what looked a complicated pattern carved into the stone. As Roberts bid me place the chest down a low noise began. A low, humming sound that was intriguing at first but began to build . . .

'What's that?' I felt as though I was having to shout to make myself heard, although I wasn't.

'Ah yes,' said Roberts, 'a security measure. Just a moment.'

Around us the walls had begun to glow, letting off a pulsing white light that was as beautiful as it was unsettling. The Sage walked across the floor to the raised platform in the middle and put his hand to a carved indent in the centre. Straight away the sound receded and the room around us was silent again, though the walls still glowed.

'So what is this place?' I said to Roberts.

'Think of it as like a large spyglass. A device capable of seeing great distances.'

The glow. The blood. This 'device'. My head was beginning to spin, and all I could do was stand and watch openmouthed as Roberts reached into the coffer with practised fingers, as though it what this was something he'd done dozens of times before, and then pulled out a vial and held it up to the light, just as he had on the day we took possession of the chest.

Satisfied, he bent to the raised dais in front of him and placed the crystal inside. And then, something happened – something I still can't quite believe – the glow on the walls seemed to ripple like mist, coalescing, not into fog but into images, a series of opaque pictures, as though I was looking through a window at something, at . . .

56

Calico Jack Rackham, as I live and breathe.

But I wasn't looking *at* him. No. It was as though I *was* him. As though I was looking through his eyes. In fact, the only reason I knew it was Calico Jack was the Indian fabric of his coat sleeve.

He was walking up the steps towards the Old Avery. My heart leapt to see the old place, even more careworn and dilapidated than ever before . . .

Which meant that this wasn't an image from the past. It wasn't an image I had ever experienced myself, because I'd never seen the Old Avery in its current state of disrepair. Hadn't visited Nassau since the true rot set in.

And yet . . . And yet . . . I *was* seeing it.

'*This is bloody witchcraft*,' I spluttered.

'No. This is Calico Jack Rackham . . . Somewhere in the world at this moment.'

'Nassau,' I said as much to him as to myself. 'This is happening right now? We're seeing through his eyes?'

'Aye,' said Roberts.

It wasn't as though I returned my attention to the image. It was simply there in front of me. As if I was part of it, inside it. Which in a way I was, because when

Calico Jack turned his head the image moved with him. I watched as he looked towards a table where Anne Bonny sat with James Kidd.

A long, lingering glance over Anne Bonny. Over certain *parts* of Anne Bonny. The dirty bastard. But then, oh my God, she looked over from the table where she sat with James Kidd and returned his look. And I mean a proper lascivious look. That roving eye I told you about? She was giving old Calico Jack the full benefit.

Bloody hell. They're having an affair.

Despite everything – despite the wonders of the Observatory – I found myself suppressing a chuckle to think of James Bonny, that treacherous turncoat, wearing the horns. Calico Jack? Well, the poxy git had marooned me, hadn't he? So there was no love lost there. But he did give us our weapons, ammunition and grub, and, well, he did have Anne warming his bed, so you had to hand it to him.

Now Calico Jack was listening to Anne and James chatting.

'I don't know, Jim,' Anne was saying. 'I haven't the faintest idea how to pilot a ship. That ain't work a woman does.'

What on earth were they cooking up?

'Tosh. I've seen a score of ladies who can reef a sail and spin a capstan.'

'And would you teach me to fight? With a cutlass, like? And maybe how to handle a pistol?'

'All that and more. But you have to want it. And work for it. There's no stumbling into true success.'

And now Calico Jack confirmed what I thought. His disembodied voice seemed to echo off the stone. 'Oi, lad, that's my lass yer making love to. Lay off or I'll cut ya.'

'Up your arse, Rackham. "Lad" is the last thing you should be calling me . . .'

Oh yes? I thought. Was James Kidd about to reveal her disguise?

James was reaching beneath his/her shirt and Calico Jack was blustering, 'Oh, is that right . . . lad?'

Roberts removed the cube from the Observatory controls and the image evaporated.

I bit my lip and thought of the *Jackdaw*. Adé didn't like our current situation. He'd be dying to make sail.

But he wouldn't do it without me.

Would he?

But now the glow that hung in the chamber before us became something else again, and all thoughts of the *Jackdaw*'s intentions were forgotten as Roberts said, 'Let's try another. Governor Woodes Rogers,' and placed another crystal cube into the console and new images formed.

We were seeing through the eyes of Woodes Rogers. Standing with him was Torres and not far away was El Tiburón. Suddenly the vision was filled with the image of a blood vial being held up for examination by Rogers.

He was speaking. 'You have a bold idea. But I must think it carefully through.'

The Observatory chamber room filled with the sound of Torres's reply.

'A simple pledge of loyalty is all you need suggest to the House of Commons. An oath, a gesture and a simple ceremonial dram of blood taken from the finger. That's all.'

Christ. Whatever Anne and Mary had been cooking up, it was nothing compared to this lot. Still trying to control the bleeding world – bleeding being the operative world. And doing it how? The English parliament.

Now Rogers was speaking. 'The ministers may give me trouble, but it should be easy enough to convince the House of Lords. They do adore an excess of pomp and circumstance.'

'Exactly. Tell them it's a show of fealty to the king . . . against those revolting Jacobites.'

'Yes, indeed,' replied Rogers.

'The crucial detail is the blood. You must get a sample from each man. We want to be ready when we find the Observatory.'

'Agreed.'

Roberts removed the cube from the console and looked at me, triumph in his eyes. Now we knew what the Templars were plotting. Not only that, but we were one step ahead of them.

The images had gone, the strange glow had returned to the walls and I was left wondering if I'd imagined the whole thing. Meantime, Roberts pulled something from the console and held it aloft. A skull. The skull in which he'd placed the vials of blood.

'A precious tool, you see?'

'Sorcery, that's what it is,' I said.

'Not so. Every mechanism that gives this device its light is a true and physical thing. Ancient, yes, but nothing supernatural or strange.'

I looked doubtfully at him, thinking, *You're kidding yourself, mate*. But decided not to pursue it.

'We'll be masters of the ocean with that,' I said. Wanting to hold the skull, reaching out to take it from him and overcome with the desire to feel the weight of it in my palm, I felt a tremble as he came forward with it, his hand outstretched. But then, instead of giving it to me, he whipped it round, striking me in the face with it and knocking me across the floor of the Observatory and over the precipice of the pit.

I fell, slamming into the stone on the way down, whipped by the vegetation that clung to the rock face but unable to get a grip on it and stop my fall. I felt a searing pain in my side, then smacked into the water below, thanking God I had the presence of mind to turn my fall into the semblance of a dive. From that height that instinct might have saved my life.

Even so my entrance into the water was a messy one. I crashed into it and floundered, swallowing water, trying not to let the pain in my side drag me under. As I broke the surface and gasped for breath I looked up, only to see Roberts gazing down on me.

'There's nothing in my code about loyalty, young man,' he taunted me, his voice echoing in the space between us. 'You played your role, but our partnership is done.'

'You're a dead man, Roberts,' I roared back, only I couldn't quite manage a roar. My voice was weak, and anyway he'd left and I was too busy trying to tend to the flaming pain in my side and get myself to safety.

When I collected myself what I found was a branch sticking from my flank, the wound colouring my robes red. I yanked it out with a scream, tossed the stick away and clenched my teeth as I held the wound, feeling blood seep through my fingers. Roberts, you bastard. *You bastard.*

Somehow, despite the pain, I managed the climb back up the walls of the pit to the Observatory. I retraced my steps, through the bridge chamber and past the corpses at the entrance, limping back down to the beach, pain-sweat pouring off me. But as I stumbled out of the long grass and on to the beach what I saw filled me with anguish. The *Jackdaw*, my beloved *Jackdaw*, had left. There was just the *Rover* anchored offshore now.

And there, where the beach met the sea, was moored a yawl, the coxswain and rowers silent sentinels with the sea at their backs as they awaited their captain – Captain Bartholomew Roberts, who stood before me.

He crouched. His eyes flashed and he smiled that peculiar joyless smile of his. 'Oh . . . your *Jackdaw* has flown, Edward, eh? That's the beauty of a democracy . . .

The many outvote the one. Aye, you could sail with me, but with a temper as hot as yours I fear you'd burn us all to cinders. Luckily I know the king's bounty on your head is a large one. And I intend to collect.'

The pain was too much. I could hold it together no more and felt myself passing out. The last thing I heard as the darkness claimed me was Bartholomew Roberts softly taunting me.

'Have you ever seen the inside of a Jamaican prison, boy? Have you?'

PART FOUR

57

A lot can happen in six months. But in the six months to November 1720 it happened to other people. Me, I was mouldering in jail in Kingston. While Bartholomew Roberts became the most feared pirate of the Caribbean, commanding a squadron of four vessels, his flagship the *Royal Fortune* at its head, I was trying and failing to sleep on a roll on the floor of a cell so cramped I couldn't lie straight. I was picking maggots from my food and holding my nose to get it down. I was drinking dirty water and praying it wouldn't kill me. I was watching the striped grey light from the bars of the door and listening to the clamour of the jail: the curses; night-time screams; a constant clanging that never ceased, as though someone, somewhere, spent all day and night rattling a cup along the bars; and, sometimes, I was listening to my own voice, just to remind myself that I was still alive, and I would curse my luck, curse Roberts, curse the Templars, curse my crew . . .

I had been betrayed – by Roberts, of course, though that was no surprise – but also by the *Jackdaw*. My time in jail gave me the distance I needed to see how my obsession with the Observatory had blinded me to the needs of my men, and I stopped blaming them for leaving me at Long Bay. I'd decided if I were lucky enough to see them again I'd greet them like brothers and tell them I bore no grudge and offer apologies of my own. Even so, the image of the *Jackdaw* sailing away without me burned like a brand on my brain.

Not for much longer. No doubt my trial approached – though I had yet to hear, of course. And after my trial would come my hanging.

Yesterday they had one. A pirate hanging, I mean. The trial was held in Spanish Town, and five of the men tried went to the gallows the day after at Gallows Point. They hanged the other six the next day in Kingston.

One of those they hanged yesterday was Captain John Rackham, the man we all knew as Calico Jack.

Poor old Jack. Not a good man but not an especially bad one either. And who can say fairer than that? I hoped he'd managed to get enough liquor down him before they sent him to the gallows. Keep him warm for the journey to the other side.

Thing was, Calico Jack had a couple of lieutenants, and their trial was to start this very day. I was due to be brought up into the courtroom, in fact, where they said I might be needed as a witness, although they hadn't said whether for the defence of the prosecution.

The two lieutenants, you see, were Anne Bonny and Mary Read.

And therein lies a tale. I'd witnessed the story,

beginning with what I'd seen at the Observatory: Calico Jack and Anne Bonny were lovers. Jack had worked his charm, tempted her away from James (that scurvy toad) and taken her to sea.

On board she'd dressed as a man. And she wasn't the only one. Mary Read was aboard ship, too, dressed as James Kidd, and the three of them, Calico Jack, Anne and Mary were all in on it. The two women wore men's jackets, long trousers and scarves round their necks. They carried pistols and cutlasses and were as fearsome as any man – and more dangerous, what with having more to prove.

And for a while they sailed the neighbourhood terrorizing merchant ships, until earlier in the year when they stopped off at New Providence. There on 22 August, the year of our Lord 1720, Rackham and a load of his crew, including Anne and Mary, stole a sloop called the *William* from Nassau harbour.

Of course Woodes Rogers knew exactly who was responsible. He issued a proclamation and despatched a sloop crammed with his own men to catch Calico Jack and his crew.

But old Calico Jack was on a roll, and in between splicing the main brace, which is to say carousing, he attacked fishing boats and merchant ships and a schooner.

Rogers didn't like that. He sent a second vessel after him.

But old Calico Jack didn't care, and he continued his piracy westward until the tip of Jamaica, where he encountered a privateer by the name of Captain Barnet, who saw the opportunity to make a bit of money in return for Jack's hide.

Sure enough Jack was boarded and his crew surrendered, all apart from Mary and Anne, that was. From what I heard Jack and his crew had caroused themselves stupid and were drunk or passed out when Barnet's men attacked. Like hellcats Mary and Anne cursed out the crew and fought with pistols and swords, but were overcome, and then the whole lot of them were taken across the island to Spanish Town jail.

And, like I say, they'd tried and hanged Jack already.

Now it was the turn of Anne and Mary.

I hadn't seen many courtrooms in my life, thank God, but even so I'd never seen one as busy as this. My guards led me up a set of stone steps to a barred door, opened it, shoved me out into the gallery and bid me sit. I gave them a puzzled look. *What's going on?* But they ignored me and stood with their backs to the wall, muskets at the ready in case I made a break for it.

But make a break where? My hands were manacled, men were wedged into the gallery seats all around: spectators, witnesses . . . all of them come to lay eyes on the two infamous women pirates, Anne Bonny and Mary Read.

They stood together before the judge, who glared at them and banged his gavel.

'The charges, sir, I will hear them again,' he called to the bailiff, who stood and cleared his throat.

'His Majesty's court contends that the defendants, Mary Read and Anne Bonny, did piratically, feloniously and in a hostile manner attack, engage and take seven certain fishing boats.'

During the minor uproar that followed I sensed somebody sit behind me. Two people, in fact – but paid them little mind.

'Secondly,' continued the bailiff, 'this court contends that the defendants lurked upon the high seas and did set upon, shoot at and take two certain merchant sloops, thus putting the captains and their crews in corporeal fear of their lives.'

And then matters of court receded into the background as one of the men sitting behind me leaned forward and spoke.

'Edward James Kenway . . .' I recognized the voice of Woodes Rogers at once. 'Born in Swansea to an English father and Welsh mother. Married at eighteen to Miss Caroline Scott, now estranged.'

I lifted my manacles and shifted round in the seat. Neither of my guards with their muskets had moved, but they watched us carefully. Beside Rogers, every inch the man of rank, sat Laureano Torres, dapper and composed in the balmy heat of the courtroom. They weren't here on pirate-hunting business, though. They were here on Templar business.

'She is a beautiful woman, I'm told,' said Torres, with a nod of his head in greeting.

'If you touch her, you bastards . . .' I snarled.

Rogers leaned forward. I felt a nudge at my shirt and looked down to see the muzzle of his pistol in my side. In the time since my fall at the Observatory I had by some miracle avoided gangrene or infection, but the wound had never quite healed. He didn't know about it, of course; he couldn't have. But he'd still somehow managed to prod it with the barrel of his gun, making me wince.

'If you know the Observatory's location, tell us now and you'll be out of here in a flash,' said Rogers.

Of course. That was why I hadn't felt the burn of the hangman's noose up to now.

'Rogers can hold these British hounds at bay for a time,' said Torres, 'but this will be your fate if you fail to cooperate.' He was indicating the courtroom, where the judge was speaking, where witnesses were telling of the awful things Anne and Mary had done.

Their warning over, Torres and Rogers stood, just as a female witness described in breathless detail how she'd been attacked by the two women pirates. She'd known they were women, she said, 'by the largeness of their breasts'. The court laughed at that until the laughter was silenced by the rap of the judge's gavel, the sound drowning out the slam of the door behind Rogers and Torres.

Anne and Mary, meanwhile, hadn't said a word. *What's the matter? Cat got your tongue?* I'd never known them lost for words before, but here they were, silent as the grave. Tales of their derring-do were told, and they never once butted in to correct anything egregious, nor even said a peep when the court found them guilty. Even when they were asked if they could offer any reason why sentence of death should not be passed. Nothing.

So the judge, not knowing the two ladies, and perhaps taking them for the reticent sort, delivered his sentence: death by hanging.

And then – and only then – did they open their mouths.

'Milord, we plead our bellies,' said Mary Read, breaking their silence.

'*What?*' said the judge, paling.

'We are pregnant,' said Anne Bonny.

There was uproar.

I wondered if both the sprogs belonged to Calico Jack, the old devil.

'You can't hang a woman quick with child, can ye?' called Anne over the noise.

The courtroom was in turmoil. As if anticipating my thoughts one of the guards behind nudged me with his musket barrel. *Don't even think about it.*

'Quiet! Quiet!' called the judge. 'If what you claim is true then your executions will be stayed, but only until your terms are up.'

'Then I'll be up the duff the next time you come knocking!' roared Anne.

That was the Anne I remembered, with the face of an angel and the mouth of the roughest jack tar. And she had the court in uproar again as the red-faced judge hammered at the bench with his gavel and ordered them removed, and the session broke up in disarray.

58

'Edward Kenway. Do you remember you once threat-ened to cut off my lips and feed them to me?'

Laureano Torres's face appeared from the gloom outside my prison cell door, framed by the window, div-ided by the bars.

'I didn't do it, though,' I reminded him, my disused voice croaking.

'But you would have done.'

True. 'But I didn't.'

He smiled. 'The typical terror tactics of a pirate: unsophisticated and unsubtle. What say you, Rogers?'

He lingered there, too. Woodes Rogers, the great pir-ate hunter. Hanging about near my cell door.

'Is that why you've been denying me food and water?' I rasped.

'Oh,' chuckled Torres, 'but there is much, much more to come. We have the little matter of the Obser-vatory's location to extract. We have the little matter of what you did to Hornigold. Come, let us show you what lies in store. *Guards.*'

Two men arrived, the same pair of Templar stooges who'd escorted me to the courtroom. Torres and Rog-ers left as I was manacled and leg irons were fitted. And then with my boots dragging on the flagstones they hauled me out of the cell and along the passageway, out into the prison courtyard where I blinked in the blinding sun, breathed fresh air for the first time in weeks and then, to my surprise, out of the main prison gates.

'Where are you taking me?' I gasped. The light of the sun was too blinding. I couldn't open my eyes. They felt as though they were glued together.

There was no reply. I could hear the sounds of Kingston. Daily life carrying on as normal around me.

'How much are they paying you?' I tried to say. 'Whatever it is, let me go and I'll double it.'

They came to a halt.

'Good man, good man,' I mumbled. 'I can make you rich. Just get me –'

A fist smashed into my face, splitting my lip, breaking something in my nose that began to gush blood. I coughed and groaned. As my head lolled back a face came close to mine.

'*Shut. Up.*'

I blinked, trying to focus on him, trying to remember his face.

'I'll get you for that,' I murmured. Blood or saliva ran from my mouth. 'You mark my words, mate.'

'Shut up, or next time it'll be the point of my sword.'

I chuckled. 'You're full of shit, mate. Your master wants me alive. Kill me and you'll be taking my place in that cell. Or worse.'

Through a veil of pain, blood and piercing sunlight

I saw his expression darken. 'We'll see about that,' he snarled. 'We'll see about that.'

And then the journey continued, me spitting blood, trying to clear my head and mostly failing until we came to what looked like the foot of a ladder. I heard the murmured voices of Torres and Rogers, and then a creaking sound coming from just overhead, and when I raised my chin and cast my eyes upwards what I saw was a gibbet. One of the stooges had climbed the ladder and unlocked it, and the door opened with a complaint of rusty metal. I felt the sun beat down upon me.

I tried to say something, to explain that I was parched and could die in the sun. And that if I did that – if I died – then they'd never find out where the Observatory was. Only Black Bart would know, and what a terrifying thought that was – Black Bart in charge of all that power.

He's doing that right now, isn't he? That's how he got to be so successful.

But I never got the chance to say it, because they'd locked me in the gibbet. Locked me in the gibbet to let the sun do its work. Let it slowly cook me alive.

59

At sundown my two friends came to fetch me and take me back to my cell. My reward for surviving was water, a bowl of it on my cell floor, just enough to dab on my lips, keep me alive, to use on the blisters and pustules brought up by the sun.

Rogers and Torres came. 'Where is it? Where is the Observatory?'

With cracked, desiccated lips I smiled at them but said nothing.

He's robbing you blind, isn't he? Roberts, I mean. He's destroying all your plans.

'You want to go back there tomorrow?'

'Sure,' I whispered. 'Sure. I could do with the fresh air.'

It wasn't every day. Some days I stayed in my cell. Some days they only hung me for a few hours.

'Where is it? Where is the Observatory?'

Some days they left me until well after nightfall. But it wasn't so bad when the sun went in. I was still crumpled into the gibbet like a man stuck in a privy, every muscle and bone shrieking in agony; I was still dying of thirst and hunger, my sunburnt flesh flaming. But still, it wasn't so bad. At least the sun had gone in.

'Where is it? Where is the Observatory?'

Every day I'm up there he's a bigger pain in the arse, isn't he? *Every day wasted is Black Bart's triumph over the Templars. There's that at least.*

'You want to go back there tomorrow?'

'Sure.'

I wasn't sure I could take another day. In a strange way I was trusting them not to kill me. I was trusting in *my* resolve being greater than theirs. I was trusting in my own inner strength.

But for another day I hung there, crouched and crumpled in the gibbet. And when night fell again I heard the guards taunting me, and I heard them gloating about Calico Jack, and how Charles Vane had been arrested.

Charles Vane, I thought. *Charles Vane . . . I remember him. He tried to kill me. Or did I try to kill him?*

And then the sounds of a short pitched battle, bodies falling, muffled groans.

And then a voice.

'Good morning, Captain Kenway. I have a gift for you.'

Very, very slowly, I opened my eyes. On the ground below me, painted grey in the dead light of the day, were two bodies. My friends, the Templar stooges. Both had slashed throats. A pair of crimson smiles adorned their necks.

And crouching by them, rifling through their tunics for the gibbet keys, was the Assassin Ah Tabai.

I assumed I'd never see him again. After all, the Assassin Ah Tabai was not the greatest supporter of Edward Kenway. He probably would just as soon have slit *my* throat as rescue me from jail.

Fortunately for me, he chose to rescue me from jail.

But – 'Do not mistake my purpose here,' he said, climbing the ladder, finding the right key for the lock and being good enough to catch me when I almost fell forward from the gibbet. He had a bulging leather flask and held the teat to my lips. As I gulped I felt tears of relief and gratitude pouring down my cheeks.

'I have come for Anne and Mary,' he was saying as he helped me down the ladder. 'You owe me nothing for this. But if you would lend me your aid I can promise you safe passage from this place.'

I had collapsed to the ground, where Ah Tabai allowed me to gather myself, handing me the leather flask once again.

'I'll need weapons,' I said after some minutes.

He smiled and handed me a hidden blade. It was no small thing for an Assassin to hand an interloper a blade. And as I crouched on the ground and strapped it on I realized I was being honoured in some way. The thought gave me strength.

I stood and engaged the steel, worked the action of the blade then slid it home. It was time – time to go and save Anne and Mary.

60

He had some distractions to set off, he said. So I was to look for the women while he saw to that. Fine. I knew where they were being held, and not long later, when the first of his explosions gave me just the distraction I needed, I was able to slip back into the prison compound and make my way there.

Then, as I drew closer, what I heard was screaming and the unmistakable voice of Anne Bonny. 'Help her, for God's sake. Fetch help. Mary's ill. Somebody, please.'

In return I heard the sound of soldiers trying to shut her up, thumping at the bars of her cell with their musket butts.

Not to be silenced, Anne was shrieking at them now. 'She's ill. Please, she's ill,' Anne was screaming. 'She's dying.'

'A dying pirate, there's your difference,' one of the men was saying.

I ran now, heart thumping, feeling the pain at my side but ignoring it as I turned a corner in the corridor of the cellblock, one hand on the cool stone wall to steady my progress and the other engaging the blade at the same time.

The guards were already rattled by Ah Tabai's

explosions and Anne's screaming. The first one turned and raised his musket but I swept my blade under and up, thrusting it through his ribcage, gripping the back of his head and wrenching it into his heart at the same time. His mate had turned at the sound of the body thumping to the stone and his eyes widened. He reached for his pistol but I got to him before his fingers curled round the grip, and with a shout leapt and struck downwards, plunging the blade into him, too.

Stupid move. I wasn't in the condition for that kind of action.

Immediately I felt a searing pain along my side. Pain like fire that began at the wound and then rolled up and down my body. In a tumble of flailing arms and legs I fell with my blade embedded in the guard, landing badly but pulling it free as I rolled to meet the attack of the last guard . . .

Thank God. Ah Tabai appeared from my right, his own blade engaged, and seconds later the last guard lay dead on the stone.

I gave him grateful eyes and we turned our attention to the cells – to the screaming.

There were two cells beside one another. Anne stood, her desperate face pressed between the bars. 'Mary,' she was pleading, 'see to Mary.'

I didn't need telling twice. From a guard's belt I liberated the keys and tore open Mary's door. Inside she was using her hands for a pillow on the low, dirty cot where she lay. Her chest rose and fell weakly, and though her eyes were open she stared at the wall without seeing it.

'Mary,' I said, bending to her and speaking quietly. 'It's me. Edward.'

She breathed steady but ragged breaths. Her eyes stayed where they were, blinking but not moving, not focusing. She wore a dress but it was cold in the cell and there was no blanket to cover her. No water to touch to her parched lips. Her forehead was shiny with sweat and cauldron-hot when I put a hand to it.

'Where's the child?' I asked.

'They took it,' replied Anne from the door. *The bastards.* My fists clenched.

'No idea where she is,' continued Anne, then suddenly cried out in pain herself.

Jesus. That's all we need.

Right, let's go.

As gently as I could I pulled Mary to a sitting position then swung her arm round my shoulder and stood. My own wound grumbled, but Mary cried out in pain and I could only imagine the agony she was going through. After childbirth she needed rest. Her body needed time to recover.

'Lean on me, Mary,' I told her. 'Come on.'

From somewhere came the shouts of approaching soldiers. Ah Tabai's distractions had worked; they'd given us the time we needed, but now the troops had recovered.

'Search every cell,' I heard.

We began stumbling along the passageway back towards the courtyard, Ah Tabai and Anne forging ahead.

But Mary was heavy and I was weak from days and nights spent hung in the gibbet, and the wound in my side – *Christ, it hurt* – something must have torn down there because the pain flared, and I felt blood, warm and wet, course into the waistband of my breeches.

'Please, help me, Mary,' I begged her, but I could feel her body sag as if the fight was leaving her, the fever too much for it.

'Stop. Please,' she was saying. Her breathing was even more erratic. Her head lolled from side to side. Her knees seemed to have given way and she sank to the flagstones of the passageway. Up ahead Ah Tabai was helping Anne, whose hands clutched at her stomach, and they turned to urge us on, hearing more shouting from behind us, more soldiers arriving.

'There's no one here!' came the shout. So now they had discovered the breakout. More running feet.

Ah Tabai and Anne reached the door to the courtyard. A black square became a grey one and night air rushed into the passageway.

Guards behind us. Ahead Ah Tabai and Anne were already across the courtyard and at the main gate where the Assassin surprised a guard who slid down the wall dying. Anne was screaming now and needing help as they clambered through the wicket door of the prison compound and out into a night glowing orange with the fire of Ah Tabai's explosions.

But Mary couldn't walk. Not any more. I grimaced as I bent down and scooped her up, feeling another tearing sensation in my side as though my wound, though a year old, simply couldn't cope with the extra weight.

'Mary . . .'

I could carry her no longer, and had to lay her down on the stones of the courtyard. From all around us I could hear the sound of tramping boots and soldiers calling to one another.

Fine, I thought. *Let them come. Here is where I'll stand and fight. It's as good a place to die as any.*

She looked up at me and her eyes focused, and she managed to smile before a fresh surge of pain made its way through her body. 'Don't die on my account,' she managed. 'Go.'

I tried to say no.

But she was right.

I laid her down, and tried to make her as comfortable as possible on the stones. My eyes were wet when I spoke. 'Dammit. You should have been the one to outlast me.'

She smiled a ghostly smile. 'I've done my part. Will you?'

Her image divided as though viewed through diamonds and I palmed tears from my eyes. 'If you came with me I could,' I urged her.

She said nothing.

No, please. Don't go. Not you.

'Mary . . . ?'

She was trying to say something. I put my ear to her

lips. 'I'll be with you, Kenway,' she whispered. Her final breath was warm on my ear. 'I will.'

I stood up and looked down at Mary Read, knowing there would be time to mourn her later, when I would remember a remarkable person, perhaps the most remarkable I ever knew. But for the moment I thought of how the British soldiers had let this good woman give birth, ripped her baby from her, then left her wounded and feverish in a prison cell. No blanket to cover her. No water to touch to her lips.

I heard the first British soldiers coming into the courtyard behind me. *Just in time to exact a little revenge before I make my escape.*

I engaged the blade and span to meet them.

61

I guess you could say I did a bit of drinking after that. And I saw people in my delirium, figures from the past: Caroline, Woodes Rogers, Bartholomew Roberts.

And ghosts, too: Calico Jack, Charles Vane, Benjamin Hornigold, Edward Thatch.

And Mary Read.

Eventually, after a binge that lasted how long, I couldn't say, salvation came in the form of Adewalé. He came to me on the beach in Kingston, and I thought he was another ghost at first, another figure from my visions. Come to taunt me. Come to remind me of my failings.

'Captain Kenway, you look like a bowl of plum duff.'

One of my visions. A ghost. A trick my poor hungover mind is playing on me. And, yes, while we're on the subject, where is my bottle of liquor?

Until, when he reached a hand to me and I reached back, expecting his fingers to become wisps of smoke, to disappear into nothing, they were real. Hard as wood, just as reliable. And *real*.

I sat up. 'Christ, I've got a head for ten . . .'

Adewalé pulled me up. 'On your feet.'

I stood rubbing my poor throbbing head. 'You put

me in a spot, Adewalé. After you left me with Roberts I should have hard feelings about seeing you here.' I looked at him. 'But mostly, I'm bloody glad.'

'Me too, breddah, and you'll be chuſſed to know your *Jackdaw* is still in one piece.'

He took me by the shoulder and pointed out to sea, and maybe it was the drink making me feel extra emotional but tears filled my eyes to see the *Jackdaw* once again. The men stood at the gunwales and I saw them in the rigging and their faces at the hatches of the stern guns, every man-jack of them looking over to the beach, to where Adewalé stood with me now. *They came*, I thought, and a tear rolled down my cheek that I brushed away with the sleeve of my robes (a parting gift from Ah Tabai, though I'd done little to honour them since).

'Shall we set sail?' I asked him, but Adewalé was already walking away, further up the beach towards inland. 'You're leaving?' I called after him.

'Aye, Edward. For I have another calling elsewhere.'

'But . . .'

'When your heart and your head are ready, visit the Assassins. I think you will understand then.'

So I took his advice. I sailed the *Jackdaw* to Tulum, back to where I had first discovered my sense and met Ah Tabai. There, I left the crew on board and went in search of Ah Tabai, only to arrive in the aftermath of an attack, walking into the smouldering, smoking ruins of an Assassin village and finding Adewalé there, too. This, then, was his calling.

'Jesus, Adewalé, what the hell happened here?'

'*You* happened here, Edward. The damage you caused six years ago has not been undone.'

I winced. So that was it. The Assassins were still feeling the repercussions of those maps I had sold to the Templars.

I looked at him. 'I'm not an easy man to call a friend, am I? Is that why you're here?'

'To fight beside a man so driven by personal gain and glory is a hard thing, Edward. And I have come to feel the Assassins – and their creed – is a more honourable course.'

So that was it. The words of Mary Read and Ah Tabai had been wasted on me but Adewalé had been heeding them. I wished I'd made more effort to do the same.

'Have I been unfair?' he prompted.

I shook my head. 'For years I've been rushing around, taking whatever I fancied, not giving a tinker's cuss for those I hurt. Yet here I am . . . with riches and reputation, feeling no wiser than when I left home. Yet when I turn round, look at the course I've run . . . there's not a man or woman I love left standing beside me.'

A new voice spoke up. Ah Tabai. 'There is time to make amends, Captain Kenway.'

I looked at him. 'Mary . . . Before she died she asked me to do good by her. To sort out the mess I'd made. Can you help me?'

Ah Tabai nodded. He and Adewalé turned towards the village and I walked alongside them.

'Mary was fond of you, Edward,' noted Ah Tabai, 'she saw something in your bearing that gave her hope you might one day fight with us.' He paused. 'What do you think of our creed?' he said.

We both knew that six years ago – Jesus, *one* year ago – I would have scoffed and called it silly. Now, though, my answer was different.

'It's hard to say. For if nothing is true, then why believe anything? And if everything is permitted . . . Why not chase every desire?'

'Why indeed?' smiled Ah Tabai mysteriously.

My thoughts collided in my head; my brain sang with new possibilities.

'It might be that this idea is only the beginning of wisdom, and not its final form,' I said.

'That's quite a step up from the Edward I met many years ago,' said Ah Tabai, nodding with satisfaction. 'Edward, you are welcome here.'

Thanking him, I asked, 'How's Anne's child?'

He shook his head and lowered his eyes, a gesture that said it all. 'She's a strong woman, but not invincible.'

I pictured her on the deck of the *William*, cursing her crewmates as cowards. It was said she'd fired shots at the men as they cowered drunk below decks. I could well believe it. I could well imagine how terrible and magnificent she'd been that day.

I went to where she sat and joined her, staring over the treetops and out to sea. She hugged her own legs and turned her pale face to me with a smile.

'Edward,' she said in greeting.

'I'm sorry for your loss,' I said.

I knew a thing or two about loss. Learning more every day.

'If I'd stayed in prison they'd have taken him from me —' she sighed as she turned her face into the breeze — 'and he'd now be alive. Might be this is God's way of saying I ain't fit to be a mum, carrying on like I do. Cursing and drinking, and fighting.'

'You are a fighter, aye. In prison, I heard stories of the infamous Anne Bonny and Mary Read, taking on the king's navy together. Just the pair of you.'

She gave a laugh that was partly a sigh. 'It's all true. And we would have won that day if Jack and his lads weren't passed out in the hold from drink. Ah . . . Edward . . . Everyone's gone now, ain't they? Mary. Rackham. Thatch. And all the rest. I miss the lot, rough as they were. Do you feel that, too? All empty inside like?'

'I do,' I said. 'Devil curse me, I do.'

I remembered a time when Mary had put her hand on my knee, and I did the same to Anne now. She looked at it there for a moment, knowing it was as much an invitation as a gesture of comfort. And then she put her own hand to mine, rested her head on my chest, and we stayed like that for a while.

Neither of us said anything. There was no need to.

62

Now was the time to start putting things right. It was time to tie up loose ends, to take care of business; it was time to begin wreaking my revenge: Rogers, Torres, Roberts. They all had to die.

I stood on the deck of the *Jackdaw* with Adewalé and Ah Tabai. 'I know my targets by sight well enough. But how will I find them?'

'We have spies and informants in every city,' said Ah Tabai. 'Visit our bureaus, and the Assassins there will guide you.'

'That fixes Torres and Rogers,' I told him, 'but Bartholomew Roberts won't be near any city. Might take months to find him.'

'Or years,' agreed Ah Tabai, but you are a man of talent and quality, Captain Kenway. I believe you will find him.'

Adewalé looked at me. 'And if you are at a loss do not be afraid to lean on your quartermaster for aid,' he smiled.

I nodded my thanks then went on to the poop deck,

leaving Ah Tabai and Adewalé to descend a Jacob's ladder to a rowing boat bobbling by our hull.

'Quartermaster,' I said, 'what's our present course?'

She turned. Resplendent in her pirate outfit.

'Due east, captain, if it's still Kingston we're sailing for?'

'It is, Miss Bonny, it is. Call it out.'

'Weigh anchor and let fall the courses, lads!' she called, and she shone with happiness. 'We're sailing for Jamaica!'

Torres, then. At the bureau in Kingston I was told of his whereabouts; that he would be attending a political function in town that very night. After that his movements were uncertain; it needed to be tonight whether I liked it or not.

So – how? I decided to take on the guise of a visiting diplomat, Ruggiero Ferraro, and before I left took a letter from within my robes and handed it to the bureau chief – a letter for *Caroline Scott Kenway of Hawkins Lane, Bristol*. In it I asked after her: *Are you safe? Are you well?* A letter full of hope but burdened with worry.

Later that night I found the man I was looking for, Ruggiero Ferraro. In short order I killed him, took his clothes and joined the others as we made our way to the party, and there were welcomed inside.

Being there took me back to when I'd posed as Duncan Walpole, when I'd first visited Torres's mansion. That feeling of being overawed, out of place and possibly even out of my depth, but chasing some notion of fortune, looking for the quickest way to make easy money.

Now I was once again looking for something. I was looking for Woodes Rogers. But riches were no longer my primary concern. I was an Assassin now.

'You are Mr Ferraro, I take it?' said a pretty female guest. 'I do *adore* your frippery. Such elegance and colour.'

Thank you, madam, thank you. I gave her a deep bow in what I hoped was the Italian manner. Pretty she may have been, but I had enough ladies in my life for the time being. Caroline waiting at home, not to mention certain . . . *feelings* for Anne.

And then, just as I realized that *grazie* was the only Italian word I knew, Woodes Rogers was giving a speech.

'Ladies and gentlemen, a toast to my brief tenure as governor of the Bahamas! For, under my watch, no less than three hundred avowed pirates took the king's pardon and swore fealty to the Crown.'

His face twisted into a bitter, sarcastic sneer.

'And yet, for all my successes, His Majesty has seen fit to *sack* me and call me home to England. *Brilliant!*'

It was a bad-tempered, resentful end to the speech, and sure enough his guests didn't quite know what to make of it. During his time on Nassau he'd handed out religious leaflets trying to persuade the merry bucca-neers of New Providence to mend their hard-drinking, whoring ways, so perhaps he wasn't accustomed to the liquor and he seemed to wobble around his own party, ranting at anyone unfortunate enough to find themselves in the vicinity.

'Hurray, hurray for the ignoble and ignorant prigs, who rule the world with sticks up their arses. Hurray!'

Moving on and another guest winced as he let fly with his whinges. 'I brought those brutes in Nassau to heal, by God. And this is the thanks I get. *Unbelievable.*'

I followed him around the room, staying out of his eye line, trading greetings with the guests. I must have bowed a hundred times, murmured *grazie* a hundred times. Until at last Rogers appeared to have exhausted the goodwill of his friends, for as he made another circle of the hall he found more and more backs were turned. The next moment he swayed, marooned in the room, looking around himself, only to find his erstwhile friends engaged in more thrilling conversations. For a second I saw the Woodes Rogers of old as he composed himself, drew back his shoulders, raised his chin and decided to take a little air. I knew where he was going, probably before he did, so it was an easy matter to move out to the balcony ahead of him, and wait for him there. And then, when he arrived, to bury my blade into his shoulder and, with one hand over his mouth to stop him screaming, lower him to the floor of the balcony and sit him up against the balustrade.

It all happened too quickly for him. Too quickly to

fight back. Too quickly to even be surprised, and he tried to focus on me with drunken, pained eyes.

'You were a privateer once,' I said to him. 'How is it you lack so much respect for sailors only trying to make their way in this world?'

He looked at where my blade was still embedded in his shoulder and neck. It was all that kept him alive, because as soon as I removed it his artery would be open, the balcony would be awash with his blood and he would be dead within a minute.

'You couldn't possibly understand my motives,' he said with a sardonic smile. 'You who spent a whole lifetime dismantling everything that makes our civilization shine.'

'But I do understand,' I insisted. 'I've seen the Observatory, and I know its power. You'd use that device to spy. You Templars would use that device to spy and blackmail and sabotage.'

He nodded, but the movement pained him, blood soaked his shirt and jacket. 'Yes, and yet all for a greater purpose. To ensure justice. To snuff out the lies and to seek truth.'

'There's no man on earth who needs that power.'

'Yet you suffer the outlaw Roberts to use it . . .'

I shook my head to put him right about that. 'No. I'm taking it back. And if you tell me where he is, I'll stop Roberts.'

Africa, he said. And I pulled my blade free.

Blood flowed heavily from his neck and his body sagged against the balustrade, undignified in death. What a difference to the man I'd first met all those years ago at Torres's mansion: an ambitious man with a handshake as firm as his resolve. And now his life ended not just at my blade but in a drunken fugue, a morass of bitterness and shattered dreams. Though he'd ousted the pirates from Nassau, he hadn't been given the support he needed to finish the job. The British had turned their backs on him. His hopes of rebuilding Nassau had been shattered.

Blood puddled on the stone around me and I moved my feet to avoid it. His chest rose and fell slowly. His eyes were half closed and his breathing became irregular as life slipped away.

Then from behind came a scream and, startled, I turned to see a woman, the finery of her clothes in stark contrast to her demeanour, a hand over her mouth and wide, terrified eyes. There was the rumble of running feet, more figures appearing on the balcony. Nobody daring to tackle me but not withdrawing either. Just watching.

I cursed, stood and vaulted to the balustrade. To my left the balcony filled with guests.

'*Grazie*,' I told them, then spread my arms and jumped.

63

February, 1722

And so to Africa, where Black Bart – now the most feared and infamous pirate in the Caribbean – continued to evade the British. I knew how he did it, of course, because in his possession was the Observatory skull, and he was using it – using it to anticipate every move against him.

As I set the *Jackdaw* in pursuit of him Roberts was stealing French ships and sailing them down the coast to Sierra Leone. His *Royal Fortune* remained at the head of his fleet and he continued sailing south-east along the African coast: raiding, pillaging, plundering as he went, constantly making improvements to his vessels and becoming better armed, more powerful and even more fearsome than he already was.

We had come across the sickening evidence of his campaign of terror in January, when we had sailed into the aftermath of not a battle but a massacre: Roberts in the *Royal Fortune* had attacked twelve ships at anchor in Whydah. All had surrendered apart from an English slave ship, the *Porcupine*, and their refusal to lay down arms had made Roberts so furious that he had ordered the ship boarded then set alight.

His men had flooded the decks with tar and set flame to the *Porcupine* with the slaves still on board, chained in pairs below decks. Those who jumped overboard to escape the blaze were torn limb from limb by sharks, the rest burned alive or drowned. A horrible, horrible death.

By the time we arrived the sea was awash with debris. Vile black smoke shrouded the entire neighbourhood, and smouldering in the ocean, almost up to the waterline, was the burnt-out hull of the *Porcupine*.

Disgusted by what we'd seen, we followed Roberts's trail south and then to Princípé, where he'd anchored his ship in the bay and taken a party of men ashore to make camp and gather supplies.

We waited. Then as night fell I gave the *Jackdaw* orders to wait an hour before attacking the *Royal Fortune*. Next I took a rowing boat to shore, pulled up the cowl of my robes and followed a path inland, led by the shouts and singing I could hear in the distance. And then, as I grew closer, I smelled the tang of the campfire. As I crouched nearby I could see its soft glow divided by the undergrowth.

I was in no mood to take prisoners, so I used grenadoes. Just as their captain was famous for saying he gave no quarter, neither did I, and as the camp erupted into explosions and screams and a choking cloud of thick black smoke I strode to its centre with my blade and a pistol at the ready.

The battle was short because I was ruthless. It didn't

matter that some were asleep, some naked and most of them unarmed. Perhaps the men who poured tar on the decks of the *Porcupine* were among those who died at the point of my blade. I hoped so.

Roberts did not stand and fight. He grabbed a torch and ran. Behind us were the screams of my massacre at camp, but I left his crew to their dying as I gave chase, following him up a pathway to a guard tower on a promontory.

'Why, who chases me now?' he called. 'Is it a spectre come to spook me? Or the gaunt remains of a man I sent to hell, now crawling back to pester me?'

'No, Black Bart Roberts,' I shouted back. 'It's I, Edward Kenway, come to call a halt to your reign of terror!'

He raced into the guard tower and climbed. I followed, emerging back into the night at the top to see Roberts standing at the edge of the tower, a precipice behind him. I stopped. If he jumped I lost the skull. I couldn't afford to let him jump.

His arm holding the torch waved. He was signalling – but to whom?

'I'll not fight where you have the advantage, lad,' he said, breathing heavily.

He laid down the torch.

He was going to jump.

I started forward to try to catch him but he'd gone, and I scrambled to the edge on my belly and looked over, only now seeing what had been hidden from me;

what Black Bart knew to be there, why he'd been signalling.

It was the *Royal Fortune*, and in the glow of her lamps I saw Roberts had landed on deck and was already dusting himself off and peering up the rock face to where I lay. Around him were his men, and in the next instant I was pulling back from the lip as muskets began popping and balls began smacking into the stone around me.

And then, not far away, I saw the *Jackdaw*. Right on time. Good lads. I picked up the torch and began signalling to them, and soon they were close enough for me to see Anne at the tiller, her hair blowing in the wind as she brought the *Jackdaw* to bear by the cliff face, close enough for me to . . .

Jump.

And the chase was on.

We pursued him through the narrow rock passages of the coastline, firing our carriage guns when we were able. In return his men lobbed mortar shot at us and mine returned with musket fire and grenadoes whenever we were within range.

Then – '*Sail ho!*' – came the British naval warship, the HMS *Swallow*, and with a lurch of horror I realized she was after Roberts, too. This heavily armed, determined warship was no doubt as sickened by the stories of his exploits as we had been.

Leave them to it? No. I couldn't allow them to sink the *Fortune*. Roberts had the Observatory skull with him. I couldn't risk it sinking to the seabed, never to be seen again.

'There is a device within that needs taking,' I told Anne. 'I have to board her myself.'

Carriage guns boomed, the three ships locked in combat now, the *Jackdaw* and *Swallow* with a common enemy but not allies. We came under fire from all sides, and as British shot peppered our gunwales and shook our shrouds, I gave Anne the order to make haste away.

Me, I was going for a swim.

It isn't easy to swim from one ship to another, especially if both are involved in battle. But then most are not gifted with my determination. I had the cover of the half-light on my side, not to mention the fact that the crew of the *Fortune* already had enough to contend with. When I climbed aboard I found a ship in disarray. A ship I was able to pass through virtually undetected.

I took my fair share of scalps along the way, and I'd cut the throat of the first mate and killed the quartermaster before I found Black Bart, who turned to face me with his sword drawn. I noted, almost with amusement, that he had changed his clothes. He had put on his best bib and tucker to meet the English: a crimson waistcoat and breeches, a hat with a red feather, a pair of pistols on silk slings over his shoulders. What hadn't changed were those eyes of his. Those dark eyes that were surely a reflection of the blackened, corroded soul inside.

We fought, but it was not a fight of any distinction.

Black Bart Roberts was a cruel man, a cunning man, a wise man, if wisdom can exist in a man so devoid of humanity. But he was not a swordsman.

'By Jove,' he called as we fought. 'Edward Kenway. How can I not be impressed by the attention you've paid me?'

I refused him the courtesy of a reply. I fought on relentlessly, confident not in my skill – for that would have been the arrogant Edward Kenway of old – but in a belief that I would emerge the victor. Which I did. And at last he fell to the deck with my blade embedded in him, pulling me into a crouch.

He smiled, his fingers going to where the blade was stuck in his chest. 'A merry life and a short one, as promised,' he said. 'How well I know myself.' He smirked a little. His eyes bored into me. 'And what of you, Edward? Have you found the peace you seek?'

'I'm not aiming so high as that,' I told him, 'for what is peace but a confusion between two wars?'

He looked surprised for a second, as though thinking me incapable of anything other than grunts and demands for gold or another tankard. How pleasing it was that in his final moments Bartholomew Roberts witnessed the change in me, knew that his death at my hands was not driven by greed but by something nobler.

'You're a stoic then,' he laughed. 'Perhaps I was wrong about you. She might have had some use for you after all.'

'She?' I said, puzzled. 'Of whom do you speak?'

'Oh . . . She who lies in wait. Entombed. I had hoped to find her, to see her again. To open the door of the temple and hear her speak my name once more. Aita . . .'

Mumbo-jumbo. More bloody mumbo-jumbo.

'Talk sense, man.'

'I was born too soon, like so many others before.'

'Where's the device, Roberts?' I asked him, tired now – tired of his riddles, even at the end.

From his clothes he pulled the skull and offered it to me with fingers that shook.

'Destroy this body, Edward,' he said as I took it and the last of life seeped from him. 'The Templars . . . If they take me . . .'

And he died. And it was not for him, nor for the peace of his soul, that I tossed his body overboard, consigning it to the depths. But so that the Templars would not have him. Whoever – *whatever* – this Sage had been, the safest place for his body was at the bottom of the sea.

And now, Grand Master Torres, I'm coming for you.

64

Arriving in Havana a few days before, I'd I found the city in a state of high alert. Torres, it appeared, had been warned of my imminent arrival and was taking no chances: soldiers patrolled the streets, citizens were being searched and forced to reveal their faces, and Torres himself had gone into hiding – accompanied, of course, by his trusty bodyguard El Tiburón.

I'd used the Observatory skull. Under the watchful eye of the Assassin bureau chief, Rhona Dinsmore, I took a vial of Torres's blood in one hand and the skull in the other. As she watched me work I wondered how I might look to her. Like a madman? A magician? A man using ancient science?

'Through the blood of the governor, we can see through his eyes,' I told her.

She looked as intrigued as she did doubtful. And after all, I wasn't sure of it myself. I'd seen it work in the Observatory, but in images conjured up in the chamber by Roberts. Here I was trying something new.

I needn't have worried. The red of the blood in the vial seemed to bathe the inside of the skull and its eye-holes burned scarlet as it began to glow and display images on its polished dome. We were looking through the eyes of Governor Laureano Torres, who was look-ing at –

'That's . . . That's by the church,' she said, amazed.

Moments later I'd been in pursuit, and followed Torres as far as his fort, where the trap had been sprung. At some point a decoy had taken Torres's place. It was he who fell beneath my blade, and there, waiting for me beneath the walls of the fort, implacable, silent as ever, was El Tiburón.

You should have killed me when you had the chance, I thought. Because when on the last occasion he'd bested me it was a different Edward Kenway he'd met in battle; things had changed in the meantime – *I* had changed – and I had much to prove to him . . .

So if he'd hoped to beat me as easily as he had before he was disappointed. He came forward, feinting, then switching sides, but I anticipated the move, defended eas-ily, hit him on the counter and opened a nick on his cheek.

There was no grunt of pain, not from El Tiburón. But in those cloudy eyes was just the merest hint, the tiniest glimmer, of something I hadn't seen the last time we'd fought. Fear.

And that gave me a boost more than any shot of liquor, and once again I came forward with my blade flashing. He was forced on to the back foot, defending left and right, trying to find a weak spot in my attack but failing. *Where were his guards?* He hadn't summoned them, believing this would be an easy kill.

But how wrong he was, I thought as I pressed forward, dodged to my left and swiped backhanded with my blade, opening a gash in his tunic and a deep cut in his stomach that began gushing blood.

It slowed him down. It weakened him. I allowed him to come forward, pleased to see his sword strokes becoming more wild and haphazard as I carried on harrying him. Small but bloody strikes. Wearing him down.

He was slow now, his pain making him careless. Again I was able to drive forward with my cutlass, slash upwards with my hidden blade and twist it in his stomach. A mortal blow, surely?

His clothes were ragged and blood-stained. Blood from his stomach wound splattered to the ground, and he staggered with pain and exhaustion, looking at me mutely, but with all the agony of defeat in his eyes.

Until at last I put him down and he lay losing precious lifeblood, slowly dying in the heartless Havana sun. I crouched, blade to his throat, ready to plunge it up beneath his chin into his brain. End it quickly.

'You humbled me once, and I took that hard lesson and I bettered myself . . .' I told him. 'Die knowing that for all our conflicts, you helped make a soldier out of a scoundrel.'

My blade made a moist squelching sound as I finished it.

'Leave this life for a lasting peace, down among the dead,' I told his corpse, and left.

65

Desperate Torres had fled. With a last throw of the dice he'd decided to seek out the Observatory for himself.

I took the *Jackdaw* in pursuit, my heart sinking as with each passing hour there was no sighting of Torres, and with each passing hour we grew closer to Tulum. Would he find it? Did he already know where it was? Had he found another poor soul to torture? An Assassin?

And then we came round the coast of Tulum, and there was Torres's galleon at anchor, smaller consorts bobbling by her sides. We saw the glint of spyglasses and I ordered hard port. Moments later black squares appeared in the hull of the Spanish galleon and the sun shone dully off her gun barrels before there was a thud and a puff of fire and smoke and balls were smacking into us and into the water around us.

The battle would continue but it would have to continue without its captain and, also, as she insisted on coming with me, its quartermaster. Together Anne and I dived off the gunwale into bright blue water and swam for shore, and then began the trek up the path to the Observatory.

It wasn't long before we came upon the first corpses. Just as the men on the galleon were fighting for their lives against the onslaught of the *Jackdaw*, so the men with Torres had been doing the same. They had been ambushed by the natives, the Observatory guardians, and from up ahead we could hear the sounds of more conflict: desperate shouts as the men at the rear of the column tried in vain to frighten off the natives.

'This land is under the protection of King Philip. Tell your men to disperse or die!'

But it was they who would die. As we passed through the undergrowth a short distance away from them I saw their uncomprehending faces go from the monolithic edifice of the Observatory – Where had *that* come from? – to scanning the long grass around them. They would die like that: terrified and uncomprehending.

At the entrance to the Observatory were more bodies, but the door was open and some men had clearly made it inside. Anne bade me go in; she would stand guard. And so for a second time I entered that strange and sacred place, that huge temple.

As I stepped inside I remembered the last time, when Roberts had murdered his men rather than let them be unbalanced by what they saw inside. Sure enough, just as I crept into the vast entrance chamber, terrified Spanish soldiers were fleeing screaming, their eyes somehow blank, as though whatever life in them had already been extinguished. As though they were corpses running.

They ignored me and I let them go. Good. They'd distract the Observatory guardians on the outside. And I pressed onwards, climbing stone steps, passing along the bridge chamber – more terrified soldiers – then towards the main control chamber.

I was halfway there when the Observatory began to hum. The same skull-crushing sound I'd heard on my first visit. I broke into a run, pushing past more frantic soldiers trying to make their escape and dashing into the main chamber where stone crumbled from the walls as the Observatory seemed to shake and vibrate with the droning noise.

Torres stood at the raised control panel, trying to make himself heard above the din, calling to guards who were either no longer there or trying to make their escape, trying to negotiate the stone that fell around us.

'Search the area. Find a way to stop this madness,' he screamed with his hands over his ears. He turned and with a lurch saw me.

'He's here. Kill him,' he shouted, pointing. Spittle flew. In his eyes was something I'd never have believed him capable of: panic.

'*Kill him!*' Just two of his brave but foolhardy men were up to challenge, and as the chamber shook, seemingly working itself loose around us, I made short work of them. Until the only men left were Torres and I.

And now the Templar Grand Master cast his eye around the chamber, his gaze travelling from the dead bodies of his men back to me. The panic had gone now. Back was the Torres I remembered, and in his face was not defeat, nor fear, nor even sadness at his imminent death. There was fervour.

'We could have worked together, Edward,' he appealed with his hands outstretched. 'We could have taken power for ourselves and brought these miserable empires to their knees.'

He shook his head as if frustrated with me, as though I was an errant son.

(And no, sorry, mate, but I'm an errant son no longer.)

'There is so much potential in you, Edward,' he insisted, 'so much you have not yet accomplished. I could show you things. Mysteries beyond anything you could imagine.'

No. He and his kind had done nothing for me save to seek the curtailment of my freedom and take the lives of my friends. Starting with the night in Bristol when a torch was flung in a farmyard, his kind had brought me nothing but misery.

I drove the blade in and he grunted with pain as his mouth filled with blood that spilled over his lips.

'Does my murder fulfil you?' he asked weakly.

No, no it didn't.

'I'm only seeing a job done, Torres. As you would have done with me.'

'As we *have* done, I think,' he managed. 'You have no family any more, no friends, no future. Your losses are far greater than ours.'

'That may be, but killing you rights a far greater wrong than I ever did.'

'You honestly believe that?'

'You would see all of mankind corralled into a neatly

416

furnished prison: safe and sober, yet dull beyond reason and sapped of all spirit. So, aye, with everything I've seen and learnt in these last years, I *do* believe it.'

'You wear your convictions well,' he said. 'They suit you . . .'

It was as though I'd been in a trance. The noise of the Observatory, the rattle of stone falling around me, the screams of the fleeing troops: all of it had faded into the background as I spoke to Torres, and I only became aware of it again when the last breath died on his lips and his head lolled on the stone. There was the noise of a distant battle, soldiers being ruthlessly despatched, before Anne, Adewalé and Ah Tabai burst into the chamber. Their swords were drawn and streaked with blood. Their pistols smoked.

'Torres awakened the Observatory something fierce,' I said to Ah Tabai. 'Are we safe?'

'With the device returned, I believe so,' he replied, indicating the skull.

Anne was looking around herself, open-mouthed. Even part-destroyed in the wake of the rockfall the chamber was still a sight to see. 'What do you call this place?' she said, awestruck.

'Captain Kenway's folly,' said Adewalé, shooting me a smile.

'We will seal this place and discard the key,' announced Ah Tabai, 'until another Sage appears, this door will remain locked.'

'There were vials when I came here last,' I told him,

'filled with the blood of ancient men, Roberts said. But they're gone now.'

'Then it's up to us to recover them,' said Ah Tabai with a sigh, 'before the Templars catch wind of this. You could join us in that cause.'

I could. I could. But . . .

'Only after I fix what I mangled back home.'

The old Assassin nodded, and then as though reminded of it he removed a letter from his robes that he handed to me. 'It arrived last week.'

They left me as I read it.

And I think you know the news it contained, don't you, my sweet?

66

October, 1722

We had good reason to celebrate. So we did. However, with my new knowledge had come a decreased interest in inebriation, so I left the exuberance in the hands of the *Jackdaw* crew, who built fires and roasted hogs and danced and sang until they had no energy left, then they simply collapsed and slept where they had stood and then pulled themselves to their feet, grabbed the nearest flask of liquor and began again.

Me, I sat on the terrace of my homestead with Adewalé and Ah Tabai.

'Gentlemen, how do you find it here?' I asked them. I'd offered it – my home – as their base.

'It will work well for us,' said Ah Tabai, 'but our long-term goal must be to scatter our operations. To live and work among the people we protect, just as Altaïr Ibn-La'Ahad once counselled.'

'Well, until that time, it's yours as you see fit.'

'Edward . . .'

I had already stood to find Anne, but turned to Adewalé.

'Yes?'

'Captain Woodes Rogers survived his wounds,' he told me. I cursed, remembering the interruption. 'He has since returned to England. Shamed and in great debt, but no less a threat.'

'I will finish that job when I return. You have my word.'

He nodded, and we embraced before we parted, leaving me to join Anne.

We sat in silence for a moment, smiling at the songs, until I said, 'I'll be sailing for London in the next few months. I'd be a hopeful man if you were beside me.'

She laughed. 'England is the wrong way round the globe for an Irish woman.'

I nodded. Perhaps it was for the best. 'Will you stay with the Assassins?' I asked her.

She shook her head. 'No. I haven't that kind of conviction in my heart. You?'

'In time, aye, when my mind is settled and my blood is cooled.'

Just then we heard a cry from afar, a ship sailing into the cove. We looked at one another, both of us knowing what the arrival of the ship meant – a new life for me, a new life for her. I loved her in my own way, and I think she loved me, but the time had come to part, and we did it with a kiss.

'You're a good man, Edward,' said Anne, her eyes shining as I stood. 'And if you learn to keep settled to one place for more than a week, you'll make a fine father, too.'

I left her and headed down to the beach to where a large ship was coming into dock. The gangplank was lowered and the captain appeared, holding the hand of a little girl: a beautiful little girl, who shone brighter than hope, just nine years old.

And I thought you looked the spitting image of your mother.

67

A little vision, you were. Jennifer Kenway, a daughter I never even knew I had. Embarking on a voyage, which went against your grandfather's wishes but had your grandmother's blessing, you'd sailed to find me, in order to give me the news.

My beloved was dead.

(Did you wonder why I didn't cry, I wonder, as we stood on the dock at Inagua? So did I, Jenny. So did I.)

And on that voyage home I got to know you. And yet there were still things I had to keep from you, because I still had much I needed to do. Before, I talked about having loose ends to tie, business to take care of. Well, there were still loose ends to tie. Still business to settle.

I took a skeleton crew to Bristol, a few of my most trusted men. We sailed the Atlantic, a hard, rough crossing, made bearable by a stay in the Azores, then continued our journey to the British Isles and to Bristol. To home – to a place I hadn't visited for nigh on a decade. A place I had been warned against ever returning to.

As we came into the Bristol Channel the black flag

of the *Jackdaw* was brought down, folded up and placed carefully in a chest in my cabin. In its place we raised the red ensign. It would be enough to allow us to land at least, and once the port marshals had worked out the *Jackdaw* was not a naval vessel, I'd be ashore and the ship anchored offshore.

And then I saw it for the first time in so long, the Bristol dock, and I caught my breath. I had loved Kingston, Havana and above all Nassau. But despite everything that had happened – or maybe because of it – this was still my home.

Heads turned in my direction as I strode along the harbour, a figure of mystery, dressed not like a pirate but something else. Perhaps some of the older ones remembered me: merchants I'd done business with as a sheep farmer, men I'd drunk with in the taverns when I'd boasted of going off to sea. And tongues would wag, and news would travel. How far, I wondered. To Matthew Hague and Wilson? To Emmett Scott? Would they know that Edward Kenway was back, stronger and more powerful than before, and that he had scores to settle?

I found a boarding house in town and there rested the night. The next morning I bartered for a horse and saddle and set off for Hatherton, riding until I reached my father's old farmhouse.

Why I went there, I'm not quite sure. I think I just wanted to see it. And so for long moments that's what I did. I stood by the gate in the shade of a tree and contemplated my old home. It had been rebuilt, of course, and was only partly recognizable as the house in which I had grown up. But one thing that had remained the same was the outhouse: the outhouse where my marriage to Caroline had begun; the outhouse in which you were conceived, Jennifer.

I left, then halfway between Hatherton and Bristol, a road I knew so well, I stopped at a place I also knew well. The Auld Shillelagh. I tethered my horse outside, made sure she had water, then stepped in to find it almost exactly as I remembered: the low ceilings, a darkness that seemed to seep from the walls. The last time I was here I had killed a man. My first man. Many more had fallen beneath my blade since.

More to come.

Behind the bar was a woman in her fifties, and she raised her tired head to look at me as I approached.

'Hello, Mother,' I said.

68

She took me to a side table away from the prying eyes of the few drinkers there.

'So it's true then?' she asked me. Her long hair had grey streaks in it. Her face was drawn and tired. It was only (*only?*) ten years since I'd last seen her but it was as though she had aged twenty, thirty, more.

All my fault.

'What's true, Mother?' I asked carefully.

'You're a pirate?'

'No, Mother, I'm not a pirate. No longer. I've joined an order.'

'You're a monk?' She cast an eye over my robes.

'No, Mother, I'm not a monk. Something else.'

She sighed, looking unimpressed. Over at the bar the landlord was towelling tankards, watching us with a hawk eye. He begrudged her the time she spent away from the bar but wasn't about to say anything. Not with the pirate Edward Kenway around.

'And you decided to come back, did you?' she was saying. 'I heard that you had. That you sailed into port yesterday, stepped off a glittering galleon like some kind of king. The big I-am, Edward Kenway. That's what you always wanted, wasn't it?'

'Mother –'

'That was what you were always going on about, wasn't it? Wanting to go off and make your fortune, make something of yourself, become a man of quality, wasn't it? That involved becoming a pirate, did it?' She sneered. I didn't think I'd ever seen my mother sneer before. 'You were lucky they didn't hang you.'

They still might, if they catch me.

'It's not like that any more. I've come to make things right.'

She pulled a face like she'd tasted something nasty. Another expression I'd never seen before. 'Oh yes, and how do you plan to do that?'

I waved a hand. 'Not have you working here, for a start.'

'I'll work wherever I like, young man,' she scoffed. 'You needn't think you're paying me off with stolen gold. Gold that belonged to other folks before they were forced to hand it to you at the point of your sword. Eh? Is that it?'

'It's not like that, Ma,' I whispered, feeling young all of a sudden. Not like the pirate Edward Kenway at all. This wasn't how I'd imagined it would be. Tears, embraces, apologies, promises. Not like this.

I leaned forward. 'I don't want it to be like this, Ma,' I said quietly.

She smirked. 'That was always your trouble, wasn't it, Edward? Never happy with what you got.'

'No . . .' I began, exasperated. 'I mean . . .'

'I know what you *mean*. You mean you made a mess of things and then you left us to clear up your mess, and now you've got some finery about you, and a bit of money, you think you can come back and pay me off. You're no better than Hague and Scott and their cronies.'

'No, no, it's not like that.'

'I heard you arrived with a little girl in tow. Your daughter?'

'Yes.'

She pursed her lips and nodded, a little sympathy creeping into her eyes. 'It was her who told you about Caroline, was it?'

My fists clenched. 'She did.'

'She told you Caroline was sick with the pox and that her father refused her medicine, and that she ended up wasting away at that house on Hawkins Lane. She told you that, did she?'

'She told me that, Ma, yes.'

She scratched at her head and looked away. 'I loved that girl. Caroline. Really loved her. Like a daughter she was to me, until she went away.' She shot me a reproachful look. *That was your fault.* 'I went to the funeral, just to pay my respects, just to stand at the gate, but Scott was there and all his cronies, Matthew Hague and that Wilson fellow. They ran me off the place. Said I wasn't welcome.'

'They'll pay for that, Ma,' I said through clenched teeth. 'They'll pay for what they've done.'

She looked quickly at me. 'Oh yes? How are they going to *pay* then, Edward? Tell me that. You going to kill them, are you? With your sword? Your pistols? Word is, they've gone into hiding, the men you seek.'

'Ma . . .'

'How many men have died at your hand, eh?' she asked.

I looked at her. The answer, of course, was countless.

She was shaking, I noticed. With fury.

'You think that makes you a man, don't you?' she said, and I knew her words were about to hurt more than any blade. 'But do you know how many men your father killed, Edward? None. Not one. And he was *twice* the man you are.'

I winced. 'Don't be like this. I know I could have done things differently. I *wish* I'd done things differently. But I'm back now – back to sort out the mess I made.'

She was shaking her head. 'No, no, you don't understand, Edward. There is no mess any more. The mess needed sorting out when you left. The mess needed sorting out when your father and I cleared up what remained of our home and tried to start again. It put years on him, Edward. Years. The mess needed sorting out when nobody would trade with us. Not a letter from you. Not a word. Your daughter was born, your father died, and not a peep from the great explorer.'

'You don't understand. They threatened me. They threatened you. They said if I ever returned they'd hurt you.'

She pointed. '*You* did more hurting than *they* ever could, my son. And now you're here to stir things up again, are you?'

'Things have got to be put right.'

She stood. 'Not in my name, they don't. I'll have nothing to do with you.'

She raised her voice to address everybody in the tavern. Only a few would hear her, but word would soon spread. 'You hear that?' she said loudly. 'I disown him. The great and famous pirate Edward Kenway; he's nothing to do with me.'

Hands flat on a tabletop she leaned forward and hissed, 'Now *get out*, no-son-of-mine. Get out before I tell the soldiers where the pirate Edward Kenway is to be found.'

I left, and when, on the journey back to my boarding house in Bristol, I realized that my cheeks were wet, I allowed myself to cry, grateful for one thing. Grateful that there was nobody around to see my tears or hear my wails of grief.

69

So – they had gone to ground, the guilty men. And yes, there had been others there that night – the Cobleighs among them. But I had no desire to account for them all; little taste for taking the lives of men given orders. The men I wanted *gave* those orders: Hague, Scott and, of course, the man who left the insignia of the Templars on my face all those years ago. Wilson.

Men who hid from me. Whose guilt was confirmed by the fact that they were hiding from me. Good. Let them hide. Let them shake with fear.

They knew I was coming after them. And I was – I was coming after them. Tonight, all being well, Scott, Wilson and Hague would be dead.

But they knew I was coming, so my investigations would have to be conducted a little more discreetly. When I left my boarding house the next morning I did so knowing I was beneath the gaze of Templar spies. I ducked into a tavern I knew of old – better than my pursuers, no doubt – and thanked my lucky stars it still had the same rear privy it always had.

By the back door I held my breath against the stink, quickly stripped off my robes and changed into clothes I'd brought with me from the *Jackdaw* – clothes I'd last worn many, many moons ago: my long buttoned-up waistcoat, knee breeches, white stockings and a battered brown tricorne. And thus attired I left the tavern, emerging on a different street a different person. Just another merchant on his way to market.

I found her there, exactly where I had expected to, and jogged the basket on her arm so she'd know I was behind her, whispering, 'I got your message.'

'Good,' said Rose without turning her head, bending to inspect some flowers. With a quick look left and right she whipped out a headscarf and tied it over her head.

'Follow me.'

A moment later Rose and I loitered near some dilapidated stables in a deserted corner of the market. I glanced at the structure, then back again with a jolt of recognition. I'd stabled my own horse here many years ago. It had been new then and convenient for the market, but the sprawl of stalls had shifted over the intervening years, its entrances had moved and the stables had fallen into disuse, fit only for loitering near, for conducting clandestine meetings, as we did now.

'You've met young Jennifer, have you?' she said.

She shifted the basket on her arm. She'd been a young girl when I'd first encountered her at the Auld Shillelagh. Ten years later she was still young but missing was that spark, that rebellious streak that had made her run away in the first place. A decade of drudgery had done that to her.

And yet, like the glowing sparks of a dying fire, there was some of her old nature left, because she'd sent me a letter requesting to meet me, and here she was, with things to tell me. Among them, I hoped, the whereabouts of her master and his friends.

'I have,' I told her. 'I've met my daughter. She's safe on my ship.

'She has your eyes.'

I nodded. 'She has her mother's beauty.'

'She's a beautiful girl. We were all very fond of her.'

'But wilful?'

Rose smiled. 'Oh yes. She was determined that she should see you when Mistress Caroline passed away last year.'

'I'm surprised Emmett allowed it.'

Rose chortled dryly. 'He didn't, sir. It was the mistress of the house who organized it, her and Miss Jennifer cooked it up between them. The first his nibs knew of it was when he woke up to find Miss Jennifer gone. He wasn't happy. He wasn't happy at all, sir.'

'Meetings, were there?'

She looked at me. 'You could say that, sir, yes.'

'Who came to see him, Rose?'

'Master Hague . . .'

'And Wilson?'

She nodded her head.

All the conspirators.

'And where are they now?'

'I don't rightly know, sir,' she said.

I sighed. 'Then why invite me here, if you've nothing to tell me?'

She turned her face to me. 'I mean I don't know where they're hiding, sir, but I do know where Mr Scott plans to be tonight, for I have been asked to take him some fresh clothes to his offices.'

'The warehouse?'

'Yes, sir. He has business items to collect as well, sir. He plans to be there personally. I've been asked to go there when night has fallen.'

I looked at her long and hard. 'Why, Rose?' I said. 'Why are you helping me like this?'

She glanced this way and that. 'Because you once helped save me from a fate worse than death. Because Mistress Caroline loved you. And because . . .'

'What?'

'Because that man, he watched her die. He wouldn't let her get the medicine she needed, not her or Mrs Scott, the both of them ill. Mrs Scott recovered but Mrs Kenway never did.'

It startled me to hear Caroline called Mrs Kenway. It had been so long since she'd been referred to that way.

'Why did he deny them the medicine?'

'Pride, sir. It was him who caught the smallpox first but he recovered. He thought Mrs Scott and Mrs Kenway should be able to as well. But she began to get such terrible blisters all over her face, sir. Oh, sir, you've never seen anything like it –'

433

I held up a hand, not wanting to hear more – wanting to preserve the image I had of Caroline.

'There was an epidemic in London and we think Mr Scott picked it up there. Even the royal family were in fear of it.'

'You didn't get it?'

She looked at me guiltily. 'The staff were inoculated, sir. Head butler saw to it. Swore us to silence.'

I sighed. 'Good for him. He may have saved you a great deal of suffering.'

'Sir.'

I looked at her. 'Tonight, then?'

'Tonight, sir, yes.'

70

And it *had* to be tonight.

'Are you Edward Kenway?' she'd said to me.

My landlady. Edith was her name. She'd knocked on the door to my room and stood on the threshold unwilling to venture further. Her face was bloodless, her voice shook and her fingers worried at the hem of her pinafore.

'Edward Kenway?' I smiled. 'Now, why would you say a thing like that, Edith?'

She cleared her throat. 'They say that a man arrived on a boat. A man dressed much like you are now, sir. And that the man is Edward Kenway, who once called Bristol his home.'

The colour had come back into her cheeks now, and she reddened, continuing, 'And there are others who say that Edward Kenway has returned home to settle scores, and that those against whom he bears his grudge have gone into hiding, but being powerful men have called resources against you – I mean, *him*.'

'I see,' I said carefully, 'and what manner of resources might these be?'

'A troop of soldiers headed for Bristol, sir, expected to arrive this very evening.'

'I see. And no doubt heading straight for wherever this Edward Kenway has his lodgings, whereupon Edward Kenway would be forced to defend himself, and there would surely be a bloody battle, with many lives lost and much damage caused?'

She swallowed. 'Yes, sir.'

'Well, you can rest assured, Edith, that no such unpleasantness will occur *here* tonight. For I'm sure Edward Kenway will make certain of it. And know this of him, Edith. It's true he was a pirate once and that he did his fair share of despicable things, but he's chosen a different path now. He knows that to see differently we must think differently. And he has changed his thinking.'

She looked at me blankly. 'Very good, sir.'

'And now I shall take my leave,' I told her. 'Doubtless never to return.'

'Very good, sir.'

On the bed was a bundle of my things that I picked up and slung over one shoulder, then I thought better of it and instead picked out what I needed: the skull and a small pouch of coins that I opened, pressing gold into Edith's hand.

'Oh, sir, that's more than generous.'

'You've been very kind, Edith,' I said.

She stood to one side. 'There's a back door, sir,' she said.

I went via a tavern where I knew to find the *Jackdaw*'s coxswain, awaiting my orders.

'Birtwistle.'

'Yes, sir.'

'Bring the *Jackdaw* to the harbour tonight. We're leaving.'

'Yes, sir.'

And then I went on to the warehouse district, using the backstreets and rooftops. I stayed low and in the shadows.

And I thought, *Oh, Mary, if you could only see me now.*

Scott's warehouse was one of many near the ports, the masts of berthed ships visible over the roofs. Most of the warehouses were deserted, shut up for the night. Only his had signs of life: flaming cressets that painted a small loading area a shade of flickering orange, empty carts nearby, and standing by the closed door a pair of guards. Not soldiers, at least – had they arrived in the city yet? – but local scar-faces slapping clubs into their palms, who probably thought this was an easy job, who were probably looking forward to a taste of ale later.

I stayed where I was, a shadow in the darkness, watching the door. Was he already in there? I was still debating when to make my move when Rose arrived. She wore the same headscarf as earlier and her basket bulged with clothes for her hated lord and master, Emmett Scott.

The two strong-arms at the door shared a lascivious look as they stepped forward to intercept her. Sticking to the side of the adjacent warehouse I crept within earshot.

'Is Mr Scott here?' she asked.

437

'Ah,' said one of the scar-faces in a heavy West Country accent, grinning. 'Well, that all depends on who's asking, don't it, m'dear?'

'I have clothes for him.'

'You'd be the maid, would you?'

'That's right.'

'Well, he's here, so you'd better go in.'

I was close enough to see her roll her eyes as they stepped aside and let her in.

Right. So Scott was in there.

In the dark I tested the action of my blade. Mustn't be too hasty, I thought. Mustn't kill him. Scott had some talking to do before he died.

I moved round the edge of the warehouse wall, and the two strong-arms were just a few feet away from me now. It was just a question of waiting for the right moment to str—

From inside came a scream. Rose. And it was no longer a question of waiting for the right time. It was a time for action. I'd sprung from the dark, covered the distance between myself and the sentries, engaged the blade and slashed the throat of the first one before Rose's scream had even died down. The second one cursed and swung his club but I caught his flailing arm, jammed him up against the warehouse wall and finished him with a blade in his back. He slid down the wall even as I crouched at the wicket door of the warehouse, raised a hand and pushed it open.

A musket ball zinged over my head as I rolled into the

entrance way, getting a quick impression of a warehouse stacked with tea chests, a gantry with offices on it at one end.

There were three figures on the gantry, one of them standing on the rail as though about to jump the twenty feet or so to the ground.

I came to rest behind a stack of crates, peeked round the edge and pulled back as another ball smacked into the wood nearby, showering me with wood chips. But my quick look was enough to confirm that, yes, there were three people on the gantry above me. There was Wilson, who stood with a pistol aimed at my hiding place. To one side of him was Emmett Scott, sweating as with trembling, frantic fingers he tried to reload another pistol to hand to Wilson.

And above them was Rose, who wobbled unsteadily on the railing, terrified. Her mouth bled. The punishment for her warning scream no doubt. Her hands had been tied and she wore a noose round her neck. All that stopped her from dropping from her makeshift gallows was Wilson, who held her with his other hand.

If he let go, she fell.

'Hold it there, Kenway,' called Wilson as the dust settled, 'or you'll have the death of the maid on your hands.'

They'd disarm me. They'd kill me, then hang Rose for her treachery.

Not if I have anything to do with it.

From my gun belt I pulled a pistol, and checked the

ball and powder. 'It was you there that night, wasn't it, Wilson? The leader? You were the one in the hood?'

I had to know. I had to be sure.

'Aye, it was. And if it had been left up to me you would all have died that night.'

I almost smiled. *You missed your chance.*

Up on the rail Rose whimpered but checked herself.

'Now throw out the hidden blade, Kenway, I can't hold her for ever,' warned Wilson.

'And what about you, Emmet?' I called. 'Were you there?'

'I was not,' he retorted, flustered and frightened.

'You would have celebrated my death, though?'

'You have been a thorn in my side, Kenway.'

'Your pride has been your undoing, Scott. Your pride has been the undoing of us all.'

'You know nothing.'

'I know that you allowed my beloved to die.'

'I loved her, too.'

'No kind of love that I recognize, Scott.'

'You wouldn't understand.'

'I understand that your ambition and thirst for power have led to the deaths of many people. I understand that now you will pay.'

From inside my robes I took a throwing knife and weighed it in my palm. *Bit different to using trees for target practice.*

I stood and inched towards the edge of the stack, taking deep, slow breaths.

Ready?

Ready.

'Come on, Kenway,' called Wilson, 'we don't have all n—'

I rolled out from my cover and darted forward and found my aim, firing my pistol and using the throwing knife at the same time.

Both met their targets. Emmet Scott span away with a hole in his forehead, his pistol dropping uselessly to the planks of the gantry, while Wilson had returned fire before my knife found his shoulder. Yelling in pain he staggered back and fell against the office wall with the blade embedded, fountaining blood as he scrabbled in vain for the second pistol.

His ball had found its mark. I felt it thud into my shoulder but couldn't let it take me down. Couldn't even let it slow me down. Because Wilson had let go of Rose and Rose was falling, her mouth wide in a scream I didn't hear above the echoes of the gunshots and the rushing of pain in my head.

She fell. And the rope unspooled behind her. And I had an image of failure, where the rope tautened and her body jerked and her neck snapped.

No.

I hit a crate at full pelt, stepped up in a run and launched myself off. I twisted, engaged my blade and with a yell of effort sliced the rope, caught Rose round the waist and the pair of us slammed heavily and painfully to the stone floor of the warehouse.

But alive.

From above I heard Wilson cursing. I snatched a second pistol from my belt and squinted through the gaps in the boards above me, seeing the light flicker and squeezing off a shot. There came another scream from the gantry then a crash as he made his way into the offices.

I dragged myself to my feet. The pain from my wound was intense, and the older wound in my flank flared up, too, making me limp as I made it to the steps of the gantry and climbed in pursuit of Wilson. I charged through the office where I found an open back door leading to steps, and at the top I caught my breath and leaned on the rail for support as I peered over the warehouses.

No sign. Just the distant clattering of ships at rest and the squawk of gulls. I concentrated, using the sense, and I heard something. But not Wilson. What I heard was the sound of marching feet as they approached the port area.

They were coming. The soldiers were coming.

I cursed and limped back inside to check on Rose. She would be okay. I ran back to follow a trail of blood left by Wilson.

71

You were safe in my cabin. Asleep, so I'm told. So you missed what happened next. And for that I'm thankful.

I reached the harbour to find that Wilson had died on the way. His body lay at the bottom of the steps. He'd been going to a ship I recognized. One that when I'd last seen it was called the *Caroline* but had since been renamed in honour of the woman Matthew Hague had gone on to marry. It was called the *Charlotte*.

Hague was in there. A man awaiting death, though he didn't know it yet. I could see poorly defined figures in the grey haze of the evening moving across the stern gunwale. Guards. But it didn't matter. Nothing was going to stop me getting on board that ship.

If the guards had seen or heard Wilson fall they probably thought he was a drunk. And if they saw me squatting by his body then they probably thought I was a drunk, too. They didn't care. Not yet.

I counted four of them as I raced along the harbour wall until I reached where the *Jackdaw* had not long been docked. In between the two ships was another smaller sailing boat held by a line that I unwound and let go, giving the stern of the craft a shove to set it off before dashing back to my ship.

'Hanley,' I said addressing the quartermaster.

'Yes, sir?'

'Prepare the guns.'

He'd been sitting with his feet up on the navigation table but dragged them off. 'What? Why, sir? And bloody hell, sir, what's up with you?'

'Musket ball in the shoulder.'

'Did you get the men you wanted?'

'Two of them.'

'I'll fetch the doc . . .'

'Leave it, Hanley,' I growled. 'It can wait. Look, there's a vessel to our starboard, name of *Charlotte*. On it is the third man I seek. Ready the starboard guns and if my plans fail blast her out of the water.'

I ran to the cabin door then stopped, screwing up my face in pain as I turned to him. 'And Hanley?'

'Yes, sir?' He had stood, his face a picture of worry.

'You'd better prepare the stern guns as well. And make sure the crew is armed. There are soldiers on the way.'

'Sir?'

I gave him an apologetic look.

'Just look sharp, Hanley. If all goes well we'll be out of this in moments.'

He didn't look reassured. He looked even more worried. I gave him what I hoped was a confident smile, then swept a wedge from beneath the cabin door as I left.

444

The sailing boat had begun its drift out to sea. I heard a shout from the deck of the *Charlotte* as they spotted it. The laughter. *Fools.* They saw the joke, not the danger. I leapt overboard, planting my feet on the stone of the harbour then racing the few yards to the stern of the *Charlotte.*

'It's Wilson,' I shouted in my best approximation of the dead enforcer as I clambered up the ladder. A face appeared over the gunwale to greet me and I planted my fist in it, dragged him over the rail and hurled him to the stone below. His screams alerted a second man who came running to what he assumed was the scene of an accident – until he saw me and the blade, which gleamed in the moonlight before I swept it backhanded across his throat.

Ignoring the last two sentries I ran up the deck towards the captain's cabin, peered through the window and was treated to the sight of Matthew Hague, an older Matthew Hague, and a worried one by the looks of things, standing by a table. With him was his draughtsman.

With a glance to see the two sentries lumbering up the deck towards me, I dragged open the door of the cabin.

'*You,*' I said to the draughtsman.

Hague dropped a goblet he'd been holding. They both goggled at me.

I risked another glance back at the sentries. I cursed, slammed the cabin door shut, wedged it and turned to meet the two guards.

They could have escaped I told myself as they died.

It was their choice to fight me. To my port the hatches of the *Jackdaw*'s gun deck were opening and the muzzles of guns appeared. *Good lads.* I saw men on deck brandishing muskets and swords. Somebody shouted, 'You need a hand, cap'n?'

No, I didn't. I turned back to the cabin door, pulled the wedge free and snatched open the door. 'Right, last chance,' I ordered the draughtsman, who practically threw himself at me.

'Archer,' wailed Hague, but neither of us was listening as I hauled Archer out of the cabin and jammed it shut behind him, Hague imprisoned now.

'Get off the ship,' I barked at Archer, who needed no further invitation, scrabbling for the stern.

Now I could hear the marching feet of soldiers as they approached the harbour wall.

'Tar!' I appealed to my crew on the other deck. 'Barrels of tar and be quick about it!'

A barrel was tossed to me from the *Jackdaw* and I set upon it, opening it and spreading it by the door to the cabin.

'Please . . .' I could hear Hague from inside. He was thumping on the wedged-shut door. 'Please . . .'

But I was deaf to him. The marching was closer now. Horse hooves. The rumble of cart wheels. I glanced to the harbour wall, expecting to see the tops of their bayonets as I emptied a second barrel of tar on the deck.

Would it be enough? It would have to do.

And now I saw them. The muskets of the soldiers as

they appeared, silhouetted along the top of the harbour wall. At the same time they saw me and pulled the muskets from their shoulders and took aim. By my side the crew of the *Jackdaw* did the same as I snatched up a torch and leapt to the ratlines, climbing to a point where I could let go of the torch, dive off the rigging and escape the flames.

If the muskets didn't get me first, that was.

And then came the command.

'Hold your fire!'

72

The order came from a carriage that had pulled up on the harbour, its door opening before it had even finished drawing to a halt.

Out skipped two men: one dressed like a footman, who arranged the steps for the second man, a tall, lean gentleman who wore smart clothes.

And now a third man appeared. A portly gentleman in a long white wig, frilled shirt and fine satin jacket and breeches. A man who looked as though he'd enjoyed many a lunch in his time, and many a glass of port and brandy to go with those many lunches.

The footman and the tall man gaped as they became aware of the many guns pointing in their direction. By accident or design they'd placed themselves in the middle: the guns of the soldiers on one side, the carriage guns and muskets of the *Jackdaw* on the other, and me on the rigging, ready to drop a flaming torch to the deck below.

The portly gentleman moved his mouth as though exercising it in readiness to speak. He laced his hands across his chest, rocked back on his heels and called up to me, 'Do I have the pleasure of addressing Captain Edward Kenway?'

'And who might you be?' I called back.

That produced a shudder of amusement from the soldiers on the harbour wall.

The portly man smiled. 'You've been away a long time, Captain Kenway.'

I agreed I had.

His lips smacked and rearranged themselves into a smile. 'Then you are forgiven for not knowing who I am. I think, however, that you will know my name. It is Walpole. Sir Robert Walpole. I am the First Lord of the Treasury, Chancellor of the Exchequer and Leader of the House of Commons.'

And I was just thinking what an impressive title that was, and how he must be one of the most powerful men in the land when . . . *Walpole. It couldn't be.*

But he was nodding. 'Yes, indeed, Captain Kenway. Duncan Walpole, the man whose life and identity you took as your own, was my cousin.'

I felt myself tense even more. What game was he playing? And who was the tall man by his side? It struck me that he had a family resemblance to Matthew Hague. Was this his father, Sir Aubrey Hague?

Walpole was waving a reassuring hand. 'It is quite all right. Not only was my cousin involved in affairs I keep at a distance, but he was a treacherous man. A man blessed, I'm afraid, with few principles. A man prepared to sell the secrets of those who trusted him to the highest bidder. I was ashamed to see him bear the Walpole name. I think perhaps in many ways, you have done my family a good turn.'

'I see,' I called, 'and that's why you're here, is it? To thank me for killing your cousin?'

'Oh no, not at all.'

'Then to what do I owe the pleasure of this visit? As you can see, I have other matters to attend to.'

The torch grumbled as I waved it for effect. From the wedged cabin of the *Charlotte* came a banging sound as Hague tried to get free. Otherwise there was a tense hush as the soldiers and the sailors peered at one another along the barrels of their weapons, both sets of men awaiting their orders.

'Well, Captain Kenway, it's exactly those matters that exercise us, I'm afraid,' called Walpole, 'for I cannot allow you to continue on your present course of action. As a matter of fact, I'm going to have to ask you to toss the torch in the sea and come down from there right away. Or, alas, I shall have the men shoot you.'

I chortled. 'You shoot me and my men return fire, Sir Robert. I fear even you yourself might get caught in the crossfire. Not to mention your friend – Sir Aubrey Hague, is it?'

'It is indeed, sir,' said the tall man stepping forward. 'I come to plead clemency for my son.'

His son had been a disappointment to him, I could see.

'Let me see your fingers,' I demanded.

Hague raised his hands. A Templar ring glittered. My heart hardened.

'And you, Sir Robert.'

His hands remained laced across his stomach. 'You'll see no ring on me, Captain Kenway.'

'Why does the idea tickle you? From what I've seen the Templars enjoy rank and status. How am I to know that I am not addressing their Grand Master?'

He smiled. 'Because no power is *absolute*, Captain Kenway, and my purpose here is not to act as ambassador for one side or indeed the other. My purpose here is to prevent an act of barbarism.'

I scoffed. *Barbarism?* It didn't seem to bother them when they were burning my parents' home. Where was Sir Robert Walpole then? Sipping port, perhaps, with his Templar friends? Congratulating himself on abstaining from their schemes. He could afford to, of course. His wealth and power were already assured.

From the cabin Matthew Hague snivelled and whimpered.

'You have returned to these shores on a mission of vengeance, I take it?' called Walpole.

'There are those with whom I have scores to settle, yes.'

Walpole nodded. 'Woodes Rogers being one of them?'

I gave a short, surprised laugh. 'Yes. He would be one of them.'

'Would it make a difference if I told you that Rogers currently languishes in debtors' prison? That the wounds you inflicted on him have left his health in a terrible state of disrepair? That his Order has disowned him? His hot temper, his continued slave trading. He is a broken man, Captain Kenway. I wonder if perhaps you might consider that matter settled?'

He was right. What more harm could my blade do to Rogers, other than to put him out of his misery?

'He is not my immediate concern,' I called. 'That honour belongs to the man in the cabin below.'

Walpole gave a sad smile. 'A silly, shallow boy, influenced by others. You must believe me when I tell you, Captain Kenway, that the principal malefactors in that particular episode are already dead by your hands. Rest assured that Matthew's current shame is punishment enough for his wrongdoing.'

I took a deep breath. I thought of my mother asking me how many I'd killed. I thought of Black Bart's cruelty. I thought of Mary Read's spirit and Adewalé's courage and Blackbeard's generosity.

And I thought of you. Because Torres had been wrong when he said I had nobody. I did have somebody. *I had you.* You who shone with hope.

'Today I should like to make you an offer, Captain Kenway,' continued Walpole. 'An offer I hope you will find favourable, that will finally draw a curtain across this whole sorry affair.'

He outlined his proposals. I listened. And when he was finished, I told him my answer and dropped the torch.

73

Except of course I dropped it into the sea.

Because he offered pardons for my men and I, and I saw their faces turn expectantly to me, every one of them a wanted man with the chance of having his slate wiped clean. He offered us all, every man-jack of us, a new life.

And Walpole had offered much more besides. Property. The chance to make something of myself with business contacts in London. When I'd finally climbed down from the rigging, the soldiers had put down their muskets and the crew of the *Jackdaw* relaxed. Then Matthew Hague had been released and run to his father and offered me tearful apologies, while Walpole took my arm and led me away, speaking of who I would be introduced to in London: the Stephenson-Oakley family, a lawyer, an assistant by the name of Birch to help me in my new business dealings.

My mercy would be handsomely rewarded, he assured me. In return he would see to it that I became the man I had always wanted to be: a man of quality.

Of course I had since gained greater expectations of myself. But money, business and a house in London would be a fine foundation on which to build a new and richer life. A fine foundation indeed.

A place I could use to attend to my other business. *My Assassin business.*

Shall we go, my darling? Shall we set sail for London?

List of Characters

Adewalé: former slave and, later, quartermaster and Assassin
Ah Tabai: Assassin
Blaney: sailor
Anne Bonny: barmaid at the Old Avery and, later, pirate
Calico Jack Rackham: pirate
Seth Cobleigh: Tom Cobleigh's son
Tom Cobleigh: Seth Cobleigh's father
Alexander Dolzell: Edward's first captain
Julien DuCasse: Templar
El Tiburón: executioner and Torres's bodyguard
Matthew Hague: unsuccessful suitor to Caroline Scott, son
    of Sir Aubrey Hague
Benjamin Hornigold: pirate founder of Nassau
Julian: friend of the Cobleighs
Bernard Kenway: Edward's father
Caroline Kenway, née Scott: Edward's wife
Edward Kenway: Assassin
Jennifer (Jenny) Kenway: Edward and Caroline's daughter
Linette Kenway: Edward's mother
James Kidd: pirate
Laurens Prins: Dutch slaver
Mary Read: true identity of James Kidd, Assassin
Bartholomew Roberts aka Black Bart: Sage and pirate

Woodes Rogers: Templar pirate-hunter and, later, governor
    of the Bahamas
Rose: servant to the Scotts
Emmett Scott: Caroline's father, Bristol tea merchant
Mrs Scott: Caroline's mother
Edward Thatch aka Blackbeard: privateer turned pirate
Laureano Torres: Templar governor of Havana
Charles Vane: pirate
Dylan Wallace: recruitment man
Duncan Walpole: Templar
Wilson: manservant to Matthew Hague

Acknowledgements

Special thanks to

Yves Guillemot
Julien Cuny
Aymar Azaizia
Jean Guesdon
Darby McDevitt

And also

Alain Corre
Laurent Detoc
Sébastien Puel
Geoffroy Sardin
Xavier Guilbert
Tommy François
Cecile Russeil
Joshua Meyer
The Ubisoft Legal department
Chris Marcus
Etienne Allonier
Antoine Ceszynski
Maxime Desmettre
Two Dots
Julien Delalande
Damien Guillotin
Gwenn Berhault
Alex Clarke
Hana Osman
Andrew Holmes
Virginie Sergent
Clémence Deleuze

He just wanted a decent book to read ...

Not too much to ask, is it? It was in 1935 when Allen Lane, Managing Director of Bodley Head Publishers, stood on a platform at Exeter railway station looking for something good to read on his journey back to London. His choice was limited to popular magazines and poor-quality paperbacks – the same choice faced every day by the vast majority of readers, few of whom could afford hardbacks. Lane's disappointment and subsequent anger at the range of books generally available led him to found a company – and change the world.

'We believed in the existence in this country of a vast reading public for intelligent books at a low price, and staked everything on it'
Sir Allen Lane, 1902–1970, founder of Penguin Books

The quality paperback had arrived – and not just in bookshops. Lane was adamant that his Penguins should appear in chain stores and tobacconists, and should cost no more than a packet of cigarettes.

Reading habits (and cigarette prices) have changed since 1935, but Penguin still believes in publishing the best books for everybody to enjoy. We still believe that good design costs no more than bad design, and we still believe that quality books published passionately and responsibly make the world a better place.

So wherever you see the little bird – whether it's on a piece of prize-winning literary fiction or a celebrity autobiography, political tour de force or historical masterpiece, a serial-killer thriller, reference book, world classic or a piece of pure escapism – you can bet that it represents the very best that the genre has to offer.

Whatever you like to read – trust Penguin.